SOMETIMES
THE HEART NEEDS
A LITTLE HELP
FROM ABOVE...

D0324518

Earthly Desires

"Susan . . ."

"Hunter . . ." they said at the same time, then paused to laugh awkwardly.

"You first," she said.

"I better get you back inside before this goes too far. Usually, I have more self-control, but I don't think I can take much more kissing." His smile was wry. "Never thought I'd say that."

Gazing up at him in the moonlight, Susan's face mirrored her thoughts so explicitly that he groaned.

"Don't look at me like that, Susan Whitten. Just don't! Not unless you want to be taken to my house and—"

"Ravished?" she supplied when he paused. "Made love to? Why not? Do you think I don't want you? I do." She laughed softly. "Brazen, aren't I? But I do, Hunter. I've never felt this way about anyone before. Maybe it's the tension, the not knowing what the night will bring, or tomorrow. Or whether I'll ever have this opportunity again. . . ."

She leaned into him, pressing close. Her voice was muffled by his shirt as she said against his broad chest, "I don't want to wait, Hunter."

Touch of Heaven

Michelle Brandon

DIAMOND BOOKS, NEW YORK

To Linda Kichline—a wonderful writer with an exquisitely eccentric sense of humor—thanks for all those hours of listening! Your friendship has kept me going.

And to Carrie Feron, my patient editor, who so kindly allows me to tag along wherever she goes.

The Arrival

1876

HOT WINDS SWEPT across a west Texas hillside, whirling in circles, stirring up choking clouds of dust that filled the air and drifted upward. The sudden dust devil left behind two people, one a white-robed man, the other a woman garbed in a farthingale and ruff. Both were coughing violently.

"Does Gabriel have to be so melodramatic about this?" the woman gasped out. Her companion shrugged between spasms of coughing.

"He does lean to the theatrical side, I suppose," he finally managed.

"God's toenails, Horatio!" the stout woman snapped as her coughing ceased. "Why didn't you tell me we were going to the moon?" She swept out one arm in a dramatic motion that indicated the barren ground studded with sagebrush and small cactus. "I thought you said I had to—"

"This is America—the New World, Tabitha, just as I told you," Horatio replied in a voice of weary patience. "We're in Texas. And I do wish you would not use such epithets."

"Eh? Oh. You mean 'God's toenails.' Sorry. I keep forgetting myself." Tabitha energetically brushed dust from her clothes; a frown knit her plucked brows. "I still don't understand why I must be forced to come to this godforsaken spot—oh, not that, either?—anyway, I've only just got to the Hereafter, and you're already plaguing me with this 'improve thyself' nonsense."

"Remember the proper vernacular, Tabitha," Horatio warned. "Your speech is important, and it could be embarrassing if you forget. Besides, you've been in the Hereafter for over three hundred years—plenty of time to improve and learn the art of suitable conversation."

Her sniff contained a wealth of disdain. "It certainly doesn't feel like that long! Time does fly, I suppose— Horatio, are you absolutely certain people really live in this desolate part of the world?"

"Positive. Just look over that ridge and you will see her ranch."

"Ah, yes," Tabitha murmured, squinting against the sun as she peered at the small ranch below. "Now, you say this girl is a descendant of mine?"

"Exactly so. And she is about to inherit the Lynnfield brooch."

Tabitha's jaw dropped, and she whirled to stare at Horatio. Her skirts spun against the dirt, and her chin jutted up out of the starched cambric ruff she wore. "*My* brooch?"

"Not yours—the Lynnfield *family* brooch, remember?"

"But this girl is—what did you call her?—an American? How can someone who isn't English inherit *my* brooch?" she demanded.

"Her grandmother was Mrs. Harriet Cabot, née Lynnfield. She married a Colonial in 1822, and—"

"How vulgar!" Tabitha muttered.

Horatio sighed.

"Sorry. Do go on," she said, attempting to smile.

"And came to America," he finished. "The Cabots moved west in 1848 when Harriet was fifty-two and her daughter Charlotte was twenty. Charlotte married in 1852, and young Susan was born in 1853. She is now twenty-three and the only living Lynnfield female."

"Good God!" Tabitha exclaimed. "All of them died out?"

"All the females, it seems," Horatio replied dryly. "I believe that Lord Neville was the last to die, and he passed the brooch on down the bloodline the best he could."

"Blithering idiot," Tabitha murmured with fire in her eye. "I cannot countenance the fact that *my* brooch has fallen into the hands of commoners!"

"Tabitha, Tabitha, all men are equal in the eyes—"

"I know, I know!" she interrupted hastily. "But not down here. That's not the way it works, and no one knows that better than I do. The Lynnfield brooch—in *America*!" She took a step forward, her heavy skirts swinging over dust and clumps of sage. "What will they do next," she blurted, "bring over London Bridge?"

"One never knows, Tabitha. At any rate, your purpose for being sent here is to help out your young descendant. She is about to be in serious trouble." With a wave of one hand he indicated a cloud of dust rolling slowly along the road. It was a small buggy, and it bowled over the ruts and rolled to a halt in front of the ranch.

"The brooch arrives," Horatio said softly, and Tabitha couldn't help an eager step forward.

"*My* brooch?"

"Tabitha, it isn't *your* brooch! It is a family heirloom that now belongs to Miss Whitten."

"I thought her name was Cabot. And besides, I have more of a right to it than anyone, don't I? I died with the damned thing pinned to my chest."

"Tabitha!"

"Well, I did! Fell right down the stairs and broke my neck quick as a flash. Didn't hurt the brooch, though."

She sniffed. "The least they could have done was bury me in it."

"It is a Lynnfield family tradition to pass it down to the next female in line, I believe," Horatio chided, and Tabitha glared at him.

"Don't I know that? How do you think *I* got it?" Her plump jowls quivered slightly. "Dreadful thing, really. I cannot forget how pale and bloodless Ana looked lying there with poison still on her lips—she was just before me, you know. I was next to inherit. Ah, well, she took her own life over a *man*—oh, it was quite dreadful! There must be something to that curse business, though it does smack of . . ."

Taking Tabitha by the elbow, Horatio tactfully switched the subject. "Shall we begin helping her instead of debating ancient history? Her ranch is about to be foreclosed on because of a long drought that has dried up all the grass for the cattle, and—"

"*Ancient history!* It wasn't that long ago!"

" . . . and it will not help her keep her father's ranch if we mull over her wretched circumstances instead of taking action. That is *your* department, dear Tabitha, and you must begin at once."

Muttering under her breath, Tabitha lifted her full skirts from the dust and set off down the slope beside Horatio. This promised to be a most uncomfortable trial for her.

There were times, Tabitha thought gloomily, when she wasn't certain exactly where in the Hereafter she had landed. The first hundred years or so had been quite pleasant, but now all this foolery about character building and other nonsense was beginning to make her think she had been duped. Perhaps this wasn't Paradise after all.

Well, there was nothing to do now but see how she could help this silly chit who had managed to inherit nothing but dust and sky. And *her* brooch!

"A drought?" Tabitha asked. "Perhaps a good rain will fix it all and I can get back before Beethoven's concert begins." She lifted her arms with a dramatic flourish.

Chapter 1

"MISS SUSAN!" DORIS Wheeler cried, racing toward her employer with a frightened cry. "Miss Susan! Flash flood!"

Susan Cabot Whitten jerked up from the chair behind her father's desk. For an instant she quivered in shock. A tumble of dark hair fell into her eyes, and she pushed it back with an impatient flash of her hand, smudging ink across her nose in the process.

"Flash flood!" Susan repeated as she came out from behind the desk, catching her skirt on an open drawer, then giving it a sharp tug that rent the material. "But it hasn't rained in months!"

"It must have rained up in the hills. . . . Oh, do hurry, Miss Susan, or we'll be drowned! Pete says it's headed right toward us, and we need to get to higher ground."

Susan groaned. "All right, I'm coming—you get Arthur for me!"

Pausing in the doorway, Doris flung her mistress a reproachful glance. "You know I don't like Arthur, Miss Susan. Let him run or swim."

"Arthur can't swim," Susan said, "and you don't have to *like* him to carry him out to the wagon, do you?"

"All right," Doris grumbled with a scowl on her plump features, "but I'd like to know what you're going to be doing while I try and find him."

"I have to get papers from the safe—and rescue my 'new legacy.' " She said the last self-mockingly.

Whatever good would an heirloom brooch do her if she couldn't sell it or use it as collateral to save her ranch? But there was no time to worry about that now. Not with a flash flood bearing down on the ranch.

She scurried toward the safe hidden in the stones of the fireplace. Nothing seemed to go right lately, she thought as she fumbled with the safe door. Not *once* had anything good happened in the past year. First her parents had died. Then the long drought had burned fields so badly that her cattle would have starved without the hay she was barely able to afford.

Susan shook her head as she drew out the small box with the strange brooch inside. Under normal circumstances some precipitation could have been a blessing; instead, the rain had turned into a flood. Now here she was, grabbing what she could and running outside like an idiot.

Doris met Susan at the door, her brown curls in wild disarray. "I can't find Arthur!" she gasped, her breath moving her heavy bosom up and down like a bellows.

Susan groaned again. "Did you look under the kitchen table? In the parlor? The pantry?"

"All his favorite hiding places, Miss Susan!"

"The root cellar?"

"Oh . . . I forgot there. . . ." Doris disappeared in a whirl of cotton skirts, and Susan could hear her muttering grim imprecations about the absent Arthur as she ran.

Susan yanked open the front door. Outside, a swiftly moving thunderhead was positioned atop her ranch. Rain poured down in a steady curtain over the ranch's dry hills and drier gullies. The air smelled of wet dust. Beyond the Lazy W the sky was blue and cloudless. Susan stood, mystified.

Well, she thought grimly, they were going to have to run for it. She could at least help Pete Sheridan bring the wagon around for Doris and Arthur.

Stepping outside, Susan could see from one corner of her eye the looming destruction of a wall of water behind the ranch. Though it was still far away, she had no illusions about how swiftly the disaster would reach her. She ducked her head and lifted her skirts up around her knees, then ran for the barn.

Pete Sheridan, foreman at the Lazy W for almost twenty years, met Susan at the barn door.

"Got the wagon hitched," he drawled, his voice betraying no hint of stress or trouble. "Whar's Miss Doris?"

"She's finding Arthur. We need to take the wagon to the front door so she won't get too wet."

Pete flicked Susan's drenched state an amused glance. Even in the face of disaster, he wouldn't have sent Miss Doris to look for Arthur. But he wasn't Miss Susan. Not once in all the twenty-three years of her life had Susan Whitten done anything remotely predictable—nor comprehensible—to the sun-hardened cowboy, and he didn't suppose she'd begin now.

"Get in," Pete said, "and I'll drive you."

Susan shook her head. "No, I'll drive us. You take care of yourself. I know how you feel about that hot-tempered stallion in the barn, and you'd never forgive me if I let him drown."

Bending over to keep the pounding rain from blinding her, Susan slapped the reins over the horses and sent them bounding forward. She made her way to the house mostly by memory; it was growing impossible to see. She'd never seen it rain like this before! And the deep gulch behind the ranch was filling up with so much water that it would soon overflow, threatening to plow down the ranch buildings.

"Doris!" she screamed over the noise of the rain and sudden clap of thunder. "Doris!"

The front door banged open, and Doris stood briefly outlined. "I'm here! And if you want Arthur to come out, you'd best come in and get him. I can't drag him out of the root cellar."

Glancing at the restive horses snorting and pulling at the reins she held firmly, Susan was torn. "Could you give it one more try?" she begged Doris and saw the plump older woman's mouth tighten into a thin line of refusal. "Oh, please do try! You know how I love Arthur! It would take a miracle for him to survive if he doesn't come with us. . . ."

Throwing up her hands, Doris disappeared back into the house. A moment later she reappeared with a squealing, struggling Arthur in her arms. But Susan wasn't looking at her. The rain had stopped, and the wall of water that had been easily visible had run off into another gully.

Susan was gazing in stunned silence at the trickle of water draining down from the gulch onto flatter land. Where had the other gully come from? She should be able to recall a ditch large enough to handle that amount of runoff, but oddly enough, she couldn't. It made her shiver. She'd ridden these gullies since she'd been old enough to sit atop a fat pony and should be able to remember a gulch there. Well, at least it had saved the ranch. No rain pelted her. The clouds had blown away as quickly as they'd come, almost as if by magic. Or a miracle.

"What stopped the flood?" She turned to Doris and saw the same astonished incomprehension on her face.

Then a smile curved Susan's mouth, growing gradually into rolling laughter. "Oh, Doris, you should see your face!" she said, still chuckling. "And Arthur looks quite disgruntled."

Dropping Arthur immediately, Doris tried to regain the dignity she had lost in dragging the struggling creature up from the root cellar.

"Miss Susan," she began in a dangerously quiet voice, "I have been with your family for over fifteen years, and I have rarely been asked to do something that I didn't want to do. But now I draw the line. No matter how much you care for Arthur, I will not go through anything like this again. Ever. He's horrible. I don't know how you can stand him."

Susan cast her companion and housekeeper a fond glance. "I'm sorry. It looks as if everything will be all right now, though." Her gaze shifted to Arthur, who looked singularly unrepentant. "Arthur," she addressed him sternly, "you've been very naughty. You've upset Miss Wheeler. Tell her that you're sorry."

Arthur turned and stuck his snout between Doris's knees, getting his head tangled in her skirts. Doris made an angry sound, and Susan laughed as she climbed down from the wagon.

"He'll learn manners when he's older," she assured the indignant Miss Wheeler as she dragged Arthur away. The plump pink pig wriggled contentedly as Susan fondled his floppy ears, then he grunted with swinish ecstasy. She sank down on the floor of the front porch and frowned as she looked out over the muddy yard. "It's been the oddest day, Doris, don't you think?"

Doris, who had been about to offer an unsolicited comment on the likelihood of Arthur's manners improving, was caught by her remark. "Why, yes, Miss Susan, you know it has. First that odd-speaking gentleman, then the dust devil I saw blow up on the hill, so queer like. No hint of rain, and then—boom!—a flash flood. It does like that a little farther east, maybe, but not out here."

"Yes," Susan murmured, pushing a wet strand of dark hair from her eyes, "that's what I thought."

A few moments later she saw Pete Sheridan striding toward the house and noted with a hidden smile Doris's quick efforts to smooth her hair. Pete walked with the rolling gait of a man who had spent most of his life straddling a horse. He was lean, with a sun-weathered look on his face that made Susan wonder if he'd been born that way.

"Hi, Pete," she greeted him and saw the way he took his hat from his head and nodded to her without really seeing her. He was busily trying not to look at Doris. "Guess we're safe, huh?"

"Yes, Miss Susan, I guess we are." Pete hesitated, then said, "Hello, Miss Doris."

"Hello, Mr. Sheridan." An awkward pause fell, then Doris added, "I suppose I should go begin supper. You will eat with us, Mr. Sheridan?" she asked as if he didn't eat with them every night except Sunday.

"Yes, Miss Doris, I'd be proud to eat with you."

"You two ought to get married," Susan observed when Doris had disappeared into the house and she still sat on the porch holding Arthur. He'd begun to struggle, and she pushed him from her lap to the porch.

Pete ignored her, watching as Arthur shook himself, then crossed the porch with his trotters clicking energetically. "I don't know why you keep that pig in the house," he observed. "It ain't natcheral."

"Maybe not for some pigs, but Arthur's special."

Pete shrugged. "So, now that we know the ranch'll still be here tomorrow, what are you going to do?"

Susan stared glumly past Pete. "I don't know. Guess I might try what some have done—ask for an extension of credit on my feed bill from the new owner of the granary."

Pete whistled long and slow. "You've heard the rumors about Carson, haven't you?"

"Mostly what Evan has told me, and you know how gossipy he is, especially for a man." There was an expression of annoyance in her lustrous dark eyes as she propped her chin in her palm and her elbow on one drawn-up knee. "I can't imagine how Evan Elliott turned out to be such a fussy kind of man. He wasn't that way when we were young."

Chuckling, Pete shook his head. "He wasn't in love with you when you were both young'uns."

Susan glared at him. Rain still dripped from the eaves of the roof and made small craters in the muddy yard. "Evan isn't in love with me—he loves himself too much!"

Pete scratched his jaw. "Miss Susan, you've always been a blunt-speakin' gal, and I admire that. But one of these days you're gonna speak out at the wrong time, and it's gonna get you in trouble."

She sighed. "You're right, Pete, I know you are. I can't help myself. I think something, and before I know it, I've said it out loud. It's a family failing, I'm afraid. You know how Mama always was."

Sheridan smiled. "Yes, Miss Susan. The missus was always outspoken, too."

They were both silent for a moment, listening to the muted *plop* of rain from the roof and remembering Susan's parents.

"Mama never did lose her Virginia drawl," Susan commented several moments later. "Even when Papa used to tease her about it."

"No, reckon she didn't," Pete agreed. "Didn't lose her fine manners none, neither."

Susan laughed softly. "Papa never could understand why Mama insisted upon a fine linen tablecloth on our table every night or the good china on Sundays!"

"Jake Whitten wasn't a man to take to those kind of things that easy," Pete said. "He always claimed he liked eatin' beans out of a can better than roast beef off a china plate." He paused, then added with a grin, "Noticed that he didn't complain too much after a while, though."

Susan's eyes stung, and to avoid tears, she rose from the porch. "Guess I'll go into town tomorrow, Pete. I'll meet this Hunter Carson and see if he's as big a rogue as Evan says he is."

"Aw, Evan's just mad 'cause Carson turned him down about a loan extension." Pete's weathered face creased into a scowl. "Don't blame Carson none, there. That Elliott boy never did learn how to manage money or cows."

"Well, Evan isn't the quickest, I'll admit that. He is my friend, though. I guess I shouldn't complain about him."

Pete was silent, then shrugged. "You've got a good heart, Miss Susan."

"And a wet dress!" she said, laughing. "I'm going to go in and change into dry clothes. Then I'll come help with any chores that still need doing."

Turning, Susan scooped up her pig and went into the house. Pete Sheridan could tell by the determined set of her shoulders that Susan planned to advance upon her quarry with daunting single-mindedness. Pete grinned.

He almost felt sorry for the mysterious Hunter Carson. Almost.

Tabitha couldn't quite meet Horatio's cool gaze. "What a country! Who would have thought a little rain would create such problems?"

An annoyed expression flickered briefly on Horatio's face. "As I've repeatedly told you, you must carefully weigh all possible consequences before acting. Perhaps, instead of a grandiose and swift solution to your descendant's problems, you should consider other options. Simpler, well-thought-out options. I may not be swift enough to avert the next calamity you cause."

Tabitha sighed regretfully. "Perhaps you're right. I suppose this calls for a more thorough examination of all the wretched chit's problems."

"Quite possibly so."

"So much for the Beethoven concert I planned to attend this afternoon," Tabitha said with another sigh. "I do so enjoy listening to him play—ah, well, perhaps I can make it back in time to listen to that new young man—what was his name? Chopin?"

"I believe so," was Horatio's dry comment. "And I would not count on that, either."

Tabitha looked at him haughtily. "How inconvenient. And how, may I ask, am I expected to solve all her problems in a short time?"

"You'll find the answer to that in the solution of them," Horatio replied. "First you must arrange your priorities."

Tabitha seemed struck by that answer and nodded in a thoughtful manner. "Aye, I suppose that is true enough. I think that I may just watch and listen for a time. Then a solution might present itself to me."

Horatio smiled. "I do believe you are improving!"

Tabitha looked pleased. "Am I? What do you mean?"

"One is supposed to carefully weigh all the details of problems before making decisions."

"Is that right? I always prided myself on making quick, instinctive decisions." She paused. "Perhaps they were not necessarily the right ones."

"Which may be the reason you are here now," Horatio pointed out.

Tabitha looked startled. "Oh! Yes, I suppose that may be true. Well, at any rate, why don't we just fade for the moment and watch and listen?"

"Excellent notion."

"But, Susan," Evan Elliott argued, "I've already told you what a ruthless bandit he is! Why don't you believe me?"

"Because I don't have any alternative but to ask for an extended loan, Evan," she replied bluntly. "Mr. Carson can only say no, after all, and what other options do I have?"

"You could sell that brooch, for one," Evan snapped. Raking a hand through his red hair, he gazed at her with soulful blue eyes. "Or you could marry me," he added hopefully. "That would end your problems."

"Oh, Evan! We've been through that so many times— and anyway, that would just double our problems. Your ranch is in as bad a shape as mine. This drought has hurt everyone in the valley." Susan rested her chin in her palm and smiled to erase any sting her words might have left. "And I can't sell the brooch, or a dire and dreadful curse will befall me. Or at least, that's what that stuffy barrister from England hinted when he gave it to me."

"It's a whopping big diamond," Evan said with a glance toward the small wooden box. "Are you sure you feel safe having it here?"

She laughed. "No one knows I have it except you. And maybe Doris, because she eavesdrops. But Doris would never tell anyone, and I know you won't, either." Rising from her chair at the kitchen table, Susan poured herself another cup of hot coffee, then one for Evan. "I have other things to worry about without wasting time worrying about a family heirloom," she said frankly. "The cattle are hungry, and even with that freak cloudburst of yesterday, the grass is dry and parched. I have to do something."

"Too bad your ranch was the only one to get any rain," Evan said gloomily. "Mine sure could have used it."

"Odd, isn't it? But if you'd seen that flood come barreling down the gully, you wouldn't have welcomed the rain!" Susan shook back a shining strand of dark hair from her eyes. "You should have seen it. And we were drenched. We looked like drowned rats."

"If I'd been here, I would have carried you to safety," Evan couldn't resist saying. "I'd never let anything harm you, Susan."

For some reason his words irritated her. Perhaps because she knew she'd never feel for Evan what he felt for her. "Don't say things like that!" she said sharply. "You know it only makes me mad to hear you carrying on like a lovesick calf."

"You get mad quicker than any blamed girl I know, Susan Whitten," Evan grumbled. "Have you ever thought of sugar-coating your words so they'd be easier for me to swallow?"

"Not for a moment," was her prompt answer. "You'd think I was sick if I did, and you know it." Her dark eyes fixed upon him, and the hint of a smile tugged at her mouth.

Evan was lost, hopelessly in love. Susan was the prettiest girl he'd ever seen, and he'd loved her for a long time. Her thick dark hair framed an oval face of exceptional beauty, and her dark eyes always sparkled with life. But it was her mouth that caused his heart to beat a bit faster, her sweetly curved lips that tempted him with what could only be considered sensuality. Evan realized Susan had no idea of the effect her looks had on men. She acted as if she'd never looked into a mirror.

Susan snapped her fingers above his head. "Evan? Evan, are you in there?"

He flushed, his pale face suffusing with color. "Yeah, I was just . . . just thinking."

She laughed, a soft gurgle of sound that made his insides wrench. "Well, it looked so painful for you!"

Grinning, he retorted, "Sometimes it is! Now, are you going to listen to me and let me talk to Carson for you?"

Her smile faded. "I don't need anyone to do my begging for me, thank you. I am quite capable of bending my own knees and hurling heartfelt pleas."

"I can't imagine anyone would refuse you anything, Susan," Evan said so fervently that she shifted with discomfort.

She hated it when he got serious. She wanted to shake him, to bring back the boy she had once gone fishing with and held hands with as they jumped out of haylofts.

Fortunately, Arthur chose that moment to intrude. "Come here, Arthur," she coaxed, using the pig as a diversion. He trotted across the kitchen floor with swinish squeals of ecstasy. She fondled his ears, and snuffling delightedly, Arthur thrust his snout in the folds of skirt material draped over Susan's knees.

Evan gazed at the pig with dislike. "Why do you insist on having a dirty pig in the house?"

Susan looked at him, irritated. "Arthur is not dirty. And I like him. He never asks rude questions."

"Only because he can't talk," Evan observed dryly as he rose to his feet. "I reckon I can take a hint."

"I'm not pushing you out, but I've got to get ready and go into Los Alamos to sweet-talk the ogre."

Evan gazed at her for a long moment. "You know I wish you luck, Susan. I just don't want that Carson fellow to hurt your feelings or your pride. Or insult you."

"The worst insult is having to ask for an extension on my credit. Jake Whitten would have shot himself in the foot before he'd done such a thing, but his daughter doesn't have his determination, I guess." Susan shook her head ruefully. "I'm not even tempted."

"You've got more determination in your little toe than Jake ever had," Evan said. He was grinning now, and more relaxed than he'd been earlier. "Well, don't you let Carson sweet-talk *you*. I heard he's got half the female population of Los Alamos panting after him already."

"All two of them? My, my, he must be a devilishly handsome wretch to make old Mrs. Simpson swoon. She's getting on to ninety if she's a day."

"Susan, you know what I'm trying to tell you!"

She ignored the edge of exasperation in Evan's voice and gave him a shove toward the kitchen door. "Go on, now. I've got to put on my beggar's rags."

Pausing in the open door, Evan stuck his head around it to say, "One of these days, Susan Whitten, you're going to give in and marry me!"

"I like you too much to do that to you, Evan. I'd end up being lynched for inhumane cruelty. Now *go*!"

When he'd gone, and the sound of his horse's hoofbeats had faded, she muttered, "He never gives up!"

Pete Sheridan echoed her thoughts later as they rode into Los Alamos over hard, rutted roads baking in the searing sun. The wagon rattled and rolled from side to side.

"He won't never leave you alone 'long as he thinks there might be a chance for him," Pete observed, squinting at Susan from beneath the wide brim of his hat. His wrinkled, sun-leathered face was creased into disgusted lines, and he leaned from the wagon to spit a stream of tobacco onto the ground.

Susan was silent for a moment. "There's nothing I can do about that," she said finally. "I've told him and told him."

"Reckon you're right," Pete said. He scratched his jaw with one hand. "Some folks just take longer to accept things than others."

"So it seems." Susan gazed across the rolling hills. "I wish he wouldn't be so hardheaded."

"Seems like there's a lot of that going around," Pete drawled, and Susan smiled.

"Are you referring to me, by any chance?"

"Your daddy would bellow like a roped bull if he thought you were going into town to ask a stranger for more money." Pete slapped the reins over the horses' rumps. "There must be another way, Miss Susan."

"If there is, I wish you'd point it out to me! I can't see anything but hungry cattle and the end of the Lazy W."

Pete's narrow lips thinned even more. "I got a little put back for a rainy day, but since we already had that rain yesterday, I'd be willing to add some to your poke. Might help."

Susan felt a sudden lump in her throat. "I couldn't take your money, Pete. And besides," she said when it looked as if he might argue, "it wouldn't be enough."

Pete shrugged. "You're probably right. Just hate to think about you having to . . . ask."

She grinned. "You meant to say beg, and don't you deny it! But if it saves the ranch, I won't mind doing a bit of diplomatic discussing."

Susan would remember that later.

Chapter 2

"HOW MAY I help you, Miss Whitten?" Hunter Carson inquired, politely rising from his chair as she entered his office.

Her first impression was of a casually dressed man wearing tan denim trousers and a cotton shirt open at the neck. Not at all the natty businessman she had expected. Her second impression was of a devastatingly handsome man. Carson's voice was deep, husky, and his words deliberate. It went perfectly with his clean-shaven, rugged features, sun-bronzed skin, hair the color of ripe wheat, and tall, muscular build. Hunter Carson exuded a blatant masculinity that Susan found almost intimidating.

She hesitated in the open doorway, suddenly feeling nervous and awkward. An unfamiliar, uncomfortable reaction. She steeled herself almost immediately and turned to close the door and gain a little time.

No reaction was evident as she sailed across the deep carpet of his office and sat down in the chair he indicated with a wave of his hand. He moved with an economy of motion, almost lazily graceful. It was irritating that he should be so politely cool and comfortable when she was writhing with sudden insecurity. Susan met his steady jade regard with a cool gaze as he took his seat behind the desk.

"I need an extension on my credit," she stated without preamble and noted the slight lifting of his eyebrows. "I am prepared to offer collateral, of course."

"Not more scorched acres of land that won't support anything but scrub and cactus, I hope," Carson said in an insultingly mocking tone.

Susan's temper began to rise. "Good land, Mr. Carson, some of the best acreage in this part of the country!"

"Yet it obviously won't support your cattle," Carson said smoothly. "Or you wouldn't be here. Am I right?"

"Only partially." Susan's hands clenched in her lap. Maybe she should have listened to Pete and Evan. Carson did not seem very sympathetic. "The Lazy W has always been able to meet its obligations in the past. This has been an unusual year."

"So I understand." Carson stood up from behind his desk. "I have a surplus of useless land at the moment. I don't need any more collateral. But . . ."

Before he could continue, Susan stood up, high color staining her cheekbones and her dark eyes glittering with a militant light. "Now, see here, Mr. Carson! I will not be put off until I've told you my circumstances! I am quite certain you have heard this same story from others in the county, but most of us are decent, hardworking people. I find it difficult to believe that you would come to Los Alamos and not want to get along with the inhabitants. It will be cutting off your nose to spite your face, and I don't know a single businessman who would do that!"

An expression of amusement flickered briefly in his eyes, and Carson inclined his head. "Very well. I'll listen to what you have to say, Miss Whitten, since you insist."

Drawing in a deep breath, Susan faced him with her chin up and her hands clenched around her reticule. "The Lazy W has a reputation as a steady producer of quality beef. This has not changed, despite the drought. I need grain to keep up that reputation, Mr. Carson, and

I have no money to pay you with. I need an extension on my line of credit with your firm. I realize that as the new owner, you are unaware of the Lazy W's excellent paying record in the past, so I am willing to forgive your presumption that we are not a good risk. I do expect, however, that you will at least give us the opportunity to prove you wrong."

She finished, waiting expectantly. What followed was a silence so deep that the ticking of the case clock in the corner sounded as loud as church bells on a Sunday morning. Susan sat back down and waited with her chin still tilted in a faint challenge, her dark eyes fixed on Hunter Carson's face.

It wasn't a bad face at all, she thought with ironic detachment, a ruggedly handsome face, in fact. If not for his eyes. His eyes were hard and green, a sharp glittering jade that held no hint of sympathy or human emotions in the depths. She shivered suddenly and wondered why.

Carson moved from behind his desk and draped a lean thigh over the corner in a casual posture that did not belie the hard gleam in his eyes. "Are you through?" he asked in a pleasant tone that sounded faintly mocking. When Susan gave a short nod of her head, he continued, "In the first place, Miss Whitten, you are wrong when you assume that I am unaware of the Lazy W's excellent record of payment. I am not a man to take over a business without doing a little investigation of the records." His hard mouth slanted in a slight smile. "In the second place, I do not want or need more dust as collateral. I would not—"

"There you go making another assumption!" Susan broke in again, her voice agitated. "I have six thousand head of good cattle—*profitable* cattle, Mr. Carson!

Please don't insult me by assuming that I would try to pass off a worthless spread—"

"Miss Whitten!" Carson's tone was suddenly harsh, and his mouth flattened in an angry line. "You have interrupted me twice now, and I would expect the same courtesy from you that I have shown since you came into my office. If this is your best foot forward, I'd hate to see your manners when you *don't* come begging."

"Begging!" Susan's face flamed with bright color, and her dark eyes looked like pinpoints of fury. "Oh, is that what you think? I suppose Evan was right, and I should have listened—you are little more than a bandit! A rich bandit, to be sure, and one who happens to hold all the cards, but it does not look like you're going to be well liked in this part of the country at all! Except maybe by the foolish women you seem to collect!" Susan gasped at her own words. What was she implying?

Hunter Carson slid his leg from the corner of his desk and stood up, his tall frame towering over Susan in a most intimidating way. He was furious. Even Susan, in her anger and disappointment, could see that. She'd obviously gone too far—drat her hasty tongue and blunt speech! Pete had been right when he'd warned her about speaking her mind.

"If you're through insulting me," he said in a dangerously quiet tone, "I have a proposition for you."

Susan swallowed. "Proposition?"

Carson's smile was nasty. "Yes. While it's quite true that I have a surplus of land as collateral, I find that the women in Los Alamos leave a lot to be desired. You are the first one I've seen who is under eighty or over twelve. So you see, your assumption that I have managed to form a collection of them is quite groundless." His voice lowered to an insultingly slow drawl, and his gaze pinned Susan to the chair. "If you will provide yourself as collateral, Miss Whitten, I will be happy to extend your credit. Otherwise, I'm afraid I do not find your suggestion very agreeable."

Susan gasped with fury. It was the most audacious suggestion she had ever heard—and the man stood there smiling at her as if it were a perfectly reasonable request!

Surging to her feet, she met his insolent gaze with a frigid stare that took all her self-control.

"As honored as you obviously think I should be, Mr. Carson, I can think of nothing I want to do less. I will find another way to keep my ranch in hay and grain, thank you!"

When Susan had stormed from his office without another glance at him, Hunter Carson leaned back against his desk. He folded his arms over his chest and crossed his legs at the ankles as he let out a deep breath. Then his anger began to fade and was slowly replaced with grim amusement. The fiery-tempered little brunette had sparked an interest without even trying. He couldn't believe he had actually made such an outrageous suggestion, but he'd been so blamed mad when she'd blurted out her accusations that he'd given free rein to his temper.

Hunter grinned. Susan Whitten just might provide him with lively entertainment before he told her that he had every intention of extending her credit. He'd been trying to tell her just that, and that she needed no collateral, but she'd interrupted him. Outspoken women usually annoyed him no end, but for some reason, Susan Whitten with her fiery dark eyes, gleaming raven hair, and classic features made him feel differently.

"Morton," Carson called. His secretary appeared in the open doorway.

"Yes, Mr. Carson?"

"If the Lazy W should request more credit, give it to them," he instructed. "But only with the stipulation that Miss Whitten speak with me first. *Only* Miss Whitten."

"Yessir, Mr. Carson," Morton said immediately. He paused, then asked, "Is there anything else, sir?"

Hunter crossed his office to gaze out the window. He looked down the main street of Los Alamos, where he could still see Susan Whitten marching indignantly down the wooden sidewalk, her spine straight, every step she took indicating her simmering rage. Her slender figure was tall for a woman, and her curves were gentle, not overblown or overstated. She was a beautiful, determined lady, he thought, probably right down to her drawers. A faint smile curled his mouth.

"Yes, Morton. Have some flowers delivered to Miss Whitten for me."

Morton was rocked with surprise. "*Flowers,* sir?"

Turning, Hunter stared at him. "Yes, flowers. You do know what flowers are, I suppose."

"Oh, yessir, I know what they are, all right. I just don't know where you expect me to find anyone to deliver flowers here in Los Alamos. This ain't Fort Worth, sir."

"No," Hunter agreed, "it certainly isn't. I hadn't thought about the limitations here. Never mind. I'll think of something else."

Not understanding at all, Morton waited politely for Carson to give further directions and, when he didn't, quietly withdrew. It didn't matter to him about the improbable impulses of the wealthy and occasionally demanding Hunter Carson. What mattered was that he had a job, and a good job with a future. Carson was exacting, but not impossible to work for. He only expected from his employees as much as he was willing to do himself. Henry Morton had already seen that much. And he certainly didn't mind doing whatever was asked of him.

Morton chuckled as he recalled Miss Susan Whitten's tight-lipped fury as she'd stormed from the office. He liked Susan—he didn't know anyone in Los Alamos who didn't like her—but he was also familiar with her usually blunt way of speaking. Evidently, she'd gotten Hunter Carson's back up, and he'd taken her down a peg or two. Morton was suddenly glad he had a front-row seat to what promised to be a very entertaining situation. He couldn't wait to tell someone about it.

Tabitha was quite annoyed. "What's the matter with that man, treating her like that?" she grumbled to Horatio. "Hasn't he had a proper upbringing? She stated her position quite clearly, yet he behaved like a scoundrel, a cad, an absolute rake!"

Horatio eyed Tabitha. "You don't think she was a trifle outspoken?"

Tabitha blinked. "Outspoken? No. Truthful, perhaps, yes, truthful. Honesty is always best. See where it has gotten me?"

"Yes, shoved down the stairs and a broken neck," Horatio murmured with a sigh. "I thought tact would have been a much better tool to use instead of blunt honesty in this situation."

"Do you? How quaint. What's the matter with honesty?"

"In most situations, nothing. But tactless honesty can be a bit dangerous, Tabitha. One must learn when to use forthright speech and when to use tact."

"Tact, guile, all the same to me. No, honesty is the best approach, Horatio, take my word for it."

"What do you intend to do now?" Horatio asked, refusing to be drawn into a debate with her. "She thinks she has no credit and has provoked Carson into a most unusual proposition."

"Men," Tabitha muttered darkly, "are full of unusual propositions. I can recall a few of them myself. Of course, men in my day dressed quite differently and were more handsome. Beards and mustaches covered a multitude of imperfections, but these crude people don't seem to know how to grow hair. And of course, in my day there was nothing more awe-inspiring than a man's well-turned leg. In this town, one can't see anything but tight pantaloons on men now, it seems, and their limbs are well covered." She seemed to realize that the conversation had wandered far from its point and said with a sigh, "But that is not my concern. I must devise a way to help this poor girl before she loses everything. If only I had thought to put a muzzle on that cad before he behaved so wickedly."

"Remember the rules," Horatio cautioned.

Tabitha gave him an indignant glance. "I remember— I can only arrange circumstances, not actual reactions. I must allow people to react in their normal manner— foolishness, I say!—and not preempt them. I still think I should be allowed just to have that tawny giant of a man give her all the credit she needs or have her marry that red-haired boy who fawns over her most disgustingly." Tabitha stared at Horatio hopefully, but he shook his head.

"They must retain free will. You are to guide, not interfere."

Tabitha waved an impatient hand. "So many rules! God's eyeballs, but I have to—sorry about that last—remember so much that I'm bound to forget *some* things."

"Try not to. You *do* want to return eventually, don't you?"

Pulling at the starched ruff scratching her neck, Tabitha sighed. "Yes. Anything to get away from here!"

One glance at Susan's face told Pete Sheridan how it had gone with Hunter Carson. He shook his head.

"Guess I don't have to ask any questions, Miss Susan. You didn't get the extension."

Her voice quivered with anger. "Oh, I got it if I want it!" she said through clenched teeth. "I'm just not certain I care for his terms."

Pete scowled. "He didn't say anything . . . wrong . . . to you, did he, Miss Susan? I won't stand for that."

Realizing that she'd been about to cause a serious feud between her loyal ranch foreman and Hunter Carson, Susan said quickly, "No, no, nothing like that, Pete. He's just rude and obnoxious, that's all."

"I don't believe you." Pete's eyes were narrowed, and his jaw was tight. "I don't care who he is. Nobody gets away with insulting you, Miss Susan!"

"Pete, whatever he said, it was my fault." Honesty made her admit it to Pete when she hadn't been willing to admit it before. "I said some rude things to him, though they were truthful enough, I guess. I should have listened to you about watching my tongue."

Still unconvinced, Pete slid a glance toward the Carson Feed and Granary offices. "Maybe he deserved to hear the truth."

"I won't argue with that." Susan slid her hand in the crook of Pete's elbow. "Walk with me to Thrasher's. I want to get something to eat."

Pete relaxed slightly. "You must be desperate to avoid an argument if you're willin' to eat at Thrasher's."

"Well, at least we know the beef is fresh, if a bit burned on the outside and raw on the inside." Susan smiled at him. "Come on. It's not like we have an entire range of restaurants to choose from. Thrasher's is the only one still open."

Surrendering to her smile, Pete allowed Susan to walk him down the wooden sidewalks. Wagons rumbled slowly past them, and a few dogs barked lazily. Other than that, it was quiet.

Los Alamos was dying slowly. It was apparent in the deserted stores, the lack of interest in those still open, and the general air of hopelessness that hung over the small town. Where once it had been a bustling center of commerce on a main route, now it had lost out to the railroad miles to the northeast. For a time the citizens had hoped that the railroad would build a spur to their small town, but that hope had died a few years before. Now it sat quietly in the searing sun and waited for the end.

"I suppose this will be a ghost town soon," Susan said as she looked around the quiet streets. Dust hung in a thick haze. "No one seems to care anymore."

Pete shrugged. "Won't matter much to the Lazy W. Have to go farther for supplies, but that's all."

"Don't you care?" Susan asked in surprise.

"Not much."

"Pete Sheridan! Where's your civic pride?"

Grinning, Pete drawled, "I'm usually sittin' on it, Miss Susan. The Lazy W has all my loyalty. You ought to know that."

"I suppose I do, but I hate to see Los Alamos die for lack of interest. My father helped start this town."

"There's that," Pete agreed. "If Jake was still here, I guess things would be different."

Susan's throat tightened. "I know they would." To avoid the sadness thoughts of her father always invoked, she asked Pete, "Where does Hunter Carson come from? I mean, all I know about him is that he showed up here in Los Alamos one day and bought the granary from Oliver Simpson. Why? I wonder. It should be obvious that he's not going to make a lot of money. Grain still has to be bought and shipped a great distance because we don't have a railroad."

Pete didn't answer until they'd entered the restaurant and ordered steaks, then he looked at Susan with a frown.

" 'Bout all I can tell you is rumors, Miss Susan. The way I hear it, Carson is from Fort Worth and owns granaries and feedlots there. He's said to be pretty ruthless when it comes to business, and in his private life as well."

"Meaning?"

"Meaning that he ain't knowed to back down when a man braces him."

"Oh." Susan thought about that a moment. "Has he been in many gunfights, then?"

"A share of them. I heard he shot the Cherokee Kid in a fair fight, and the Kid was known to be one of the best."

"I see." Susan began to revise her first impression of Carson slightly. "He's no natty businessman, like I thought he might be," she murmured over the rim of her coffee cup. "And he certainly doesn't mince words when he gets his back up."

Pete watched her closely. Her face had colored when she spoke of Carson, and he wondered again just what had been said. Knowing Susan, she had given Carson ample cause to insult her, but he still wouldn't stand for it. Susan Whitten was almost like a daughter to him.

"Some men don't mince words," Pete said. "Carson's one of them. Give him a wide berth, Miss Susan. We'll figure out some way to keep the Lazy W."

"It will take a miracle," Susan said with a sigh. "And I don't think miracles happen anymore."

Pete shook his head. "No, they don't. Not like that." He looked up and past her, and his dark eyes narrowed. He gave a grunt of irritation that made Susan turn her head. "No," he said quickly, "don't even glance that way. It's Greet Duncan."

"Greet Duncan? The man I fired last month?"

"Yeah. And he don't look none too happy at seein' us here. I'd just as soon you pretend you don't see him."

"That shouldn't be too hard, since you won't let me turn around and look," Susan shot back, but a faint smile curled her mouth. "I guess he's still mad because I fired him for stealing."

"Probably. Men like him don't never take the blame for what they do."

"I think I've met another man like that," Susan said and shrugged when Pete looked at her. "Mr. Carson seems to be as arrogant as they come."

Pete didn't reply, but she could feel him studying her. A faint flush rode her high cheekbones, and Susan reflected that sometimes Pete Sheridan knew entirely too much about her.

Chapter 3

TRY AS SHE might, Susan could not get Hunter Carson off her mind. She thought about him at the most inconvenient times, remembering his insolent, insulting drawl and the way he had looked at her so closely, his jade eyes raking her with an assessing gaze that had made her squirm. No man had ever made her feel that way before.

It had been a week since Susan had met with Carson, and she had not figured out a way to save the ranch yet. The last of their hay was being doled out, and she didn't know what she'd do in the coming days if something didn't turn up.

The drought had ended, but the ground was still parched and the streams mostly dried up. It had rained too late to help several other ranches. She'd heard from Doris that the Andersons had given up and moved on to east Texas, where the rain was a little more steady. So had the Taylors, but they'd gone even farther west, to California.

Staring out over the rolling acres of the Lazy W, Susan sighed. Her discussions with the bank had been fruitless, as she had suspected they would be. Everyone in the county had appealed for loans. There was no help for it. She'd have to go back to Hunter Carson and ask for grain on credit. It was her only option.

Susan watched the sun set over distant hills. Not even Arthur could brighten her mood, and her hand lay idly upon his silky head. The pig grunted and twisted in her lap, then finally lay down at her feet to sleep. Susan sat on the wide front porch and dreaded the coming day. To have to go back, to humble herself in front of Hunter Carson, to see his mocking smile and hear his low, drawling acceptance was almost more than her pride could bear. But pride was little comfort when facing homelessness. Yes, she *would* visit Hunter Carson, and she *would* do her best to make amends and watch her tongue.

This was the hardest thing she'd ever done, Susan thought as she sat in Carson's office. She had taken great pains with her style and wore her best Sunday gown and hat. If she was to go a-begging, she would do so in style.

Hunter leaned back in his chair. As if he knew how she hated being there, he was deliberately slow in getting to the point. He would not allow her to talk about her credit but steered the conversation away from the topic.

"I understand, Miss Whitten," Carson said in his easy, deep drawl, "that you are the sole owner of the Lazy W now. It must be difficult for you to run a ranch that size."

"Not really." Susan cleared her throat of the tightness in it and managed a casual smile. "I have Pete Sheridan to help me. He was my father's foreman and has stayed on. I also have several loyal ranch hands willing to stay until things get better."

Carson smiled. "There's nothing more valuable than loyal employees. Your father must have been a fine man."

"Yes. Yes, he was." Susan itched to end the casual chitchat and get on to the purpose of her visit, and he knew it, damn him. His lazy gaze rested on her face with detached amusement, and she damned him again for looking so blamed handsome. She shifted uneasily and wished he would let her get to the point of her visit.

"You said, I believe, that you have six thousand head of cattle? That's a large number. What are your plans for them?"

Hunter was enjoying himself. Susan Whitten looked as if she would stand up and holler at any moment. Though her large dark eyes were fringed with incredibly long lashes, they could not hide the banked fires smoldering in their depths. Her mouth—full and tempting—was thinned into an irritated line despite her obvious efforts to be pleasant, and her small, determined chin was thrust out in a pugnacious tilt. Oh, yes, he was definitely enjoying himself! Let her squirm; it was the least she could do after attacking his character the last time she had sat in his office.

Halfway through her rambling explanation of what she planned to do with the cattle, Susan stopped.

"You're not really listening to this, are you?" she asked flatly. "And you don't really care what my plans are for the cattle. You've already made up your mind about extending my credit, haven't you?"

"Ah, you are a clever young lady, Miss Whitten." Hunter smiled. "Yes, I have already made up my mind."

Desperately Susan rose to her feet, her gaze fixed on him. "Mr. Carson, I am not a person who is prone to pleading my cause too eloquently, but I would like to ask—"

He stopped her, scowling. "I detest begging. Don't demean either of us by descending to that level. Do you recall my suggestion the last time you were here?"

Susan's cheeks flamed, and her mouth tightened. "I do."

"It was unfair of me."

Relief flooded her. "Yes, it was. And quite vulgar, too, I might add."

"Always tactful, aren't you?" Carson said dryly. "Never mind. I have another proposition for you."

She eyed him warily. "You have?"

"A bargain of sorts." Hunter rose from behind his desk and came around the front, reaching out to take Susan's hands between his large palms. "A compromise."

Her heart began to thud with erratic thumps that made her eyes grow larger and her breath shorten. She didn't dare draw her hands away, not until she heard him out.

Putting out her tongue to moisten lips suddenly grown quite dry, Susan said in a sort of croak, "What kind of bargain?"

She could see his eyes quite clearly now, and they were very, very green. A deep green, almost jade, sharp and flecked with tiny hazel specks that made them look hard. She noticed a small scar that puckered the end of his left eyebrow; it was almost unnoticeable unless one was close, very close, and it made him look even more dangerous—if that was possible. Rather piratical, Susan decided, and hoped she didn't blurt it out.

Hunter's deep, husky voice sent a shiver down her spine. "I think a kiss would be collateral enough to satisfy me."

"A kiss?" She tried to jerk her hands away from his grasp, but he held them tightly.

"Surely you don't object to a simple kiss, do you, Miss Whitten?"

"This is absurd!"

He shrugged. "Life is absurd. A kiss for your future, Miss Whitten. What do you say?"

"You're a madman!"

"I must be. Nonetheless, that is what I want."

Susan hesitated. A kiss wasn't that awful. She'd kissed Evan when they were children, and Race Lassiter at a party one evening. And she sometimes kissed Arthur atop his pink little head. And if it would save the Lazy W . . .

Putting up her chin, she said finally, "All right. One kiss."

Hunter almost laughed. She looked so martyred, as if he had suggested she strip naked and lie upon a sacrificial altar. He would enjoy showing her that one kiss could be a lot more than she'd bargained for.

Pulling her into the sinewy circle of his arms, Hunter tilted back her head with one strong finger under her chin. Susan closed her eyes and pursed her lips chastely. He smiled again, in anticipation this time. She obviously had no idea how to really kiss, and he found that this knowledge intrigued him.

Sliding his left hand around to her back to draw her closer, Hunter felt her sudden leap of alarm. "I'm just going to put my arms around you," he murmured. Her hands clutched his upper arms, and he felt the gentle pressure of her fingers on his muscles.

He slowly pulled Susan closer to him, until she could feel the brush of her breasts against his chest. His shirt buttons dug into her even through the material of her gown, and she could feel the long, hard length of his body all the way down her legs. His thighs were close—shockingly close—and she could feel the prod of his belt buckle against her stomach. Her nerves were stretched tautly, and her breath came in short gasps as she kept her eyes tightly shut. Dratted man. Why didn't he just kiss her?

Then she wished she hadn't been so hasty, because she felt the warm whisper of his lips over hers just before they touched her mouth briefly, then lifted. Thinking it was over, Susan opened her eyes.

"That wasn't a kiss," he said softly. "You're too tense."

"You didn't specify an untense kiss," Susan pointed out.

He shook his head. "Are you a welsher, Miss Whitten? Do you go back on your word?"

"You said—"

"A kiss, not a peck."

He didn't give her time to protest; his fingers gripped her chin firmly, and this time, his mouth moved across her lips in a scalding kiss that made her knees grow weak and her head spin. His tongue slipped between her lips with a startling efficiency that shocked the proper Miss Whitten to her toes. She'd never imagined a man would kiss with his tongue!

And worse, she'd never imagined that she would like it.

An invading heat spread through her body like wild-fire, leaving her nerve-ends flaming and her normal responses raging out of control. She was no longer certain she could give Hunter Carson his simple kiss and be done with it; she wasn't certain of anything but that she had begun to hold on to him with fierce desperation as his mouth moved on her lips. She had to. If she let go, she would slide to the floor in a bone-less heap.

The kiss didn't stop; it seemed to go on forever, until Susan was making strange, moaning noises in the back of her throat and Hunter was breathing fast. Then suddenly he put her away from him and stepped back.

Susan felt strangely bereft. She wasn't quite certain what had happened or why it had stopped. Her eyes were huge in the sunlight streaming in the window, fixed on Hunter with a dazed expression.

Because she felt so odd, and because she wasn't really certain what had just happened to her, Susan blurted out the first thing on her mind.

"There's a great deal of difference in kissing you and kissing Arthur!"

A tawny brow shot up, and Hunter's eyes narrowed the slightest bit. "I suppose I should be flattered, but not knowing Arthur—at any rate, Miss Whitten, you have kept your end of the bargain quite admirably."

"Do I get the extension?"

"Oh, you've had the extension since before your first visit," Hunter said and enjoyed the sudden widening of her eyes. Once again he had the advantage. He hadn't particularly cared for her comparison, whoever Arthur was.

"What do you mean by that?"

"I never allow business and pleasure to mix. As I told you, I examined the records thoroughly. There was never any doubt that the Lazy W would receive a credit extension."

"But you said—!"

"No, you never let me finish saying anything, or you would have heard me say that I expected no collateral from the Lazy W. Its payment record speaks for itself."

"Why, you scoundrel! You blackmailer! You . . . you . . ."

"Bandit?" Hunter supplied helpfully.

"Worse!" Susan's cheeks flamed, and her hands curled into tight fists. Hunter Carson was grinning wickedly at her, and his green eyes were dancing with laughter.

If she hadn't been so chagrined, and appalled that he was right, Susan might have seen the humor in the situation. As it was, she was indignant. She wished she could loftily declare that she had no intention of accepting the extension but knew that would be madness.

Rather grimly, she said, "I hope you enjoyed this little charade."

"Immensely."

"I intend to pay you back."

"For the grain? Or the kiss?"

Susan glared at him. "Both!"

"You came into my office and insulted me," Hunter reminded her with a shrug. "What was I supposed to do?"

Grudgingly she muttered, "Get even, I suppose."

"Would it make you feel better if I told you I didn't enjoy the kiss?"

Startled, she stared at him. "You didn't?"

"I didn't say that. I just asked if it would make you feel better if I said that."

Twirling away, Susan walked toward his office door with as much dignity as she could muster. She could hear his muffled laughter even after she slammed out of the building, and hoped fervently that she never had to lay eyes on the man again.

Tabitha whirled across the desert floor, her long skirts making waves behind her. The hem caught on a cactus, and she disengaged herself with muttering grumbles.

"Cad," she said distinctly, adding, "bounder, churl, caitiff, knave," and a few other choice epithets to her litany. Horatio listened silently. Folding her hands in front of her, Tabitha fixed him with a stern gaze, as if he was directly responsible for Hunter Carson's behavior.

"He has a free will of his own, you know, Tabitha."

"Aye, so you keep telling me." She gave an indignant sniff and tossed her head as best she could. The effect was something less than she desired, as her curled, crimped hair caught on a jewel pinned to her ruff. Disentangling herself, she gave a long sigh.

"Oh, Horatio, the poor girl is bound to make a fool of herself over him. I see it now. He's bewitched her."

"Do you really think so?"

Tabitha sighed again. "No. Not yet, anyway. But he's certainly put her into a tizzy, I'll tell you that."

"Maybe she'll enjoy it."

Drawing her chin up and giving him a frosty stare, Tabitha said, "That is a typically male response, Horatio, and I had thought you above all that."

"It was a simple observation."

"Fie! It was arrogantly rude, just the sort of remark Hunter Carson would make." Tabitha turned her back on him and stared down at the small town nestled on the prairie. Her plucked brows drew together in a thoughtful frown. "I wonder," she said slowly after several moments had passed, "if familiarity would not breed a certain contempt on her part. After all, he's so obviously wrong for her, and once the . . . uh . . . *attraction* part was overcome, she'd see it quite clearly."

"Do you think so?"

"Of course." Tabitha nodded wisely. "It will be just like wearing a shoe that's too tight: the friction will make her miserable, and she'll give him his comeuppance."

"And that will fix everything?"

Tabitha looked surprised. "Why shouldn't it? She has the loan, after all, and will make a go of the ranch. Now, if she can only rid herself of that nuisance, her life will rock along quite smoothly."

"If you say so, Tabitha."

Of course, Susan told herself, in a town as small as Los Alamos, they were bound to run into each other. Even if she'd remained on her ranch, she would have eventually had to face Hunter. In the end, when they met again, it wasn't as bad as she had anticipated.

"We meet again, Miss Whitten," Hunter said when he saw her outside the bank several days later. "What a surprise."

Susan's heart did a funny kind of flip-flop in her chest, but her voice did not betray her. "*I'm* not surprised, since we both live in the same town," she said and enjoyed the way his mouth squared into a broad grin.

He looked unbearably handsome. Sunlight made his golden hair gleam like raw silk, and his eyes were narrowed with laughter, green and warm. She stifled the urge to blurt out an admiring comment about his looks and smiled instead.

"Ever the diplomat, aren't you?" he inquired. His mouth curled with humor, almost making her forget the touch of those sensuous lips against her own. Almost.

"I do try my best." Susan matched his careless smile. "I fear that I'm late for an appointment now, Mr. Carson, so if you'll excuse me?"

"If you mean Mr. Cadwallader, forget it. He's closeted with some official today and won't be able to keep any of his appointments," Hunter said.

"Oh!" Susan's brow furrowed. She glanced up the street to see if Pete was still in sight, but the ranch foreman had disappeared, probably into one of the two saloons. She sighed. She should have come alone. That's what she'd wanted to do, but Pete had insisted upon accompanying her.

"Tell you what," Carson was saying, "since I couldn't see Mr. Cadwallader, either, why don't we have lunch? My treat," he added when he saw the doubtful look in her eyes. "And it's in broad daylight, so you can be assured I won't molest you."

The quick memory of his warm lips against hers slid into Susan's mind, and she remembered the fiery warmth that had spread from her neck to her toes.

"What makes you think I don't want to be molested?" Susan asked before she thought, then flushed when Hunter burst into laughter. When would she ever learn to think before she spoke?

"Somehow," Hunter said, still laughing, "I have the feeling you'd renege if I took you up on that. Don't worry. I'll be a gentleman."

"There's a first time for everything, I suppose," Susan observed tartly but allowed him to escort her to Thrasher's.

It was crowded. Being the only restaurant in town, it had the dubious distinction of being patronized by most of the inhabitants at one time or the other. As soon as Hunter entered, three waiters rushed over to vie for his attention and show him to a table.

"I eat here every day," he confided to Susan when she remarked that no one had ever treated *her* like visiting royalty. "I think Mrs. Thrasher is afraid I'll do the sensible thing and hire a cook if they aren't nice to me."

Seated across from him, Susan regarded Hunter steadily for a long moment. He confused her. Just when she began to think he was a complete blackguard, he showed a more charming side of his personality. How? Did she dare think differently of him because he could converse lightly and waiters liked him? No. He was still the same man who had tricked her into kissing him.

"So why don't you?" she asked abruptly, and he shrugged.

"Why don't I hire a cook? I don't know. I'm not really domestic. I don't usually care anything about extravagant meals. I only want something filling."

"Then you should be satisfied with eating here," Susan said wryly. "If your only requirement was that your stomach was filled, you could graze out on the prairie."

"Cactus spines get between my teeth," Hunter said. He eyed Susan's face for a moment, his gaze shifting from her wide-spaced dark eyes to her lips, then to her sculpted cheekbones. "I bet you have a cook."

"The best. Doris. She's been with us for years, ever since I was small."

"I have someone like that at home in Fort Worth. She runs the house, though, and I'm not allowed to cross her."

Susan arched her brows. "Somehow, I find that hard to believe. You don't seem like the kind of man who would allow anyone to argue with him."

"No?" Hunter crossed his arms atop the table. "What kind of man do I seem like to you, Miss Whitten?"

"Hard. Like a pirate, maybe. You know, used to taking what you want without regard for others' feelings." She flushed when he didn't smile. "I always say what's on my mind, Mr. Carson. Maybe you've noticed."

"Oh, I've definitely noticed," Hunter said in his easy drawl, and the hint of a smile touched his lips. "So when do I get a dinner invitation?"

Susan stared at him. "Excuse me?"

"Dinner. A homecooked meal. You said you have Doris, and she's a great cook. Would you deny a hungry man food?"

Relaxing slightly, Susan smiled. "I only said that to tease you."

"It worked."

"Tuesday?"

He grinned. "Tuesday is fine. I'm surprised you were so easy, Miss Whitten. I thought I'd have to do a lot of coaxing to wrangle a dinner invitation from you."

She leaned forward, lowering her voice. "I intend to get my revenge by doing the cooking myself, Mr. Carson."

Laughing, Hunter shook his head, and Susan had the sharp thought that he was very much at ease for a man who held the future of the entire town in his hands. She wondered what he wanted from her and sensed that it wasn't just repayment of her debt. Despite his affable front, Hunter Carson had a steely undercurrent that showed through at times. It made her vaguely uneasy.

"The nerve of that man!" Tabitha snapped to Horatio. "I'm surprised that a relative of mine can't see through his handsome facade to the rogue beneath!"

"So you think Carson dishonest?" Horatio inquired.

"I'm positive of it! Well, I've done all I can do. She just refuses to see it. I'm ready to return."

"I don't think you're finished here, Tabitha."

Her mouth pursed with dismay. "What do you mean? It's up to her to work things out now."

"But things have not been entirely resolved, have they? There's still Mr. Carson, and there are still her taxes to be paid. Not to mention the fact that someone wants the Lynnfield brooch."

"*My* brooch?" Tabitha was indignant. "I won't have it!"

"Oh? Then I think you'd best linger a while. . . ."

Chapter 4

DORIS GRUMBLED, "I don't know why you're making all this fuss. Isn't this the same man who's walked out with half of Los Alamos?"

A wave of irritation washed over Susan. "Probably. Why should that make any difference?"

Eying her mistress, Doris's blue eyes were sharp with speculation. "Are you trying to sweet-talk him into something, Miss Susan? Is that why you invited him to dinner tonight?"

"Actually, I have no idea why I invited him," Susan said frankly. "The invitation just came out before I thought about it. And I already have a credit extension."

Shaking her head, Doris muttered, "This doesn't make any sense, but I can't say anything you've ever done has—Arthur! Get out of there!" She swatted the pig with a rag. "Does this pig have to stay underfoot while I'm trying to cook?"

"He wants you to share." Susan shooed the stubborn pig toward the door. "My, my, Arthur, you're growing," she said, panting as she pulled him from the kitchen.

"Mark my words, Miss Susan, one of these days you won't be able to get that pig through the back door. Then what will you do?"

"Let him sleep in your room," Susan said with a wicked grin. "I don't know why you carry on so over Arthur. He's housebroken and much tidier than a dog. And he likes you."

49

"Only because I always smell like food to him—now, go on with you—both of you—or this cake won't be done in time."

Susan left the kitchen with Arthur, half-dragging the reluctant pig from his favorite room. She wondered why she felt so nervous about Carson coming to dinner. He was just a man—even if he was a man who was fast becoming the most talked about man in Los Alamos. She'd heard rumors of his business deals, some of them ruthless, some of them quite sympathetic, if one could apply the word *sympathetic* to Hunter Carson.

And she had invited him to dinner. Sudden qualms assailed her about being with Carson, having him in her home. Whatever had possessed her to do such a thing? He was dangerous. Everyone said so. Even Pete, who normally gave a man enough rope to hang himself.

"Don't rightly know why, but I think he's got more up his sleeve than he's tellin'," Pete had said.

Susan put her palms on her scalding cheeks and briefly closed her eyes. She must have lost her mind. Or close to it. Because when she thought of Hunter Carson, she thought of his kiss, his searing lips touching hers. She didn't think of Pete's doubts, or of Doris's blunt warning, or even of Evan's accusations—she thought of Hunter's arms around her and his mouth hovering over hers. She was shameless, she supposed, utterly shameless.

Remembering that, Susan met Hunter with a cool reserve that lifted his eyebrows.

"Good evening, Mr. Carson," she said in a demure tone that teased a smile from him.

"Good evening, Miss Whitten." He stepped down from his horse and looped the reins over the hitching post in front of the house, then stepped up on the porch. He hadn't quite expected to find her waiting on the front porch for him, nor had he expected the awkward greeting. "I'm not too early, am I?" he asked, and she shook her head.

"No, not at all. I said six o'clock, and it's exactly one minute to. You're very prompt."

Hunter gazed at her for a brief moment, then held out a small package. "This is for you."

Startled, Susan took the package, jerking her hand away when her fingers accidentally brushed against his warm hand.

"Thank you," she managed to say calmly and pried open the lid of the box. It contained bonbons, all neatly contained in small slots. She looked up at Hunter. "I've never received candy from a man before. Am I supposed to eat it now or save it until later?"

He looked at her gravely. "That depends on your mood. Since we haven't had dinner yet, maybe you should save it."

She shut the lid on the box and noticed that it had a big red taffeta heart on the top. A faint flush stained her cheeks, and she hoped he didn't notice.

Hunter did notice and was hard pressed not to laugh. Despite Susan Whitten's outspoken nature and heavy responsibilities, she retained charming naïveté.

"Am I invited inside?" he asked when several more moments passed.

Susan looked startled. "I'm not sure—I mean, I guess that would be proper—if you won't try to kiss me again."

She flushed, suddenly aware of what she had blurted. Now he would know she'd been thinking about his kiss, and she'd wanted to avoid that. Drat! Why did she always have to say what was on her mind?

Hunter was looking amused, and his gaze lingered for a long moment on her lips as if to tell her that he had no intention of making wild promises. His words, however, were coolly polite.

"After you, Miss Whitten." He reached around her to open the door, ignoring her flustered leap of alarm.

Why had she ever invited him out to dinner? And why did he have to look so devastatingly handsome, dressed in a red vest, snug-fitting cords, and a navy shirt open at the collar? He wore guns slung around his lean waist, and she realized with a shock it was the first time she had seen him wear them. They weren't the serviceable type of revolvers the cowboys on the Lazy W wore. They weren't ornate, by any means, but looked beautifully deadly.

"Expecting trouble with the menu?" Susan said, pointing to his guns.

He grinned. "It's a nice ride from Los Alamos to the Lazy W, and I wanted to keep it that way."

Nodding, Susan led him into the neat parlor with its carved cherry tables and lacy cloths. Hunter Carson looked out of place in the dainty room, just as her father had always looked. Jake Whitten had been a big man and had only stepped into his wife's parlor when forced to do so. He'd much preferred his masculine study, and looking at Carson as he sat on the settee, dwarfing it with his large frame, Susan understood her father's reluctance. Some men just looked uncomfortable sitting on floral-print settees.

As Susan cast about for a subject of conversation, Doris appeared in the doorway. "Are you ready to serve, Miss Susan?"

"Perhaps Mr. Carson would like a drink before dinner," Susan said and turned to him. "What would you like?"

"What do you have?" Hunter asked, correctly guessing

from the feminine appointments that his choices of drink would be limited.

"Blackberry wine, a cordial, or rye whiskey that we keep for emergencies," Doris said in a disapproving tone.

"Since this isn't an emergency, maybe I'll pass on the drink." Hunter twirled his hat in his hands and began to wish he hadn't come. Why had he begun something like this anyway? Susan Whitten was not the kind of young woman he usually formed an attachment for. None of his attachments lasted long, and he liked it that way. His business life was complicated, so he liked his personal life light and free.

At the moment his only consolation was that Susan obviously felt just as uncomfortable and awkward as he did. Maybe he should do the generous thing and end the evening as quickly as possible.

Susan smoothed the watered-silk material of her skirt and managed a casual smile. Hunter stared down as he continued to twirl his hat in his hands. Susan cleared her throat.

"Mr. Carson . . ."

"Miss Whitten . . ." they both said at the same time, then paused. "Go ahead," Hunter offered.

While Susan tried to think of something witty to say, Hunter gazed at her with polite attention. His gaze admired the smooth texture of her hair and the tiny mass of dark ringlets that dangled in front of her ears, and he thought for a moment of how sweet her lips had been before he tore his attention from that direction. Best not to think of such things at a time like this.

Fortunately for both of them, Arthur chose that moment to come into the parlor, creating an instant diversion.

Arthur trotted up to the startled Hunter. Immediately

the pig seized his hat. "Oh, you naughty pig!" Susan cried. She leapt up from her chair and went to try and wrest the hat from him, but Arthur resisted. "Doris!" Susan called over her shoulder. "Doris! I thought you put Arthur in the root cellar."

"Arthur?" When Hunter reached out and managed to pry the pig's teeth from the brim of his hat, he asked, "Is this the Arthur you referred to in my office?"

"Did I? I don't remember." Susan tugged Arthur away from Hunter with an effort.

"I do." Hunter's voice was faintly grim, but a suggestion of amusement flickered in his eyes. "You compared kissing me to kissing Arthur. I assume you meant this Arthur?"

"Oh!" Susan looked up at him guiltily. "Are you offended?"

"I'll let you know when I'm more closely acquainted with Arthur," Hunter replied, putting his hat safely out of the pig's reach.

Susan began to laugh, and Hunter grinned. By the time Doris announced that dinner was served, they were both more comfortable with each other.

"So just why did you buy out Simpson?" Susan asked him over dessert. "You said it seemed like an excellent investment, but I find that difficult to believe. Los Alamos is not exactly a boomtown, and even though there are quite a few profitable ranches in the area, without the railroad, the town is doomed."

Hunter shrugged. "Let's just say I'm a man who likes to take chances."

"So I've heard." When his eyebrow lifted, Susan added, "The Cherokee Kid. Someone told me you beat him in a fair fight."

Hunter's green eyes cooled slightly. "Gossip and rumors are never to be trusted, Miss Whitten. Keep that in mind."

"You mean it wasn't a fair fight?"

His gaze warmed, and a smile curled his mouth. "You have a knack for speaking out, don't you?"

"I've been told that," she confessed. "I try and watch what I say, but sometimes it just pops out. So—was it a fair fight?"

"Fair enough. I let him draw first and have the first shot."

Susan's eyes widened. "And you still shot him?"

"Ghoulish curiosity, Miss Whitten?"

"Admitted."

Hunter grinned. "Yes, I still shot him. He didn't leave me any other option."

Propping her chin in her palm, Susan gazed at Hunter across the table and the remnants of Doris's white satin cake. "You *are* a dangerous man, Hunter Carson."

"Only to people who insist upon shooting at me when I've requested that they stop," Hunter said lightly and pushed his empty plate away. "I cannot eat another bite of food, Miss Whitten. You have fulfilled your boasts most admirably, and I concede Doris's wizardry in the kitchen."

"I'll tell her. Would you care for an after-dinner drink or something?"

"If it's blackberry wine or cordial, no." Hunter rose as Susan stood up, and he put out his hand. "Let's take a walk."

Despite a small warning voice in the back of her mind, Susan walked outside with Hunter. Dusk shrouded the land, and the buildings sprawling beyond the main house were black silhouettes against a paler night sky. A thin

moon was barely visible. Lights glowed in the bunkhouse, and the lowing and gentle movements of cattle
could be heard in the distance.

Susan walked in comfortable silence beside Hunter,
and Arthur trotted behind them.

"You're the only woman I know who has a pet pig,"
Hunter remarked, and Susan laughed.

"Arthur is unique."

"So are you."

His husky voice sent a shiver down her spine, and
Susan said lightly to cover her sudden awkwardness, "I
didn't mean to keep him as a pet, really, but he was so
small and defenseless, and as he got older, he'd grown
attached to me. I couldn't just put him out with the other
pigs, so here he is."

"You seem to collect strays," Hunter said softly, and
when they reached the dark shadow of a huge oak and
Susan turned to ask him what he meant, he drew her
into his arms.

She'd been half-expecting it—anticipating it, really,
and didn't protest. Instead, she closed her eyes and put
her face up for his kiss.

Hunter's fingertips stroked down the side of her cheek,
stingingly warm, oddly stimulating. His hand moved to
cup her chin in his palm and hold her head still as his
mouth brushed over her parted lips. Lightly at first, then
with a firm pressure, he slid his tongue into her mouth
and heard her faint gasp of surprise. One strong arm
bent behind her back and held her close against him,
so close he could feel the thunder of her heart beating
against his chest.

Susan's head whirled, and she knew then that she had
gone far beyond all rational thought. She had almost
thrown herself at Hunter, but somehow that didn't matter

at this moment. What mattered was that he was holding her closely and kissing her, and that she liked it.

Lifting her arms in an artless motion, she put them around Hunter's neck, her slender body pressing against him as she did. Hunter responded to her proximity, to the pressure of her firm breasts against his chest, but he knew that she wasn't aware of how she affected him. As artless and naive as she was, Susan Whitten had no idea what havoc she was wreaking with his endurance. It amazed him. She'd been brought up on a ranch—didn't she have some idea of what went on between men and women, or had her education been confined to the animal world? Maybe Susan didn't know that it could be dangerous to tempt a man at times.

Schooling himself, Hunter kissed Susan long and thoroughly, much more thoroughly than his body could bear, then set her away from him. He was breathing roughly, and his eyes were hot and green as he looked down at her lovely face. Her eyes were still closed, and her mouth open and bruised from his kisses.

He gently touched her cheek. "I think that's enough for now, Susan."

Her lashes flew up, and she looked disappointed. "But I was enjoying it!"

Rather grimly, Hunter muttered, "So was I, but if I keep kissing you, I'm going to want to do much more." He gave her a gentle shake. "Understand?"

Suddenly she did, and her cheeks grew warm and pink. "I think so. I just didn't consider that. It . . . it's different for a man than it is for a woman."

Hunter fumbled in his vest pocket for his cigarettes, drew one out to gain time and keep control, rolled it, lit it, and took several puffs before he said, "Yeah, I believe it is different."

He leaned back against the broad trunk of the oak and surveyed her moonlit face. Lights from distant buildings provided a faint glow that took the edge from the deepening night shadows.

"So tell me, Susan Whitten," he said after a moment, "why aren't you married?"

She shrugged. "Because I couldn't find a man who'd have me."

"I find that unbelievable." Hunter narrowed his eyes against the stinging curl of smoke from his cigarette. "Are you just choosy?"

"You could say that," she agreed. "I want more than just friendship. I want . . ." She paused, uncertain how to say what she felt without sounding foolish or childish. "I want whistles and horns, I guess," she ended lamely.

"Whistles and horns?"

"You know—something out of the ordinary to happen when I fall in love. I'd rather spend the rest of my life alone or with Arthur than take what's available just because I can't find what I want."

"Ah, I forgot Arthur, the kissing pig."

She laughed. "Arthur doesn't kiss—I *kiss* Arthur."

"Somehow, I find that less than flattering," Hunter said wryly. "And I'm not about to ask where I rate against the illustrious Arthur."

Susan slanted him a curious, half-laughing glance. "So why aren't you married?"

He hesitated, then said, "It's hard to find a woman who can keep a man's interest for a long time, much less long enough to get married." Hunter shrugged at her questioning look. "Most women only want one thing from a man."

"And that is—?"

"Undying devotion, all his attention, heart and soul

and body and mind—I don't think I left anything out."

"That's more than one thing," Susan pointed out with a laugh. "And it sounds perfectly reasonable to me. After all, if a woman is going to trust a man with her heart, shouldn't she expect something back?"

Hunter tossed his cigarette to the ground and crushed it with his boot, then smiled down at Susan. "I should have known you'd see logic in that. Any woman who keeps a pig in the house couldn't have a surplus of logic."

"If that's supposed to be insulting, you missed."

Another heart-stopping smile curled Hunter's mouth, and he lifted Susan's chin in his palm as he studied her upturned face intently.

"You are the most intriguing woman I have ever met, Susan Whitten," he said softly. "I don't think I understand half of what you say, but you're not boring."

A shiver traced her spine as he bent his golden head and kissed her lightly, and when he drew back again, she somehow found her voice.

"I think you're the most dangerous man I've ever met, Hunter Carson, but I'm not afraid of you."

Some of the humor left his eyes. "You should be."

It wasn't until much, much later, after he'd left and Susan was alone in her bedroom with Arthur curled on his rug on the floor, that she took the time to mull over his words. She wondered why he'd come out to the ranch, and why he'd acted so polite and charming. Although it wasn't in Susan's nature to be devious, she had a feeling he was putting on some type of a show tonight.

Maybe she should heed his warning. . . .

Chapter 5

SPLUTTERING, TABITHA SAID, "Did you see that? He kissed her again! Horatio, I tell you, girls today are entirely too brazen and—"

"Tabitha."

She paused and looked at him, and her thin, plucked brows lifted inquiringly. "Aye?"

"I seem to recall much more than stolen kisses in the court of Elizabeth."

"Oh. Well, of course, we *were* a bit impetuous at that, but I was certainly never brazen enough to—well, I'm sure that if I did, I did penance for it."

Horatio's austere face seemed amused. "Hypocrisy ill becomes you, Tabitha. And I believe that you may have more to remember than a few innocent kisses in the moonlight."

"Forsooth—sorry. Of course, you're right. So, now that my little kinswoman has managed to get starry-eyed," she said in a scathing tone, "I suppose I am to arrange for *him* to fall in love with her, too? It's obvious that he will do what men like that always do, if I don't."

"Which is?" Horatio seemed interested, locking his hands behind his back and gazing at Tabitha.

"Which is, he will have his way with her, then leave her behind like an old shoe." Tabitha nodded wisely. "I've seen it happen many times." A faint frown creased her brow. "Not to one of my relatives, however."

"Tabitha, remember," Horatio cautioned, "that you can only arrange circumstances, not—"

"I know, I know!" She drew herself into an indignant knot. "But all the same, I do think that this Master Hunter Carson should be schooled a bit."

"I tell you, Susan, the man's after more than just a walk in the moonlight with you!" Evan's voice was bitter and tight. He leaned on the corral fence and stared at her.

"It's really none of your business, Evan." Susan yanked at the stirrup strap and readjusted its length, her gaze determinedly fixed on the worn leather of her saddle, avoiding Evan's angry face. It was vaguely humiliating to have everyone know she'd been kissed in the moonlight by Hunter Carson, but there were few secrets on the Lazy W. Especially if one allowed one's self to be held and kissed in the open where anyone could see. What had she expected?

"Maybe it ain't any of my business," Evan continued stubbornly, "but I'm making it so! Carson is dangerous. And if you think it's you he's after, you're wrong."

Her mouth twisted wryly. "I suppose you're right. Why would any man be interested in me alone?"

"Aw, Susan, I didn't mean it that way and you know it!"

"Do I?" Her frosty gaze met his at last. "You certainly don't convince me."

Evan had the grace to flush, but his eyes were still angry, his fair complexion mottled. "Look, Susan. He's swallowed up several ranches around here, and you know it. Don't fool yourself into thinking he'd avoid picking up the Lazy W because of your pretty face."

"Evan, I don't think this is a subject you and I can discuss rationally," Susan said tightly. She slid a hand down the worked leather of her saddle, letting her fingers linger over the carefully tooled pattern. "For all your good intentions, you're not my father. I appreciate the sentiment but not the interference."

"You always were hardheaded," Evan growled. "And if it works out like I think it will, you'll be sorry quick enough."

"Good. Then you can say 'I told you so,' and we'll all rest easy." Susan flashed him a furious glance and stepped up into her saddle. Her mare took a few prancing steps to the right and tossed its head.

Evan's jaw was clenched tightly, and his hands knotted into fists. Suddenly she was sorry they'd come to these kind of words. He meant well; she knew he did. But she had no desire to be lessoned when she was all of twenty-three years old!

Something told her that Hunter Carson could be trusted in business matters. He was not dishonorable, just astute. Those who spoke against him in town were the same men who managed their ranches poorly. Only Evan seemed to think him a thief and worse. But then, Evan *did* have a cause, she reminded herself, feeling slightly guilty.

"Evan, I'm sorry," she said with a sigh. Her smile flashed briefly. "I've had so much on my mind lately. I won't be too trusting, I promise. And as for the other, it was a simple kiss, no more."

Even as she said it, Susan knew she was telling a big, fat fib. It had been no simple kiss. Not for her. For Hunter Carson, perhaps, but not for her. There had been something so . . . hungry . . . in her response to him that it had been slightly shaming.

Well, it was not likely to happen again. He had not seemed overly taken with her and had left with only vague comments about returning. Nothing definite. She probably was, as Evan said, a fool. But she could be nothing other than what she was, and she knew it.

"Where are you going, Susan?" Evan's hand was on the toe of her boot, and she glanced down at him in surprise. She'd almost forgotten he was there, or where she was. Her attention had drifted far from the present.

"I have to ride into town and check with the granary. There was some confusion about the last order. Not enough alfalfa and too much sweet feed."

"Can't someone else do that?" Evan frowned.

"No," Susan answered patiently. "Pete is busy with the branding, as are most of the other men. It's springtime, Evan. You know how busy it is around here."

Her glance seemed to accuse him of being less than concerned with his own ranch, and Evan flushed.

"Yeah. I've been busier than a dog with two tails myself lately." He paused, looking up at her from beneath the felt brim of his hat as if he wanted to say something else, but when he shook his head, she shrugged.

"I've got to go now, Evan. See you Saturday."

"Saturday—oh, yeah. The dance." He forced a smile. "I don't suppose it will do me any good to ask, but—"

"Doris and I are going together, along with Pete," Susan said to forestall his invitation. "We're taking some of Doris's famous fried chicken."

"Yeah, I thought you might." Evan stepped back and away from Susan's horse. "See you there."

Susan couldn't help feeling guilty as she rode into town. Poor Evan. It must be terrible to want someone to love you back. She didn't know. She'd never been in love. It sounded like much too dangerous an emotion.

Hunter Carson's image flashed into her mind, and she dug her heels into the bay's sides with a grimace. She certainly had not felt love the other night; she wasn't stupid. She recognized lust, pure and simple, for what it was. Susan had no knowledge of flirtation; she was far too direct. And she knew what she'd felt had not been starry-eyed love but a physical response to an attractive man.

A hot flush rose in her cheeks. She still felt it.

"Oh, Lord," she moaned aloud, "I must be crazy! It's the heat. Just the heat. That's all."

Hunter Carson was suffering from the same kind of crazy heat. He stared out the window of his office, ignoring the pile of paperwork on his desk. His dark brows were furrowed, and his hands knotted behind his back.

A slight breeze blew over Los Alamos. Dust boiled up in the street, wafting on slow currents of air that hung in a murky haze. Commerce had picked up slightly. The general store had generated more business, and with the easing of financial pressure on some of the ranchers, more people were in town. A normal reaction to loan extensions and more credit. It might even save the town eventually.

Hunter's hard mouth curved into a slight smile. Of course, he knew something that would really revitalize the sluggish economy. All he had to do was wait.

He leaned forward and rested his weight on knuckles pressing into the wooden windowsill as he saw a familiar figure riding slowly into town. There was the cause of his discontent. And she looked damnably pretty astride a prancing bay, her golden skin gleaming in the harsh sunlight.

Straightening, Hunter left his office without bothering to tell his clerk where he was going.

By the time Susan reached the granary offices, Hunter was outside waiting on her. A faint smile curled his mouth, and his green eyes were veiled by long, thick lashes.

"Hullo," Susan said, sliding from atop her bay and looping the reins carelessly over the hitching rail. Hunter noted the delectable sway of her hips in the fitted riding skirt she wore, the split sides skimming over long, slender legs as she crossed to the porch. She was smiling at him, and her full lips parted teasingly. "Is business so slow that you come out to drag customers in from the streets?" She stepped up on the low porch and dragged her hat from her head, slapping it against a gloved palm and sending dust spiraling into the air between them.

Hunter shrugged. "Just special customers."

Laughing, Susan arched a delicate brow at him. "Ah, you're a smooth one, Hunter Carson! And now you're probably going to say that I'm a sight for sore eyes and pretty enough to charm coyotes, right?"

He grinned. "I can't fool you, it seems. Am I that predictable?"

"Most men are." She peeled off her gloves and stuffed them into her hat, then raked a hand through the tumbled strands of dark hair that clung damply to her neck. "I've heard it all before."

Thoroughly amused now, Hunter said, "Aren't you supposed to pretend shyness and modesty at this point? Then murmur how shocked you are by my forwardness?"

"Probably." She twirled her hat in her hands, and there was a soft glow in her thick-fringed brown eyes. "But I've never been very good at that. I usually end up looking and sounding like a fool if I try."

"Ah." Hunter swung open the door to his offices. "Then come inside and we'll stick to business. I assume that's why you're here?"

"Yes," she said with a laugh, "but don't disappoint me! I expected more flowery phrases and attempts at seduction, not this easy surrender."

Hunter waited until they were in his private office and the door was closed behind them before he replied. He simmered with heat when he looked at her and wondered if she could see it.

"I can certainly continue with the seduction," he said, "if you like. With or without the flowery phrases." His voice was deliberately soft and husky, and he saw from the sudden widening of her eyes that it had the desired effect on her.

"Oh. Well, you know I was only teasing you," she said after a moment and shifted uneasily to toss her wide-brimmed felt hat in a chair when he reached for her.

"Were you?" he murmured. "Now, where did I get the idea that you weren't?"

She turned back to him with a startled glance. Her eyes were wide burning pools in her dusky face. "Mr. Carson . . ."

"Hunter." His hand cupped her elbows and drew her close to him. "I think we know each other well enough to bypass formality, don't you, Susan?"

"No. I mean yes, we probably do, but is it safe?" She squirmed out of his hold and stepped out of reach.

"Safe for who?" He spread his arms wide. "I'm not even wearing my guns."

Susan's gaze flicked briefly over his body in the tight denim pants, shirtsleeves rolled up to expose a muscled, stretch of forearm, and the collar open at the neck. Her eyes moved back to his face with an odd tautness.

"Ah, then it's only you who are in danger." She awkwardly reached for her gloves, trying to keep her hands busy. The leather fingers of the gloves shook slightly with her reaction to him, and he smiled at her.

His senses quickened, and he wondered at it even while he resisted. Susan Whitten had a strong effect on him. He wondered if she even suspected it. Somehow, he thought that she didn't. She looked as if she was having trouble knowing just what to think.

"Am I in danger, Susan?" The mocking smile widened. "Mortal, maybe?"

She laughed, but less easily this time. "Definitely. I often have that effect on men, hadn't you heard?"

"As a matter of fact," he said more seriously, "I had heard."

"Oh? And who told on me?"

"Evan Elliott."

Her smile faded. "Evan!" She looked faintly startled. "What on earth did that rattlebrain have to say?"

Definitely enjoying himself now, Hunter leaned back against his desk and crossed his long legs at the ankle. This was getting to be too much fun. A prudent man would resist going on with this. But he didn't.

"Only that you and he have been promised to each other since you were children, but that you weren't quite ready to make it official yet." He bent closer. "Mr. Elliott expects you to be his wife any day now."

"Does he!" The gloves slapped briskly across her open palm, and her dark eyes flashed with anger.

"So I was made to understand."

"That snake!"

Hunter laughed. "I thought the same. Glad to see that you agree."

She glared at him. "Don't you dare say anything unkind about Evan! *I* can say things about him, but only because he's my friend."

Nodding, Hunter didn't disagree. In fact, he was rather glad she'd defended Elliott. At least she had loyalty, even when it was—in his opinion—misplaced.

Susan's fine brown eyes sparkled. Her chin lifted with what he recognized as trampled pride. "So, now you probably think I'm hanging out after you like the rest of the women in town. I imagine Evan was not overly tactful."

"No, he wasn't, and no, I don't necessarily think you are 'hanging out' after me." His dark brow rose slightly, and he shifted position against the desk. "But then, I was not aware that the rest of the town was hanging out after me, either, as you have implied."

An impish gleam lit her eyes. "The Widow Simpson has been making eyes, I hear, not to mention Lyla Wentworth."

"Ah. Lyla. And that constitutes the entire town?"

Susan's brows had drawn into a slight frown. "You speak of Miss Wentworth as if you are familiar with her. Are you?"

Hunter stilled the impulse to laugh and said gravely, "Not in the sense you may mean, Susan."

"Oh!" Her cheeks flushed. "I didn't mean that quite as it sounded, you know. I only meant, that Lyla is— blast it, don't laugh at me!"

"Sorry, but you have to be the most transparent female I have ever met," Hunter said. He couldn't resist her bald honesty. And he could not resist leaning forward to take her into his arms again.

Susan offered a brief resistance, then sighed. "I guess we might as well get this over with. Then we can talk about alfalfa and sweet feed."

"Good idea."

Hunter brushed his lips over hers, lightly at first, still amused. But when she closed her eyes and leaned against him, his amusement quickly altered to a fierce pleasure in the feel of her soft body. The gentle thrust of her breasts against his chest was intoxicating, as was the faint fragrance of wind and lavender that emanated from her gold-tinged skin. In spite of himself, Hunter discovered that he responded to her much more quickly than he'd thought. Or should. Or even wanted to.

Moving his mouth more firmly over her lips, his arm flexed behind her, drawing her closer so that her thighs were pressed against his legs. He could feel the rapid thud of her heart, could hear the quick intake of her breath, and her genuine response generated a fierce heat within him. It also effectively removed any restraints he'd held against kissing her quite thoroughly.

His arms tightened around Susan's quivering body, and he half lifted her from the floor. His tongue slipped past the flimsy barrier of her lips into her mouth, touching lightly and sending shivers down her spine. He felt them beneath his palms, and his throat tightened. Shifting slightly, he pulled her into the angle of his stomach and thigh, letting one hand drift back to cup her chin. He held her face in that unguarded embrace for a moment, his fingers making small circular motions on the curve of her cheek, his mouth drawing silken response from her lips.

When his fingers caressed down her cheek to the slim arch of her throat, then came to rest on the thrust of her breast, he felt her hesitation. He wasn't surprised; he would have been surprised if she hadn't. But that didn't mean he intended to back off, either.

His palm lightly touched the rigid peak of her breast, not exactly threatening, but definitely arousing. Though she held herself away from him, he could feel her instant reaction to his caress and pressed home his advantage. Before she could bring up her arms to fend him off, he put his other hand on the back of her head to press her mouth to his again, his lips fierce and ruthless, binding her closer, muffling her protests.

Her hands folded between them, not pushing away, not caressing. He increased the pressure on the swell of her breast only the slightest bit. His tongue stroked warmly inside her mouth, mimicking the rhythm of sex, and she squirmed against him, pushing closer, opening her mouth to him, returning the thrusts until he pulled away with a groan.

Hunter was an old hand at seduction, and he recognized from Susan's innocent, strained reactions that this was all very new to her. So much for Evan Elliott's claim.

"Susan," he whispered, nipping lightly at her throat and hearing her soft moan, "God, you're sweet."

The heels of her palms pressed against his shoulders without much conviction, and her head fell back and her long hair drifted in silky wisps that tickled his bare arms in places. Hunter looked at her flushed face, at the long, spiky wings of black lashes lying on her cheeks, and her parted lips and felt the overpowering urge to move her over to the Persian carpet and do what his body was urging him to do.

It was crazy. Why did she have this power to arouse him so quickly and powerfully? He'd lied when he'd said he had not noticed the attention from eligible females in

Los Alamos; he'd done more than notice. But somehow, none of them held the raw power to interest him that this one slender girl did.

He ached with it; and somehow, he felt as if she would not deny him. Her quivering responses were evidence of her own passion. But he wouldn't take her. Not like this.

Amazed at his newfound scruples, and wondering wryly why he had suddenly grown so fastidious about sex, Hunter set Susan on her feet with an effort. She hung in his embrace for a long moment, her forehead pushing against his chest.

"I didn't want you to stop," she said after a moment, her voice husky and oddly childlike.

He had to clear his throat before replying, "I didn't want to stop."

"Then why did you?"

Muffled by his shirt, the raven swing of her hair, and her down-bent head, Susan's voice sounded even more vulnerable than before. Hunter winced.

"If I don't stop now, Susan, I won't stop until it's too late. For you."

"I see."

He wondered if she did but didn't take his arms from around her quaking body. He felt the same weak quivering in his own body and had the stunned thought that it hadn't been like this for him since he'd been thirteen.

Inhaling deeply, Susan gathered herself and stepped back and away from Hunter. Her eyes looked glazed, and her entire body throbbed with feeling; it felt raw.

"I feel as if Blaze has dragged me through acres of cactus," she said frankly, meeting his narrowed jade eyes. "I don't think I like this."

Some of the amusement crept back into Hunter's eyes. "No? I can't say that frustration is my favorite emotion, either."

"Oh. Is that what this is—frustration?"

"Are you that much of an innocent, Susan Whitten?" His voice betrayed his exasperation. "Surely, some man has held you in his arms before and made you feel something!"

"Oh, yes. I've been kissed, and I've felt something." Her liquid brown eyes held his gaze. "Usually a raging desire to escape. I didn't feel that with you."

"I'm flattered. I think."

"Are you? You sound angry." Susan looked down at the floor. "I suppose now you will think I'm fast and loose, and it will be all over Los Alamos and Callahan County that I'm little more than a brazen slut."

He knew it would be wrong to laugh. "No, not a slut. Brazen, maybe, if you'll be disappointed at nothing being said."

She mulled over his comment. She knew he was only teasing her, but there was an undercurrent of tension now that hadn't been there earlier. It was because she had allowed him liberties. Doris had warned her about such things, which Susan had always felt unnecessary and simply ridiculous, seeing as how there was not a man in the entire county she desired to kiss. Except maybe Race Lassiter, and he was a little too savage for her tastes.

Hunter Carson, now, he was a man who stirred response in her breast. She flushed when she thought of how easily she'd allowed him to touch her, but it wasn't because of the more physical aspects. Somehow, it was vaguely embarrassing that she had committed some kind of social error and wasn't quite certain how she could have done it otherwise.

"Well," she said briskly, gathering her composure, "now we can get on to our discussion over my last order. There was a mistake. Instead of six hundred pounds of sweet feed and twelve hundred of alfalfa pellets, I somehow got more sweet feed. I don't understand it—I checked those bags myself, but it's a fact." She frowned slightly, then shook her head. "You know sweet feed is too heavy to feed horses or cattle in this heat. The molasses gets them too hot. Actually, I think just a few oats and plenty of hay does them better, but Pete insists on the alfalfa. Says it keeps them cleaned out much better—what did I say?"

She stared at him, perplexed. He was laughing, one hand over his face, his eyes covered by his long fingers.

"Nothing. I think I overestimated my charms, that's all. You're a priceless jewel, Susan Whitten, but I guess you know that."

"No, I didn't. Thank you for sharing that with me." She began to feel as if there was a jest at her expense; she waited for him to explain, but he just waved his hand negligently.

"Do whatever you like, and tell Harry—Henry—whatever my clerk's name is, that I approved it. I trust you." His big shoulders shook slightly, and the glance he gave her was faintly rueful. "I think I've learned an important lesson this morning, Susan. I'm not certain I wanted to learn it, but learn it I have."

Since she had no idea what he was talking about, she stood uncertainly for a moment. "Well. Well, good. I'm glad I've been of assistance." Shifting awkwardly from one foot to the other, Susan cast about for another subject of conversation. A safe subject.

"Are you going to the dance Saturday night?" she said finally, seizing on what she hoped was a neutral topic.

"The dance. Oh, yeah, down at the Civic Center." He gave her a smile. "I hadn't thought about it, to tell the truth. Will you be there?"

Nodding, Susan reached for her gloves and hat, then realized that her gloves were somewhere on the floor. She bent to retrieve them, bumped heads with Hunter, who had bent to do the same, then straightened, awkward and embarrassed.

"Yes, with Doris and Pete. Fried chicken. Lots of food. Do come. See you there, maybe."

Susan fled, ignoring his faintly startled expression as she strode swiftly from his office and out the front door of Carson Feed and Granary. She just hadn't been able to look at him anymore, seeing the amusement in his eyes and knowing that he obviously considered her some sort of sideshow. Like the tattooed man at the fair that came through Los Alamos on occasion. Or maybe the two-headed calf. Susan shuddered at the thought.

She wanted Hunter Carson to regard her in a more serious light. Like he had when he'd kissed her. There had been no amusement in his face then, or in the lips he'd pressed over her face, mouth, throat, and even a little lower.

Shameless, that's what she was. Shameless. She hadn't wanted him to stop, and she'd actually blurted that out to him. He must think her worse than any lightskirt. But *God*, she'd give anything if he'd only do it again. . . .

Chapter 6

SATURDAY NIGHT WAS clear and surprisingly cool. Music trilled in the air, lively and quick, fiddles and violins and guitars competing with skilled abandon. The grounds around the Los Alamos Civic Center—a grand name for a rather innocuous building on the edge of town—pulsed with excitement. In a town the size of Los Alamos, any public function generated a crowd. It seemed as if every citizen within a hundred-mile radius had gathered to celebrate.

"What's the occasion?"

Evan Elliott turned from his lazy perusal of the crowd to see a well-dressed man at his elbow. He raked him with a curious glance, then shrugged.

"Twenty-fifth anniversary of the town charter. And the end of the drought, too, I guess. New in town, I take it?"

The man smiled. "Yes, I am." He stuck out his hand, and Evan took it. "Peter Thorne, here."

Staring at him closely, Evan frowned. "You've got a strange accent, Mr. Thorne."

"Ah, that. I'm from England. It's rather evident, I presume."

"England?" Evan's interest was aroused. He thought about Susan's inheritance, the valuable brooch that was more of a hindrance than a help, since she couldn't use it for anything. It had come from England. "How did you find a small town like Los Alamos, Mr. Thorne?"

Seeming slightly amused, the tall, lean Englishman rocked back on the heels of his highly polished demi-boots. "I had an acquaintance tell me that this was the Wild West. I came to see what entertainment could be found."

"And have you found any?"

"Not yet. No Indians, no gunfights in the street, just a very tame time of it."

"Disappointed?" Evan's eyes narrowed slightly, and he shifted from one foot to the other.

"Rather." Thorne cocked his head to one side. He held a gold-headed cane in one hand, and he swung it negligently from side to side. "Perhaps you could direct me to more lively pastures. You look to be a man of some consequence."

Evan laughed. A faint flush colored his jaw, and he swung his gaze from Thorne to the crowd. A man of some consequence? He could only wish. If he were, maybe Susan would do more than smile kindly and offer platonic words that made his gorge rise. His hands tightened at his side, and he loosened them slowly.

"I don't know about lively pastures, Mr. Thorne," he said after a moment, "but I'll be glad to introduce you around. And if you stay late enough tonight, there's sure to be a fight or two. There always is when a few of the hands get a bit too much to drink at the wrong punch bowl." His mouth turned down at the corners. "Not very exciting, but that's about it in this part of the country. The only Indians we've seen lately are too old and too hungry to cause much trouble. And we like it that way."

"Yes, yes, I can see that." Thorne's steady gray eyes fixed firmly on Evan. "So, old chap, lead on! I do believe that you and I will deal well together."

Slightly amused now, Evan shook his bright head. "Now, I don't know about that. I'm not cut out to be a guide."

"Oh, and what are you cut out to be, Mr.—?"

"Oh. Sorry." He stuck out his hand. "Evan Elliott."

Thorne took his hand, keeping his gaze on Evan. "And I repeat, Mr. Elliott—what are you cut out to be?"

Evan stared at him. There was something strangely intent about this man, something compelling.

Tabitha frowned slightly. "That Thorne—he seems a bit familiar to me. Does he you, Horatio?"

"Can't say that he does." Horatio looked at her with a steady gaze. "Perhaps it's just his type of personality that seems familiar to you."

"Aye, that would be it, I suspect." Giving a thoughtful nod, Tabitha turned her attention back to the dancers. They whirled in a blur of bright colors and laughter. Her toe began to tap to the rhythm of the lively music, and after a moment or two she began to experiment with some of the calls.

"Allemande left—what in the name of God's little green apples can that mean?" she grumbled to herself, sweeping her skirt through the dust on the slope above the square. "And do-si-do? Ah, I see it now—here, give me your hands, Horatio. No, don't be stubborn, just cooperate for a moment or two. How am I to understand Susan if I can't understand what's going on in her life?"

Looking pained, Horatio allowed Tabitha to lead him through a few steps—during which she caught her skirt hem on a cactus and narrowly escaped tumbling him into the spiny plant.

"Enough, I say!" He pulled his hands from Tabitha's and gave her back a glare. "I do not consider square dancing a necessary part of your training, Tabitha. Perhaps you should concentrate on Susan instead of promenade left or right."

Tabitha expelled a sigh and nodded. "Very well. But I shall never put you on any of *my* guest lists!"

She glanced at him sharply when he muttered a soft, "Thank God!" but said nothing as Susan arrived in Los Alamos for the celebration.

Susan looked up eagerly as the ranch wagon rocked over a rut and finally came to a halt. She could hear the music, the laughter, and the shouts and smell the delicious fragrance of sizzling beef.

"They started without us," she said to Doris and leapt from the buckboard to the ground. Her calico skirt swirled prettily around her ankles, and she fingered the lace collar of her off-the-shoulder blouse for a moment.

"Did you expect 'em to wait on you, Miss Susan?" Pete asked with wry amusement, and she made a face at him.

"No, and *you* know I didn't!" was her swift retort. "I just meant that things are probably in full swing now, and we're late."

"Whose fault is that?" Doris asked as she allowed Pete to swing her down from the buckboard. "If it wasn't for that wretched pig—"

"Now, don't go blaming Arthur for what happened." Susan smiled at the resigned expression on Doris's face. "You should have known he wouldn't be able to resist delicacies within his reach, Doris."

"Within his reach, indeed," Doris grumbled. "He grabbed the tablecloth in his teeth and pulled until every sweet in the house was on the floor!"

Susan's laughter made even Doris smile. "And he did look so surprised to be wearing pudding!" Susan exclaimed.

"Greedy pig." Doris looked at Pete for confirmation, and the grizzled cowhand shook his head.

"Ain't never held with keeping a pig in the house. You should thank your lucky stars the fool swine didn't jump up on the table. He should be bacon by now."

Susan did her best to look shocked. "You're a hard-hearted man!"

"Who's hard-hearted?" a husky voice asked, and Susan turned to see Hunter Carson approach. Her throat closed, and she felt a lurch of her stomach.

He looked especially handsome tonight: his tall lean frame was clad in denims and a chambray shirt; his boots were dusty but obviously expensive; and his gunbelts were slung around slim hips in a deceptively casual manner. Oh, yes, he was definitely a handsome man—and quite, quite dangerous.

"Pete is," she managed to reply without stammering. "He wants to cook my pig."

"I'm with Pete." Hunter's grin eased the flat comment, and Susan laughed.

"Cannibals!"

"Are you suggesting we're swine, Miss Whitten?" Hunter said mockingly.

Hunter noticed Pete Sheridan was watching him with steady regard, not unfriendly, but just watchful. It was clear to everyone there that he was assessing Carson.

Hunter did not seem the least perturbed by Pete's perusal. He met it coolly; returned it just as steadily.

Susan reached into the buckboard and took out a wicker basket. "Here," she said, "stop staring at each other like two bucks and carry this to the trestle tables.

They're set up under the oak trees, I think."

"Miss Susan," Pete drawled, "you're about as sensitive as a rock."

"I know it. But even rocks have their uses." Her smile was bright, and both men relaxed slightly. "Now, come on. I want to celebrate before all the food is gone!"

By the time they reached the long tables that groaned under culinary burdens, Pete and Doris had wandered away from Susan and Hunter. Doris's face was turned eagerly up to the taciturn foreman as she drank in his every word, and he seemed boyishly pleased.

Bright paper lanterns were strung in trees, and a wooden platform built of old oak planks had been erected for dancing. Musicians sat and stood behind the dance floor, and the tables formed a right angle to one side. They took a shortcut across the edge of the dance floor, and Hunter spread a hand on her back to guide her. The touch sent jolts along her spine.

Susan looked at him through the lowered wing of her lashes. "How did you know when I'd get here? In town, I mean." She dodged a drunken man who stumbled toward her, and felt Hunter's arm against her back as he braced the clumsy dancer.

"I didn't."

"But you were right there when we—" She paused. "Were you even looking for me? Maybe not. I just assumed, since you were right there, and we'd just come in—Lord, I think I've made an idiot of myself again." Her knuckles whitened as she gripped the basket handle more tightly.

Hunter's hand shifted slightly; his fingers pressed warmly against her waist. "No, you're right. I was waiting on you. And I didn't know when you'd get here. I just took a chance."

"You're used to taking chances, I hear," Susan said with a laugh, and Hunter nodded.

"Especially when it comes to pretty ladies."

"Aren't you the gallant! I'll bet you say that to every woman carrying a basket of Doris's fried chicken." Susan smiled in what was meant to be a teasing manner. He gave her one of his heart-stopping smiles, and she gulped. This was too much. She was making a complete idiot of herself over this man, yet she couldn't seem to stop. She'd taken extra care with her appearance this evening and had hoped he would come to the celebration. Now it seemed as if he'd been waiting on her. Did that mean—?

"Why *were* you waiting on me? Do you feel something for me?" Susan asked him bluntly, then could have cheerfully bitten off her tongue. A hot flush stained her cheeks when he gave a shout of laughter.

"True to form, no beating around the bush for you, I see," Hunter observed when his laughter faded. "Yes, Miss Susan Whitten, I like you. I wouldn't have waited to see you if I didn't."

"Oh."

"Just 'oh'? Nothing else?"

"I talk too much." Her voice was slightly subdued. "I always say the wrong thing. Just 'oh' is a welcome change, I'm certain."

Sliding an arm around her waist, Hunter took the basket from her with his other hand. "I prefer honesty, Susan. I never realized it before, but I do. And you're refreshingly honest, I have to admit."

"Tactless, Pete says. And Evan. He says I have as much guile in me as a randy bull in a pen full of cows."

"Does he?" Hunter choked out. "Lovely thing to say to a woman."

Susan flashed him a mischievous glance. "Evan and I were always trying to top one another as children. I can do him one better if I choose."

"I have no doubt of that." Hunter's gaze locked with hers, and she felt the warning thump in her chest again. It was easy to see why some people considered him dangerous; *he was*. She'd never felt so tinglingly alive in her life, and so close to the brink of disaster.

It was startling. Though her life had never been exactly boring, neither would she have considered it fraught with peril. Now, because of Hunter Carson—and her reaction to him—she did. Susan sighed.

"Don't be so hard on yourself, Susan." Her head jerked up, and he smiled. "I meant it when I said I like your frank speech."

"That's only when I say something you want to hear. Wait until I point out things you'd rather not hear." Her smile faded slightly. "My mother used to tell me that the women in our family had a bad habit of being too blunt, and she was right. But it's so hard to change."

"Then don't. Not for me, anyway."

They'd stopped at the far end of the tables, and Hunter was looking down at Susan intently. The wicker basket was still in his hand, and his other hand had taken her wrist in a gentle grip. She felt it from her toes to her nose.

"Well, well," came a mocking voice that made Susan turn in surprise.

"Evan."

Elliott strode toward them, his fair face flushed with anger and his blue eyes pinpoints of fury. Even though Susan pulled guiltily at her wrist in Hunter's grip, he did not release her; nor did his hold on her lessen. He stood quietly relaxed, watching Evan.

With his gaze on Hunter, Evan said in what could almost be considered a snarl, "I thought you were coming in with Doris and Pete, Susan!"

"I did," she said crossly. "What's the matter with you? Stop behaving like a sore-tailed bear. We just got here a few minutes ago."

"I've been waiting for you for hours!"

Susan kept her voice calm with an effort. "All right, Evan. I can see that you're upset. But if you could manage to look at the basket in Hunter's hand, you will see that I have just arrived."

Elliott's gaze snapped from Susan's face back to Carson's, and over the wicker basket he held. It didn't seem to defuse his anger.

"Didn't take you long to find each other," Evan said in a tight, accusing voice.

"You got a problem, Elliott?" Hunter asked softly.

Evan recoiled slightly from that hard green gaze but didn't back down. "Yeah. But I reckon that's something you and I can talk about later."

"Yeah, I reckon so."

Susan leaned forward to take the wicker basket from Hunter. "Stop acting like two dogs fighting over the same bone. I'm not a bone. And I'm not flattered."

Ignoring her, Evan looked at Hunter with narrowed, distrustful eyes. "Tell me something, Carson—why are you still here in Los Alamos? It can't be for the exciting night life." He shifted a bit at Hunter's piercing gaze and added stubbornly, "As I understand it, your business is in Fort Worth, not here. Los Alamos is just a little dot on the map to you. I ain't the only one who wonders why you're hanging around."

"I have a business here, remember?"

Apparently, Evan also chose to ignore the dangerous edge to Hunter's voice. "The granary? That ain't nothing, and you know it. You could leave that with a manager and go back to Fort Worth and never miss it. Or be missed."

"Kind of you to consider my welfare and contentment, Elliott, but you're going too goddamned far."

Susan shot Hunter a quick, startled glance. Though his words were short and his tone flat, the ruthless light in his eyes was terrifying. She moved as if to come between them and felt Hunter's arm flex to bring her back out of the way. Tension vibrated like visible waves in the air between them, and she sought frantically for something to say. Fortunately, it wasn't quite necessary.

"My, my," interrupted another voice, soft, liquid, with an accent that reminded Susan of the barrister who had brought her the Lynnfield brooch. "Is this the fighting you promised me, Mr. Elliott? Somehow, I thought it would involve firearms."

Though Susan turned to look at the new arrival, Hunter kept his wary gaze on Evan, who returned it belligerently. The noise around them made everything seem slightly distant and false, as if she were watching a play instead of this confrontation between her childhood friend and Hunter. Now this foreigner, politely watching in a gray suit and shining boots, added yet another weird dimension to the night.

"Who are you?" Susan asked bluntly.

He bowed slightly from the waist. "Peter Thorne, miss, at your service." He smiled. "And I have the honor of addressing—?"

"Susan Whitten."

"Ah. Delighted, Miss Whitten." He swept her another bow with a flourish that made her frown.

"You're English, aren't you?"

"Yes, Miss Whitten, I am. Very perspicacious of you."

"Yes." Susan stared at him. "I suppose so." She tried to think what that meant, then decided that it must mean the same thing as smart. "What did you mean about the fight and firearms, Mr. Thorne?"

"Only that Mr. Elliott seemed to think that before the night was over, there would be an altercation of some kind. I was told, you see, that the Wild West had a wide range of such circumstances."

"Stick around," Hunter advised, not taking his eyes off Evan, "and you may see one yet."

Susan turned back to the two men facing each other with hackles raised and bristling like cactus. "You both look ridiculous!" Susan snapped. "I don't want to see either one of you! I'm going to get something to eat."

She marched off, shifting her wicker basket from hand to hand and disappearing in the swirling crowd. As she pushed past the celebrators, anger warred with fear. She wondered if Hunter or Evan had any idea of how silly they'd looked glaring at each other. And that man, Peter Thorne, had seemed so satisfied that they were close to a quarrel. Men! Always looking for a chance to fight. What was there about coming to blows—or even bullets—that so intrigued them? She'd never understand it. Even her father had seemed to enjoy a rousing good fight once in a while, "embroiling himself just for pure cussedness," her mother had said.

Susan was greeted by several women she knew and invited to place her food on the cloth-draped table. She managed to smile pleasantly as she rested the wicker basket and removed Doris's platters of chicken. Fluffy biscuits, Doris's specialty, filled a small sack, and she set them out, too. With all the other food people had brought, she hardly saw how anyone would notice more, but she spread it out in a pleasing array.

For several minutes, she was too busy helping to fill plates to think about Peter Thorne or Evan, or even Hunter. People filed past, greeting her with teasing comments or smiling nods, neighbors she'd known all her life. Finally she had a moment to herself and leaned back against a wide oak tree to rest, fanning her face with a small pasteboard fan that advertised "Gilbert's Saloon" in big block letters. She chatted easily with women who'd known her mother and exchanged comments about the end of the drought and the coming year. Then she saw Evan approaching and excused herself.

"You sure do look pretty," Evan said, coming up and giving her a hangdog glance. "I meant to tell you."

Susan glared at him. "Do I? And how would you know? All I've noticed you doing the past hour is behaving like a northbound mule's south end!"

"Aw, Susan, don't be mad—"

"And how dare you tell Hunter Carson that we're about to be married?" she said softly, well aware of curious ears close by. "We're no such thing and you know it!"

"Does it matter so much to you that Carson thinks we're that close?" Evan asked in a painfully tight voice.

Susan paused. His eyes looked bleak, and she wished for an instant that she could tell him no. But she couldn't. And she couldn't let him think she felt more for him than friendship. A quick cut was much kinder than a slow burn.

"Yes, in a way it does, Evan. Not just Hunter Carson, but anyone." Lantern light made long shadows of her lashes, and Susan looked away from Evan's pained stare. "You know how I feel, Evan. I've made no secret of it. And this isn't the time or the place to—"

"Right." He cut her off. "We'll talk about it again later. Thorne is waiting on me, and I promised to show him around a little."

"Who is this Peter Thorne?" Susan's brows dipped lower over her eyes. "He seems awful familiar with you for a man who just got into town."

"I could say the same thing about Carson!"

"Oh, Evan! It's not the same thing, and you know it!"

"Do I?" His look challenged her. "Thorne is a stranger here, and he's asked me to show him around a little. That's all. And a hell of a lot less than Carson wants from you."

"Are you back to that again?" Susan glared at him.

"No. I'll leave you alone, Susan." Evan's voice was peculiarly soft, and a faint flicker of raw pain speared the anger in his eyes. "But don't come crying to me when Hunter Carson takes your ranch and leaves you like an old shoe."

"Good Lord!" Susan sputtered furiously, hoping that no one close by could hear their conversation. It was just like that infuriating Evan to say things people might take the wrong way. Or the right way.

Evan walked away, quickly mingling with the crowd of denim-clad cowboys and ranchers. Suddenly the gay atmosphere didn't seem quite so gay, nor so bright. Evan's surly attitude had cast a pall on what had promised to be a wonderful evening, and Susan wished suddenly she could just go home.

But she couldn't, and she knew it. Doris would have been crushed, and she couldn't spoil her evening. Besides,

what excuse could she give? So Susan stayed, serving
food to the crowd with a bright smile on her face, trading
quips with neighbors she rarely saw. She had no desire
to join in the games, or the dancing. Not now. She was
left feeling strangely restless, strangely—waiting.

As the evening wore on, Susan found that she couldn't
help looking for Hunter Carson. He'd not sought her out
again. She wondered if she'd made him mad with her
sharp tongue. It was possible. Evan never got mad, or
stayed mad, anyway. But Hunter wasn't Evan.

And *that*, she told herself miserably, was what had
attracted her to him. Hunter was too self-contained, too
confident. He wouldn't hang after her like Evan did.
While that had certain advantages, there were certain
drawbacks, too.

"How are you, dear?" someone was saying in a thin,
querulous voice, and Susan blinked.

It was Mrs. Johnson, and she was staring at Susan in
such a curious way that she realized the woman must
have been speaking to her for several moments.

"Hello, Mrs. Johnson. I'm fine. I was just . . . uh . . .
I was thinking that we might need to put out some more
biscuits. What do you think?"

"More?" Mrs. Johnson gave a startled glance at the
plate piled high with fluffy biscuits. "Perhaps in a little
while, dear."

"Yes. You may be right." Susan searched for something else to say, but Mrs. Johnson seemed to have
chosen a topic already.

"I understand that you and Evan are finally going to
be married, Susan. That's so nice. I've always thou—"

"We are *not*!" Susan snapped before she thought. "I
mean to say, we're just friends, Mrs. Johnson. Nothing
has changed between us."

"Oh." Mrs. Johnson seemed perplexed. "Then what I heard about you and Mr. Carson—oh, dear. Perhaps I should not have said that."

Exasperated, Susan bridled. "Why not? Everyone else seems to know more about me than I do myself. What is it that Mr. Carson and I are supposed to be doing?"

While Mrs. Johnson grew more flustered, Susan became infuriated. Apparently, everyone in Los Alamos had decided her future for her. Or had at the least been discussing what she should or shouldn't do. How maddening to be discussed like that.

"Don't you know, dear?" Mrs. Johnson squeaked at last.

"No, I don't know!" Susan ground her teeth together. "I do wish someone would be so kind as to tell me!"

"I'll tell you," an amused male voice said from behind her, and Susan turned, chagrined. Hunter Carson approached with his curiously graceful stride that made her think of a hunting lion. What wonderful timing.

"I'm not certain I want *you* to tell me," she began, but he cut her off.

"I think Mrs. Johnson is too embarrassed." Grinning, he took Susan's hand in spite of her attempt to shove it into the pocket of her skirt, and held it between his broad palms. "If what I hear is correct, we are—lovers."

Mrs. Johnson squealed and scurried away, and Susan stared up at Hunter with her mouth hanging open. "What?" she managed to whisper after a moment. The music seemed much too loud, and the dancers were a blur of bright calico and gingham just out of the range of her vision. "L-lov—"

She couldn't finish, but Hunter had no trouble. "Lovers. Us. Together. Alone. *Close*. You know—"

"I know what it means!" She snatched her hand away as if burned. "Ridiculous."

"Is it?" Hunter's jade-colored eyes narrowed slightly, and he leaned closer to her. "Why do you say that, Susan Whitten?"

"Because it's true." She edged away from him, feeling as if her entire body were seared. Why did he have to have this effect on her? It was silly, really. He was only a man. *But what a man . . .*

Dragging her gaze from the scarred gray trunk of the tree behind Hunter back to his face, Susan said calmly, "I don't even know you, Mr. Carson, and—"

"Hunter."

Ignoring him, she finished, "—and when I do, I may not want any more to do with you. After all, we've only just become acquainted with each other, and—"

"And you're already attracted to me." He smiled at her furious gasp. "Don't deny it. It's all right. I'm attracted to you, too." Shrugging, he added, "Damned if I know why, and I have to admit it's inconvenient as hell, but I like being with you."

"Don't do me any favors!" Susan sidled farther away, glancing desperately around for an avenue of escape. Where was Doris? Pete? Anyone who could offer her a reasonable excuse for escaping Hunter? She'd run into deep water here, thrown herself over a ledge into thin air without hope of support to help her. Suddenly she was afraid of him. Afraid of how he made her feel. Afraid of getting in so deeply she would find herself hopelessly mired and left to flounder.

Hunter gazed down at her, his dark brows snapping down over the bridge of his nose. There was a calculating look on his face that made Susan pause, and when he reached out for her again, his hand closing firmly around her wrist, she wasn't surprised. Just chokingly wary.

"Come with me, Susan. We need to talk."

It would have been more embarrassing to resist than to be seen going with him, and Susan barely had time to gasp over one shoulder that she'd be back in a moment before she was tugged around the broad trunk of a tree and past the perimeter of the celebrations. The crowd thinned, and beyond a few curious glances from the women serving food, no one remarked upon their leaving.

"Please," Susan said when Hunter had pulled her into the murky shadows of the adobe building that housed the Civic Center. "Everyone will think—"

"They already think it," Hunter interrupted, and before she could protest, he pulled her hard against him.

The shock of his embrace rendered her immobile, and when his mouth covered hers, Susan was lost. He kissed her fiercely, as if branding her, his lips hot and searching as he took hers. He kissed her until her knees grew weak and her legs trembled, and then he pushed her up against the cool adobe and leaned his body against hers, his hands spreading on the wall behind her. Bright moonlight played across half of his face, and there was the sharp set of desire on his features that she easily recognized.

His face was detailed in the stark play of silvery moonshine that washed over them, the perfect planes and hard-curved angles of shadow and light. His eyes gleamed like jade stones beneath the heavy, thick curve of his lashes, raking her face with wary speculation, hiding his thoughts when she wished desperately she could read them.

Susan shivered. She could feel his heart beating against her breasts, could feel the press of the buckles on his gunbelts biting into the soft flesh of her stomach, and the insistent nudge of his groin against her upper thighs. It was as exciting as it was frightening. And for a moment she wondered why she should be frightened at all. Wasn't this natural? Wasn't this how Nature had intended it to be? This sweet, wild sweep of longing that made her want to yield?

Yes, yes, but not without love. . . .

Clinging to that truth, Susan wrenched her mouth from his with a gasp. But she couldn't move away; his hands were still against the wall on each side of her head, his arms bent so that his body rubbed enticingly over her.

"No," she murmured in a strained voice that made him laugh softly.

"No? Your lips may say that, but the rest of you"—he stroked a hand from her throat down the middle of her body—"says yes." Hunter cupped her chin in his palm and turned her to face him. "Susan, we've both wanted the same thing since we met. Can you keep pretending we don't? Are you going to lie to me and to yourself?"

"I can't speak for you," she said wretchedly, "but I can for myself. And I'm not some heifer to be serviced by any bull who wanders by!"

"I know that." Hunter's grip tightened on her chin when she tried to look away. "Do you think I want that? If I did, there are any number of women here who will oblige me. Sex is easy to get—"

"Ah, so says the great Hunter," Susan scoffed, stung by his reference to other women.

"—it's deeper emotion that's not so easy to come by," he finished grimly. His long fingers tilted up her face. "I do admit I like kissing you, and I want much more, but not just because you're the only willing female in Callahan County."

Susan slapped his hand away, and he let it drop. Anger sparked in his eyes, and she met it evenly.

"Don't treat me as if I had no say in it! You didn't bother to *ask* me to come with you—you ordered it. I'm not a pet dog to be commanded."

He seemed faintly surprised. "Did I *command* you to do anything?"

"You gave me no choice about accompanying you." She noted the faint brown specks clustered around the irises of his green eyes. Ridiculous. Men shouldn't have such beautiful eyes or such long lashes. Light gleamed on only half his face, leaving the other half in shadow, making him look mysterious, somehow, and distant in spite of the soft glow in his eyes. She looked away from him. She couldn't look at his elegantly cut mouth or the beautiful green eyes so vivid and shiny in the cool wash of moonshine. Moistening her lips with the tip of her tongue, she tried to remove herself from the need he awakened.

"Susan." When she wouldn't look at him, he took her chin in his palm again. "Susan, I only wanted you to come with me. I thought you wanted to come."

She shifted uneasily. She *had* wanted to come. She'd wanted him to kiss her like he'd just done. How could she say that without looking brazen?

"Well," she muttered, "*ask* me next time."

He laughed softly. "All right. I will. And then if you don't come, I'll drag you."

She laughed. "I think I knew that already." Leaning her head back against the adobe wall, she relaxed. Hunter was not what she'd first thought him, that was for certain. He was arrogant, yes, but he didn't belittle others. He was just—confident. Very confident, assured that things would go his way. Maybe that's what appealed

to her so much. Jake Whitten had been that way. It was
an arrogance born of confidence in one's own abilities to
see a task through, and her father had had that in abun-
dance. So did Hunter Carson, and he was the first man
she'd ever met who compared favorably with Jake.

Susan inhaled deeply and looked at Hunter with a
smile. He was still much too close, but it was no
longer alarming, despite the quickening of her pulse
as he dragged his hands down her arms to grasp
her wrists. He turned her hands palms up and kissed
the softer skin. Susan was slightly embarrassed. She
didn't have the smooth, soft skin he was probably
used to seeing on a woman. Her hands were rough
in places, with small calluses. She worked too hard
on the ranch to be able to cultivate the luxury of soft
feminine hands.

Susan drew her hands from his grasp and shoved them
into the pockets of her skirt.

Hunter misunderstood her action. He levered his body
away from hers, straightening and looking at her down-
bent head with a slight frown. The aching need he felt
wasn't in the least assuaged by her drawing away from
him, and he wanted to ignore decency and throw her
over his shoulder and take her to his house and make
love to her until the sun rose the next day. Or the
next.

It was a primitive, elemental reaction and he knew
it, but he didn't care. If he said aloud what he felt,
she would run like a spooked mustang; if he didn't do
something to ease his need for her, he'd do something
crazy. He knew that, too. He wasn't used to wanting
so badly without relief. Come to think of it, he wasn't
used to wanting any woman the way he wanted Susan
Whitten. If he didn't have this damnable ache in his

groin, he might be able to figure out why *she*, of all the women he knew, caused this reaction. As it was, all he could think about was relief.

Hunter Carson was experienced at seduction. And he knew how to attract and seduce willing women. He usually didn't bother with the reluctant ones. Why should he, when there were so many willing ones out there? Yet now he wished he'd cultivated that particular skill. And in the next moment he knew he could never have done anything to hurt Susan. She was too honest, too vulnerable, and he was not the kind of man to prey on the innocent.

Dammit.

"Look, Susan," he said, his voice much harsher than he intended. "I think maybe I've made a mistake. If I offended you, I'm sorry for it. I guess I thought you were more . . . ready."

Raking a hand through his pale hair, he took a step back, and she flung him a startled glance. "Wait!"

He paused and lifted a brow, but his eyes narrowed a fraction. She flushed, then looked down at her feet, and a shaft of light sprayed over her again, highlighting the dark raven's gleam of her hair. Hunter smiled.

"It's all right, Susan. I understand, I guess. I don't have to like it, though."

She looked confused, and when she met his gaze again, her bottom lip was flattened into a thin line. "I'm glad you understand," she said tightly, "because I have no idea what you're talking about!"

A rumble of laughter shook him, and he reached out to take her hand again, tucking it into the crook of his arm and his elbow. "Let's go back where there's more light and I can watch your face," he said dryly. "I have a feeling I'm missing a lot."

"So are the folks who'll be looking at us like we've rolled in the mud when we get back," she said with a shaky laugh.

"Ignore them."

"Ignore them? That might be a little hard."

"Not for me. I'm willing to bet there's not a saint nor an angel in the entire town of Los Alamos." Hunter gave her hand a squeeze. Shadowed light played across her upturned face in a wavering pattern, revealing her anxiety. "Shove their curiosity in their faces, and they won't dare say a word."

"Really, Hunter," Susan began, her eyes indignant at first, then growing wide with shock when loud shots sounded in the distance. "What was that!"

Hunter was already turning back toward the lighted square, his gun filling his hand. "Come on," he said in an impatient tone that brooked no argument, "you need to take cover."

Susan half stumbled, half ran beside him. After the first spate of shooting, only loud voices could be heard as they drew nearer. An occasional feminine scream punctuated the rumble of male voices.

"Comanche!" someone shouted, and Susan felt a chill ripple down her spine.

"*Comanche?* But we haven't had any trouble with them in several years."

Hunter was pushing her toward someone, his face set, and she had only a brief glimpse of cold green eyes as he released her hand.

"Take cover, Susan."

"But—"

"Dammit, don't argue!"

Susan gaped at him. No one ever spoke to her in that hard tone. She felt Doris's hands on her, heard her voice in her ear telling her to come along to the building to hide with the rest of the women and children; she tried not to lose sight of Hunter, but he had disappeared.

"Comanche," Doris was saying in a half sob. "Oh, God!"

Susan finally turned to look at her, seeing the pinch of fright in the older woman's face. She remembered then how Doris's first husband had been killed, along with her parents, in the raids of years earlier. For a long time now the Comanche had not bothered them. It looked as if the peace was over.

Tabitha was almost dancing with excitement. "Wild Indians! Oh, how absolutely terrifying!"

Staring at her, Horatio shifted uneasily. "You did not summon them here, did you?"

Seeming surprised, Tabitha looked at him. "Of course not. How would I do that? But I must admit, it certainly does help."

"Help? I don't see how, Tabitha. Though I admit there has not been an overabundance of mule skinners in my acquaintance—and those whom I have met have a quite *interesting* turn of phrase—I hardly see how their massacre can help Miss Whitten with her ranch."

"Not the ranch." Tabitha wadded her thick skirts behind her and sat down on a rock. She wiggled until she was comfortable and gazed at the chaotic scene below. "Hunter. He's mad for her. Can hardly stand it until she yields. It will be just the thing, I think. Wealthy men make good husbands. Hunter will save her ranch. And the brooch. It will be simple—they'll do what it looks as if they're going to do anyway, and he'll be honor-bound to marry her."

Horatio's question erased the satisfied smile from her face: "How do you know he'll marry her? This isn't the fifteenth century anymore, you know. Honor doesn't mean as much."

"Sixteenth," Tabitha corrected absently. "Well, I can't be that mistaken about him. He may be a bit impetuous and uncivil, but he doesn't seem like a *complete* bounder. No, he'll do the right thing by her."

"Your definition of the right thing and his may vary greatly, Tabitha."

"I don't think so." A faint scowl creased her brow, and her thin brows dipped lower over her pale eyes. "That Peter Thorne, now—he's not the thing. Not quite the thing. I don't care for the man. In fact, I think that he may turn out to be a problem."

"Not as big a problem as the Comanche, I believe."

Starting at Horatio's dry tone, Tabitha looked back at the town and saw clouds of dust in the far distance.

"Comanche," she murmured. "I've never seen one up close. They keep to themselves, over in that broad field of high grass and trees they call the Happy Hunting Ground." A gleam lit her eyes. "What an excellent opportunity!"

"Tabitha—"

"Oh, don't go preaching at me again, Horatio! I vow, you are becoming like an old maid! Harping and preaching. I know the rules." She flounced irritably on the rock, and her stiff hoops flew up. Shoving them back down, she gave a sigh. "Deuced uncomfortable attire in this heat. This ruff is scratching my neck so badly, I can hardly think."

"Then change."

"Oh. Yes. Yes, I can, can't I?" Tabitha smiled, and in a moment she was wearing a buckskin dress patterned with brightly painted beads and quills. Moccasins covered her feet, and she wore a long, trailing headdress of eagle feathers on her head, not quite covering her tightly curled hair. "What do you think, Horatio?"

Clearly taken aback, he covered his eyes. "Not much, I'm afraid. Tabitha, only the men wear those long headdresses. If I'm not mistaken, that is a warbonnet. Somehow, I had the thought you might choose to wear something sensible like a skirt and blouse, perhaps."

"Ordinary. You have no imagination, Horatio." Tabitha rearranged her buckskin skirt, smoothing it over her plump knees. She looked thoughtful. "Now, we must see what we can do to get Hunter and Susan together. That Evan Elliott will stop it if he can."

"You're certain a marriage is the answer for Susan?" Horatio shook his head, and his long robe swayed slightly in the hot, dry wind.

"Aye. Aren't you? Through the centuries marriage has always been the answer to a woman's problems. An *advantageous* marriage, that is."

"Perhaps times have changed, Tabitha."

"Pooh. Not that much. He's still hot for her, the rutting stag, and she's as hot for him. She's said so, the outspoken little wench." Tabitha nodded sagely. "Yes, get those two alone together long enough, and her problems will be solved."

"I hope you're right—"

"Of course, I am." Tabitha's smile was confident. "All I have to do is make the proper arrangements. Fortunately, the Comanche have begun it for me."

Chapter 7

IT WASN'T COMANCHE. At least, they were not attacking Los Alamos yet. An outrider had ridden in, shooting his pistol into the air and reeling in his saddle before someone managed to help him from his horse. It was he who had caused the shouting with the dreaded word *Comanche*.

Most of the men in town were unarmed. Only a few had worn their guns to the dance.

"A hundred braves, maybe," the outrider managed to say between gulps of hot air and warm whiskey. "Don't know if they're headed here or not."

"Anders, you say they attacked a mule train on the Salt Flats?" someone asked, and the sweat-drenched cowboy nodded.

"Yeah. Killed all the skinners, took the mules, set the wagons on fire. Don't know who's leadin' em."

Hunter handed Anders another cup of whiskey. "How about calling in the soldiers at Fort Griffin?"

"Fort Griffin?" A shake of his head killed that hope. "Maybe Fort Concho . . ."

"Yeah, that's closer," someone commented, but Hunter shook his head.

"Most of their force are out in the field. Food and ordnance comes from the railhead in Fort Worth, through Weatherford, to Richardson, then Griffin to Concho. From there, they take it out to the columns in the field. Not to mention that every stage, cattle herd, or wagon

train moving west from Richardson requires an escort."
He rubbed his jaw with one hand. "Fort Concho has
reinforcements from Fort Richardson, some of the Tenth
Cavalry. They should have men to spare us. Look, if
these Comanche were part of a larger group, they'd
be here by now. The fact that they hit the mule skinners, then left the area, means it's not that big a war
party."

"Who are you to know so much?" Evan said with
a sneer. "I didn't realize you were a big Indian fighter."

Hunter stared at him coolly. "I've done my share
of fighting Apache, Cheyenne, and Comanche. Even
Pawnee. I may not know much, but I'm willing to bet
I know more than you."

The wounded man thrust his empty tin cup back into
Hunter's hand. "Well, it don't matter none now. They
ain't right behind me, but I sure would look to outlying
ranches. They're liable to hit as many as they can and
steal all the livestock."

"That's usually their tactic," Hunter agreed. "But do
you really think we should run around like scared chick-
ens? Maybe we should prepare for the worst here, where
the women and children are, not spread ourselves too
thin."

Pete Sheridan looked pained. "I think we should all
go back home and look to ourselves," he said in a
mutter. "And we should be prepared for the worst, like
Carson says."

Shrugging, Hunter said, "If that's what you're going
to do, I'll stay here and protect the women and children.
If the Comanche are bold enough to attack Los Alamos
for the herds on the feedlot, someone will need to
be here."

Evan snorted. "Yeah, the big Indian fighter is going to be safe in town, while we're out—"

Hunter stood up in a smooth, lithe motion. He towered over the younger man, and his face was tight with anger in the incongruous glow of the bright paper lanterns swinging overhead.

"I've heard enough, Elliott. This isn't about Susan, it's about Comanche. Don't mix the two."

"I wasn't!" Evan glared back at him, but he took a few steps away. "And if you think everybody staying here would make a big difference, you're wrong. It'll only mean more deaths. I've seen what those red devils can do, and I know what I'm talking about."

His belligerence couldn't disguise the truth; Hunter knew it, and every man there knew it. Anders was the only man to say it aloud, however.

"Damn, them Comanche can be ruthless. I 'member not many ranches 'round here escaped some sort of trouble a few years ago, whether it was Comanche, 'Pache, or those damn dog soldier Cheyenne." Anders shook his head. "This town is a big prize, too, since there ain't much of it left and there's all those cattle, and the horses in the pen behind the livery stable." His eyes lifted and met Hunter's. "Them Comanche ain't *that* far away."

"Then maybe it'd be best to stick here for a while, see what they're going to do—" Hunter began.

"So you're suggesting all the men stay in town and let the Comanche make off with everything else?" Harold Tanner demanded in a harsh tone. "Not me. I've lost before, and I ain't goin' to sit safe and quiet while they burn down my house and steal my stock. I'm goin' home."

Several others agreed, and before a few minutes had passed, most of the men had decided to return to their ranches to save what they could. The women and children would be left in town for safety, but the men were riding out.

"How 'bout you, Elliott?" Tanner asked. "You goin' to stay or go?"

Trapped by his pride, Evan was forced to say, "Go, of course. I don't have any womenfolk to hold me back."

Pete Sheridan turned to Hunter. "I'm going. But I want to leave Miss Susan in town, which ain't going to be easy. She'll fight about it like a treed cat. You stayin' here to keep watch?"

"Yeah. Looks like it. I've got some hired hands who can go with you. Or if you think you'll need me—"

Shaking his head, Pete said, "I'd feel better if you were here with the women, but I'll take some of your men, if you can spare 'em."

"I'll see who's willing to go." Hunter didn't glance at Evan as he turned away, but felt his furious gaze. Too bad. He certainly didn't have time or the inclination to soothe ruffled feelings. Let Elliott stew; he had work to do.

Los Alamos was not a large town, and most of the buildings were wooden. A well-placed fire would easily raze the entire town. Though Hunter didn't much think the Comanche would bother with the town even with the lure of the feedlot full of cattle and the horses milling in pens, he didn't want to take any chances. There were too many examples of other towns that had been caught unprepared during the Red River War two years before.

Hunter supervised the erection of barricades at both ends of the wide main street and posted men with rifles at strategic points. Using the trestle tables as barricades, he weighted them down with bags of feed from the granary. It was getting late; a full moon rode high in the sky, and he swore softly as he made the rounds, checking to be sure everyone knew what to do in case of attack; then he sought out Susan.

He found her with the other women in the Civic Center, the only adobe structure in Los Alamos. The women were talking softly or sitting in small groups. Most of the children were asleep on pallets. The long windows had been covered with blankets, and only a few candles were lit. He stepped just inside the door and paused. It took a moment for him to find her in the murky gloom, and when he did, he smiled.

Susan held a child on her hip, a sleepy-eyed, wailing toddler with dark curly hair and chubby cheeks. Hunter leaned against the doorframe and watched her for a moment as she tried to quiet the sobbing little boy.

Susan. God, it made him feel as if he was missing something when he looked at her. Why? He knew plenty of women, women who were available to him for a pleasant evening or all night, if he wished. But Susan Whitten had touched some deeply buried emotion in him, and he didn't know how or why. Now, seeing her with a child in her arms and looking for all the world like a dusty Madonna made him realize that he was missing something in his life.

And it made him hungry, with an animal hunger that awoke him to everything he'd lost. Or never had. . . .

It all seemed to rest in this one girl now, this slim, dark-haired girl with shining eyes and a trusting soul. God, he must be insane to even think what he was thinking, but he couldn't help it. And he couldn't help wanting her.

He might have backed out the door without ever speaking, if she hadn't looked up then, her face revealing her delight at seeing him. Hunter watched as she gave the now-quiet child to Doris with a murmur and soft caress of the silky curls, then came toward him.

Her skirts swayed seductively around her ankles, though why he should consider the simple way she walked seductive, he wasn't certain. Maybe it was because he wanted it to be.

"Mr. Carson," she said softly, and when he lifted a brow at her, she glanced meaningfully toward the women nearby. "Have you come with news for us?"

"Yeah, I guess I have." *Ridiculous, to feel so awkward.* "One of the scouts rode in to say the Comanche don't seem to be in this area. Either they've gone, or they've chosen another target."

"It would be more sensible if they attacked a remote ranch," Susan said with a frown, her voice soft. "Do you think we're safe here?"

Shrugging, he swept off his hat and raked a hand through his hair. "That's anybody's guess. It's certainly the right night for an attack. All that damn moonlight— a Comanche moon. Damn. If they were Apache, we wouldn't need to expect anything until just before dawn. Now . . ."

He let his voice trail off, and she glanced back again at the women nearby. "And now you think we're pretty safe. Is that what you're saying?"

Hunter followed her glance. The knot of women hovered close, trying not to appear too anxious, but it was evident from their lined faces and twisting hands.

"Yeah, I think we're pretty safe for now," he said in a louder tone. "Of course, we still need to be quiet and keep a close watch."

Susan's mouth curved slightly. "I agree. As long as you're here, Mr. Carson, would you mind coming with me to see if there are any cracks in the windows? I'd like for this building to appear unoccupied from the outside, and if we need to put out the candles, we will."

He understood her broad hint. "I'll be glad to oblige you, Miss Whitten. I think it's safe enough to check outside." Holding out his arm for her to take, he tried not to let his satisfaction show.

Once they were outside, Susan flashed him a mischievous glance, her dark eyes dancing. "I had to think of an excuse to talk to you. Since we're already reputed to be lovers anyway, I didn't think it mattered."

Hunter grinned. "Shameless wench," he said in the same soft voice she'd used. "It looks as if our minds run along the same track." He curled a hand around her arm and drew her close to him.

Silvery moonlight glittered over the quiet street; it was more quiet than Hunter had ever seen it, the silence eerie, ominous. In the distance a coyote howled, and was answered. He felt Susan shiver.

"Cold?" Hunter looked down at her; her long lashes made faint shadows on her cheeks, but she looked up quickly and flashed him a smile.

"In this heat?" Hot, dry winds blew across the empty street, stirring up dust; somewhere a canvas wagon top flapped loudly. "No, I don't think so."

"Then you're afraid." His arm slid around her waist, and he drew her closer. "Don't be."

"Then there really isn't much danger?"

"I didn't say that." He looked up at the full moon riding the sky. "I'd feel a lot better if that damned moon weren't so bright."

Susan nodded; he felt her stiffen beneath the palm he had riding on her hip. Her voice was slightly shaky.

"A Comanche moon. I remember how—a long time ago—I used to cry at the full moon. It made me afraid because I knew that they would come again."

"Did they raid your ranch often?"

"No, not at first. After we'd been here a while, my father said. At first they were accepting; not friendly, maybe, but not overtly hostile. Of course, my father was prudent enough not to make a big deal out of a few missing cattle once in a while. He said they got hungry same as the rest of us." Susan drew in a soft breath, then let it out again. Her voice was low, as if there were ears around them. "Then, when more and more settlers started coming, and the army—there were raids. On nights like these. Papa would hide my mother and me in the cellar under the house, and we would sit in the dark and listen to the shots and yells—I hated it. I had nightmares about it. But I always knew my father would keep us safe."

"He did an admirable job of it."

They'd reached the end of the porch running along the front of the Civic Center and stepped down into the dust and sparse grass. Hunter steered her into the shadows next to the adobe building. She felt soft and warm and feminine beneath his palm, and he turned her to face him.

A slight smile curled her lips; it made her dark eyes glow, and even in the shadows he could see the faint tint of a blush on her high cheekbones. She put a hand on his chest, her fingers spreading over the chambray and burning into his skin through the thin material.

"See any chinks of light, Mr. Carson?"

He blinked down at her. "What?"

"Light—the reason we came out here, remember?"

"That's not the reason, and you know it." He pulled her to him, heard her soft gasp, swallowed it as his mouth closed over her parted lips.

Pulling her up against him, he splayed a hand over her back, held her close, his mouth searching hers, finding the sweep of response he sought. This was what he'd brought her out here for, this—this burning that made him half-crazy with wanting her. And she knew it. She had to. No woman could be that blind to the hunger in his eyes. Or touch. Or kiss. *God.*

"This is crazy," she whispered when he released her lips to draw in a breath, and he nodded.

"Yeah. But I feel crazy tonight."

"So do I." She slid her arms around his waist and pressed closer, tilting up her face to look at him; her breasts flattened against his chest and made him swallow a groan of frustration.

Hunter pushed back a strand of ebony hair from her cheek; then he stuck his hand in the thick mane and tugged it free of confining pins. It fell in a midnight drape over her shoulders, stark against the ivory of her blouse, silken skeins beckoning him.

"You've got beautiful hair," he muttered, wanting to say more but knowing it wasn't the right time, the right place. Maybe there never would be a right time or place for them. It seemed as if he'd begun like this before; there had been others and it had always ended. Sometimes quickly, sometimes with bitter words and feelings, but it had ended.

"Hunter?"

"Yeah?"

"Kiss me again. I'm afraid, and when I'm with you, I'm not so frightened."

"Happy to oblige," he muttered, but it wasn't quite true. He couldn't keep kissing her; not without some sort of satisfaction. More than he was getting; he was so tight now he was as taut as a strung bow. Too many kisses, and he would snap. He knew it. Couldn't she feel it in his touch? The slight quiver of his arms around her?

He was breathing raggedly when he pulled away from her again. Damn. He wanted her but not taken in the dust and street. She was too fine for that. He wanted it to be right for her their first time.

"Susan . . ."

"Hunter . . ." they said at the same time, then paused and laughed awkwardly.

"You first," she said on the wings of her laughter. "I don't think I can remember what I was going to say anyway."

"I better get you back inside before this goes too far. Usually, I have more self-control, but I don't think I can take much more kissing." His smile was wry. "Never thought I'd say that."

Gazing up at him in the moonlight, Susan's face mirrored her thoughts so explicitly that he groaned.

"Don't look at me like that, Susan Whitten. Just don't! Not unless you want to be taken to my house and—"

"Ravished?" she supplied when he paused and clenched his teeth together. "Made love to? Why not? Do you think I don't want you? I do." She laughed softly. "Brazen, aren't I? But I do, Hunter. I've never felt this way about anyone before. Maybe it's the tension, the not knowing what the night will bring, or tomorrow. Or whether I'll ever have this opportunity again. . . ."

She leaned into him, pressing close. Her voice was muffled by his shirt as she said against his broad chest, "I don't want to wait, Hunter."

There was a long moment of silence. The wind sent a dry tumbleweed skittering down the street; the moonlight sprayed over them in sharp detail, and Hunter remembered why they were there. His hands closed around her upper arms, and he pushed her gently away.

"I'm supposed to be watching for Comanche."

"There are enough other people watching for them. If they come, you can—" She jerked to a halt and buried her face in her palms. "I'm a shameless hussy. I'm sorry. . . ."

"No, wait," Hunter said in a tortured voice when she slipped away from him. "You only said what I was thinking. God, Susan, you must know how I feel about you."

She stared up at him, and he saw doubt in her eyes, and the soft glisten of embarrassed tears. Damning himself and the night, Hunter dragged her to him and kissed her again, his mouth hard and ruthless.

"Damn the Comanche," he said in a thick mutter when he lifted his head again. Susan looked up and past him.

"Hunter—look!"

Turning to look where she was pointing, Hunter was surprised to see a huge bank of clouds skid across the sky to hide the full moon. Even more surprising was the hiss of rain that fell in a wave.

"Where on earth did that come from?" he wondered aloud, shaking his head. Rain began to fall harder, sinking into the parched earth, drumming on the rooftop of the Civic Center.

"I'm getting wet."

Her voice brought him back to the moment, and he took her hand in his and pulled her with him. Instead of running back into the building with her, Hunter tugged her toward the livery stable. It was a hundred yards away, across the street and flanked by several scrawny trees. He shoved open one of the double doors.

Susan was laughing as he pulled her inside. "What's so funny?" he asked, peering at her in the dim light. Rain made a loud noise on the tin roof so that he had to lean closer to her to hear.

Sweeping a hand down the front of her skirt and blouse, Susan said, "I'm glad you brought me in out of the rain."

Hunter stared. She'd gotten drenched in their dash across the street. Her pale blouse clung to her curves in a wet, transparent drift of cotton, and her calico skirts hung around her legs in wilts of fabric. It was a most enticing sight.

His hot eyes shifted back to her face; she wasn't laughing now but looking back at him with an intent stare. Hunter took a deep breath and released her hand.

"So am I. Now let's see about getting you dry."

Nodding, Susan flicked a glance around the interior of the livery stable. "Is there anyone guarding the stock?"

"Not here. We moved them all to one place. They're at my feedlot at the other end of town. There weren't enough men to guard it all."

He'd been pulling her with him as he answered, and they were in the center of the empty stable now. He found and lit a lantern, turning it down low, then turned to her. The smell of hay and dust filled the air, mixing with the scent of rain from outside.

"The rain is a blessing," Susan murmured. "The Comanche won't attack tonight. Not here."

"Probably not. I wouldn't place bets on predicting them, though. Not safe."

Stripping out of his drenched shirt while he spoke, Hunter hung it over the top of a stall, spreading it out to dry. Susan watched silently, her arms hugged close to her wet body, her eyes big in the shadows and faintly flickering light of the lantern.

Hunter looked at her. "You're really wet. Cold?"

"Yes, I am." She shivered slightly. "Are there any blankets in here?"

"Yeah, I'll look for 'em." Hunter moved away from her before he lost control, grabbed her, and kissed her again. The rain had made her clothes almost transparent, and he could see the darker blossom of her nipples through the thin material of her cotton blouse. A surge of desire hit him so strongly that he broke out into a sweat in spite of his damp, chilled skin. It sent a surge of blood into his groin that was almost crippling in intensity, and if he didn't move away from her, he might do the unthinkable and push her into a pile of hay and take her. It was faintly humiliating to realize he had so little control of his own body or urges, and Hunter damned himself as he found several blankets and took them back to where she waited.

"Here," he said, handing her one of them. "Take off your clothes and wrap this around you."

She took it, slanting him a shy glance. "What are you going to do? You're just as wet as I am."

"I'm used to it." He shifted uneasily, wondering if she noticed his arousal in the tight, wet pants, hoping she had not. "I'll spread some blankets on a pile of hay, and we can sit there when you're comfortable."

It was his way of giving her some privacy; when she had stripped, hung her clothes over a stall door, then stepped into the stall where he was smoothing out the last edge of a blanket, she wiggled bare, impudent toes at him.

"I'm wet to the skin," she said cheerfully, and as he turned to look at her, dragging his gaze up from her bare feet and calves to the patch of tawny skin showing beneath the folded edges of the rough blanket she had wrapped around herself, his reaction must have been evident. Susan took a quick step backward as he straightened.

Neither of them had forgotten their need. It was a palpable throb in the air; tension and a kind of waiting hung between them, and as Hunter moved silently toward her, Susan wet her lips with the tip of her tongue.

"Let's sit down here on the hay," he said in a voice he didn't quite recognize; it was husky, almost raw with need for her.

Susan picked her way delicately across the hay, her bare feet curling up slightly at the prick. Her hands were curled inward as she held the blanket rather awkwardly, not quite able to look up at Hunter's face, it seemed. He didn't blame her. If any of what he felt showed on his face, she was probably wishing she was a hundred miles away.

Sprawling beside her when she was seated on the mound of blankets and hay, Hunter leaned on one elbow and stuck a stalk of straw in his mouth. He chewed on it, watching her face, trying to think of something to say. Why did he feel so damned awkward?

"You know all about me," Susan said after a moment of silence where nothing was heard but the gentle patter of rain on the roof. "I don't know anything about you, except that you're from Fort Worth, that you've managed to do pretty well for yourself, and that your housekeeper terrifies you."

He smiled crookedly. "What else is there to know?" The end of the straw moved up and down as he spoke, and his damp blond hair felt wet and heavy against his neck.

Shrugging, Susan met his eyes, and he saw her suck in a deep breath. "Everything," she said then, her eyes soft brown challenges boring into him. "Your favorite color.

The best thing that happened when you were a child—things like that."

Hunter shifted uncomfortably. "I don't usually think of the past." He flicked the straw to the floor of the stall.

"What do you think about?" She lifted her chin, and her dark hair shimmied in a silken ripple down her back. "Don't you have any favorite memories?"

"None like you mean." Hunter managed a tilted smile. "I have a feeling you're going to give me some, though."

"Only memories? How about a future?" Her voice grew tight with pain. "I don't know anything about you, Hunter. You keep yourself so mysterious, so—hidden—and I don't know if I've fallen in love with a man who'll return it or who'll hurt me." Her eyes were huge bruises in her face, and she caught her lower lip between her teeth and looked away from him. "You frighten me, Hunter Carson, and I don't know what to do."

Hunter caught her chin in his palm when she turned away with a flush of embarrassment. He didn't know what to say or how to tell her what she wanted to hear.

"Don't be frightened," he said in a low, rough voice. "I want the future with you."

Susan stared at him for a long moment; then she leaned forward. "I think I love you," she said softly, then kissed him.

Hunter felt a surge of raw emotion and closed his eyes against it. He focused on the soft satin of her mouth, on the tantalizing fragrance of her hair and skin, and the velvety smoothness of her shoulders beneath his palms. He put both hands on her shoulders, and when the blanket slid to one side and she tried to catch it, he stopped her.

Lost, lost, he was utterly lost. Nothing mattered now but this one slender girl with the soft brown eyes and even softer mouth.

His hand clutched the blanket in a reflex action, and he met her startled gaze steadily.

"Don't. Let it go. Let me cover you with kisses, Susan." Not waiting for her reply, he scraped his hands over her shoulders to cup her chin in his palms. He held her head still while he kissed her brow, her closed eyelids, the tip of her nose, then her lips again. His kisses were soft and subtle, and he held tightly to what was left of his self-control.

He knew he should wait; he knew he should. But he could no longer deny himself Susan. He'd waited weeks; he'd wanted her from the first time they'd met, and now that she was here, naked and willing, he couldn't wait. He'd make it up to her later. But now . . . but now there was this, the soft skin under his exploring hands, the honeyed lips opening for him, the sweet, full breasts with coral tips that made his entire body ache. . . . Oh, yes, there was all this, and he was only a man after all, though decency demanded he be honest and fair.

Hunter gave it one more valiant try: "Susan, sweetheart, are you sure you want me?"

All his scruples vanished without a trace when Susan touched him tentatively, her hands sliding up over his bare chest in a light caress, and Hunter groaned softly. His mouth left the soft hollow at the base of her throat, and he pushed her slowly back into the bed of straw and blanket.

Arching to meet his kisses, feeling his mouth scorching over her breasts, closing wetly over a coral-tipped nipple and sucking slowly, Susan surrendered to the raging fire he had started in her. It swept out of control; her hands moved up and down his bare back, skimming over small, old scars, the ridge of his spine, sliding around his rib cage to play over the smooth flex of muscles on his chest.

He still wore his pants, but he'd taken off his gunbelt and laid it aside earlier. She felt the cold press of his belt buckle nudging against her bare stomach, felt the rough scratch of his denim trousers against her thighs. It was oddly stimulating.

This was all so new to Susan; not just the act, which of course, was, but the feelings Hunter released in her. She had never thought about giving herself to a man like this. As any girl brought up on a ranch, she was familiar with what went on between men and women. Somehow, she had never applied what she'd seen or heard to herself. Now she was lying naked in Hunter's arms with his mouth on parts of her no man had ever glimpsed before, and she didn't know what she was supposed to do.

Following instinct, Susan touched him back, twisting so that she could reach him, tugging impatiently at the buckle of his belt, her hands skimming over the hard, flat bands of muscle on his flat belly. His muscles contracted when she touched him there, and he groaned softly, looking at her with glazed eyes.

It was heady stuff to discover that she could make him look at her like that, and Susan lay her palm lightly on the front of his pants. He pulsed beneath her hand, surging to meet her, and she closed her fingers around the hard detail of him.

Through clenched teeth, Hunter said softly, "I can show you what to do with it. . . ."

"Would you?" Her hand stroked him, and he thrust closer to her. "But maybe I'd like to find out for myself."

Beads of sweat dotted his upper lip, and when his jaw tightened, she noted the dark stubble of beard-shadow on his face. Hunter's eyes were half-closed, sultry with hot green lights, and his mouth was a taut slash. Susan began to unbutton his denims, and when he couldn't stand it anymore, he pushed her hands aside and finished it.

Shoving his pants off, he came back to lie over her, and she felt her throat close. He was beautiful, beautiful enough to make tears come to her eyes; his body was well muscled, golden, perfect.

She shivered, and he pulled her next to him, holding her against the velvety steel of muscle and sinew and fine-sculpted contours. His tawny head lowered, blocking out the glow of lantern light as he bent to kiss her again, and she closed her eyes.

"Open your eyes, sweetheart," he murmured against her mouth. "I want to watch your soul burn in them."

Her lashes lifted, and she sucked in a deep breath as he moved over her, his knees nudging her thighs apart. When her mouth opened, he covered it quickly with his again. She finally relaxed as he coaxed searing kisses from her, feeling weak and small and lost.

"Hunter . . ." She couldn't finish; she didn't know what she wanted to say, what she wanted to ask. It seemed that he did.

"Easy, love, easy. I won't do anything you don't want me to do," he said softly. "This is for you, for us, for the future and whatever we want to make of it. Hold me, honey. Like this. . . ." He took her hand and moved it between their bodies, curling her fingers around him, catching his breath when she gripped him. "That's right . . . not too hard. I don't want to go too fast for you. . . . God, Susan, you taste so good," he said next, putting out his tongue to scrape it across the tip of her breast again.

When his mouth closed around the peak, hot and moist and making her jump, his hand moved to cradle her other breast. Susan felt the fires burning in her belly leap almost out of control, and her hand tightened around him so fiercely that he groaned.

He blew his warm breath across her wet nipple, and she writhed beneath him gasping, her hands moving up to cup his broad shoulders. "Hunter, this is so . . . so strange and good, and—I don't know what to say, what to do . . ."

"Hold on, sweetheart, because it gets better." His hand slid down, stroking softly between her thighs, feather-soft and light, teasing, making her skin quiver. Her legs opened for him when he rubbed his palm across the dark, silky nest of curls, and as he lavished attention on her breasts and kept his hand on the gentle mound, Susan moaned.

Then he dragged his thumb across the most sensitive part of her, and she arched against his hand. A shocked gasp tore from her throat, and if she could have uttered more than an inarticulate cry, she might have told him to stop, that he shouldn't do that, that it was too mind-rending to bear. But she couldn't, and he didn't move his hand or his thumb but kept stroking it over her and making her spiral into a flaming column of need.

Hot spears of fire shot from the pit of her stomach up, threatening to consume her, making her pant for the sweet ache of release. She didn't know what would ease the hot, wild throbbing, but Hunter had to know.

Trembling, she writhed beneath his hand and mouth, her breath coming faster and faster, her body convulsing; when a shattering explosion rocked her, Hunter muffled her cries with his lips, inhaling them and giving them back to her with a hoarse mutter.

Half-sobbing, she turned her face into his shoulder. "I had no idea it was like this." She shuddered again as he moved his hand from between her thighs and held her close. She could feel his heart beating strongly against her cheek and throat. He was still aroused, his erection pulsing into her stomach, hot and heavy and insistent. Susan realized in that moment that this had only been the beginning.

Shifting so that he pressed heavily on her, his weight bearing her down into the soft cushioning of hay and wool, Hunter moved upward. Susan felt the throbbing heat of his male body between her thighs, nudging against her entrance. She moved to accept him, her arms around his neck, her face lifting for his kiss. Her hips arched closer, and she bit her lip at the burning pressure of his rigid body.

Hunter's breath was a harsh scrape of air entering and leaving his lungs; she felt the muscles in his belly jerk as she dragged her fingers over them in a light whisk, and one hand moved to grip both her wrists, pulling them gently over her head to pinion her to the blanket.

"Easy, honey, easy," he muttered against her ear, his breath husking over her neck and making her shiver. His big body inched closer until he probed the soft, downy folds of her in a burning entry.

Swallowing a cry of pain, Susan gave herself in to the kisses he quickly pressed on her, until finally she was quaking with need for him again. Tension rose swiftly; her skin burned for his touch. She ached for him, and there was a wild, throbbing pulse deep in the pit of her belly that made her writhe restlessly.

Hunter pressed forward, one arm straight and his palm digging into the hay beside her head, the other hand still holding her wrists in a light clasp above her head. The slow, relentless thrust of his hips eased him partially into her, and when he gave a quick, hard thrust, he finally succeeded in burying himself completely. He groaned with the effort and rested his forehead against her bare shoulder.

Breathing raggedly with the effort to hold back and not hurt her, he didn't move for a long moment. Susan brought her arms down and held him. Her breasts were flattened under his weight; she felt the harsh rattle of his breath. A tear trickled from her eye down her cheek, and when Hunter lifted his head and saw it, he flinched.

"Damn, I hurt you," he said softly. "I'm sorry, love. I wish—it shouldn't hurt again. Not like this time."

Susan managed a shaky smile at the true regret in his eyes. "It's all right. But, Hunter—?"

"Yeah?"

She moved restlessly. "Please *do* something to help me. I mean—oh, God, I don't know what I mean. Only that I feel like there's something more. . . ."

He laughed; dropping to his elbows, he lay atop her and shook with it. Then he lifted his head to look down into her indignant face again.

"Oh, yes, sweet Susan, there's more. A lot more. And I guess you're a lot more ready than I thought you were." His smile was tender and loving, and when he kissed her again, she sighed.

He began to move, and at first it hurt; not like before, but a raw, burning scrape that was uncomfortable. But he was patient and tried not to hurt her, and after a moment it stopped hurting, subtly yielding to a surge of urgency. The buildup began slowly, then mounted higher and higher until she was clutching him, her hips matching his thrusts with increasing fervor, her heels digging into the blanket.

The shock of his invasion altered to a fierce pleasure that heightened her senses; she heard the rhythmic patter of rain on the roof, the rough cadence of his breathing, the straw crackling beneath their movements. She could smell the sweet fragrance of new-mown hay, the sharp, dusty scent of rain outside, the clean masculine smell of Hunter. It was almost as exhilarating as his touch.

Susan burned wherever he touched; she ached for him with a searing need, rose to meet him, gave him back his own softly muttered love-words, sex-words, words that were unfamiliar but vaguely arousing.

He was pounding into her faster and faster, his loins rocking between her thighs, his body filling her with his heat and strength.

Quivering waves of sensation radiated throughout her body; when Hunter tucked his hands beneath her hips to lift her, pulling her up onto him with a shattering cadence that made her cry out, Susan felt the splintering shards of release break over her, carrying her along on a hot, wet tide of relief.

Hunter caught her response, gave her his in a final hard thrust as her soft internal muscles clenched around him with her climax. She was half sobbing, but heard his muttering growl of satisfaction as he held himself tautly for an instant, then let out his breath in a gust of air and dropped his head back on her shoulder.

His hair was damp with sweat, and his body glistened with it in spite of the chill. Susan's own skin glistened mistily in the shadows, and she shivered as she finally began to feel the cool air. Hunter wordlessly drew a blanket up over them and shifted to one side, pulling her into his arms and cradling her against his chest.

Time stood still. It was enough for the moment that they were together.

Chapter 8

TABITHA WORE A smug smile. "See? They're in love. I think I've made my point."

Still averting his eyes, Horatio didn't look convinced. "There is a big difference between love and lust. And I wasn't aware there were any promises made between them."

"Not necessary." Tabitha smoothed the buckskin skirt and caught her finger on the sharp end of a painted quill. She muttered a low imprecation—for which she had to apologize profusely—sucked at her injured appendage, then observed in the same satisfied tone as earlier, "I know these things and I say they're in love. He's smitten with her. And the girl is definitely taken with him. Before the day is over, they will be betrothed, and I will be back lying on silk cushions and listening to Beethoven play the Moonlight Sonata."

"So, this will be a job well done, heh?" Horatio rocked back on his heels with his hands clasped behind him, and bent a sour gaze on Tabitha. They sat high above the town of Los Alamos, where there was no rain and the moonlight was strong and bright. "What of the brooch?"

Tabitha still sucked at her finger. She glanced down at her decorated dress, and the warbonnet slipped to one side, hanging half over her face in a shimmy of eagle feathers. "What of the brooch? It's safe enough, I suppose."

Horatio made an exasperated sound. "You look like a

turkey buzzard that has been run over by a train, Tabitha. Do fix your headdress." He cleared his throat, then raised his brow when she changed the fringed buckskin and feathers for a red satin dress that ended just above her ankles. Black mesh stockings covered her pudgy legs, and the low-cut gown displayed much more of Tabitha than anyone should see. She, however, looked inordinately pleased.

"Tabitha," he asked in a strangled voice, "what— where did you see a dress like that?"

"Some shop. Gilbert's Saloon, or something like that. I'm not quite sure what sort of salon 'tis, but I must say, at least the women in there know how to adorn themselves with plenty of ornaments. You know, in Elizabeth's court, we all had ropes and ropes of pearls, diamond buckles, brooches, and even the men sparkled and glittered—oh, my, but we were lovely!"

"Yes. Well, that is no longer the fashion. Unless one happens to be a dance hall girl. And unless one is quite, ah, disreputable."

"Oh?" Tabitha frowned. She looked down at the elbow-length gloves she wore. Several bracelets winked in the moonlight. "Dance hall girl. Disreputable. I suppose you mean whores?"

Horatio winced. "Yes, though it is hardly for us to judge. That is left to—"

"Oh, please! Do not go into one of those long-winded tirades again. I'll change." Another blink of the eye, and she wore a decent shirtwaist with a bustle in the back. She made a face. "Almost as bad as a farthingale and ruff in this dreadful climate. But when in Rome—now, we were talking about my going back. My duty is clearly finished, and surely you do not think that this Hunter Carson has any designs on Susan's brooch!"

"Oh, no. Not him."

"Then who, pray tell?" Her voice was sharp. "Don't be mysterious. I hate that. And I hate being left out. I don't like being the only one who doesn't know something."

"I believe you already know."

"Do I? Oh, yes, I suppose I do. Thorne. Dreadful fellow. How does he know about it? And what does he mean to do?"

"The only way to find out the answers to those questions is to remain a while longer."

Sighing, Tabitha flounced on the rock, and the bustle hunched up in the back to hover near her shoulder blades. "I can't think why they sent you along, when you're making me do all the work. Very well." She wrestled with the bustle a moment, then added with another sigh, "I'll see what happens. But I'm getting tired of this, though I must admit young love is always nice."

"You're a saint, Tabitha," Horatio observed dryly.

She looked pleased. "Do you really think—?"

"Let's concentrate on one thing at a time," he cut in hastily, and Tabitha rose from the rock.

"I suppose you are right, though I do think Saint Tabitha has a nice ring to it. So . . . saintly." She started down the rocky slope. "Come along. Don't dawdle. I need to get this over with."

Wrapped cocoonlike in shadows and satisfaction, it took a while for either of them to notice that the rain had finally slackened. It was only a gentle spray against the tin roof now.

"Susan," Hunter said softly against her ear, "you need to go back."

She heard his voice through layers of contentment which wrapped around her like cotton gauze. The sweet smell of hay engulfed her, sharp and close. His arms around her were warm and comforting, making her feel secure in any storm. Safe. That was it. She felt safe again. Hunter made her feel as if nothing could touch her when she was with him.

"Whistles and horns," she murmured. Hunter shifted to look down at her.

"What?"

"Whistles and horns. I heard them when we made love."

He laughed, softly, his breath stirring her hair and making her smile. "I'm glad."

Without opening her eyes, she reached for him. Her arms went up and around his neck, skimming over the smooth brown column of his throat. She tangled her hands in the gilded strands of his hair, long, fine, and silky tumbling through her fingers, then dragged him down to her mouth. His lips were warm, pliant; when she flicked her tongue against them and he opened for her, drinking her in, the kiss subtly changed in intensity.

He kissed her fiercely, and his arms coiled around her body in a tight clasp that made her wriggle closer to him. It was a sensual slide of bare skin against bare skin, his chest scraping over her sensitive nipples so abrasively that she gasped and arched upward. She could feel the flat, hard band of muscles ridging his belly move against her as he shifted, and it brought every sense in her body alive with longing for him.

"No," he said after a moment, the word a tortured groan of sound as he wrenched away. "Not enough time. God. You make me crazy." This last was said in a mutter as he levered his body up and away from her. His palms pressed into the hay with a slight crackling. A faint, wry smile slanted the hard lines of his mouth when she looked at him with disappointment. "If we don't get you back soon, any shred of a decent reputation will be gone."

"I'm certain that it's already useless, but if you insist . . ." She twisted to a sitting position, captured his face between her palms, and gave him a last, hard kiss. It was hard for her to look at him and remember all the things she'd said in the heat of passion, and hard not to remember. A faint flush warmed her face when Hunter rocked back to his heels and gazed at her for a moment, his mouth squaring into a wolfish grin.

"You look good enough to eat, sweetheart."

"Is that an invitation . . . ?"

Rising smoothly to his feet, he shook his tawny head with real regret. "For later. Here—put your clothes on, and I'll check outside for trouble."

The fear returned. Comanche could be terrorizing the town at that moment. She felt a pang of guilt that she'd forgotten, even for a moment.

"Do you think the Comanche are close?" she asked as she caught her clothes, and he turned to look at her, surprised.

"Comanche? No. I was thinking more of those nosy old biddies like Mrs. Johnson or Mrs. Simpson. If they get wind of this . . . well, I'd just as soon you not have to listen to any of it." He grunted sourly. "Comanche are a lot less dangerous."

Hunter picked up his denim trousers from where they'd been discarded and stepped into them. He didn't button them as he bent to pluck a pistol from his holster, and Susan's gaze drifted over him with open admiration. His smooth body was so well made, so blatantly masculine; the open waist of his pants made her flush again as her eyes followed the narrow strip of hair curling down his belly. She glanced away, then glanced back.

"Hunter! You've been wounded!"

"What?" He looked at her, half-turning back as she rose to her knees and plucked at the material of his pants leg. "What are you talking about?"

"Blood—there, on your pants leg. Oh, let me see where you've been hurt. . . ."

He looked down at the smears of blood staining the tan denim, then laughed softly. "Susan. That's not my blood. That's yours. These were under us." There was a brief, awkward silence. "You know," he added in a gentle tone that brought a quick surge of heat to her face.

"Oh." Her throat convulsed with embarrassment. "I guess I thought . . . well."

Her blood. Of course. The proof of her virginity. And now he wore it. Humiliating in a way, but she wasn't ashamed of it. No, she wanted Hunter with all the honest emotion in her. There was nothing to be ashamed of in that. He tenderly cupped her chin in his palm.

"I'll be right back, sweetheart. You get dressed."

Bending, he brushed the top of her head with his lips, then crossed to the double doors of the stable. Susan watched him. In the soft gloom his golden body glistened, light playing over his broad shoulders and the smooth flex of his muscles. She tried not to watch him too closely; there was something so appealing, so arousing about his half-clad body in the shadows that it made even her throat ache.

She struggled into her skirt and blouse, looked for her shoes and slipped her feet into them. By the time Hunter came back to where she sat in the straw, she was trying to braid her hair into a neater plait. Raking her fingers through the dark, silky strands that curled defiantly with a life of its own, she found it hard to face him.

Hunkering down on his heels beside her, he smiled, a soft smile. Her gaze remained fixed on the straw and tumbled blankets. She didn't want to look at him, but he was too close. Daring a glance upward, she saw and felt his gaze at the same time.

"Safe?" she asked lightly, tucking the ends of her hair into the last twist and winding it deftly into a knot. God, why did he have to look at her like that?—with that hot, smoldering glow in his eyes, and the heat of their passion still curling inside her like a banked ember, needing only the slightest provocation to flare out of control again.

"Safe enough." He slid a hand through his hair in the gesture she had come to regard as endearing and typically Hunter, and rested his arms on his thighs, his hands dangling over his knees. "I'm not worried about Comanche as much as I am some stalwart, honest citizen with an itchy trigger finger and a queasy imagination. Maybe I oughta go out first."

"Swell idea. Then when they shoot you, I'm left all alone to explain how I came to be lying in a deserted stable with you." She shook her head, and the ghost of a smile traced her lips. "No chance, Cochise. We'll face whatever's out there together."

"Together?" The word seemed to take him back. Then he relaxed slightly and grinned. "Yeah, I guess we can. I can always hide behind you, I suppose."

"Oh, wonderful!" Laughing, she stuck out her tongue at him and rose to her feet. "And I was thinking you're so brave and strong."

He rose, too, and grabbed her into his arms for a swift, fierce embrace. They were both quivering when he stepped back and shrugged into his shirt and tugged on his boots. Susan stood silently as he buckled on his guns and searched for his hat, then they left the stable and stepped into the cool, damp air that smelled of fresh rain and wet dirt.

In the distance there was a low rumble of thunder; dark clouds still hung overhead. An east wind blew with a soft, sloughing sound down the street. The moon was gone and it was dark now, velvety black shadows surrounding them as they walked the short way back to the adobe building where no lights showed through the covered windows.

The musical sound of rain dripping from the eaves was a soft accompaniment to the kiss he gave her at the door of the Civic Center, then she eased inside with a lingering smile and his whispered promise that he'd see her later.

Later. It would have to do.

No candles broke the gloom when she slipped inside; only Doris was still awake. "Caught in the rain?" the older woman asked.

She nodded gratefully, if a bit guiltily. Doris peered at her in the murky shadows, her body covered by a gray wool blanket that made her seem part of the floor. "Thought so. It's been a long day. Let's get some sleep."

Susan spread out some blankets near Doris, then lay awake on the hard pallet for quite a while before she fell asleep. And when she did, her dreams were of Hunter Carson.

Morning brought the realization that no Comanche had raided. Nor were any sighted nearby.

"I guess we can ride back out to the ranch," Doris said as they folded up the blankets. Her attention was on the chore, not on Susan. It was quiet in the huge room; only a few women and children remained. Doris's voice sounded a bit louder than usual. "Do you think it's safe?"

"Didn't John Bradley come and tell us it was?" Susan asked. "They attacked a homestead thirty miles from here, then left the area. I guess we'll be all right."

She found it hard to look at Doris; surely the night before would be evident in her eyes. It should be. She still felt it. She still felt Hunter's mouth on her, his hands, the weight of his body; she still heard his sweet, soft words in her ear.

What would she say when she saw Hunter today? This was outside her realm of experience, and she wasn't certain how she was supposed to react to a man after . . . after.

"Susan."

She jerked guiltily. "Yes, Doris?"

Doris pushed at her hair; she stared pointedly at the clock on the wall. "I think it's time we started back to the ranch."

"You're right." Susan flashed a glance at the door and sighed. He hadn't come. Where was he? She felt so awkward, so obvious. Did Doris see it? She managed a smile up at her companion. "How about eating first? I don't think I want any more cold chicken and biscuits. We can eat at—"

"Thrasher's, I presume," Doris said resignedly, and when Susan laughed, she smiled. "All right, I'll go. It'll make me appreciate my own cooking even more."

Thrasher's was crowded. Apparently, others had the same idea. A loud hum of chatter filled the room, the rattle of dishes, the clink of cutlery, the jangle of spurs from the men. Here and there an occasional voice would rise above the others in laughter or irritation.

Wooden tables lined the walls haphazardly, filing like

drunken soldiers in columns down the middle of the large room, resplendent in red-and-white checked table-cloths. Mismatched chairs staggered at each table. Susan grabbed the first table that came empty, and they slid into the uncomfortable chairs with smiles of relief.

"After last night, even Thrasher's food looks good," Doris murmured, glancing around at the crowded café. "I was terrified that at any moment those murdering devils would be down on us. It was a restless night."

"For me, too," Susan said after an awkward moment slid by. She picked up a menu and pretended to read it. "I'm just glad it rained. Hunter seemed to think the bad weather helped keep them away."

"Probably." Doris peered at the soiled menu she held. "Well, I only hope that Pete and the others out at the Lazy W are all right, too. We'll have no way of knowing until we get there."

"Do I detect a hint of worry about the handsome Mr. Sheridan?" Susan couldn't help tease, and Doris colored hotly. She didn't say anything until they had ordered and the harried waitress left their table. Then Doris leaned forward and glared at Susan.

"Handsome? That piece of weathered rawhide?" She shook her head a bit too vigorously. "But he is almost a part of our little family, so of course I worry. I also worry about Henry, Burton, Miguel, and some of the others who have been with us a long time."

"And Arthur?"

Doris snorted in a most unladylike manner. "That pig!"

"Don't disparage my pig," Susan said around a gurgle of laughter. "Besides, he likes you."

"Hmmph. I'd like him—on a platter with an apple in his greedy little mouth."

"Doris, Doris—he's only a pig. How is he supposed to act? You can't expect him to go against his nature, now can you?"

"Maybe not, but that doesn't mean I have to like it." Doris was almost smiling, but when she looked up and past Susan for a moment, her smile stiffened.

Catching her expression, Susan said, "Oh, come on, Doris. Arthur isn't that bad. Admit you like him."

"Yes, yes, he's wonderful," Doris said so quickly that Susan sat back in her chair and looked at her in surprise.

"Well. That was easy. Too easy. Don't you want to tell me how greedy he is again? And nosy? And messy? Are you going to give up after over a year of complaining?"

"Susan—"

"Oh, look at you! You look as if you've just been poleaxed! Is it so hard admitting that you actually like Arthur a little bit?"

"Susan . . . Susan, that's not it."

"Are you thinking about Pete, then? You know you and he are going to have to admit one day that you love each other." Susan shook her head. "Give in, Doris. You might as well. Why, I've known how you two—"

"Susan," Doris broke in desperately, and there was such a concerned look on her face that Susan paused with her mouth still open. "Don't turn around. Not now. Just sit here and pretend that you don't see him."

"Pretend I don't see who? And it's easy to pretend when I *don't* see who you're talking about." Susan laughed. "Why are you being so—"

Half turning as she talked, Susan saw immediately why Doris had looked so distressed. It was Hunter. And he was not alone. He was with Lyla Wentworth, of all people, and the slender blonde was flirting her garters off, smiling and simpering and running her hand over his broad chest while Hunter just stood there with a silly smile on his face and didn't move.

Susan's heart dropped to her toes. He actually looked as if he liked it. As if he was used to it. As if he wanted her to do that. Another conquest, perhaps? She'd heard the rumors—but, oh, that was before . . . before she'd told him she loved him. Before last night. Before she'd lain with him in a sweet-smelling pile of hay and felt his hard man's body on hers and his mouth touching her where she'd never been touched before. No. Hunter would not betray her like this. She just didn't believe it. It had to have meant more to him than to be with another woman only hours later. . . .

She didn't realize she was standing up until Doris hissed at her to sit down, and Susan looked at her blankly.

"Don't you see, Susan? That's all you need, is to have everyone in town whispering about you!"

Susan made an impatient motion with her hand. "Is talk that important? Besides—besides, there's already enough talk. I don't care."

But she did care about being held up to ridicule, and she knew that if she made any kind of public spectacle, she would be. She sat back down slowly and, with her back to Hunter, began to breathe more easily. For several moments she had felt a crushing vise squeezing off her breath. Now, with her back to him and Lyla, she could inhale.

She did and looked up at Doris. "What are they doing?"

Doris shifted uncomfortably and looked down at the plate of food that had been set in front of her. "Lyla is still rubbing on him. Oh, I hate this. Don't look so dreadful, Susan. Everyone will know. Eat."

Susan looked at her plate and didn't remember ordering her food. She certainly didn't want it now. But dutifully she began to eat, forking bites into her mouth and chewing while she pretended that her world had not just reeled on its axis. He would explain. There was a simple explanation. There had to be. After all, he could have just run into the blond flirt and come into the restaurant with her out of courtesy—but would that justify allowing her to publicly rub on him?

No, and no, and no!

She tried not to think about that. She'd known when she suggested coming here to eat before going back to the ranch that Hunter was likely to be here. After all, it was the only restaurant in Los Alamos. She'd hoped that he would come in, see them, and naturally join them. It would have been so easy. Yet now it wasn't easy. Now it was painful.

They ate in silence, and Susan didn't even hear the noise around them. She was far too aware that Hunter had not approached them, that he was seated at a table in the far corner with Lyla Wentworth, and the blonde was laughing gaily. Occasionally she heard the deep rumble of Hunter's voice over the crowd, and her eyes would inexplicably mist with tears. She didn't let them fall, of course. That would be the worst humiliation.

"Susan, let's go," Doris said after an interminable amount of time had passed. "We can't sit here forever."

Susan made a wry face. "Too bad! It would certainly help."

Doris smiled weakly at Susan. "Good trooper! Don't let anyone know how you really feel."

"Is he still here with Lyla?" She didn't dare turn to look.

Doris nodded. "Yes. Don't look."

An odd twist of her heart made Susan pause. Doris knew, of course. She knew about last night. And now she also knew that Evan had been right and Susan was just one more conquest. But how could he have said such sweet things to her, held her so tenderly, told her they had a future together?

Susan straightened her spine and stood up. She smoothed the wrinkles from her skirt and tilted her chin proudly. No one else would guess that she was drowning with anguish inside. No one. Not even Hunter.

They were almost out the door before Susan heard him call her name. Her heart gave an odd lurch, and she quickened her steps. If only she could get outside away from curious eyes, then she could face him.

By the time they reached the wooden sidewalk, Hunter caught up to them. She felt him just behind her, his physical presence like a sharp blow, an explosion to her lacerated senses. His voice held no hint of betrayal; it was the same: husky, deep, shattering. Intimate. *Oh, God!*

"Susan—wait."

Wagons rumbled past, dogs barked loudly, and horses trotted down the already dried mud of the street with faint, clopping sounds. Susan was aware that the barricades had been removed, that it was business as usual. And that her heart had somehow turned to stone in her chest.

She turned slowly and forced her gaze to his face. He was smiling at her, his green eyes half-shaded against the bright day by his long lashes. He wasn't wearing a hat, and a hot blaze of sunlight made his pale hair glimmer like gold. She looked away.

"Good morning, Mr. Carson," she replied stiffly.

His eyes narrowed a little bit. He looked uncertainly from Susan to Doris's set face. His spurs jangled as he shifted position on the wooden sidewalk, and he rested one hand on his hip, fingers curled under.

"Good morning, Miss Whitten." It was said with a hint of sarcasm. His boots scraped on the wooden planks beneath his feet. "I thought if you're ready to ride back out to your ranch, I'd go along as a guard. It may not be quite clear yet, and—"

"No, thank you," Susan put in firmly. "Doris and I are quite capable of managing. I appreciate your offer, however. Perhaps you are more needed in town."

She started to brush past him, still not looking at him directly. Hunter put a hand on her arm. His touch unnerved her, but she didn't shake loose. His voice was impatient and exasperated.

"I'm sure I'll be sorry I asked, but what's the matter with you? Did you get bad news or something?"

Susan fought the urge to laugh, feeling that it would sound more hysterical than amused. "No, no bad news." She met his gaze for an instant. It jolted her to her toes; hot and potent and filled with masculine hunger. She stiffened. "I just feel the need to go home."

"Isn't that what I said?" He smoothed back his hair in the familiar gesture. "Your buckboard's still here. I had it taken up to the granary after we hauled it out of the street. I'll put a team to it and take you home."

She glared at him, her knuckles white as she gripped handfuls of her skirt. "No, thank you! I'm extremely capable of driving my own team—"

"Pete took them. You don't have one here."

She set her jaw stubbornly. "Then I will hire what is necessary, or leave the wagon, or walk, if I have to, but I do not require your help in getting home!"

Susan felt Doris at her elbow, knew that she was making an issue out of it, but knew, too, that she could not allow him to see the depth of her hurt. He was staring at her with a narrowed look of concentration. She looked away from him again.

"Susan—" He reached for her arm again, the one word taut and filled with insistence, and before she could speak or react, feminine footsteps hurried across the planking.

"Hunter! There you are. I thought you were coming right back."

Susan didn't have to turn to recognize Lyla Wentworth. She knew that voice, that soft, syrupy tone Lyla used when she was around a man. It had been the same in their adolescence, and Lyla had kept more boys hanging around her with that sugary tone than there were flies in the cow yard, Susan thought glumly.

Blond, smiling, tiny, and dressed exquisitely, Lyla made Susan feel like a clumsy, dowdy old maid. Especially in the wrinkled skirt. Lyla smiled of lilac water, while Susan probably still smelled of the stables. And Hunter. Her heart lurched. She turned to smile politely at Lyla, and saw that the blonde didn't even glance at her.

Hunter looked faintly bemused as Lyla put a possessive hand on his arm. "I didn't know you were waiting on me," he said shortly.

Her laugh tinkled softly, somehow rising above the noise in the streets. "Of course I was, silly! We're still not through with our business."

"Business? Oh." He shook her hand off his arm. "That can wait. No hurry on it."

"But, sugar, my daddy's in a powerful hurry to talk to you about that land." Lyla smiled prettily. Her blue eyes were wide and fringed by long, curling lashes that swept up and down with usually devastating effect. "He's anxious to buy some of it now that you have so many foreclosures."

Susan stared at Hunter. He stared back at her, his jade eyes challenging. *Foreclosures.* Evan had been right. Once again she had acted impulsively and come to regret it. She'd slept with the enemy, bedded a rattlesnake, invited in the Huns. She was doomed. The Lazy W was doomed. Pete, Doris, Miguel, Henry—everyone who depended on her would lose. All because she'd let Hunter Carson sweet-talk her, and because she'd thought she could handle him and make deals with him and not lose her shirt. He'd call in that loan, and she wouldn't be ready. He'd have the ranch, and she'd be out on the prairie eating cactus.

"Don't say it," Hunter hissed when Susan opened her mouth to tell him what she thought of him. His eyes flashed menace at her, and for some reason, she decided to listen to him. About this, at least.

"You have no idea what we're talking about, Miss Whitten," he added when she shut her mouth again. Susan gave him her sweetest smile.

"Nor do I wish to, Mr. Carson. Pray, do continue your important discussion about the proper distribution of stolen property in comfort. Doris and I must get back to the ranch. While we still have it."

"Have I interrupted something?" Lyla asked with feigned innocence. Her eyes blinked. "Oh, my!"

Still gritting his teeth, Hunter said, "Miss Wentworth, you know Miss Whitten, don't you?"

Lyla barely flicked Susan a glance. "Of course. Are

you ready to go now, Hunter? I promised my father that we would be back soon."

"Don't let me keep you from your *pleasures*," Susan said, and when Hunter would not release her arm from his tight grip, she looked down at it pointedly. "Please, Mr. Carson—even you cannot expect to spread yourself so thin."

"Susan, dammit, don't be stupid." He sounded impatient, and she flashed a glance at Lyla, who looked suddenly interested in the exchange between them. Susan's chin lifted slightly.

"Excuse me, Mr. Carson, but I believe that your rudeness cannot be excused. Now, if you will release my arm, I will be on my way."

"I have no intention of letting you get away that easily. I want to talk to you."

Susan pried his fingers loose, her nails cutting into his skin. Her hand was shaking, and she hoped her voice was steady when she said, "There's nothing to say. I don't want to talk to you."

"Dammit!" Hunter began, but Doris cut in.

"Mr. Carson. Perhaps you don't mind being gawked at by half the townspeople, but we do. Unless it is your intention that Susan and I be ogled, you will be kind enough to allow us to go our way. Whatever your business with her, it can be discussed at a later date."

He released Susan's arm. "Fine. Rest assured, I will be out there to discuss it."

Susan met his hard gaze. "We'll be terribly busy for a while. I'm afraid that I won't have much time for visiting, so I'll let Pete take care of any business."

"That ought to be interesting," Hunter drawled with a lift of his brow, "considering the nature of my business."

A faint flush stained her cheeks, but she turned away with all the dignity she could muster. "Any other business is over with."

"Not by a long shot, Miss Whitten," Hunter said as she walked away. "Not by a long shot."

Chapter 9

HUNTER WAS SO mad he wanted to kick something. Or somebody. Since it would look pretty foolish to do either, he decided to do the next best thing—he would nurse his anger in the smoky interior of Gilbert's Saloon. He didn't usually hang out in saloons, but there were times it was the best thing a man could do. It kept him from going after Susan and making her madder than she already was, and he had no doubt that he was too frustrated to choose his words with care.

Dammit, what bee did Susan have in her bonnet now? And why was it women always seemed to think a man could read their minds and know why they were angry? It made him want to pick her up and shake some sense into her, but he was too mad to act on *that* impulse. And Lyla Wentworth was standing on the sidewalk and looking at him smugly as she waited for him to reply to whatever stupid thing she'd said now. He looked at her.

"What?"

"Let's go to my house. My father will be there in a little while."

Impatiently, he shook his head. Hunter looked past her to where Susan had disappeared around the corner. "No. I'll talk to him later."

"That's what I said, silly." Her voice lowered to a soft, sensual purr. "He won't be there *until* later, and we can be together until then."

147

Hunter frowned. Her insinuation was unmistakable now. Before Susan, he would have taken her up on it. Now it only made him edgy.

"I've got another appointment," he said abruptly and saw her shock at his refusal. "Tell your father I'll call on him later to discuss those land contracts. Goodbye, Miss Wentworth."

"But—"

Lyla found herself talking to empty air as Hunter pivoted on his heel and stalked down the sidewalk. She stood where he'd left her and gave an angry stamp of her foot when he turned into Gilbert's Saloon.

It took a moment for Hunter's eyes to adjust to the dim light in the saloon, and he paused just inside, cautiously. Even in a small out-of-the-way town like Los Alamos, there could be trouble. Maybe especially in an out-of-the-way place like this. Remote towns drew men on the run, men with bad tempers and bad reputations. He'd gone after men like that once.

Once. Another lifetime ago. Then a woman had changed it all for him. Turned it around, in fact. A faint smile tucked the corners of his mouth, and his eyes narrowed slightly as he stepped toward the bar.

It was that look that the bartender saw, and he glanced at the Winchester he kept under the bar, then back to Hunter. "What can I get ya?"

"A bottle of whiskey and a clean glass." Hunter tossed his money on the bar, took the bottle shoved toward him, and moved to a table in the back. By habit, he took a chair that faced the doors, and one where no one could sneak up behind him. Yeah, it had been a long time, but he still held to the old habits. They died hard. Self-preservation was strong.

Leaning back in his chair, Hunter sipped at his whiskey and tried not to think about anything. The saloon was close to empty; only two or three customers were there, and a tired-looking saloon whore draped over a man at the far end of the bar. Her red satin dress hung unevenly, and black net stockings sagged in places; frizzled hair waved around her head. He let his glance slide past her to the men just coming in the doors, then swore softly.

Evan Elliott and Peter Thorne. Somehow, the duo seemed a perfect fit. He sipped at his whiskey again. For some reason they looked guilty. Although it was probably his dislike of them that colored his opinion; if they were guilty of anything, they certainly wouldn't walk into a public saloon where anyone could—and would—report them. He knew firsthand about Los Alamos gossips.

Elliott didn't see Hunter sitting in the back. He and the dapper Englishman walked to a table behind a low wooden partition and sat down with a bottle and two glasses. Hunter could hear them as clearly as if they were at the same table with him.

"Please," the Englishman was saying in his cultured, clipped accent, "be still, Evan. You make me nervous with your shillyshallying."

"What do you want to tell me?" Elliott's voice was quick and furtive. "And why act so secretive? You brought me all the way back from my ranch to meet me in a saloon? Don't sound as if what you want to say is that important."

A low laugh thrummed in the air, and Hunter heard the scrape of chair legs, as if Thorne was moving closer. "My dear fellow, I had to be certain whomever I chose to be my partner would be worthy of the decision."

"Partner? In what? All you said was that you could make me some money."

"And so I shall, if you will only put in a modicum of effort." After a splash and gurgle of pouring liquor Thorne continued softly, "It requires only a little time on your part, and perhaps a bit of conversation."

"With who?"

"Miss Whitten."

A brief silence flowed, and Hunter felt his muscles tighten. His hand curled harder around his glass of whiskey.

"Susan?" Evan said at last. "I don't know if I want to involve her in anything. What do you mean, anyway?"

"Ah, Evan, Evan. Surely you must realize that I would never ask you to harm your lady-love. I know full well how you feel about her."

"Damn you!" There was the sound of glass slamming on wood. "Don't you dare make fun of how I feel about Susan!"

"Is that what I said?" Thorne demanded sharply. "No, it is not. I merely mentioned your friendship with her. It can be of great advantage to us both."

"How?"

"Don't glare at me so suspiciously, Evan old chap, and I shall be happy to tell you." Silence, and the creaking of a chair; then: "Very good. It is this—she has recently come into the possession of a very fine antique brooch. It is English, handed down from daughter to daughter. My employer has empowered me to purchase it from Miss Whitten. I am prepared to offer a handsome amount, and you, as the mediator, will be given a more than generous finder's fee."

"Finder's fee?" Evan asked suspiciously. "How much? And what do I have to do for it?"

Hunter mentally cursed the greedy Elliott, and his lips tightened into a thin line. Damn him. If he hurt Susan . . .

"Two thousand dollars for your portion, Mr. Elliott. Does that sound fair?"

"Two thousand—you must be crazy! No damn piece of jewelry is worth that! Not that one, anyway. I've seen it. It's just a fair-size diamond in an old-fashioned setting."

"That 'fair-size' diamond, sir, is worth a small fortune in its way," Thorne said dryly. "To a collector only, of course. It is English and should never have been brought over here, you understand. My employer is quite sentimental about such things."

I bet he is, Hunter mused. *More sentimental about small fortunes in jewels is my guess. . . .*

"So, all I have to do is talk Susan into selling it?" Evan asked after a moment. "I've already tried that. Back when she needed the money so bad." His voice was bitter. "That was before that bastard Carson extended her loan. Now she doesn't need it. She won't sell for sure."

"Perhaps you could find a method to persuade her. Two thousand dollars is not a small purse," Thorne said softly. Silence spun between them again, then he added, "If you can arrange it within, say, a week, perhaps I can persuade my employer to add a bonus to your fee. Would five hundred dollars be adequate?"

"Wheeoo!" Evan whistled softly. "How much are you offering for the brooch, if you're willing to give me that much money just to arrange it?"

"As much as it costs to get it."

"Your boss must have more money than brains," Evan said flatly.

"Quite. He's not loathe to part with whatever it takes to get it." Thorne coughed politely. "The duke specifically bade me return with the brooch or I should be sacked."

"Fired? For not getting it?"

"As I said, the duke believes it belongs in England. And I agree with him. Will you help us, Mr. Elliott?" The hesitation drew out, and then Thorne said, "If Miss Whitten receives a large amount of cash, she will no longer be forced to do business with undesirable businessmen, am I correct?"

"You mean Carson."

"Whomever she must placate to continue running her ranch."

"Yeah, that goddamn Hunter Carson, the bastard!" There was the sound of glass hitting wood again, hard. "Yeah, if she didn't have to deal with him—"

"Lower your voice!" came the quick, hard warning, and Evan subsided. "So, you'll help me?" Thorne prompted.

Hunter's eyes narrowed when he heard Evan say in a slow, measured voice, "Yeah, I guess I will. I'll have to eat some crow with Susan, but I think she'll come around."

"Do you?" Thorne laughed. "Eating crow sounds quite undesirable, but then, the money you earn will more than make up for it. Very wise of you, Evan. And I imagine that if you are solvent once more, Miss Whitten will realize how valuable you are to her."

"Do you think so?" Elliott sounded eager. "Yeah, she only got so mad at me after all this happened. Said I was lazy, that I didn't take ranching seriously." His voice grew hard. "Yeah, she'll see that I do, that I can make a go of it. Then she'll come 'round."

"And if she doesn't?" Thorne asked after a moment. "As I have stated, my employer is quite insistent about acquiring the brooch. It was in his family at one time, you understand. Here—let me fill your glass for you. Now, if Miss Whitten refuses to sell, do you suppose that you could, ah, detect its location and sell it for her? I assure you that the money would be generous," he added when Evan made a harsh sound. "And you wouldn't have to allow her to discover you had been behind its disappearance. Why, then, Evan, you would be in the position to give her any amount of money she desired, if you wanted to handle it that way. Think how grateful she would be."

"And she wouldn't have to know I took it?"

"No, no, indeed. Why should she? My employer would have the brooch, you would have the money, and as your *wife*, Miss Whitten would share in the proceeds. Everyone would be happy, do you see?"

"Yeah, yeah, I do!" Elliott laughed suddenly. "In fact, I think I like that last idea better. She don't ever need to know who got it—and then she'll see that I can support her, and it won't matter once we're married."

"Good, very good. I think we'll deal well together."

There was the clink of glasses, and Thorne told Evan to meet him there the next day at the same time to discuss their plans.

"I'll be here," Elliott promised, and there was the scrape of chairs being shoved back.

Hunter pulled his hat over his face and sat there for a while after they left, just to make sure they didn't see him. He needn't have worried; neither of the men even glanced toward his table.

Worried, Hunter knew Susan would never listen to him if he repeated what he'd overheard; not now, anyway. She was mad at him for something stupid, probably, and he'd have to wait her anger out. Dammit, what could have made her so mad at him?

Tabitha let out a howl of rage that started every coyote in Callahan County to a fever-pitch of yowls. Horatio put a worried hand on her arm.

"Now, Tabitha . . ."

"That lackbrained, addlepated numbskull! What does he think he's doing, trafficking with a man of Thorne's ilk? Peter Thorne is far too clever a rogue for that trusting boy—oh, you needn't stare at me like I've lost my wits, Horatio! I'm just angry!"

"So I see."

"Well, I intend to go right down there and set that twit straight—"

"No. You can't, Tabitha. That would be ill advised."

Tabitha stared at Horatio. "What do you mean—can't?"

"Simply that your advice would not only be ignored, it would be dangerous."

"Dangerous? What can he do—kill me?" Tabitha laughed. "I'm a step ahead of him there."

"No, no, not to you. Must you equate everything to your own needs, Tabitha?"

She paused, pushed at the bustle which had somehow twisted around to her left hip, giving her a lopsided look, and heaved a sigh. "Hmm. P'raps you're right. Let me but think a moment. . . . Ah, I've got it!"

Horatio sighed softly. "May I ask what you've got?"

"Hunter shall tell Susan all about it. Then she will put an end to it, of course." She twitched her skirts with a grunt of satisfaction. "Take the Lynnfield brooch, will he? Not as long as it's in the possession of a true descendant, he shall not! No, not as long as I live— oh, you know what I mean."

"Are you certain that will work?"

Tabitha looked up at him in surprise. "Why shouldn't it? She'll listen to him."

"Do you really think so?"

"Well, any fool can see that he loves her, and he would not harm her, so I cannot imagine that she would not listen to him."

"Like *you* have always listened?"

Drawing herself up into an indignant knot, Tabitha opened her mouth to retort, then closed it, opened it again in a fishlike motion, closed it. "I listened," she said finally. "I just chose not to hear."

"Ah. A distinction, however fine, is always welcome."

"You're trying to tell me something!"

"Don't snap at me, Tabitha."

"Well, aren't you? I declare, Horatio, there should be an end to interference when one is dead. I mean, it's the outside of enough that I must come to this godforsaken— desolate—spot, then to find myself embroiled in a messy affair like this . . . well, I hope to tell you that I have seen how I could have benefited, perhaps, from a few well-chosen words myself, but Susan is different."

"Is she? Does your descendant listen so much better?"

That took her by surprise. "God's holy hands, I hope so!" was the fervent reply a moment later.

Susan sat on the front porch and fondled Arthur's ears. He responded with a pleased grunt, then snuffled at her free hand.

"Greedy pig," she murmured, more to the air than to the creature beside her. She fed him the last bite of bear sign that Doris had just taken from the oven; the light, flaky pastry held no appeal for her just now.

Not much appealed to her lately.

Hunter hadn't followed her.

Oh, she knew she'd told him not to, but she'd still expected him to ignore her words. Not that she wanted him to, she told herself hastily, but still, he did owe it to her to at least put up a protest when she told him to go away. It was the least he could have done.

"Miss Susan."

She blinked, then saw Pete standing at the bottom of the steps looking up at her. Susan flushed. How long had he been standing there trying to catch her attention?

"Miss Susan," he pushed on, seeing her gaze come to rest on him at last, "I thought you'd exchanged that sweet feed for alfalfa pellets."

"I did." She stared at him. "I know I did. You know I did."

Scratching his head, Pete nodded slowly. "Yep, thought both of us knew that. But damned if I know how—we've got more sweet feed than alfalfa again. Now, Miss Susan—I went and picked up the order myself. But I swear to you that it has gone and got messed up again."

"Someone is playing pranks, maybe. Have you checked the contents?"

Pete gave her a reproachful stare. "Yes, Miss Susan. We checked them."

"Then how—?"

"Beats me. Might ask Carson, though."

Her flush returned, beating hot and strong along the bones of her face. "Yes, that would be one alternative, but I don't think we need to do that. After all, we knew what was in them when we left Los Alamos, didn't we?"

"Thought we did. Guess we didn't."

Exasperated, Susan snapped, "Well, someone here must have switched them! Find out who it is!"

Pete gave her a long, considering look. Susan's hands clenched helplessly. She knew what he had to be thinking; he was right. She'd become as mean as a snake since—since the night of the party.

"I'm sorry, Pete. I'm just tired, I guess." She managed a smile. "It's been a long day, and by the time I got through with those account books, I'm afraid even Doris's bear sign didn't cheer me up."

Pete brightened. "She baked bear sign?"

Laughing, Susan said, "Help yourself! I'm sure she won't mind letting those dirty boots in the back door. Just don't leave tracks on her clean floors."

When Pete had gone around the house to the back, Susan stood up. Arthur stood up with her, his trotters clicking on the wood planking of the porch. Small piggy eyes gazed at her expectantly. His pink body wriggled.

"Pig," Susan muttered with a smile and scooped him up to settle him against her shoulder. It was a lot harder than it had been; Arthur was growing, and soon she wouldn't be able to lift him at all. Groaning a little bit, she put him back down.

Arthur immediately trotted down the steps and into the yard. Susan followed, her steps lethargic, her thoughts wandering again. As usual, they drifted back to Hunter. She tried not to think about him, but she couldn't help herself.

Two days. Two days since he'd held her, whispered sweet words in her ear he hadn't meant. And she had not seen or heard from him since leaving him standing on the sidewalk in Los Alamos.

Damn him. Damn her. Damn everything. That's what she got for being so trusting. For giving herself to the first man who made her heart beat faster. She should have waited, should have known better.

Her fingers curled into her palm, leaving half-moon depressions in her skin, and she relaxed slowly.

"Well," she muttered to Arthur, "I guess I'll stick to pigs from now on, right?"

Arthur glanced up at her and wiggled his snout. Then he returned to rooting along the ground, searching for any small delicacy that he could find under an occasional rock.

Susan was standing by the corral fence watching some of the men work a few green-broke horses when someone said, "Rider coming."

Her heart lurched, as it had every time a visitor came to the Lazy W. At least, as it had since she'd met Hunter Carson.

This time her expectations were right.

Hunter rode toward the corral on his big chestnut; dust boiled up in small clouds behind him. He reined in several yards away, swinging easily out of the saddle as Susan turned with an uncertain glance. She felt like running into the house, wondered frantically if there was dirt on her face, if her hair was neat, if her clothes were rumpled—then she steadied herself. What did she care? What did *he* care?

She focused on Hunter as if he were the only man in Texas. His movements were lazily efficient, casual. The big chestnut walked behind him. Hunter paused and glanced toward Pete, nodded. "Sheridan."

Shoving back his hat, Pete nodded. "Carson."

Susan felt a quiver of irritation. Men. Those curt acknowledgments could have meant anything. Whether they were hostile or friendly certainly didn't show in their greetings. Maybe she should learn to do the same.

Pressing back against the corral fence, she folded her arms over her chest—mainly to stop the quivering of her hands—and regarded Hunter coolly. She hoped he couldn't see through her pretense. Inside, she was seething with indecision. Damn him for being so heartbreakingly handsome, so beautiful, like a pagan god set down in Texas to steal away her soul. Her chin lifted, and she met his gaze with a calm she hadn't known she still possessed.

"Mr. Carson."

His mouth twitched slightly, and his eyes were narrowed and hard beneath the brim of his hat. Casually looping his reins over a fence post, he touched his hat and said just as coolly, "Miss Whitten."

With everyone standing around, casting curious sideways glances at the two of them, it would have been impossible to say or do anything more personal anyway, and Susan inhaled deeply.

"What brings you to the Lazy W?"

"I think you know," he drawled, refusing to release her eyes. "Is there somewhere we can talk privately?"

"As I told you, Mr. Carson, Pete will handle anything you need to dis—"

"No."

His hand curled around her wrist, and he pulled her away from the fence. That action had the immediate effect of jerking Pete forward a few feet, and Susan saw from the corner of her eye that several of the men had stiffened warily.

"My business is with you, and you know it," Hunter said.

"Hunter . . . Mr. Carson," she said in a choked voice. "I don't want to talk to you."

"Let her go," Pete said flatly as his right hand dangled over the butt of the pistol at his side.

Susan flinched slightly. Pete was liable to draw, and she couldn't risk that. He'd be killed; she trusted Hunter's reputation as a fast gun, if not the man himself.

"No, Pete. It's all right. I do need to talk to him . . . about the feed."

Pete's jaw stuck out belligerently. "I don't like the way he treats you, Miss Susan. Ain't no man gonna grab you like that in front of me. Or any other time, if I can help it."

"He'll let go of me. Won't you, Mr. Carson?" Susan looked up at him and saw the faint press of a smile at the corners of his mouth. Idiot! Didn't he know—or care— that seven armed men were glaring at him with murder in their eyes?

Shrugging, Hunter released her arm. "As long as you come with me."

Bridling, Pete took another step forward, and Susan put out a hand to stop him. "I'll come with you, since you ask so graciously, Mr. Carson." She flashed him a grim glance and stalked past him. Arthur trotted along behind her, his snout up and testing the air, giving an occasional squeal.

Hunter's long strides brought him even with her, and she could feel his assessing gaze on her. Her cheeks grew hot, but she felt a chill skip down her spine.

"Why did you come out here?"

Ignoring the hostility in her low voice, Hunter said, "I thought you'd had enough time to get over whatever was bothering you a few days ago. And I have something to tell you."

She gave him a quick glance. "I don't think we have any business to discuss that Pete can't handle," she said, contradicting herself.

"The hell we don't."

Startled by his ferocity, she paused and half turned. Hunter put a hand under her elbow and steered her back around. "Don't stop unless you want your hired hands all over me."

"That's not a bad idea!" She let him guide her toward the house, her arm tingling where he kept his hand around it. "You must be crazy," she said. "Did it ever occur to you that they might shoot you when you grabbed me?"

"Yeah, it occurred to me."

"I suppose you think you're fast enough to take on seven men, then?"

"No, I just knew I wanted to talk to you." His voice was slightly mocking. "Would you have let them shoot me?"

"I might have."

"But you didn't."

"Don't press your luck, Hunter Carson!" He laughed softly, and she bristled. "I can always correct my mistake, you know."

"I suppose you can, sweetheart. That one, anyway."

"Don't call me that," she said quietly.

Susan didn't say anything else until they were in the house, and the cool shadowed rooms provided some relief from the heat.

"Come into the study," she said, ignoring Doris, who hovered anxiously in the doorway. Hunter tipped his hat to her, and Doris gave him a chillingly polite nod, then went back into the kitchen, Arthur trailing behind her.

Shutting the study door behind them, Susan found that it was even harder meeting his eyes when they were alone than it had been in front of her men. She paused and looked at the familiar room with its masculine appointments of deer horns, rifle cases, and thick bear rugs scattered on the floor. Hunter looked so *right* standing there.

"What do you want?" she asked gruffly as she moved to stand behind her father's desk. She toyed idly with one of the pens and the ink bottle. Account books still littered the surface, and her neat rows of figures looked like hieroglyphics when she tried to concentrate on them.

"I want to know what the hell's the matter with you," he said, tossing his hat to the desk. "Do you blow hot and cold, dammit?"

"Obviously."

"Stop avoiding me, Susan." He moved too quickly for her to evade his grasp, catching her by one arm and pulling her toward him, his hands rough on her. Half across the desk, his fingers digging into the tender skin of her upper arm, Susan flung back her head to face him.

"Let go of me!"

"No." His grip tightened slightly, and he moved around the corner of the desk to drag her closer. "What burr have you got under your saddle?"

"Nothing I care to discuss with you, Mr. Carson."

"Mr. Carson." Hunter's mouth tightened. "Don't call me *Mister Carson,* so cool and distant, like we haven't lain together and I haven't been inside you, little girl." Both hands were on her now, tucking her against his body, against the hard angle of his chest and thigh. "I want to know what's the matter."

Struggling to hold on to her composure, Susan looked away from the demanding look in those hard green eyes.

"I don't feel like talking about it. Besides, there's nothing between us to discuss."

Lame, lame, lame! He'll never buy that!

Hunter gave her a slight shake. "Look, there's something between us, and you know it. After the other night I thought—"

"Yes!" she said in a half-snarl. "Let's talk about the other night! Or maybe the other morning, you snake!"

He frowned, and his green eyes grew cold. "Say what you've got to say outright."

Jerking away from him, Susan rubbed at her arms, meeting his fierce gaze with one of her own. Pain and anger choked her, so that her words were a tumble of gasps and half-formed thoughts.

"You said—at least you *acted* like you cared, and then you didn't even bother to—well, I guess when Lyla showed up, you found something you liked better!"

"Lyla!" He looked stunned, then a faint smile curled his mouth. "Is that it? Lyla?"

"No, that's not it!" Susan sucked in a deep breath to steady her voice. "You lied to me. You've been foreclosing on ranches."

"I never said I wouldn't."

"Liar!"

His eyes glittered, cold and green and dangerous. She took an instinctive step back.

"Don't call me a liar, Susan. I never said I wouldn't foreclose on any ranches. If I foreclose, you can bet I gave them every chance to make good."

"Oh, certainly you have! A regular philanthropist is in our midst!"

"Dammit, Susan, don't mix business with personal matters. What is between us has nothing to do with the granary or any of my other business deals."

"That's what you think!" Pressing her curled hand to her mouth in a tight fist, Susan fought back the surge of tears that threatened to fall. Ridiculous. Tears for a man who thought nothing of turning out decent, hardworking people? Who would probably think nothing of turning her out?

"I don't see how you make that connection," he said in a tight, flat tone that sent a chill up her spine.

"Hunter, these people are my neighbors, friends. What affects them affects me. To be turned out of their homes, penniless and left to fend for themselves, is a hardship I cannot condone for anyone."

"I don't think we're talking about the same thing. Who have I turned out without a penny? I paid good, hard cash to the bank for the foreclosures I bought."

Susan looked at him, wanting to believe him. "But Lyla said—"

"Lyla Wentworth is an empty-headed flirt! She doesn't understand the first thing about business and couldn't make the distinction between a foreclosure and a fence post."

A bubble of amusement rose in Susan's throat, but she shoved it back down, not quite willing to release her anger yet. "Obviously, you aren't interested in her for her intelligence. I didn't notice you pushing her off you, though."

"Was I supposed to slap her in public? Nothing less than tossing her in the nearest horse trough would have got her off me."

"Well . . ." Susan stood uncertainly. Hunter didn't look so angry now, though his eyes were still wary. Maybe she should have given him a chance to explain.

"Well what?"

She managed a sheepish shrug. "Well, maybe I jumped to conclusions."

"You jumped like a damn bighorn sheep." He eyed her for a long moment. "I don't like being put in the position of having to defend myself, Susan. Unless I've done something wrong and you *know* it, don't do it to me again. It's a damn uncomfortable feeling."

Shifting from one foot to the other, she found it hard to look at him. She'd been so sure that he'd only been toying with her and had immediately remembered every bad thing Evan had ever said about him, and now she was ashamed that she'd not trusted him more.

"I truly apologize, Hunter. I don't usually go around accusing people of things they haven't done. . . ." She paused and bit her bottom lip when he didn't say anything. His spurs jingled when he took a step forward, and she looked up as he reached out to catch her to him.

"Aw, hell, Susan, you can make me madder than I ever thought about being." He grazed the top of her head with his jaw. "I'm not good at this kind of stuff. Just give me a chance next time."

Sighing into his shirt, she put her arms around him and nodded. "I will. I won't doubt you again." She felt his chest shake with amusement.

"Yes, you will, but just ask me about it first. For a woman who can be too outspoken, you picked a heck of a time to practice tact."

Susan was too busy breathing in the familiar scent of him to respond for a moment, then she lifted her head. Her dark eyes glimmered. "What do you mean, *tact*? I thought you said I was refreshingly honest."

"Yeah, well, that was before you turned on me." His arms tightened when she tried to pull away, and he was laughing. "You know I'm only teasing you."

Curling her fingers into the edge of his shirt, she rubbed her cheek against his chest. "Brute. What was the other thing you came out here for? Besides to throw yourself on my mercy, I mean."

"Mercy—! You little witch."

Hunter kissed her thoroughly, his lips searing across her open mouth in a scalding kiss that took away her breath and left her hanging limply in his arms when he lifted his head. She could feel his heart thumping against her breast and wondered if he could feel hers. A fire had been ignited in her, and it flickered heatedly. She was breathing in a ragged rhythm that kept pace with his, and she knew from the pressure of his body against hers that he was as aroused as she was.

Clearing his throat, Hunter muttered, "Give me a minute or two. I can't think too straight right now."

Susan snuggled against him, not really caring why else he had come. He'd come. That was enough. It was more than enough at the moment.

Chapter 10

WHEN HUNTER SAT her down and began to tell her what he'd overheard in the saloon, Susan stared at him numbly.

"That can't be true," she said, shaking her head. "Hunter, you must have misunderstood."

"Susan—"

"No!" She jerked to her feet. "Evan can be irritating, even hateful, but he wouldn't stoop to—to *that*!"

Hunter rose to his feet and put a hand on her shoulder. "I didn't say he intended to murder you, Susan. I just said you needed to keep an eye on him."

"On Evan? We grew up together! Evan would never hurt me. Not deliberately. Not for a piece of old jewelry, for heaven's sake!"

"No," Hunter said coldly, "not for heaven's sake—for his. He's desperate. This Peter Thorne is looking for the brooch you inherited and will pay well. Evan agreed to try and get it for him. Now, you can believe me, or you can decide I'm lying. Which is it?"

"This can't be put in black or white, Hunter. There are areas of gray here!" Susan stared at him in frustration, seeing the anger grow in his eyes again.

"I should have known you wouldn't believe me, but after what you just said—" His mouth twisted with wry mockery. "Your promise didn't even last five minutes."

"This isn't the same thing. You're accusing a child-hood friend of plotting to rob me for his own gain."

"You know Elliott's desperate. His ranch is going under, and instead of trying to work it, he's looking for the easy way out. Like he always has. That's why I wouldn't give him a loan extension. He would have been in the same shape in six months or a year, and all it would have done was delay the inevitable."

Susan's face was pale, and her lower lip trembled. "Oh, Hunter, don't you understand? He's never worked it. His father didn't make him do anything he didn't want to do when he was younger, and when his parents died, he just didn't know how to cope. He's tried, really he has, but—"

"But he won't take advice, and he won't put any effort into it." Hunter shrugged. "It's not my problem. He made it this way. He can solve his own problems."

"You're being hard-hearted."

"Yeah, well, I didn't have anybody cleaning up behind me when I was growing up, and I've had to figure things out on my own." His eyes glittered coldly. "Maybe I don't have any patience with Elliott, but it's not because I haven't been in his shoes."

Susan stared at him uncertainly. She knew nothing about Hunter Carson, she realized suddenly, absolutely nothing. Only what gossip had circulated, and that was no more reliable than the wind. Her throat tightened, and she looked at him as if seeing him for the first time.

He was still the Hunter she'd fallen in love with, still handsome and reckless with that faint scar at one corner of his brow, lines of amusement fanning from his eyes; but there was a subtle difference. There was a stamp of ruthlessness carved into his face, into the grim set of his mouth, and the hard, implacable gaze of his eyes at times. She remembered how he'd looked when they'd heard Comanche were coming, and how harsh his voice and face had been. She'd thought it was because of the danger, but maybe it was the way he reacted to any threat to what he wanted.

"Decided my fate yet, sweetheart?" he asked softly, his voice lightly mocking, and Susan flushed.

"I don't know what you mean."

"Yes, you do. You're standing there looking at me as if I've suddenly grown two heads, and you're trying to figure out if I'm as hard and dangerous as you heard. Well, I told you I was, and I am. Not quite like you may have heard, maybe, but I don't cotton to lazy men who want to take what they haven't earned, that's for sure."

"You mean Evan."

"I mean any man who's too lazy to work an honest day. I told you—I don't ask anybody else to do what I'm not willing to do."

Susan felt suddenly sick. She believed Hunter. She knew he was right. But he was asking her to choose her loyalties, and she couldn't.

"I'll talk to Evan," she began, and when he swore at her, she glared at him.

"Little idiot," he growled, grabbing her arm. "Why give him a warning? He wants to cheat you, for God's sake, and you plan on asking him why?"

She jerked her arm away. "No, not quite like that. I'm not as stupid as you obviously think."

"You mean as you act." Hunter raked an impatient hand through his tawny hair. "Look, I just wanted you to be on guard, that's all. I don't give a damn about your blasted brooch—or a hundred hunks of jewelry. I don't want you hurt."

"And you think Evan would actually hurt me? All he wants is to convince me to sell my brooch. He's tried it before, and when he couldn't, he left me alone. I don't know why you're convinced he'll rob me."

"He said so, for one thing," Hunter said dryly. "It's not so much Elliott as Thorne I'm worried about. He's slick. And I've got a feeling. If he's offering that much money, Susan, he wants it bad. He'll do what he has to do to get it, and he'll use Elliott as the fall guy."

"What are you talking about?" She quivered with anxiety and frustration and glared at Hunter. His expression was as exasperated as hers must be, and she tried not to say what was on the tip of her tongue. "What do you mean?" she asked again, more calmly this time.

Hunter turned and looked out the window, leaning one hand on the wooden frame. His body was tense, one leg bent at the knee, his back muscles taut beneath the thin cotton shirt.

"It's an old game, Susan. I've seen it done a hundred times. Hell, I've done it myself, a long time ago."

Susan felt a thump of dread. "Done what?"

Hunter turned back to her, crossed his arms over his chest, and leaned against the wall. Sunlight gilded his hair and made a glowing halo around his head, leaving his face in shadow. He looked to Susan like a fallen angel, with his guns and his pitiless green eyes and the aura of light.

"You have to understand—I don't know Thorne. I only know his kind of man. Elliott didn't see through what he was saying, but I did. Thorne intends to get that brooch come hell or high water, and if an outcry is made, it will be your precious Evan who takes the fall. Thorne will be a long way away with the brooch, Elliott gets the blame—there will be plenty of evidence against him, trust me on that—and he'll hang for it. Thorne wins, you and Elliott lose."

"I don't believe you. This is all too fantastic—oh, I don't mean that like it sounds," she said quickly. "I just mean it sounds too crazy to be true. Isn't there a chance you're wrong?"

He shifted uneasily. "Maybe. I don't think so, though."

Susan ran to him and put her arms around him; his came around her more slowly, and she could feel his hesitation.

"Don't be mad, Hunter. I can't help but believe in my friends, and you have to admit that you and Evan have never liked each other."

"True." His jaw rubbed across the top of her head. "But I'm not deaf, and I know what I heard."

"But you're going on what you *didn't* hear, just what you think is true!"

"Dammit, Susan, will you just be on guard?" Hunter said. "I didn't suggest you call him out in the middle of the street and gun him down."

Her cheek paused in rubbing against his shirt. "No," she said after a moment, pushing away, "I have a feeling you intend to do that."

He made an impatient movement with his hand. "I don't call men out in the street."

"But you don't back down when they call you."

His eyes met hers. "No. I don't."

"And if Evan gets angry enough to draw on you, you'll meet him."

"Susan—"

She put her hands over her face. "What kind of man are you, Hunter Carson?" The words were muffled by her fingers, but they hung in the air between them for several minutes before he answered.

"Do you really want to know?" She looked up at the cold clip of his voice. His eyes were frost-green, rimmed with a hardness that could have pierced steel. "I'll tell you," he said without waiting for her reply. His hands came to rest on her shoulders with savage force, and his mouth tightened into a straight slash. "You've heard part of my reputation, sweetheart, but you didn't hear all of it."

"Hunter—"

"No. You asked. You'll listen." His fingers dug into her skin, and he dragged her a step closer, though when he looked at her, Susan had the feeling he was seeing something—or someone else—in the distant past.

"I was married, Susan, a long time ago. We were young and foolish and quarreled a lot. I was a deputy then and wasn't home often. She left me. With my best friend. I went after them. I don't know what I intended to do when I found them, maybe ask why, maybe ask her to come back—it doesn't matter. I tracked them to some mining shack up in Colorado; they were in bed. Curled up together, his arms around her as they slept— I just stood there looking at them, and then I saw the pistol on the table. It was mine. She'd taken it with her, I guess." His mouth twisted. "I was accused of killing them. It couldn't be proved, but it seems that the verdict didn't matter. I went free, but I lost my job as a deputy, of course."

Susan felt sick, and she felt a sweeping surge of sorrow for him. And fear. "Oh, my God, Hunter . . ."

"Yes. Well, after the trial, I left the territory. I wandered around a while, and it seemed that I was always running up against someone who wanted to see if I was fast with my gun. I couldn't ride into any backwater shantytown without facing some fool in the middle of the street before I rode out again." He laughed, a harsh, bitter sound. "A bad reputation travels a lot faster than a good one, I can tell you that. It felt strange to be on the other side of the law. . . . Damn, I couldn't begin to count the number of men who called me out. And I killed them because I didn't care. They were just part of it, part of the nightmare."

Releasing her, he turned back to the window again. She grabbed the edge of the desk to keep from sinking to the floor, feeling suddenly weak. Fading sunlight tangled in the thick strands of his hair, and she thought of the halo she'd seen on him earlier, the tarnished gold, the fallen angel.

Hunter, Hunter, I'm so sorry. . . .

"I never saw my father after the trial," Hunter said in a soft, bleak voice. "He never knew if I was innocent or guilty. Never asked. I didn't have the courage to go home and see him." Sucking in a deep breath, he said more strongly, "When he died, he left me the family business in Fort Worth. I sold it and took the money. Hell, I knew I wasn't a damn merchant. But I had worked on enough ranches that I felt I knew cattle. I got a job in the stockyards in Chicago, and when I had enough experience and enough money, I went back to Fort Worth. I started my own company. I've still got it. And I've got more. When I get enough, I'll sell them all and buy my own ranch."

Turning, he met her gaze. "That's one reason I came out here."

"To buy up ranches?" Susan asked in a quavery voice and saw his brows snap down in a scowl.

"No, to buy *a* ranch. One of my own. I want my own place built with my own hands."

"I see."

"Do you?" His smile was disbelieving. "I don't think so. I think you'd like to see, but you can't."

"Did you do it?" she couldn't help asking. "Kill them, I mean?"

"Not according to the law." His gaze was cool. "Would you believe me if I denied it? A jury of twelve believed me, sweetheart—would you?"

Twisting her hands together, Susan inhaled deeply and said, "Yes. I do believe you. I don't think you would kill anyone in cold blood."

"But I've killed many a man in the middle of the street while people hid inside and watched."

Angry, she snapped, "Are you trying to convince me that you *did* do it? I don't care how many men have called you out. That's not your fault. I don't think you could kill your wife and your friend."

"Ah, sweetheart, you've never stood there and seen dust and ashes in place of dreams before, I guess. Yes, I felt like killing them. I wanted to. I picked up the gun and I aimed it at them."

"But you didn't do it." She was near tears, and a sob caught in her throat. "You didn't!"

He grabbed her roughly, jerking her into his arms, burying his face in her dark, soft hair. "No, sweetheart, loyal Susan, black-eyed Susan—I didn't shoot them. I could never kill something I loved."

She wept against his shirt and felt as if she'd been dragged behind a wild mustang as he held her. The past week had been one of the most shattering she'd ever experienced. Too much had happened, and she was being assaulted by too many different, alien emotions. Old loyalty warred with the new. Fear, love, danger— she shuddered, and he pressed her harder against him.

"Be careful, Susan," he said in her ear, his breath warm and soft and shattering across her skin. "Just be very careful. I can't lose you now."

Her head tilted back and she sought his mouth, her eyes blinded by tears, salt streaking her cheeks, smearing on his lips and transferring to her own. She tasted them, felt them on his lips. It didn't matter. Nothing mattered right now but Hunter, but being in his arms, but loving him.

"Make love to me," she whispered, and when he groaned, she added, "please!"

"Sweetheart, sweetheart—you're too fine to take on the floor. The stable was bad enough—God, don't do that."

Susan's hands unbuttoned and slipped inside his shirt, her fingers scraping across his bare skin, feeling his hard muscles contract beneath her touch. She was suddenly frantic for him, consumed with a raging desire that she didn't understand.

Hunter did. It was fueled by fear, driven by denial. He captured her hands in his and held them.

"It's not the right time, not the right place."

She shook her head, silky black wisps of hair whipping across his face in stinging slaps. "It is right—anytime we are together, it's right."

"Susan." Her name was a groan on his lips.

She didn't understand, didn't know what he wanted for her. For them. Her hands were feverish in his grasp, twisting and turning, and he finally let them go. Susan put them immediately back inside his opened shirt, fingertips skimming an invitation across his skin.

"Witch," he muttered against her hair, and his arms closed around her. "The door isn't locked."

"Doesn't matter," she said into the space between the cotton shirt and his throat. Her lips worked across the flat expanse of skin, tasting sweat and soap and man. It was exhilarating. She couldn't bring herself to tell him that

Doris knew, that she might guess they needed privacy. "Doris won't come in. No one will come in without being invited."

"Unless they think I'm hurting you." His hands closed over hers in a last desperate grasp at control. "I don't think I'm very welcome here. Susan, for the love of God . . ."

Susan's mouth moved over his chest, pausing at the pulse beating in his throat; her hands spread on his chest. She pulled the shirt over his shoulders, down his arms, and let it fall to the floor in a drift of blue cotton. His heart thundered against her with response, she could feel it in every nerve, every fiber of her being. He was just being practical and cautious with her, and she loved him for it.

But it didn't ease the wanting.

When she looked up, she saw the thick brush of his dark lashes close over his eyes, his throat cord with restraint, and his mouth tauten. Wickedly, knowing he could not hold out, she bent her head and trailed a path of hot, steamy kisses down the middle of his smooth chest, pausing to lavish a band of muscles with the tip of her tongue. Then her clever tongue dipped into the cup of his navel, wetting it thoroughly, flicking against the curl of hair fleecing him. His belly contracted sharply, and his hands moved to tangle in her hair and draw her head back up.

"Dammit, Susan," he said roughly, and she turned her face up to his. Her palms smoothed over him, found and caressed the hard ridge of his body through his pants, and she saw her triumph reflected in the sudden flare in his eyes.

His mouth covered hers, not gently but rough and fierce and filled with all the passion she could have wanted. She leaned into him, giving herself up to him, her hands cupping his shoulders and holding herself against him. The lips that had haunted her sleep, her every waking thought, clung to hers relentlessly, stealing her breath and her sanity.

He took her down with him to his knees, moving with swift ease to lay her back on the thick bear rug sprawled on the floor. Susan's arms were around his neck, and his hands spread beneath her hips to lower her gently.

Her breasts rose and fell in rapid drags of air; her dark eyes stared up at him as he bent over her.

"This is crazy," he muttered, but he was working at the buttons of her blouse. Fading light still caught in his fair hair like angel-fire, and his lips trapped hers again in a stinging, searing kiss as the blouse was whisked away. She shivered suddenly, felt his hands at the waist of her calico skirt. Her hips lifted when he tugged, and skirt and short boots were tossed into a pile.

Her eyes opened slowly when she heard the clink of the buckle on his gunbelts. He worked the buttons on his pants, slid them down, came to her in a sweep of heated skin and softly muttered words.

"Love me," she whispered against his mouth, "love me."

There was an urgency in their movements that dictated every caress, every kiss. Hunter's mouth found her lips, her cheek, the slim column of her throat, the firm thrust of her breast. He lingered there, hot and wet and driving her into arching against him.

"Susan," he muttered against her breast, the word feathering over her taut nipple and making her shiver and reach for him. Her palms shaped to the wide curve of his shoulder, drew him down, her mouth seeking to kiss him anywhere she could reach: biceps, flexing and veined and hot, the ripple of his pectoral muscle flowing down into the knotted ridge of abdominal muscles delineating his flat stomach. Susan kissed them all, and Hunter arched his back and groaned softly.

"Susan," he whispered again, hoarsely, smoothing the flat of his palms up her naked hips, fingers kneading the supple skin with rhythmic motions. Feathering strokes of his fingertips along the curve of her inner thighs, pausing to tangle his hand lightly in the silky nest of curls at the juncture, Hunter dragged his hand in a tantalizing move across her satin folds of skin. She gasped, arched against his hand, dug her nails into him in a reflex action. He didn't slow his movements, but brought her to a moist, writhing heat that had her clutching at him and begging him for relief.

"All right, sweetheart, all right," he muttered. Beads of sweat dotted his upper lip, trickled down his face as he caressed her. Kneeling between her legs with his thighs pressing them apart, he lowered himself quickly, almost desperately, his hands moving to hold her by the shoulders.

Susan felt the soft cushion of the rug beneath her back and hips, felt his hard weight above her. She arched her hips again, her hands at his lean waist, urging him closer. She couldn't wait, didn't want to wait. She was burning up with a raging inferno that needed this, needed to feel his hard man's body inside her.

Shameless, shameless, shameless. God, it felt too good not to be right. . . .

Kissing her fiercely, Hunter cupped his palms beneath her hips and lifted her at the same time as he drove forward, pushing into her with a sweet, wild urgency that made her gasp. It wasn't as painful as the first time, though there was the burning invasion that dulled the burst of pleasure for a moment. His body scraped along the most sensitive inner part of her in a thrusting penetration that tore a gasp from her.

Pausing, he buried his face in the curve of her neck and shoulder, his body poised motionless. "Am I hurting you?"

His voice was thick, strained, and Susan shook her head. "Don't stop, Hunter. . . ."

Tightening his arms around her, lifting her slightly to ease his entry, Hunter pushed again, this time succeeding in burying himself deeply inside her. Her inner muscles contracted in an involuntary ripple that forced a groan from him. His breath came swiftly and raggedly, almost like short sobs, gasps for air.

"Susan," he groaned softly, several times, her name a litany of passion between them as he began to move again.

Pulling her toward him, his hands pressed solidly into her buttocks, he lifted her up into his battering rhythm of passion. Susan wanted to cry out with the soaring feelings that beat in her breast, but she couldn't. Her breath would not come to voice her pleasure; it strangled somewhere in the back of her throat.

She dug her heels into the soft fur of the rug and arched upward to meet his thrusts, her body convulsing around him and driving them both to the edge. Her hands fluttered aimlessly against his back, his sides, the curve of his buttocks as she sought relief. Hunter's deep, hard thrusts pinned her back to the floor, threatened to drive her into the rug and wood. And he took her with him on that great, shattering wave of passion, up and up and up to the summit before taking her over the pinnacle in a single powerful drive that tore a cry from her.

Quickly covering her mouth with his, he inhaled her cry and gave it back to her in breathless kisses as she throbbed under him. A shudder passed through him, and he grew taut with it, groaning with his own release as his body pulsed into hers.

It was exquisite torment, pleasure, all rolled into one shattering emotion, and they held each other tightly as the late-afternoon shadows drifted into the room and shrouded them.

Chapter 11

DROWSY, SUSAN'S LASHES lifted slowly. Hunter lay on his side, his breath coming in deep regular lifts of his chest. Her heart contracted. He looked so soft and vulnerable lying there like that; the thick brush of his lashes lay in dark wings against his cheeks, gilded by the bright dying rays of the sun slanting through the windows.

Outside, a dog barked. She could hear Doris in the kitchen, rattling pots and pans. Susan flushed. She glanced at the window, then back at Hunter. He was looking at her through the veil of his lowered lashes, and a faint smile curved his hard mouth.

"We're going to have to stop meeting like this," he said softly and grinned at her deep blush. Rising to one elbow, he stroked a broad hand from her throat down to the small mound of her stomach; his palm lifted with the tiny quiver. "Maybe we should do something about this," he said then and lifted a brow at her questioning look. "Something a little more comfortable than stables and floors."

"Complaints already?" She pushed his hand away and sat up, feeling suddenly awkward.

"Oh, no, Susan Whitten, no complaints." A finger dragged down the ridge of her spine, and his hand spread over the small of her back, sending shivers from shoulder to hip. "I think, sweet Susan, that we're going to have to make better arrangements from now on. I want you again"— his hips shoved forward to prove it, and she felt him hot and heavy against her thigh—"and I can't do anything about it."

"And you have an idea how we could arrange things in a better way?" she managed to ask lightly, reaching for her blouse and skirt, unable to look at him, unable to stop the flush that covered her entire body. She couldn't think with him touching her, with his hard man's body nudging against her with the evidence of his desire. And it didn't help at all that she wanted him, too, that just the thought of it made her throat ache and her stomach twist.

"I do," he said, curling his body into a sitting position and taking her hands between his. "And when I get some of this mess straightened out, I'll show you."

"Ah. Until then we meet in stables, I take it."

"Are you complaining now?" His voice held a thread of laughter, and she looked away from him.

It wasn't quite what she'd wanted to hear. She didn't want *someday*. She wanted now. She wanted this, him, with her at night, during the day, forever. But she didn't say it aloud. She couldn't. She'd been brazen enough. If he had not taken the hint—or did not want her the same way—there was little she could do about it without completely tossing away any pride she had left.

"I'm not complaining," she said lightly. "Planning."

Another rumble of laughter sounded low in his throat. "I knew I could count on you."

But could she count on him? Susan bent her head and let her hair swing forward to hide her face as she dressed, not looking at him, hearing the sounds of his dressing too loud in the quiet room. The metallic clink of his belt buckle, the whisk of tan denims, whisper of cotton shirt, rustle of leather as his gunbelts were wrapped around him sounded as loud as thunder to her ears.

Too quick, too quick, the time was over too quick.

"Well," she said matter-of-factly, jumping slightly at the sound of her own voice, "since it's late, maybe you can stay for supper."

Notching his buckle, Hunter slid the leather end through the metal ring and looked up at her. "Don't go away from me again, Susan."

She gave a start. "What do you mean?"

He took her wrist and turned her hand palm up. Stroking a finger across the small pink ridges, he said, "You know what I mean. You've put some distance between us. Why?"

"Really," she said with a forced laugh, "I don't know what you're talking about." She bit her lip when his head lifted and he looked at her.

He released her hand. "Dammit, you can put up walls faster than any woman I've ever seen. Where did your blunt honesty go?"

Recognizing the frustration in his eyes, she said, "I can't be honest when it's so important. It's dangerous."

"Is it?" He raked a hand through his hair, silky tumble of light strands mixing with darker sliding between his spread fingers. "You're not the only one involved in what's between us, you might remember that."

"But how deeply are you involved?" she blurted out, then stopped, flushing again.

Hunter reached out and pulled her against him, pressing her face into his chest. "As deeply as a man can get. Is that what's bothering you?" His index finger curled under her chin to lift her face to his, and he said softly, "Look at me, Susan," when she avoided his gaze.

Drawing in a deep breath, she met his eyes and saw the soft amusement in them. "Don't laugh at me!"

"Ah, sweetheart," he said, flexing his arm to drag her back against him when she tried to jerk away, "I'm not laughing at you. I'm laughing at me. As many times as I've played the game, this is the first time I've been serious, and you don't believe in me."

"I certainly appreciate knowing that you're experienced at this," she muttered testily, refusing to let him coax her into laughter. "And besides—you were serious once before, if I heard you correctly."

His arm tightened. "Yes. I was. But not since then."

Susan flinched at the flatness of his voice. She shouldn't have brought up his wife, even obliquely. It was not fair, and she had always thought she played fair.

"I'm sorry, Hunter. That was uncalled for." She felt his shrug and said in a rush, "I've never felt any of this before, and I can't understand why I feel so many damned conflicting emotions. It's making me crazy. I don't know if you really want me, or if I'm just a temporary amusement, or if what I feel is . . . is real. I don't know any of those things, and when I start thinking about them, I begin to feel panicky." Her fingers curled into his shirt, and her throat tightened. "Don't you see?"

Rubbing his jaw across the top of her head, Hunter gave a sigh that stirred her hair and said, "Yes, I see. Maybe I don't understand things as well as I thought I did."

They parted rather awkwardly, and Susan looked past him to the window. Pale golden light softened the harsh lines of the hills beyond the ranch, suffusing the world with a gentle haze. It shimmered slightly, and she saw the blues and purples of dusk shroud the high peaks that marked the east boundary of the Lazy W. She turned back to look at Hunter.

"Well, do you want to stay for supper?"

He smiled at the mundane question. "Yes. If Doris will let me."

"It's not Doris that worries me as much as Pete." Susan smoothed her skirt with one hand and looked down at her feet. "I want them to like you."

Grinning, Hunter said, "Pete can only shoot me. Doris will kill me with kindness."

Susan had to laugh. "You've figured out her secret, I see. When she takes a dislike, she's so overly polite I feel like saying something hateful just to make things normal again."

"Maybe I'll pass on the supper invitation after all. I don't think I want in the middle."

"Coward."

"Survivor." Hunter caught her to him again and gave her a swift, hard kiss that made her breath catch in her throat and her heart lurch.

When he released her, she took a tentative step away and managed a smile. She was lost, irrevocably lost.

"Why must I remain on the fringe of things?" Tabitha asked. Her voice was plaintive, her brows drawn down into a knot. " 'Tis ridiculous. That great huge block of a man only made things worse with his bumbling." She gave a grunt, half of disapproval, half admiring. "He certainly managed to stir her up though, didn't he?"

"Tabitha," Horatio said wearily, "I think—"

"Oh, pother! 'Tisn't what we think that's important. 'Tis what they think." Tabitha's frown deepened, and she paid no attention to Horatio's startled expression. "They need to listen to each other. They're both saying the same thing, but neither of them is listening. And they're going in circles."

"Are you thinking you can direct them?"

Tabitha gave him a severe glance. "I'm certain of it. I think if I was able to point out a few things to Susan, she would better understand the situation. If someone doesn't take charge, she's liable to make a mess of it."

"I see."

"Do you?" Tabitha seemed surprised. "Good. I was afraid you might disagree."

"Oh, no, I believe that you seem to have things well in hand. At the moment."

"Do you! How agreeable!"

"How do you propose to talk to her?" Horatio asked. "I assume you will just show up at the doorstep and present your case?"

"Oh. I see. That would be a bit awkward, wouldn't it?" Tabitha's thin brows snapped down over her eyes again. "If she won't listen to that green-eyed cowboy, why would she listen to me . . . hmmm. All right, I have it!" Her mouth curved into a delighted smile, and she sat up so straight her bustle shimmied. Shoving at it with one hand behind her back, she said, "I'll be an old friend of her mother's! I can say that I just wanted to meet Carlotta's daughter, and that—"

"Charlotte," Horatio interrupted. "Her mother's name was Charlotte."

Tabitha flapped an impatient hand at him. "Charlotte, Carlotta, whatever! Daresay the girl will know."

Burying his face in an open palm, Horatio seemed to be praying for a moment. Tabitha watched him silently. When he lifted his head, he smiled thinly. "Do go on, Tabitha. You were saying?"

"Well . . ." She flounced uncertainly on the rock where she sat, then looked down at the ranch garbed in the glowing colors of dusk. "As I was saying, I shall engage her in conversation and during the

course of it convince the silly chit that she must
not trust Peter Thorne. Or Evan Elliott. Blackguards,
both of them! Bloody thieves, and—I shan't say that,
of course."

"You must not name names, Tabitha."

"What?"

"It's not allowed. No names. You cannot predispose
a person against another."

"God's blood! What shall I say then? How can I warn
her about them?"

Sighing, he murmured, "You must decide that."

"Sweet Je—hoshaphat. Well. So be it. I shall endeavor
to use tact."

"Like Susan does?"

"Heavens, no! Girl hasn't an ounce of it in her. It
defies logic how she has managed all these years with
that outspoken tongue of hers." Tabitha shook her head.
"Shouldn't be surprised if that brawny cowboy doesn't
box her ears for it one day."

"And do you think he will?"

Tabitha considered for a moment. "No, I don't think
he will. Lord help us, with that murderous glare of his,
he doesn't have to resort to such things. But enough of
this. I think I'll pop in for sherry and biscuits tomorrow.
Do you think that's acceptable?"

"Sherry and biscuits or popping in?" Horatio asked in
his driest tone.

"Both."

"I think," he said slowly, his gray brows lifting, "you
will find both acceptable."

Tabitha smiled. "Good. Very good."

Susan stared uncertainly at the plump woman who was
garbed in a bustle and flounced skirts. The high-necked

starched dress she wore looked much too uncomfortable in the heat.

"Well, m'dear," the woman was saying chattily, "aren't you going to ask me in off your portico?"

"Of course," Susan said with a start, holding open the door and looking past the woman with a frown. "Did you walk here, Mrs.—"

"Tid—no. Not that. Lynnf—eather, Tabitha Lynn-feather," the woman said in a sort of gasping stutter. "Excuse me. Stubbed my toe. Dear God!"

A loud screech followed that exclamation, and Susan turned from looking for a horse and buggy to see Arthur tangled in the woman's skirts. Pink floppy ears waggled indignantly, and he was snorting and squealing and trying to release himself from under the multitude of voluminous petticoats as the stout woman swayed alarmingly.

"Oh, my!" Susan said as she leapt forward. "Don't fall, Mrs. Lynnfeather, please don't fall!" *It'd kill Arthur.* "Here, let me help you. . . ."

Mrs. Lynnfeather's bonnet had been knocked awry in her struggle to remain upright, and a gleaming mahogany table had been sent to the floor, but other than that, there were no casualties. Arthur trotted hastily across the floor with shrill squeaks of distress, and Mrs. Lynnfeather pushed the ostrich feather now dangling in her eyes back atop her hat.

"My, my, wherever did that dreadful pig come from?" she asked, brushing at her skirts and fixing Susan with a glare.

"The kitchen."

"Ah, you like fresh meat, I take it." Mrs. Lynnfeather shook her head. "Take some advice and slaughter your meat outside, m'dear. Much tidier. Now, I was telling you that I am a friend of your poor mama's, and as she has passed and I was in the neighborhood, I thought I'd drop in to see her daughter." She beamed at Susan, who was setting the table upright again.

Susan blinked. "In the neighborhood—? My nearest neighbor is twelve miles from here. As the crow flies."

"Yes, yes, m'dear, I'm well aware of that. Dreadful trip. Long, dusty—never dreamed there could be so many cactus in one place. Never dreamed of a cactus at all, in fact." Mrs. Lynnfeather gave Susan a brisk pat on the arm. "Journeys give one such a voracious appetite, don't you agree?"

Taking the hint, Susan said, "I shall have Doris prepare a tray—you will stay for tea and pastries?"

"Pastries, yes, but tea is a bit—well, I need something rather more vivifying." She smiled, lifting her thin, plucked brows. "Don't you agree?"

"Ah, I have some cordials and liqueurs that you may prefer. I'll have Doris bring them out . . . if you'll excuse me a moment?"

"Of course, child, of course." Mrs. Lynnfeather waved a magnanimous hand. "Take your time. I'll sit here on this soft settee . . . God's blood, but it's been a millennium since I've sat on anything but rocks—pay no mind, child. Do go."

Susan flicked her a wary glance and took a step back, then turned and went into the kitchen in much the same manner as Arthur had gone.

"Doris," she said, her voice slightly shaky and making the older woman turn around to look at her strangely, "there is the oddest woman in our parlor."

"Here?" Doris seemed surprised. "How did she get here?"

A nervous giggle burst from Susan's mouth, and she put a hand over her lips to stifle it. "God only knows! There is no carriage, no buggy, no horse—she just showed up on the front porch and said she knew my mother."

"Well, she certainly didn't walk!" Doris shook her head with practical assurance. "Too far for anyone. And if she's an old friend of Miss Charley's, well, she's too old to have hiked anyway. Pete must have taken care of her carriage."

"Yes, probably so. Well, at any rate, she wishes to speak with me, and she's hungry and wants something rather more *vivifying* than tea, so be sure to bring out all the cordials we have." The giggle threatened to erupt again. "I dare not disappoint her. And since she's here, she probably intends to stay the night."

"Wonderful." Doris shook her head. "I'll make up the guest room and set another place at table." She looked quickly at Susan. "Are we expecting Mr. Carson for supper again?"

A faint flush stained her high cheeks as Susan shook her head. "No, I don't think so. He had to go to Fort Worth for a few days."

"Ah."

Doris didn't follow up that interjection with another comment, but Susan knew she was thinking about two days before when Hunter had stayed. It had been an uncomfortable evening for all of them. Doris had been killingly polite, Pete vaguely hostile, Hunter so cool and collected it had the effect of irritating all of them. Well, it promised to be another long, long evening, with the appearance of the odd Mrs. Lynnfeather. What kind of name was that? And she certainly didn't recall her mother ever mentioning her.

"She didn't?" Mrs. Lynnfeather asked around a mouthful of cream pastry. "Well, I'm not surprised your mother did not mention my married name. Did she perhaps mention my maiden name? Oh, I'm certain she did, and you've just forgotten it. How long has she been gone now? Five years or more, wasn't it? Ah, how time flies. Well, well, well. So, you're little Susan."

Resettling herself on the flowered settee after she selected another tidbit from the tray Doris had brought, Mrs. Lynnfeather muttered an imprecation as her bustle shot up in a soft rustle of crepe material, nudging her shoulder blades.

"Damn thing. Forgot to tie it down, I suppose. Stupid wire cage. Ridiculous how fashions go from bad to worse over the years, don't you agree?"

Susan watched in fascination as Mrs. Lynnfeather shoved at the bustle with one hand and stuffed a tart in her mouth with the other.

"Why do you wear it?" she asked. "I mean, I can imagine why you would want to be in fashion back East, but out here where it's hot and just keeping the wind from blowing your skirts over your head is a feat of endurance, it seems rather tiring to wear a bustle."

Mrs. Lynnfeather paused and looked at her. "Very clever of you, my child. I shall remove it." She thought a moment and added, "Later."

"Yes, later would be best." Susan stared at her with a kind of helpless amusement. In spite of herself, she rather liked the woman. She was a bit overbearing, with an odd manner about her, but pleasant in a smothering sort of way.

"Will you stay the night, Mrs. Lynnfeather?" she asked when the woman paused in a ceaseless flow of conversation to select another pastry. "It will be dark soon, and I am certain you don't want to travel at night."

"Stay the night? Now, there's an interesting possibility I hadn't considered." She nodded sagely, and the ostrich feather in her bonnet bobbed in an energetic motion. "Stay the night . . . do you have feather mattresses?"

Susan blinked in surprise. "Why, yes, of course. Are you allergic?"

"Allergic?" It was Mrs. Lynnfeather's turn to blink in surprise. "By the holy rood, I should hope not! I'm Church of Eng—Protestant, I mean."

Confused, Susan stared at her. "Maybe we're not talking about the same thing."

"P'raps not. Would you care to tell me why you wished to know such a thing? I find it most disconcerting."

"Sorry. I should have realized that you could not wear that hat if you were allergic to feathers."

"I have no notion a'tall what you're about, my child. Whatever do you mean—allergic?"

"I only wondered if feather mattresses made you . . . made you sneeze."

"Ah. No, of course not. Are they supposed to?"

Laughing now, Susan shook her head. "No, but my great-aunt had an allergy to them. She had to sleep on mattresses that were stuffed with a special kind of moss, or balls of cotton."

"How fascinating." Mrs. Lynnfeather tried to lean back on the settee and found the bustle preventing it. She gave a sigh and sat forward again. "And where is your great-aunt now?"

"Dead, I fear."

"Oh. How sad. Was it sudden?"

With her lips twitching from suppressed laughter, Susan embarked on a discussion with Mrs. Lynnfeather about her family, what she knew of them. She found the older woman to be full of questions, and by the time Doris announced that supper was served, there wasn't a single family member who had not been discussed at some length.

"I never knew I remembered so much," Susan said dryly, putting away the family Bible. "You've challenged my memory tonight, Mrs. Lynnfeather."

"Have I?" She smiled. "Just because they're dead and gone, they should not be forgotten. Of course, they would not forget you, either."

Susan turned to look at her. Her face was strained. "Not a day goes by that I don't remember my parents," she said softly. "I miss them terribly."

"Ah, I am certain you do, poppet. Do not despair. They know it, I'm convinced, and are smiling at you."

"Do you believe in the afterlife, Mrs. Lynnfeather?"

"La, what a question!" was the quick answer, given with a wave of her hands. "Do you?"

Nodding, Susan paused, then smiled. "I greatly fear that if we don't get to the table before Doris's meal is cold, we'll discover the afterlife much more quickly than we thought!"

Doris had managed to coax Arthur to the root cellar, so dinner was a fairly quiet affair, with gleaming lamplight, a fine linen cloth on the table, and the good dishes in honor of their guest. Susan slid Doris a speculative glance when she saw the Wedgwood. When Hunter had joined them, the everyday china had been used. Doris ignored her ironic glance and accepted Mrs. Lynnfeather's compliments on the meal.

"Roast beef! My, it's so tasty! Your culinary expertise is beyond compare," Mrs. Lynnfeather enthused, and Doris blushed with delight.

"Thank you, ma'am. I do like my beef juicy and tender instead of charred like some others I know prefer it." Her glance at Susan was received with a serene countenance.

Pete Sheridan seemed less inclined to conversation and, after eating his meal in almost virtual silence, excused himself and left the table. Susan watched him go with only slight envy. Her head was beginning to ache from the strain of keeping Mrs. Lynnfeather occupied, and she wished that she had not been so quick to extend an invitation to stay the night. She was tired and wanted to go to bed and think about Hunter.

She stifled a yawn, then propped her chin in the cradle of her palm and stared down at her plate. Pushing the last of her roast beef around with her fork, Susan slowly became aware that she was being spoken to. Her head snapped up, and she saw Doris looking at her and Mrs. Lynnfeather smiling.

"I fear that I've been a burden, Susan dear," Mrs. Lynnfeather said, and when Susan opened her mouth to offer a polite protest, she was told, "Tut, tut, don't argue. I find that I cannot accept your hospitality for the night, but I do wish to speak privately with you before I leave."

Fighting her relief, Susan said weakly, "Of course, but it's so late and you really should stay. Last week, Coman—"

"Nonsense. It's not that late, and I'm not at all afraid of the dark. Or Comanche. What I have to say won't take long, I assure you."

She was true to her word. When the meal had ended and Susan sat with the plump woman in the parlor again, Mrs. Lynnfeather fixed her with a smile and said, "Now, what is this I hear about your dilemma?"

"Dilemma?"

"Yes, your problem. I'm not here simply for a visit, you know, though you are a delightful girl. No, I'm here to warn you of a man who might bring some harm to you."

Susan shifted uneasily. "Warn me of a man?"

Nodding, Mrs. Lynnfeather fixed her gaze on Susan and said firmly, "He means you ill, my dear. Do not trust him."

Susan sat quietly, not speaking, her dark eyes focused intently on the woman. Mrs. Lynnfeather frowned.

"Do you understand my meaning? I know what he's about, you see. I cannot divulge how I know, or exactly what I know—though it would be much easier, and I told Horatio that—but still, you must believe me. I have no reason to wish you ill, while your *friend* does." She reached out and gave Susan a pat on the hand. "You do know the man I mean? He may have loved you once, but not as much as he loves the idea of wealth. 'Tis your decision, of course, and I cannot do aught but advise you, but I think if you dwell on it a while, you will see I am right."

Nodding woodenly, Susan said through stiff lips, "Yes, I think I know who you mean." She swallowed the surge of nausea that rose in her throat. She couldn't say his name. She just couldn't. Blinking, she looked gravely at the woman staring at her so anxiously. "Perhaps I should forget him then and marry—"

"Yes, yes, that is exactly what you should do! Then your worries will be over." She leaned forward to pat Susan on the cheek. "Wealthy men make the best husbands, m'dear," she said obliquely. "Wed your fair lad and be happy."

Unable to sit still another moment, Susan rose to her feet and Mrs. Lynnfeather did, also. She smiled kindly at her, and Susan managed a smile back.

"Thank you for coming," she said when it seemed as if something was expected from her. "And . . . and don't worry. I appreciate your warning and will heed it."

"Excellent, excellent! Well, I must go now. Perhaps the concert has not yet ended—I'm certain you will be quite all right now, child. I've enjoyed meeting you."

Susan didn't move from the porch for a long time after Mrs. Lynnfeather had climbed into a buggy that had appeared seemingly from nowhere to wait for her. Dust drifted in hazy clouds behind the vehicle as it rolled down the long, curving road that led to the house, then disappeared. Not even the faint echo of the wheels and hooves remained.

"Peculiar," Doris muttered under her breath, "most peculiar." She looked closely at Susan in the dim light of the lantern. "Are you ill, Miss Susan? You look pale."

"Just tired."

"Shall I—"

"No, don't do anything. You must be tired, too. I think I'll stay out here and look at the stars for a while." She sliced her a quick smile. "Don't worry. I'm fine."

"If you say so. Want me to let Arthur out of the cellar now?"

"Yes. He's probably eaten everything within reach."

Susan's throat ached with the strain of holding back her tears. Alone on the porch, she wandered to one side and stood looking up at the sprinkling of stars overhead. It was a clear night, with the dark silhouette of the mountain peaks in the distance and the sweet sweep of the wind over the land, but she was remembering a rainy night. And Hunter Carson.

Hunter. Even strangers warned her about him. Could it be true? Why would she believe a woman she'd never seen in her life before, except that her words had echoed the trend of Doris's warnings, and even Pete had been reluctant to speak out for him.

She'd been reluctant to believe what Hunter had said about Evan, and still could not make herself believe that her childhood friend would try to harm her. Caught between two loyalties, she'd confided in Pete. He always tried to be fair, always tried to see both sides of an argument.

Pete had been first wary, then thoughtful when she had told him what Hunter had overheard.

"Well, now, Miss Susan, I've known Evan Elliott since he was a kid in short pants and skinned knees, and I'll be the first to say he's as lazy as they come," he'd drawled. "But I ain't never thought of him as mean. Not Evan. He just ain't mean enough to think of something like Carson claims he's planned."

"Hunter says Peter Thorne is behind it." Susan watched him closely as he thought that over, his sun-weathered face creased into faint lines. "And he says they won't balk at hurting me to get what they want."

At that, Pete had shaken his head. "Nope, don't believe that of Evan. Might be tempted to steal, yeah, but not to hurt you. Hell, Miss Susan, that boy's crazy about you. He would never hurt you."

It was what Susan had thought, too. Though she'd wanted to believe Hunter—and she thought he was telling her what he truly believed—she had not been able to believe that Evan would harm her.

Mrs. Lynnfeather had, with her well-meaning warning, only confirmed what she'd been fighting against.

Susan lay her head back against the side of the house. In the distance a coyote howled, then another. A few yips sounded, punctuating the mournful wails, and then faded into silence. She could hear the men in the bunkhouse as they laughed and played cards, a horse snorting and stomping in the stables, and cattle lowing softly. It was all normal. She should be at peace.

Except that for some reason, Hunter wanted her to hate Evan Elliott, and she didn't know why. And it made her want to scream with frustration and anguish.

Why, why, why?

Chapter 12

HUNTER SWUNG DOWN from his horse and led it into the small stable behind the house he'd bought in Los Alamos. It was late, and he was tired. He'd ridden all day to get back home. Damn. It was crazy, but he didn't want to be away from Susan for so long.

Rubbing a hand over his jaw, he took care of his horse, unsaddling, brushing down, feeding, before he went inside. He'd been in the saddle for two days, and he needed a bath and a drink. The house was quiet; he'd given up trying to find a housekeeper to live in and had hired old Mrs. Purdy to come in a couple of days a week to clean it. God knows, she was no cook, but she could keep it clean.

He lit a lamp and poured himself a drink, then sagged into a chair in the small parlor. Sticking his long legs out in front of him, he lay his head back against the chair and thought about what the next few weeks would bring.

Would Susan understand? He hoped so. On top of everything else that had happened lately, the results of his survey couldn't have come at a worse time. He grimaced and took another sip of whiskey.

He should never have let Susan matter so much to him. It was a complication, and he hated complications. Hadn't he learned anything in all these years? Apparently not, he answered his own question. It was crazy, crazy, crazy. That first day she'd walked into his office, filled with fire and righteous indignation, he should have turned her over to his clerk and forgotten about her. But he hadn't. He had let himself be interested in a pretty face that he knew spelled trouble.

Susan Whitten, lovely heiress to the Lazy W—a debt-ridden, struggling ranch miles from anywhere, worthless to almost everyone but its owner—and the Texas and Pacific Railway. And the railroad intended to plow right through the northeast corner of the Lazy W and angle down to Los Alamos. Unfortunately, it would also cut through some of her best grazing land.

It would make Susan rich, if she cared to sell. If she didn't—he scowled. The terrain wasn't suitable, and it would cost too much to go around. If she didn't sell to the railroad, a spur wouldn't be built to Los Alamos, and not only would the town lose a lot of money, but everything he had planned for the past seven months would be endangered.

Damn, damn, damn!

She'd never believe that he didn't have something to do with it, something to gain by her friendship. Not after their last argument about Evan Elliott and Peter Thorne. Why hadn't he guessed that the railroad would go through her land? He should have. He usually paid close attention to details. But he'd been thinking of soft brown eyes and dark hair, and the velvety feel of her body under his hands, and he hadn't thought of anything but Susan.

Susan, Susan, black-eyed Susan. No, she wouldn't believe him. She might say she did, but she wouldn't. And there would be no way to convince her he hadn't known, because he *should* have known.

Rubbing a hand over his face, Hunter drained the last of his whiskey and set the glass on the table. There was another way. He could always go back and survey the land north of Susan's and cut through the edge of Elliott's property. He didn't want to.

It would cost more, take longer, be less efficient, and he would have to bear the brunt of the cost. He'd lobbied for this spur because it affected him directly, because it would give him the means to transport grain and feed and cattle at a lower cost; he had friends in high places now, where ten years ago he couldn't have spoken to the dog catcher without taking the chance of being arrested.

Money, Hunter had discovered, was power. But he'd known that for a long time. Now he had money and power and stood to gain a lot more—and lose something very important along the way.

There didn't, he reflected bitterly, seem to be much of a choice about it. Gain money, lose Susan. A simple enough equation. Except he didn't want to lose Susan. And he didn't give a damn about the money, but it wasn't just all his risk. He had partners in this venture; they would look at him as if he had lost his mind if he said he didn't want to take the obvious solution because he'd fallen in love with the owner of the Lazy W, and she'd think he was up to no good if he tried to buy so much as an inch of her land.

A faint smile curled his mouth. She'd been so mad when he told her about Elliott. What would she say if he turned around and offered the dissolute wretch a small fortune for acres of arid scrub and cactus?

Too bad the government had stopped handing out land grants to the railways. It would have been a lot simpler, but they'd halted that practice six years before; and still collected every time federal shipments were made. Low, low prices were to be charged for every item shipped by the federal government, but new days were coming. New men were coming, men better than Fisk and Gould and

Drew, who had almost bankrupted the government with their schemes.

Back in '69, Fisk and Gould had created a national emergency by buying all available gold on the stock market to hold until the price rose; President Grant ruined their plan, on Black Friday, releasing gold from the United States Treasury to drive the prices back down. It had stopped them for the moment, but they'd escaped unscathed and turned their hands to buying up more railroads.

Fisk was dead. Now Gould intended to dabble with the Texas and Pacific line running from Fort Worth to Abilene, and Hunter was in his way.

It had started out so simply; Hunter had needed a new granary, Los Alamos had one for sale with ready-made customers close by, and he had invested in the railroad. A spur to Los Alamos would be no problem. But actuality had been quite different, and he had found real people behind the cold words of the reports when he'd come to Los Alamos. People like Susan Whitten.

Damn, and damn, and damn. Business was one thing, he'd told Susan, and personal another. So why wasn't he taking his own advice?

Closing his eyes, Hunter rubbed them with his thumbs. He was too tired to think about it anymore. It was all he'd thought about for days, weeks. And really, he knew what his decision would be, even without thinking. There wasn't much of a choice as far as he was concerned.

Yawning, Hunter got up from his easy chair and went to bed. He was asleep almost as soon as he'd stripped and fallen onto his bed.

Rest didn't come easily to Evan Elliott. Not that night. He had too much to think about, too much to do. Tomorrow he would see Susan. And he would talk to her, try to tell her how important it was that she listen to him about that damn bastard Carson.

Shivering with nervous tension, he paced in the dingy front room of his house. It needed repair, new furniture, new drapes, a new roof—there was so much that could be done with it if he had the money. It was within his grasp, money and Susan. It hovered just out of reach, an unattainable goal until Peter Thorne had come into town.

He disliked the Englishman, didn't trust him, but he offered an opportunity that Evan couldn't pass up. Not now. Not when Susan was farther away from him than she'd ever been in their lives. Evan wasn't quite certain how it had happened, only that it had. And it seemed to him that it had happened when Hunter Carson had come to Los Alamos.

Hatred burned high in him. Damn that cold-eyed bastard. Did he think because he had money he could buy everything? He couldn't. Not Susan, anyway.

Until now he hadn't thought anyone could buy Susan. Until now . . .

Now it looked as if Hunter Carson could. And had. And Susan seemed to like it.

Frustration burned in Evan like hot coals, searing him and making him throb with raw pain. Susan, Susan, his Susan since childhood, and another man would have her. Or had her already.

Shutting his eyes, Evan Elliott thought fiercely, No, no, he won't have her, if I have to kill him first!

When the sun rose, Evan was ready for daylight and had cleaned himself up and saddled his horse. He'd see Susan today. Today he would convince her that she should trust him and only him to take care of her.

*   *   *

It was surprisingly easy. A lot easier than he'd thought it would be. Slightly bewildered, Evan looked at Susan's wan face.

"What'd you say?"

She smiled. "I said, that would be fine, Evan."

"You'll go with me?"

Resting her chin in her palm, her elbow propped on the kitchen table, Susan sighed. "You did say you wanted to take me on a picnic, not China, am I correct?"

"Yeah, but I didn't think you'd agree," he blurted out, then flushed when she stared at him.

"Why'd you ask me if you didn't think I'd go?"

The flush still reddened his cheeks, diffusing the tan freckles on his face, and Evan shook his head. "Hell, Susan, I don't know! I mean, I thought you'd say no at first and I'd have to talk you into it. I didn't think you'd say yes right off the bat like that."

"Surprise."

He grinned. "Yeah, it is. But if you're willin'—hey! I know! We'll go to the old swimmin' hole where we used to go as kids—remember?"

A slow smile curved her mouth, and she nodded. "Yes, I remember. I remember getting in trouble for going with you when we were thirteen. Mama said I was too old to be doing that."

Evan's eyes lit at the memory, and for a moment they were both caught up with visions of their youthful, innocent prank. It had not occurred to either of them at the time that there were sound reasons for not swimming naked in the old pond. Later, they'd been made to feel foolish and uneasy about themselves. They'd never gone again, nor talked about it.

"Well," Susan said, "we're too old for that now, too,

but I don't see any harm in taking a picnic basket out there and sitting under the shade trees."

"Sounds good to me," Evan agreed, standing up and holding out his hand for her. "Let's go now."

The swimming hole was on the northeast side of the Lazy W, tucked beneath a grove of fig trees, shady and cool and inviting. Layers of salt lined the pool, rendering it unfit for drinking but just right for swimming; it made swimmers more buoyant, and if they didn't mind the gritty feel the water left on them, it was perfect.

As children, Susan and Evan had considered it perfect. As adults, it was a pleasant spot to revisit fond memories.

They raced the last half-mile to the slope overlooking the pond, just as they often had as children, their horses cutting up the ground and sending dust boiling into the air as they ran stretched out. Susan's horse, Blaze, won by a nose. A long-legged, gleaming bay, black mane and tail whipping in the wind, the animal seemed as delighted as its owner to have won.

"Not fair," Evan accused, laughing, his blue eyes alight as he slid from his rangy black to the ground. He grabbed at Susan's reins. The bay danced out of his reach with another toss of the head, and Susan pushed her hat from her head to laugh down at him.

"You always say that when I win! It's only fair when you win!"

Grinning, Evan said, "Yeah. But I had to carry the basket, remember."

"Oh, a little wicker basket isn't going to slow you down that much," Susan shot back, sliding from her horse to the ground.

"Little? Doris packed enough food in here for eight people. . . ."

"Which ought to take care of *you*!"

They teased each other the entire time they spread out the blanket under the trees and set out the lunch Doris had insisted on packing for them. It was only when they'd eaten that an awkward silence fell, and Susan was the first to feel it.

For a while she had pretended that everything was the same, that she and Evan were children again, teasing each other and racing their horses. But reality had returned, and with it the restraint she'd felt in his company for several months. Maybe it was the way he was looking at her, the speculative gleam in his eyes when he watched her. Or maybe it was just because he wasn't Hunter.

That was it, she thought glumly. Evan wasn't Hunter, and Hunter was the man she wanted to be with. Nothing was the same, nothing felt right. Only with Hunter did she feel truly alive. Evan was part of her past, part of what she had once been but no longer was. Hunter was her future.

Or had been . . .

To her shock, Evan leaned quickly forward and took her in his arms. He ignored her sudden stiffness and bent his head and kissed her. His lips moved across hers softly at first, with a longing that penetrated Susan's shock, and she put the heels of her hands against him to push him away from her.

"No," she gasped out when he lifted his mouth. "No!"

"Susan . . ." His voice was ragged, his breath coming in harsh gasps and pants for air, and he tried to kiss her again, his mouth hard this time, brutal. She could feel her lips swelling and pushed him more forcefully.

"Stop it, Evan!" Her fists beat against his shoulders. "Stop it!"

He released her abruptly, gulping in air in great pants that shook his frame. "Dammit," he said softly. "Dammit."

Trembling, Susan sat back on her heels and watched him as he moved away from her. He seemed to be trying to regain control of himself, and after several minutes he stretched out on the grass and blanket. Evan bent his arms under his head and looked at Susan gravely.

"It's not the same, is it, SuSu?" he asked, reverting to his childhood pet name for her.

"No, it isn't the same."

Evan nodded. "We used to experiment with kissing, do you remember that? We practiced, and it was only a game." A minute or two ticked past, then he said softly, "It's not the same at all anymore. Nothing is."

She tried not to look at him but drew her knees up and put her arms around them, resting her chin on denim as she stared at the ruffled waters of the pond. Wind rustled the branches of the trees, and the leaves danced; it curled under her hair and lifted it from her forehead, cooling her damp skin. A dust cloud boiled up in the distance, hanging briefly on the horizon as if someone had ridden past. Cattle. Or maybe buffalo.

Evan was right. She couldn't pretend it was the same when it wasn't. He knew it, and much as she wanted to be able to force an emotion she didn't feel, she knew she couldn't.

"No," she said at last, "nothing is the same. I guess we've grown up."

"Yeah." Evan plucked a grass stem and stuck it in his mouth. He chewed on it a moment, looking past Susan to the blur of peaks in the distance. Heavy waves of grass gleamed under the sun, rippling like ocean waves as far as he could see. Flat-topped ridges smoothed out the horizon in places. Susan followed his gaze. She flinched when he said, "I want you to marry me, SuSu."

A long silence fell. Then she looked at him with her dark eyes filled with pain and regret. "I'm sorry, Evan."

Tossing away the pulpy grass stem, Evan flashed her a crooked smile. "So am I." He sucked in a deep breath, then said, "Susan, you know how I feel about you. I'll always feel that way about you. You're mine. I think I fell in love with you when I was five years old."

"Evan, please . . ." Her voice was strained, but he gave a quick shake of his head.

"No, let me finish. We've got a lot of years behind us, Susan. That counts for something. My father used to say you had to be friends before you could love someone, and I know he was right." Evan's hands curled tightly into fists. "If you would just give it a chance, we could be more than only friends. Maybe we don't feel the same because we're not. We aren't kids anymore— we're grown up. I love you. I know you love me. We could make it together if you'd give it a chance."

"Evan, stop! It's not the same because we're not the same, because we want different things!" Susan shook her head, and her dark hair shimmied around her flushed face. A wave of agony creased her features for a moment, and she closed her eyes against it. When she opened them, Evan was staring at her intently. "I can't," she said simply. "If I never get married, I can't marry you. It wouldn't be fair to either of us. I don't love you that way."

"Yes, you do. You just can't see it because you're blinded by—"

"Don't say it!" Curling to her feet, Susan stood over him, her dark eyes flashing. "Don't say what you're about to say, Evan. I don't think I could bear it."

"Dammit, Susan," he snarled, coming to his feet to stand over her, "that bastard has you so tied up in knots you don't know what you're doing! Can't you see what everybody else in Callahan County can see?"

"Apparently not!" She took a step back, suddenly wary of Evan. He looked furious, his fair complexion mottled with rage and his eyes a burning blue. She'd never felt afraid of Evan before, but now there was a look on his face that made her want to run. "I'm going home, Evan," she said abruptly.

Bending, she scooped up her hat and put it on her head, then began to toss empty food containers into the basket. A hot press of tears stung her eyes, but she blinked them back. This should never have happened. She almost hated Hunter for being the cause of it but knew in the next moment that the day would have come without him. She just didn't love Evan the way he wanted her to.

"You're making a big mistake, Susan," Evan said in a soft, strange voice, and she looked up at him. He was calm, but there was an underlying current in his tone that made her even more uneasy than before.

"I don't think so," she managed to say quietly. "I hope not. I love you for friendship's sake, Evan. I would never hurt you."

He shrugged. "Don't worry about it. Sometimes a little pain is necessary. That doesn't mean it's over."

"What do you—?"

"It's all right, Susan," he cut in. "You don't have to worry about it. I'll take care of everything. It will all be all right again, I promise."

"Evan—"

"No. I don't want to hear you say you don't love me any more." His words were short, sharp. "It don't matter.

Not now. Later. Later, we'll talk about it. Now I just want you to know that I'll take care of it all. And you. You won't be hurt."

"Evan, you're making me nervous! Would you stop talking in riddles and tell me what you mean?"

He smiled at her, a thin stretching of his lips that looked more ominous than amused. "Why, I mean to show you how much I love you, SuSu. That's all."

Hunter's warning echoed in her mind, but Susan saw no malice, no evil in Evan. He was hurt, angry, but not dangerous. Not to her, not to anyone. Evan could never do her harm, and she knew it.

Forcing a smile, she said softly, "I know you love me, Evan. And I love you. As a friend."

"Sure. That's right. We're friends. And we'll always be friends. We made a pact when we were kids, remember?"

"Yes. Blood brothers, of sorts. I still have the scar on my wrist."

"So do I. Our blood is mixed, just like our lives. We won't ever be apart. Not for long. Not forever."

"Not in our hearts," Susan said gently. "But our lives may take us apart."

"No. Not that either." He shook his head, then glanced at the sky. "Let's go back. It's getting late, and I have to take care of some things."

Attempting to ease the disquiet between them, Susan said, "How's your ranch doing?"

"It's all right. Not great. I had to sell most of my herd because I couldn't feed them, and by then they were so lean I got three cents a pound for what I could get to market."

Susan felt a pang of guilt. She'd not even asked him about his welfare lately. She'd been so caught up in

Hunter Carson that she'd not thought of anyone but him. She was selfish. She should have asked, should have offered to help in any way she could.

"Three cents isn't bad, considering the market," she said in a placating tone, and he grimaced.

"Not as good as I could have got, and you know it. But things will get better. I've got some plans."

Again the disquiet. Susan stuffed it determinedly to the back of her mind.

"Plans to start again?"

"Sort of. I'll tell you about it sometime. I'm still trying to work it out."

Susan wanted to tell him what Hunter had overheard, ask him if it was true, but she couldn't. She couldn't bring herself to even give credence to the wild tale by giving it voice to Evan. Odd, her usual bluntness seemed to have been drowned out by an unwillingness to cause him even more pain than she had. Once, she would have said what was on her mind without thinking twice about it—or even once.

Now her ease with Evan had been destroyed. It was sad.

When she was at home again and Evan had ridden away, she sat in her father's study and thought about the day. It would never have occurred to her a few months before that she would feel so awkward and ill at ease with Evan, but now she could not enjoy the simplest time with him without feeling that way.

Hunter hadn't caused it, she realized. It had been that way before he'd come. She sucked in another deep breath and tried to rationalize everything that had happened. Hunter's warning was uppermost in her mind, contradicted by the oblique warning of the eccentric Mrs. Lynnfeather. All her instincts had told her that

Evan could never do what Hunter thought he would, yet today—today, he'd been so strange. So remote, with an odd, watchful look in his eyes. Perhaps she didn't know how desperate he was. Perhaps Hunter was right.

And there was that. What if Mrs. Lynnfeather was right? What if Hunter was playing a cruel game of some kind, using her, using Evan, using the entire town? There had been a very real warning behind the kind, rather foolish face. She had felt it; it had reached out, almost palpable, curling around her with menace. Yes, there was something wrong, but it was so hard, so hard to think that Hunter would be the one.

Swinging around in her father's huge desk chair to look out the window, Susan wondered bitterly if everything she touched was doomed to fail. Look at the trouble she'd had this past year. The troubles with the ranch, her unease with her own nature, Evan, and now Hunter.

Hunter.

She rose abruptly from the chair and tried not to look at the thick bear rug spread on the floor. It brought back memories she wanted to avoid right now, memories of Hunter and his lean, golden body sprawled across the rug in a blaze of masculine beauty that brought a lump to her throat when she remembered.

Closing her eyes, Susan tried desperately to think of something else, anything else. She'd go mad if she didn't.

Moving without thinking, she went to the fireplace and raked her hand across the smooth gray stones until she found the niche that opened the safe. She swung it open and took out the metal box that held important documents. And the Lynnfield family brooch.

Taking it out carefully, Susan held it in her palm and gazed at it with a frown. It was lovely, in a sort of old, antiquated way. The huge square-cut diamond winked in the press of light streaming through the window, and the gold filigree setting was delicate and fine. It felt heavy in her palm, and she wondered how anyone had enjoyed wearing it. Of course, styles had changed, and what would look only out of place and presumptuous now would have looked quite proper on the old style of dress.

Turning it over in her hand, Susan toyed with the catch for a moment, then pinned it to her left breast, thrusting the pin through the thin material of her blouse and feeling faintly foolish. Silly, to play dress-up with an heirloom, but it made her feel as if she had a link to the past to have it, a link to the women who had preceded her, who had loved and laughed and perhaps worn this brooch at fancy balls.

She was suddenly glad to have inherited it. The jewelry gave her a feeling of continuity, to know that there were women who had been part of her family and cherished this very same piece. What was it the barrister had told her about its history?

Oh, yes, something about a woman, Catherine, she thought was her name, doing a brave, courageous deed for King Richard the Lionhearted. She'd helped rescue him from his brother's treachery, restoring the kingdom to him and getting him out of an Austrian prison, and in gratitude the king had presented her with the brooch. It had been handed down from daughter to daughter, female relation to female relation, a symbol of feminine courage.

Susan straightened. Of course. This wasn't just a piece of lovely, antiquated jewelry. This was a symbol. She could not be less than her ancestor, could she? What would Catherine think if she knew that a Lynnfield heiress had bowed beneath a challenge? Not much, she was certain.

After carefully removing it from her blouse, Susan was placing the brooch back in its small velvet box when Doris knocked on the door.

"Come in," she called and held up the brooch when Doris entered. "This looks too pretty to be a curse, don't you think?" she asked lightly, and Doris recoiled.

"What are you talking about?"

Susan laughed. "A curse. The brooch is cursed. Or at least, that's what Mr.—Greaves? Grimes? Graves, that's it. The barrister who brought it to me. He said it was cursed."

"Cursed. Oh, Miss Susan—"

"No, no, it's quite true, according to family legend." An impish smile curled her mouth as Susan replaced the brooch in the metal safe. "He said—let me think of his exact words—'It is said that a curse attends those who have inherited it, Miss Whitten, and I feel that I must pass that warning on to you along with the brooch. It seems that murder was done in order to inherit the brooch.' That was back in the sixteenth century, of course. A long time ago."

"Murder!"

"According to old Graves. He said that the wearer, a Lady Tabitha Lynnfield, had the bad fortune to be a rather scatty old cat, and her heir was a greedy woman who owed a mound of debts. Inheriting the brooch would, the woman thought, help clear those debts with the moneylenders. Not so at all, but she did not discover such a thing until she had given Lady Tabitha a hearty shove down the stairs. Broke her neck quite cleanly. . . ."

"Miss Susan!" Doris cut in, and Susan laughed with

delight at the expression on her face.

"Don't look so upset, Doris. That was several hundred years ago. It's over now. And anyway, when it was over with, the wicked lady found that she could not use the brooch for barter and ended her own life by leaping out a window." Susan grinned at Doris's shocked face.

"Good Lord!" Doris murmured, and Susan nodded wryly.

"That's what I said. Graves just nodded politely and informed me that he was passing along the information with the brooch."

"How kind of him," Doris said faintly. "Is it . . . is it true, do you think?"

"Are you that superstitious?" Susan shook her head. "I have never considered myself so, but I *did* have the bad taste to ask Mr. Graves if he thought it was true."

"And he said—?"

"The oddest thing." Susan frowned, remembering. She had no intention of telling Doris more. She worried too much.

"Do you believe it?" she'd asked skeptically, and the barrister had lifted an eyebrow. His reply had been slow.

"Not really, Miss Whitten. It's an inanimate object, quite incapable of fostering evil. Evil lies within man, however, and that is what inspires most of our problems."

Well. No point in bringing that up with Doris. Not in view of some of the things that had happened lately.

"He said no," she told her housekeeper and smiled at the look of relief on Doris's face.

It had been an interesting tale, and Susan had enjoyed hearing it, though she'd not been at all affected by it. Now she began to wonder. Not about a curse; she wasn't the type to dwell on that, but on the evil that was inspired by greed. And by need.

Evan again. Would he stoop to robbery to meet his needs? He might, if he thought the need great enough, and if he thought he could justify it. Anyone might, given the right circumstances, and Evan was weak.

Susan shifted uneasily. Hunter had seemed so certain, and after listening to Evan today, seeing the odd expression in his eyes and hearing the note in his voice, she didn't know anymore. She wasn't sure of anything anymore, not even herself.

"God's holy heart!" Tabitha exclaimed, leaping up in fury from the flat rock where she sat. "I was *murdered!*"

Horatio seemed unmoved by this proclamation. "Why not Tidwell instead of that ridiculous Lynnfeather, may I ask?"

She fixed him with a baleful eye. "The name seemed a bit more in keeping with my disguise."

"Disguise? You mean masquerade—"

"Enough! Did you know that I was murdered?"

"Of course."

"Ahh! I was murdered for that brooch! Lady Emily, of course, the little thief!" Striking one curled hand into the other, Tabitha paced the hill above the ranch, her eyes blazing with fury. "Murdered," she moaned, "cut down in my prime! Ah, cruel fate, O how thou hast erred!"

"Do you think so?" Horatio murmured politely. She turned on him.

"Of course I think so! I was still young enough to enjoy life, to relish my little—wait. I haven't seen Emily since I've been . . . been there. Where is she?"

Horatio was silent, his gray brow still lifted in mild inquiry. After a moment Tabitha smiled and sat back down.

"Good. Serves her right, the little bitch. I hope she's boiling in oil."

"Nothing so archaic, I assure you. Torment is often what is in one's own mind and actions, you know." Horatio put up a hand when Tabitha opened her mouth to speak. "That is all you need to know now. I believe that matters have not progressed with your descendant quite as you had thought they should."

"Ah, yes." Tabitha frowned. "How *do* these people make such a muddle of things?" She shook her head. "Well, I shall do what I can, though the girl is making it very hard for me." A faint smile curled her lips. "At least she has enough sense to appreciate the brooch."

Making a steeple of his hands, Horatio asked mildly, "What do you intend, may I ask?"

Gloomily Tabitha responded, "Lord only knows!"

"Ah."

"Oh, for the love of—I have to think, Horatio. Can you believe that there is so little communication between two people who think they love each other?" She shook her head. "It defies logic. They should be put in stocks until they come to their senses."

"And you think that would help?"

"It might. A little solitude and time to dwell on how much they care for each other might do them some good."

"I see."

She shot him a narrow glance and shifted, smoothing the crepe skirts over her knees with one hand. The bustle was gone, and the back of her dress dragged along the ground when she stood up and began to pace.

"Then again," she said after a moment, "it might not do them any good. Look at how swiftly they begin to doubt each other when apart. *Jesú*, how irritating they can be!"

Whirling around and stirring up dust with her trailing hems, Tabitha said in loud triumph, "I have it! They must be forced to endure each other's company until they talk it out! And then that great bloody nodcock may tell her that he loves her instead of just assuming that she knows it. Men. Idiots, every one of them." She flicked a glance at Horatio. "Sorry. No offense meant, of course. I don't think of you as a man."

"No offense taken," Horatio said with a patient sigh.

Chapter 13

"COMPANY TO SEE you, Miss Susan." Doris looked disturbed, and Susan flashed her a surprised glance.

"Who is it, Doris?"

"That Carson fella."

"Oh." That explained it. Doris had made several veiled references to the fact that Hunter Carson had seemed to make Susan unhappy, and her displeasure was obvious. Susan, however, felt her heart leap at the news that he was there. She rose from the bedroom chair where she'd been trying to read and ran a hand through her tousled curls. "Where did you have him wait on me?"

"The parlor."

Susan couldn't help a nervous laugh. "He probably looks as out of place in the parlor as a steer!"

"Don't care 'bout that none." Doris met her quick gaze with an uplifted chin. "Ask me, that man don't need to be made to feel too comfortable here. He upsets you, Miss Susan, and you know it."

"Yes, he does upset me at times," Susan said as she moved to her dressing table and caught up a hairbrush. "But I can handle it."

Doris's snort told her what her housekeeper thought of that statement.

"Don't you think I can, Doris?"

"I don't think you can see beyond the end of your nose when it comes to him, Miss Susan."

"Well. I guess that's blunt enough." Susan made a wry

face at her reflection in the mirror. "Don't ask what you don't want to hear, right?"

"You said it. I didn't."

Turning, Susan stared at Doris. The older woman's face reflected worry and love, and it made Susan feel suddenly guilty as well as apprehensive. She looked at the brown hair lightly streaked with gray, at the familiar, sensible blue eyes and stubborn chin, and smiled.

"You don't want me to be with Evan, either. Is there any man good enough for me, Doris?"

"Maybe. Time will tell that. It isn't Evan Elliott, that's for sure. And I'm not at all sure it's this Hunter Carson. The man's a mile too bold as far as I'm concerned. And nobody knows anything about him but what he tells." She shook her head. "I'd feel better if he came from around here."

"So you'd know his history?" Susan teased. She felt better. Doris didn't dislike Hunter because of anything bad she felt about him, but because of what she didn't know. It made sense, knowing Doris. Knowing Hunter.

Crossing to her, Susan gave Doris an impulsive hug. It was quickly, fiercely returned. "I just can't stand the thought of you being hurt, child. You mean a lot to me, and have since the first day I came here."

"I know. I really do. And I love you for it. You've been a mother and a friend to me, Doris, and I would never hurt you. I just hope that when I do choose a husband, you will love me enough to accept him."

Doris looked down at the hands she still had on Susan's arm. "I guess that's your way of telling me that you love this Hunter Carson."

"Is it?" Susan was faintly startled, then realized in a rush of comprehension that Doris was right. She did love him. "In a way. I don't know if he's the right man for me, but I hope so." Susan managed a reassuring smile when Doris looked up at her face with searching eyes.

"Does he know how you feel? Does he feel the same?"

"He hasn't said. I haven't asked." She bit her bottom lip. "He hasn't asked me to marry him, but still—"

Doris cut her off with a wave of her hands. "He won't think about marriage until you mention it. Men never do. It is not a subject that occurs to them naturally as it does a woman. You have to throw out hints so wide they fall into them, and even then it sometimes takes a while for it to sink in."

"Are you instructing me on how to coax Hunter into a proposal?" Susan couldn't help teasing.

Doris stiffened, but the hint of a smile tugged at her mouth. "No. You'll have to figure that out yourself."

"Does this mean you'll be nice to Hunter?"

"Well, I'll be polite—"

"Oh, no! No more of that icy courtesy that's deadlier than rattlesnake venom, if you please! It's always better to hear what's on your mind, and you know it!"

"That works two ways, Susan Cabot Whitten."

Susan paused. Of course it did. And she had always been that way. Until Hunter had gotten her so confused that she wasn't certain what she felt, and unsure of what to say to anyone. Maybe that was it. Maybe she should just tell him what she'd heard, ask him outright if it was true. He'd have to tell her the truth. Yes. That was what she would do. And then she'd know if he was what she thought he was, if he was honest or if he was what Evan named him.

"You're right, Doris. Tell Hunter I'll be down in just a moment. I want to change into something pretty."

"I won't tell him that last. Let him think you wouldn't dress special for him. Take him down a peg or two."

"Oh, Doris!"

Even dressed in her prettiest gown and with her hair becomingly brushed in loose curls around her face and over her shoulders, Susan felt nervous at seeing Hunter again. It had been four days since she'd seen him, since he had come out to the Lazy W and made love to her on the rug.

Her throat closed, and she forced her hands to be still as she clutched them in the folds of her skirts and stepped lightly down the last few stairs and into the hallway. She saw him waiting, looking out of place and impatient in the neat, feminine parlor. She steeled herself.

"Hunter."

He turned at the sound of her voice, and she was achingly aware of his male beauty. His regular, carved features, the thick tawny mane of hair that looked as if it needed trimming, the hard, glittering green eyes beneath the thick brush of dark lashes, all combined to make her heart beat more rapidly and the blood pound through her veins. A slow smile curved his hard mouth, and she saw the flash of appreciation in his eyes as she moved toward him.

It was quickly replaced by something else, a wary glint that made her look up at him uncertainly. He nodded gravely at her.

"Come out onto the porch with me, Susan."

Slightly startled by his chilly invitation, Susan went with him to the wide porch. A square of lamplight from the parlor fell across the wooden planks, and evening shadows darkened the sky. Hunter stood against the house, his face turned toward her, half in shadow, half in light. He was watching her, and she forced a smile.

"To what do I owe the honor of this visit, sir?"

His mouth twisted. "Enjoy your picnic yesterday?"

Susan looked at him more closely. There was a brittle edge to his words that made her cautious.

"I always enjoy eating Doris's food. Don't you?"

His cool gaze seemed to mock her caution. There was a fine tautness to his expression that made her swallow the question she'd been about to add, and she just looked at him. As if sensing her uneasiness, Hunter cupped her chin in his palm and bent to kiss her lightly.

When he drew back, he said, "You taste the same. I'd almost think you hadn't been kissing someone else if I didn't know better."

Susan blinked, and then it dawned on her that he must have seen her with Evan. Evan. Good God, if he knew Evan had kissed her, he must have seen them by the swimming pond the day before.

"What were you doing out there?" she blurted out. "On my land, I mean."

"Ah, so you've figured out where I saw you already? You are a pretty quick study, Miss Whitten."

Susan pushed his hand away. A spurt of irritation seized her. "Don't act like a schoolboy. If you were spying, you should have been bold enough to come ask questions."

His spurs jangled as he took several steps away from her, and Susan saw his hand tighten on the hat he held. "I don't think I'd be throwing around names just now if I were you," he said softly. "You might get some thrown back at you."

"What?"

His jaw tightened. "I thought we had an understanding."

"Understanding." Her mind raced swiftly. Did he mean the obvious? No, he couldn't. Men didn't think the same way women did about those things, and as Doris had reminded her earlier, they rarely thought about marriage until a woman put it into their heads. "I suppose we do," she said slowly when his eyes narrowed into ominous slits. "Why?"

"Somehow, I thought when there was an understanding between two people, that meant certain liberties were a bit restricted, shall we say."

"Liberties? Do you mean—" She inhaled deeply. "Hunter, are you mad because Evan kissed me?"

"Very good, Miss Whitten." His polite words barely masked a tightly leashed violence, and Susan recoiled from it. His smile at her recoil was awful, chilling and fierce at the same time. "Ah, so now you're frightened of me?"

"Hunter, I don't think you understand—"

"No," he cut in, "I don't. Dammit, Susan, after what I told you, you still went off with the man. I can only take that to mean that either you think I'm a liar or you want Evan Elliott."

"Wonderful choices," she said with rising irritation, "but quite, quite wrong!" She glared back at him. "Can't you get it through your head that Evan has been my friend since we were children? I still think of him that way."

"Forgive me for doubting you," Hunter said in a snarl that made her eyes widen, "but the kiss I saw didn't look very childish."

"Oh, that!"

His hands flashed out to grab her, and Susan winced at the biting pressure of his fingers on her arms. " 'Oh, that'?—hell, yes, oh, *that*! By God, Susan, I wanted to ride down that hill and kill him, and you stand there as cool as ice and say *oh, that* to me. . . ."

Susan sucked in another deep breath, seeing the fury

in his eyes, feeling the harsh grip of his hands on her, and remembered that he'd been accused of killing his wife for being with another man. If his wife had looked into his eyes and seen the same cold glitter she saw, she'd probably died of fright, not a bullet.

Swaying instinctively into him, Susan lay her cheek against his chest. He shuddered at her action. She felt the raw power in his body, leashed, trembling, shaking beneath her with the effort to hold back. All her outrage, her doubt of him, was subdued by the naked jealousy she saw in his face. Whatever else, Hunter cared about her. It made her throb with need and love for him.

"Hunter, I love you. I don't want Evan. I don't want anyone but you."

"You love me?" He laughed harshly, a savage sound that she'd never heard from him before. "So much that you were kissing someone else not a full day ago . . ."

"Hunter—"

"No. Don't say it. If you value your life, don't say it to me, sweetheart." He flexed his fingers into her wrists in an involuntary motion and let out a deep breath. "God, I wonder how I can be such a fool sometimes. . . ." She could feel the tension in him, the tightly coiled steel of his muscles, and knew he was struggling for control. Knowing that made her even more frightened; it also made her aware of how easily she could hurt him. He loved her. He must, or she would not have the power to hurt him.

"I love you, Hunter," she said again, softly, snapping his head down as he stared at her in the dim shadows.

Susan lifted her head from his chest and looked up at his face. His green eyes were intense, his expression grim. But she finally felt the slight easing of his taut frame.

"You say that mighty easy for a woman who was kissing another man yesterday."

"I didn't kiss him," she began, adding quickly as she saw the hot, fierce light ignite in his eyes again, "*he* kissed me. There's a difference."

Hunter didn't move for a moment; he just stood with his hands still curled around Susan's wrists, loose now, but not letting her go.

"Did he try to . . . hurt you?"

She shook her head. "No. No, of course not. I told you, Evan would not hurt me."

Disgust curdled his voice as he said, "Right, Susan. I forgot how noble he is. That's why he plans on stealing your jewelry and forcing you into marrying him."

"Are we back to that again?"

"Damn straight," he snarled so viciously that she took a step away, half-afraid, her eyes flying to his face in alarm. He still held her wrists, and he pulled her slowly back. A faint, terrible smile curled his mouth when he saw her face. "Hell, Susan, you just won't listen. Maybe I'm expecting too much from you."

"Or too little from Evan. Hunter," she forestalled the snarl she saw on his lips, "give it a little time. I'll be careful, I promise. Just don't go jumping to conclusions or thinking that I want anyone but you."

Dropping her wrists, he raked a hand through his hair. The fierce green of his eyes softened slightly. "All right," he said finally. He bent and picked up his hat, kneading it between his fingers with a look of intense concentration. "I won't. But maybe we ought to do something about the other."

"What do you mean?"

His glance lifted and held hers, and Susan saw the uncertainty in those hard green eyes. "I won't share you," he said flatly. "Not even with a kiss for old times' sake. Do you understand what I mean?"

Susan leaned against the porch post and stared at him. A sweep of joy tore through her, but she dared not give in to it until she was certain he meant what she hoped.

"Is this a marriage proposal?"

She said it lightly, with just the right trace of teasing in case he hadn't meant that at all, but there was no need.

"Damn right it's a marriage proposal." He shot her a dark look. "What'd you think it was?"

"Well, you're so romantic, Mr. Carson, I wasn't sure." Susan glared at him, half in exasperation, half joyous. He shrugged.

"I didn't want to rush it, but you're not leaving me much choice. If I don't marry you quick, you're liable to run off with a damn tinker or something."

"You're wise to move so quickly. The last tinker who came through here was devastatingly handsome. He had three teeth and no hair, and I swooned when I saw hi—"

Hunter jerked her into his arms, smothering the rest of her sentence with his mouth. He kissed her long and hard, forcing her mouth open with his tongue, filling her with it until she couldn't breathe, couldn't think, couldn't move. His arms tightened around her, holding her close from chest to knee, pressing her so closely Susan could feel the state of his arousal.

Pushing her back against the outside wall of the house, Hunter leaned his body into hers. She smelled the heat of him, the musky male scent of soap and leather and wind and dust that seemed to surround her, make her entire body ache with wanting him. Raking her hands up his sides, feeling his muscles contract beneath her light touch, she was aware of the strain slowly leaving him, replaced by another, more sexual tension.

They were on her front porch, and the barn and stable and bunkhouses were scattered across the wide expanse of the yard, tiny dots of light from the house. But inside, Doris sat listening, and Susan knew that it was madness to give in to what was swelling inside her.

"Hunter," she managed to whisper against his mouth; he caught his name, inhaled it, gave it back to her with his kisses, his warm breath feathering across her face. Sliding his hands down her sides, he gripped her hips, lifted her, ground his body into hers, the wall at her back providing a stable prop. She felt him hard against her, his erection nudging her body, making her legs spread to give him freer access. Her arms went around his neck, she melted into him, not caring anymore what anyone saw or said.

When her hands slipped up the powerful, taut curve of muscle in his back to curl around his neck and draw him into her, Hunter broke loose. He levered his body away from her, ignoring her soft moan of protest; he grasped her hands, held them to his mouth for an instant, his breathing harsh and ragged.

"Not here," he muttered roughly. "Dammit, there's never the right place or time for us. . . ."

"Hunter?" His name was a sigh on her lips, and her palm fluttered from his light grasp to curl around his neck again and draw his mouth back down. "Please kiss me. . . ."

Dazed by the response pounding through her, Susan did not hear anything but her own desire, and when Hunter snapped his head away from her and gave her a rough push behind him, she was bewildered and bereft.

"What . . ." she mumbled in confusion, then saw the dark shape loom up on the porch steps and launch itself through the air. A short scream erupted from her throat as she heard Hunter's soft curse. Brutal gasps, pants, and thuds followed, mixed with more curses, and everything moved so fast that it was over at about the same time as she identified Evan as the shadow.

By then he was sprawled on the porch floor glaring up at Hunter, blood streaming down his face. "Damn you, Carson," he muttered. "I think you broke my nose."

"You should have thought about that before you jumped me, Elliott."

Hunter's cool reply broke Susan from her daze. She glanced at him and saw that he wasn't even winded. He still stood warily, his hands curled into fists and held slightly in front of him, one leg bent at the knee and in front of the other, his feet spread for balance.

Turning back to Evan, Susan said, "Why did you do that? And why are you here?"

Evan lurched to his feet, holding one hand up to his face as he pulled the neckerchief from around his throat. When he had it pressed to his nose, he flicked Susan a look that plainly said he'd expected more sympathy.

"I came to talk to you." His words were muffled by the cloth but his anger was evident. "And when I got here and saw you . . . with *him*, I thought he was hurting you."

Hunter gave a disbelieving grunt, and Evan's eyes swung to him. Fury flared for an instant but disappeared when Pete Sheridan came up the steps, his spurs rattling.

"Hey, what's going on up here? Thought I heard some noises I didn't like."

"You may have, Pete," Evan said, slashing another

glare at Hunter. "Carson was manhandling Susan, and I thought I was coming to her rescue. I didn't know she liked it."

"Evan!" Susan said at the same time Hunter took a step forward. She put out a quick hand to stop him. "No. Leave him alone. Please," she added when Hunter glanced at her angrily. "I hate fighting. Especially when it's over nothing but a mistake."

Her inference was not lost on Pete. The foreman's dark eyes slid from Evan to Hunter, then back to Susan. "Miss Susan, what do you want me to do?"

"Maybe you should help Evan stop the bleeding and then get him on his horse," she said softly and almost winced at the pained look Evan shot her.

"Is that the way you want it, Susan? You've made your choice?" Evan asked thickly.

"Yes, Evan. That's the way it is. I love Hunter. We're going to be married."

She felt Hunter stiffen, heard Evan's hoarse denial, and saw Pete's surprise all in the same instant, it seemed. Confused, not knowing why Hunter didn't seem to want her to say they were to be married, Susan hesitated.

"Is that true, Carson?" Evan demanded roughly. "You going to marry Susan?"

"Not that it's any of your business," Hunter said after what seemed an eternity to Susan, "but yeah. If she'll have me."

Relief flooded her; he didn't sound like a deliriously happy fiancé, but that could be because he disliked Evan so much.

Evan reeled, and Pete put a hand on his shoulder. "I'll help you take care of th' bleedin', Elliott. Come on over to th' bunkhouse with me."

"No." Evan jerked away from him, and his glance at

Susan was dark and bleak. "No, I don't want anything from anybody at the Lazy W."

"Evan—" Susan put out a hand, but Hunter's quick grip on her arm stopped her. She half turned to look at him, and Evan laughed bitterly.

"You've made a bargain with the devil, SuSu. I hope you don't regret it. He's already roping you in, and you're so blind in love—or maybe lust—that you can't see it. Go ahead and marry him. You'll be sorry quick enough, I can tell you that." His short laugh was harsh. "It ought to be right funny when you find out what a whorin', murdering bastard he really is." Evan half turned and took a few steps toward the edge of the porch, then looked back at her. "I rode out here to tell you that I found out some very interesting news about your lover. Ask him about the railroad, and where it intends to cut through. Then ask him what interest *he's* got in it. You might find his answers pretty interesting."

Pete Sheridan stood on the top step, one boot on the porch, his hand resting on his hip by the butt of his gun. He looked at Susan, then Hunter as Evan brushed past him. No one said anything for a moment. Hunter returned Pete's gaze coldly.

Pete pushed back his hat. "I'd like a word or two with you, Carson."

"Concerning?"

"Miss Susan." Pete didn't back down from Hunter's icy gaze, but his hand dropped slightly nearer his gun. There was a taut wariness about him, as if he half expected Hunter to draw on him. "See," he said slowly, "I feel like I'm responsible for her since her daddy died. I've known her since she was a little girl, and I don't intend to let her marry some gunslick that don't care about her."

"Sounds fair enough," Hunter said after a moment, and Susan looked at Pete.

Her voice trembled slightly. "I'd like to talk to him first, please. There are some questions he needs to answer for me."

"I think I know what you want to ask me, Susan," Hunter said softly. "My answers are one of the reasons I didn't ask you to marry me weeks ago."

A lump formed in her throat, and Susan nodded slowly. "I see. Would you like to tell me exactly what a railroad has to do with my land? And if it has anything to do with why you were on Lazy W property without telling anyone yesterday?"

Shifting from one foot to the other, Hunter said in a low, rough voice, "I'm a major stockholder in the Texas and Pacific; we're laying tracks this way, and a spur to Los Alamos needs to go through your land. The northeast corner. I did the survey. We're willing to buy or lease."

"My best grazing land."

"Yes."

"I see." Susan crossed her arms over her chest and looked up at him. "And when did you propose to bring this up? After we were married, by chance, and I would have very little to say about what my husband did with our property? I know that's the way it works—what's mine becomes yours after a marriage."

"It works the other way around, too." Hunter's voice was just as angry as hers. "Don't start doubting me again. Dammit, I don't need a wife who doesn't trust me!"

"Then maybe you don't need a wife at all!" Susan shook away the hand he put on her arm. "No. No, I don't think so, Hunter Carson. I don't think you need *me*, anyway! I don't think you need anyone!"

Jerking away from him, she ran into the house, pushing past Doris, who stood in the doorway. Pete and Doris exchanged glances but didn't speak. Hunter put on his hat, gave Pete a cool nod, and stepped down off the porch without looking back. No one said anything as he stepped into the saddle and swung his chestnut around, spurring him into a canter.

Upstairs, through the open window, Susan's muffled sobs could be heard. Doris winced, and Pete walked over and put a hand over hers.

They stood that way for a little while, as the moon rose in the sky and the stars glittered coldly. Nothing was said, but nothing needed to be said. Both of them knew the other's heart; and both of them ached for the girl they loved.

Chapter 14

JULY BLEW IN on hot winds, and along with it horrible news from Montana.

In late June General Custer had fought and died along with the Seventh Cavalry, massacred against incredible odds by the Sioux. There were no white survivors of the attack. Newspaper headlines proclaimed the golden-haired general a hero, but some soldiers spoke up in small voices to remind how he'd ignored the best advice of his captain and scouts.

The Indian situation was growing more tense by the day, and none of the men on the Lazy W rode out without loaded rifles and plenty of ammunition. The Comanche had not returned to the area, but with the new unrest, no one felt safe.

With the enforced restriction, Susan stirred restlessly under the restraints; late one afternoon found her out by the stables, gazing wistfully at her bay mare. She needed to keep busy, to keep her mind from straying, but Doris had run her out of the kitchen in exasperation because of her distraction.

"You don't have your mind on canning, that's for sure," Doris had said. "Go outside and see if Pete has something you can do!"

So she'd gone, but after cleaning stalls and throwing hay, there was little left for her to do. She leaned on the fence and watched the horses mill in the small corral.

"Don't be thinking 'bout ridin' out alone, Miss Susan," Pete advised, and she nodded.

"I'm not. But if I don't do *some*thing, I'm liable to start baying at the moon like the coyotes."

Pete looked at her. "Bayin' at the moon ain't so bad. Long as you can outsing the coyotes."

A faint smile curled Susan's mouth. "Well, is there any man who can ride out with me today?"

Shaking his head, Pete said, "Dempster's down sick. Murdock's hung over—without pay—and Fisher's out fixing the fence at the northeast section."

"Comanche again?"

Pete nodded slowly. "Or rustlers. Can't tell how many cattle are missing yet."

Susan grimaced. In the past three weeks scores of cattle had come up missing. Men had been shot at, horses stolen. It was as if someone had a personal grudge against the Lazy W. Her mouth tightened. Someone like Hunter Carson, perhaps. Her mind shied away from thinking about him, just as she had trained herself to do since the night she'd sent him away. She looked back at Pete.

"Anyone ride in to report it to the sheriff?"

"Can't spare a man. We're goin' in for more feed tomorrow, though. We'll report it then."

"Well, we need to get these cattle as fat as we can as quick as we can. I want to get them to market soon. I have a debt to pay."

Pete shuffled his feet in the dirt and looked down at his boots. "Thought Carson sent back your accounts marked paid in full."

"That doesn't mean they were paid. I intend to honor the rest of that debt. I refuse to owe him."

"Yeah, can't say as I blame you." Pete's guileless gaze drifted, then came to rest on her face. "Might have to talk to him then."

Susan bridled. "Whose side are you on?"

"Yours. Always yours, Miss Susan. Don't you ever forget that. I'm on your side more than you are."

"And what's that supposed to mean?"

Shrugging, Pete said, "Nothing." He looked at her. "Did you hear 'bout Carson gunnin' a man in town last week?"

Susan's throat tightened. She tried not to show the sudden fear she felt. "No, I didn't. How would I? I haven't been away from the ranch, and all Evan can talk about—what happened?" she finished lamely.

"Seems like Charley Franks got liquored up, ran into Carson, had a few words. From what I hear, Franks pulled his iron first. I wasn't there, so I don't know, but Carson ain't in jail."

"Does that mean—is Hunter innocent?"

"Franks is dead." Pete shrugged. "Ain't gonna be no trial, anyway. That ought to tell you somethin'."

Silence stretched between them. It was hot, and the heat made Susan's blouse stick to her shoulder blades. Heat and fear. She could feel the beads of sweat trickle down her spine, and turned away irritably.

"Maybe I'll ride into town with you tomorrow. You can get the feed, and I'll get some other things I need."

Her chin lifted at Pete's curious gaze. She had no intention of allowing Hunter Carson to keep her away from town just because of the enmity between them.

Enmity. Was it? Was that what that sweet, wild longing had changed to? She wondered sometimes, late at night when it was hot and the open windows allowed in only a trickle of a breeze to cool her heated skin. Then she felt hot and heavy inside, with an ache that she couldn't acknowledge and couldn't ignore.

And then, lying there looking up at her ceiling in the

dim shadows of her room, she thought of Hunter. She would think of his mouth on her, his hands, the shivering ecstasy that he could summon with his touch. She knew now what it was to have a man inside her, where before there had only been vague longings, hazy and not quite sharp enough to torment her.

Now she knew, and now she missed Hunter with a clarity of thought and feeling that kept her constantly on edge. She felt Pete's eyes on her and stiffened. No one would know how she longed for him, wept for him during the night. She'd thought it was forever. . . .

"Let's leave early tomorrow," she said to Pete, her voice sharper than she intended. "I don't want to be caught out late on the way back."

"Yes, Miss Susan. I had planned on it."

Pete's soft assurance mocked her tart words, and she nodded briefly.

She was no less sharp the next morning, when dawn trailed rosy fingers across the sky and a cool breeze eased the heat. The horses stamped restlessly, metal bits jangling and sounding overloud in the still quiet. The huge wooden wheels of the buckboard rattled as Lonny Wyatt brought it up, and Sam Murdock, still looking hung over and slightly sheepish, sat on the high seat beside him.

"Is this all that's going?" Susan asked, glancing at the well-armed men.

"No, Miss Susan." Pete turned to look at her. "I'm going, and so is Dempster."

"I thought he was sick."

"He's all right. A little green around the edges maybe, but right enough to ride and shoot. Most of the men are out on the line, and we're leaving plenty here. Don't hardly think we'll be much of a draw to any Comanche, not with the horses I put to the harness."

Susan flicked a glance at the team. They were the scrub horses brought in off the range, not the sturdy bays or chestnuts they usually used. She smiled.

"I guess they won't catch anyone's eye, but I've never known Comanche to be greatly concerned with beauty."

Pete grunted. "At least they don't eat 'em, like the Apache do."

"Well, I'll ride Blaze, I guess," Susan said, referring to her leggy bay. "No room in the wagon anyway, and I feel like I need a good run."

Shrugging, Pete said, "Suit yourself, Miss Susan. Just don't get any ideas about runnin' off and leavin' us behind on your little gallop."

"Now, would I do that?" she teased with a slight smile.

"Not if I can help it."

But it was hard to keep Blaze in hand, and Susan had to keep a tight rein on her mount. It had been too long since she had exercised the frisky mare, and she danced and tossed her head, long black mane whipping the air and Susan's face.

"Damn you," Susan muttered when the mare took several sideways steps, neck bowed and chin lowered to grip the bit between her teeth. "Behave!" She could feel Pete's narrowed gaze on her and knew he was worried that the mare would take off with her.

She was an excellent horsewoman; she'd practically grown up on a horse. But there were times the horses won a round or two, and this wasn't a good time to allow it.

By the time they reached Los Alamos, Susan's arms were sore and tired from restraining Blaze. She left her at the livery stable, sliding from the mare with more than a few feeling comments on her nature. Pete grinned.

"Glad you got your exercise this morning, Miss Susan."

She shot him a disgusted glance. "I bet you are. I may ride back in the wagon." Pulling her hat from her head, she raked a hand through her sweat-dampened hair. "Guess I'll go over to the sheriff's office and report those missing cattle. Then I'm going to the dry goods store and down to the seamstress. I'm almost threadbare when it comes to decent clothes." She stopped and bit her lip, fully aware that she was chattering. She let her hat dangle down her back.

"I'll take care of the feed," Pete said casually, "unless you want to—"

"No. No, you take care of it. I intend to stay at this end of town."

Pete nodded silently and walked off, spurs jangling and his stride slow and assured. Susan smiled. She depended on Pete and didn't know what she'd do without him. He was a part of the ranch, just like the buildings and the land itself.

She often wondered what she would do if he ever left, though she didn't think he would. Not because of her, because of Doris. She smiled. When would he and Doris finally admit they loved each other and do something about it? It wasn't as if they weren't together all the time anyway, but at least then there would be more than longing looks across the dining table every evening.

Susan tore her thoughts from her ranch foreman and back to the situation at hand—missing cattle. Surely, Sheriff Barton could do something about it. The Lazy W couldn't be the only ranch in the area suffering from the Comanche. Or rustlers.

Pete tended toward the latter theory, said the Comanche operated differently, didn't pick and choose and take them off the same way rustlers would. And the tracks he'd found around the watering hole up in the northeast corner were those of shod horses, not the unshod horses of Comanche.

It would be interesting to see what the sheriff would make of it.

When Susan pushed open the door of the small clapboard and brick building that was office and jail combined, she saw Barton at his desk. He was leaning back, feet propped up, talking to a visitor. And when her gaze went to the man sitting in a chair opposite Barton, her heart dropped to her toes. She stood indecisively for an instant, just long enough to draw both men's attention.

Hunter Carson stood up immediately, his green eyes as vivid and cold as she remembered them. Susan took a step back.

"Sorry. Didn't know you had business already. I'll be back, Sheriff—"

"Don't bother leaving." Hunter gave her a quick, hard smile. "I was through."

Susan stood, frozen to the spot. It was just as well that he leave. She didn't think her legs would carry her very far, certainly not back up the street.

Sheriff Barton was standing, too, rubbing a hand across his clean-shaven jaw, peering at her from beneath bushy gray brows. His deep voice cut into the haze surrounding her as he said, "Miss Whitten, I'm glad you're here. I was going to ride out to the Lazy W to talk to you. Now you've saved me the trouble."

"Have I?" she murmured, unable to really concentrate on anything but Hunter. He seemed to fill the room, his broad shoulders and height blocking out everything.

Though he'd said he was leaving, he still stood there, lean and hard and handsome, making her heart beat so fast she was certain it could be heard all the way down at the church. "What did you need to talk to me about, Sheriff?" she managed to ask.

"Saving the town." Barton smiled at her, his beefy face creasing into a mask of cajoling humor when she looked at him suspiciously.

"What has that got to do with me?"

"Well, it seems that—no, don't leave, Carson. This concerns you, too. Maybe you can explain it better than I can."

"I don't think Miss Whitten will listen to me."

Hunter's mocking gaze still rested on her face, and Susan knew suddenly what it was about. A flash of fury shot through her, followed quickly by an odd twinge of pain. He didn't need *her*. He only needed her land, rights to put his damned railroad spur across the northeast corner of the Lazy W. She stiffened.

"Mr. Carson is right, Sheriff. I don't want to listen to anything he's got to say. And I don't intend to discuss a railroad, either. I came in here to talk to you about the cattle that are missing from my spread. Rustlers, Pete thinks, not Comanche. It seems that—"

"Miss Whitten," Barton broke in, his gray brows drawing down into a scowl, "I don't think you know how important this railroad spur is to the town. It means the difference between a livelihood and moving. Do you understand? If Los Alamos gets that spur, more business will move in, more jobs for the folks here, a boost for the economy. All Mr. Carson wants you to do is lease him the rights for that stretch of ground, and hell, Miss Whitten, it'll make you more money than cattle!"

Susan knew that. She'd already argued it out in her

mind. It wasn't railroad rights that bothered her; it was the way Hunter had proposed to get them. And she would rather see Lazy W go under and be sold for taxes than let him do that to her. Or at least, that's what she told herself when she was mad. When she cooled down, she knew that it meant more to the ranch than it did to Los Alamos.

Tossing back her head, her chin tilted, she looked hard at Hunter. "Come to the sheriff for help, Mr. Carson? Are you going to have me arrested, maybe, if I don't agree?"

His eyes narrowed. "Don't be stupid."

"That's not stupid. It's working. And it's probably quicker than breaking me by stealing all my cattle." Her voice was tight, her hands curled into fists at her sides. "But of course, you can afford to wait me out. I can't stand losing many more heads of cattle."

She had to look away from Hunter, could not bear the fire and ice of his harsh gaze on her. A faint, ironic smiled curled his lips, but it did nothing to soften the anger in his eyes. She felt his anger, felt it rising off him like steam; and along with it was something else, an emotion that beckoned dangerously.

Susan forced her gaze to the sheriff, who was looking at both of them with something like confusion on his face.

"Well," he said. "Well. Am I to take it that you came in to lodge a complaint against Mr. Carson, Miss Whitten?"

"Not especially him. Whoever is stealing my cattle." Her gaze shifted to Hunter now, open and direct, a mocking challenge in her eyes. Let him deny it or confirm it. Let him know that she wasn't fooled by him any longer. "It's not the Comanche. Unless they're riding

shod ponies now. And unless they're trying to run me
out of business so I'll sell a piece of my land." It was said
more to Hunter than Barton, an accusation, a gauntlet
thrown down.

Hunter's reaction was unexpected. "That does it," he
growled furiously. Then he moved forward in a graceful stride, took her by the arm, and propelled her out
the door.

At first Susan was too stunned to do anything. She
let him turn her around and steer her down the street
several yards before the shock wore off. Then it hit her,
and she was aware of Sheriff Barton standing in the open
doorway of his office, staring after them with a faintly
amused smile on his face. Humiliation heated her face
and made her careless.

"What do you think you're doing?" she snapped,
jerking her arm free of his grasp. He immediately
captured it in a hard grip again and jerked her close.
Her riding skirt swung against his legs in a whirl of
material. She could feel the heat of his body pressing
against her, felt the controlled anger in his grip.

"Dammit, Susan, enough!" The words brushed her ear
in a breath of exasperation.

She tried to pull away, and his fingers coiled tightly
around her wrist in a punishing grip that made her flinch.
"Let go of me, Hunter Carson."

"Not until you promise to listen."

Her head flung up, and she glared at him. "Listen! To
what? More lies?"

"Lies?" His jaw tightened, and she saw a hot flare in
his eyes that made her swallow nervously. "Not lies.
Truth. You just don't want to listen, but by God, you
will!"

"I have no intention of listening to anything you have

to say to me, Hunter Carson." Her chin came up in a stubborn tilt that made his hands tighten on her wrists. "I've listened to too much already."

"Do you think so? I don't. And you will listen to me, or I'll drag you down the middle of the street to someplace where you'll have no choice."

"Do you really think no one would come to my rescue?" she snapped. "Try it and see!"

"Gladly. But don't say I didn't warn you." He gave a harsh laugh. "Do you really think any man in this town would brace me after last week? I'm already reported to be a killer—and everyone here knows you're going to marry me."

"I won't. Not anymore. I've changed my mind."

"Too bad. I haven't."

"What . . . what are you doing?" she choked out when he pulled her with him, his long strides covering the ground and making her half run to keep from being literally dragged along the street. Furious, she jerked at him. "Pete will come after me—"

"Let him."

"He'll shoot you, you fool!"

"He can try."

Half shouting now: "Hunter—people are looking . . . I'll scream, I swear I will!"

"Go ahead." He didn't even glance at her, and Susan saw that people were, indeed, pausing to stare uncertainly. She felt a hot flush stain her cheeks and ground her teeth angrily when Hunter said, "They all know we're going to be married anyway, remember? Your precious Evan spread the word to everyone. I can't walk ten feet in the damned town without someone stopping me to congratulate me, so go ahead and give them a good show. They'll just think it's a lover's quarrel."

Startled, angry, half-afraid, Susan trotted to keep up with him. She hadn't thought of that. She hadn't thought of anything but her grief over Hunter's treachery. Of course, everyone would be expecting a wedding if Evan had told them she was marrying Hunter. And now there wouldn't be one, and it would be just as humiliating to try and explain that as to try and explain why Hunter was dragging her down the middle of the main street.

"Did you tell them the wedding's off?" she asked when he paused for a moment. He flicked her a sardonic glance.

"No. Why should I? As far as I'm concerned, it's not."

Susan stared at him. "But—"

"We'll finish this discussion inside," he cut in and spread a hand on her back to nudge her forward.

Susan blinked, realizing that he had taken her to his house. He'd pushed open the front door, and when she was inside, he shut it behind them.

"What?" she mocked, glancing at his hand on her arm and the closed door. "Aren't you going to lock me in?"

"If I need to, I will." His eyes met hers, and there was a challenge burning in them.

She stiffened. "If you think I'm here willingly, and that I want any part of you, Hunter Carson, you're—"

Flexing his arm, he jerked her hard against him, and his mouth came down over hers, cutting off her angry words. Covering her half-parted lips, Hunter took immediate advantage and slid his tongue inside her mouth. Hot, hard strokes rasped over her tongue, exploring, fencing, making her writhe against him. She hung in his embrace, toes barely brushing the floor, the arms she'd put up as a barrier between them curling around his shoulders to hold her upright.

He was so achingly familiar, the scent of his heated skin arousing and surrounding her, making her shudder under his heavy hands. Her anger was dissolving into a hot, heady sensation that curled from the pit of her belly upward, leaving her weak and heavy. She clung to it desperately. When her head fell back and she saw his narrowed green eyes gazing down at her, she tried to push away again, but her efforts only brought her up harder against him when he tightened the arm he held around her waist. He pulled her dangling hat over her head by the string and tossed it to the hall tree. It caught on a hook and swung there.

A faint, merciless smile curled his mouth. "Don't fight me, sweetheart. You won't win, and you don't really want to anyway. Not in this. . . ." His hand slid from the small of her back to cup her buttocks in his palm, lifting her up and against the hard bulge in the front of his pants.

Susan gasped, pushing futilely at him, but her own body was betraying her with a sweeping flush that threatened to leave her shattered. Damn him, damn him for touching her, making her want him like this. And he knew his own power, of course, or he wouldn't have brought her here, wouldn't be holding her like this.

That knowledge brought a surge of pride to her defense, a stubborn wave of resistance to his unfair tactics.

"I do," she managed to say as tremors racked her body and gave the lie to her words. "I do want you to let me go. I don't want you, Hunter. *I don't want you. . . .*"

Hunter pulled her even closer to him, notching her body between his hard thighs, insinuating himself so close it was as if they were already naked and in bed; she could feel every detail of his body and closed her eyes.

"Open your eyes, damn you, Susan. Open your eyes

and tell me that you don't want me. That you don't love me."

Dragging her lashes up, Susan stared at him, her throat working soundlessly for a moment. His eyes were a dark, fierce green, the sensual lines of his mouth curved into a wicked snarl that made her tremble. He looked danger-ous, he looked as if he could murder her if she didn't say what he wanted to hear. She summoned her courage, remembered her anger.

"I . . . I don't love you," she whispered hoarsely and saw the harsh glitter in those green eyes go opaque, unreadable in the shadowy light of the dim hallway.

"Then it will be without love. But you won't leave me, Susan. I won't let you."

She stared at him, uncertain, half—no, more than half afraid. This was a Hunter she didn't know, hadn't seen before. Not this angry, this determined, this—hurt. Pain and rage glittered in his eyes, and she was afraid of him. For him. For herself. Of herself. . . .

"Fine, then," she heard herself say, her voice sounding as if it came from a great distance away. "Go ahead. Take me to bed if you think that will make a difference. It won't. You'll just be a rutting stallion. I still won't tell you I love you."

His fingers tightened painfully on her. "Won't you?" he said in a low, awful whisper. "Won't you? Dammit, I bet you will."

Closing her eyes, she moaned a protest when he put one arm under her knees to lift her against his hard chest. He paid her no attention but strode down the dim, cool hall to kick open a door and slam it shut with his foot.

Susan realized that he'd taken her to his bedroom, that he didn't intend to take no for an answer, that she had lost. Then she realized she didn't care. She didn't. God help her, she wanted him as badly as he wanted her. The barriers she'd put between them suddenly wavered. *Not now.* She couldn't keep them up. Not when he was kissing her again, his mouth moving hot and fierce over her brow, cheek, lips, down the arch of her throat as her head fell back.

Her throat corded as she half groaned, half cried, "Why didn't you stay away from me? Why?"

He lay her on the bed, following with his body over hers in the same smooth motion. She felt the mattress give beneath their weight; his words were as hot as his eyes and hands on her, working at buttons, tugging at her blouse.

"Damn you, Susan, I stayed away. But no more. No more."

His mouth and weight forced the air from her lungs in a hoarse gasp. Her bare breasts raked against his shirt; the buttons dug into her tender skin in a stinging prick, and she tried to twist away. Struggling, she shifted under him, but he slid one hand down her body, over the thrust of her breast to cup its weight in his hand. His other arm pressed against her shoulder, trapping her effortlessly as she squirmed.

"Hunter, you know why I can't do this," she managed to say between deep gasps for air. "It isn't right anymore. There's too much between us. . . . Leave me alone, please leave me alone."

His hand stilled briefly in her hair, brushing it back from her temples, watching the silky black tendrils trail over his palm. "No," he said flatly. "Not for those stupid reasons." His head lowered again. "Not for any reasons. . . ."

Bruising her lips with his kisses, he wouldn't let her speak, wouldn't let her argue; he held her in his harsh embrace, and she knew the ending was inevitable. He intended to make love to her, to make her feel something, respond to him whether she was willing or not.

When her lips parted in protest, his tongue moved between them in slow, drugging strokes, sparking shivers in her. No, she couldn't let him wrest the response he sought, not like this, not when he was angry and there was no understanding between them. Not until he understood why she was so afraid of him. Afraid for him and for herself.

"Hunter, please," she choked out when his mouth left hers and he lifted his body for a moment. He curled his fingers into the edge of her blouse and yanked it over her head, paying no attention to the soft rending of cotton.

"Please?" he mocked. "Please what. Please stop? Or please keep doing this. . . ." His thumb and forefinger circled her nipple, making sensations shoot from her breast to the warm pool of her stomach, and she tried to push his hand away.

Relentlessly he brushed aside her efforts, pulling her chemise off and tossing it carelessly aside. He straddled her thrashing body, holding her in the vise of his steely thighs, not letting her twist away from him as his hands caressed her. Kneading her flesh gently, his fingertips stroked over the curve of her breasts, circling her nipples then swooping down over the arch of her rib cage to nudge beneath the waistband of her skirt.

A sob caught in her throat, a sob of defeat mixed with frustration and need, and Susan bit her lip to hold it back.

Teasing her with clever fingers, dragging his thumb across the rigid peak of her breast and then lowering his head to take the taut nipple in his mouth, Hunter ignored her futile efforts to avoid him. He sucked at the coral tip in rhythmic motion while his hand teased her other breast; she gasped and arched upward, her hips moving seductively in spite of herself.

It was crazy; a hot, damp heat spread from the center of her stomach, oozing upward, trailing fingers of fire in its wake. She couldn't resist him, craved the sweet agony of his hands on her. *Crazy, crazy, crazy . . .*

A soft moan escaped when Hunter forced her hips to move against his in the rhythm of sex, scraping over the hard ridge of his arousal. He heard her moan and lifted his head at the sound of her surrender.

Triumph flared briefly in his eyes, making them hot and hard and green. "That's right, sweetheart," he said softly, sliding his hands beneath her hips to lift her up into him.

Gasping, Susan moaned incoherently. Shifting to lie between her thighs, he spread her legs apart with his knees, then lowered his body against her. Her long skirts hampered his movements, but they hampered hers, too. She heaved to buck him off, but his weight and determination kept him in place. He lowered his head and kissed her again until she quieted.

"Stop fighting me, Susan," he murmured against the soft skin of her throat. His breath was warm across her skin. "I won't hurt you. I'd never hurt you. I told you that."

"Hunter, please get off me. . . ."

"No." He caught her hands when she tried to push at his shoulders. "I won't get off, honey. I want you, and you want me, too." Brushing a kiss at the corner of her mouth, he shifted slightly to push up her skirts. "Dammit," he muttered, realizing that the split skirt would not be pushed up around her waist. He worked at the buttons at her waist for a moment, freed them, then tugged the material down her legs in spite of her struggles. He caught her wrists in one hand when she tried to pull him away, and held them tightly while he removed pantalets, stockings, and short boots.

Only the diffused light from the shade-covered windows brightened the room, and Susan was suddenly glad for it when Hunter looked down at her. Her chin lifted slightly in defiance, and he grinned. Still holding her wrists over her head and propping himself up with that hand pressed into the pillow, Hunter traced a leisurely hand down over her body. Lightly trailing his fingertips from her throat to her breast, pausing to etch circles around the pinkish tip beaded into an impudent knot, he slid his hand over the flat mound of her abdomen and down to the silky nest of curls below.

"Stop it!" she hissed desperately. His hand paused.

When he lifted his gaze, it was hot and flaring with lights she recognized. He released her wrists and dragged his free hand down her throat, fingers resting on the pulse throbbing at the base.

Susan knew what came next, knew that her entire body was throbbing with need for him. It was galling to her pride to be made to feel this emotion against her will, and she damned her body at the same time as she twisted beneath his touch.

His hand came between her thighs in feathery strokes that made her jerk; then his fingers touched the small dark fleece at the center, sliding over the hidden folds. When she cried out, he slid up over her and bent quickly to kiss her, probing her mouth with his tongue. Still kissing her, he moved his hand again, pushing at her clenched thighs.

"Open your legs for me, sweetheart," he said against her mouth when she shuddered.

Her fingers dug into his shoulders, nails raking across the material of his shirt, clenching convulsively as he wedged her thighs apart. His hand was warm, hard, searching against her, making her quiver. She remembered how he could coax a wave of release from her with his touch, how he had held her and stroked her there until she was panting with it. She'd been helpless beneath his touch then and held tightly to her control now.

But Hunter had no intention of allowing Susan to stop him from giving her pleasure. "Spread your legs, Susan," he said against her mouth again, and when she hesitated, he dragged her thighs apart and quickly held them with his knees braced against her. "I only want to love you, honey."

"No—" It was torn from her, that one word of denial, of accusation, and his mouth tightened.

"Yes." His hand moved wickedly, stroking across the sensitive folds of her body in a tantalizing touch that made her arch upward into his palm. He smiled then, a taunting, cruel smile that mocked her efforts to avoid him. "Oh, yes, sweetheart. And you want it, too. You weren't so reluctant last time, or the time before when I wanted to wait until it was right." His thumb grazed the most sensitive part of her, making her gasp. "Well, now it's right. We're in my house and my bed, and I have no intention of allowing you to leave."

"Hunter . . ."

"Yes, say my name," he said fiercely. His thumb moved up and around, creating sparks of fire and a pleasure so intense she couldn't breathe. When she arched against him, opening her legs wider for him, unable to stop the motion of her hips, he rubbed his hand over the aching spot more swiftly.

Another gasp tore from her throat, and her nails dug

into his back as she called his name again and again. When his mouth closed over her breast again, hot and wet and unbearably exciting, she felt the faint tremor deep inside escalate to a thundering roar. It drowned out everything, that shattering release, sweeping through her veins in a raging tide that made her entire body convulse in a series of quivering spasms.

"Hunter, Hunter," she sobbed into his chest, "Hunter."

"Yes, sweetheart," he muttered thickly, aroused by her climax, "I'm here. And I'll never leave you."

He moved briefly away from her; she felt his absence in a kind of dazed way, then felt the mattress dip beneath his weight again as he moved back over her. Bare flesh skimmed over her, exciting, arousing, sensual. He was as naked as she was, and Susan swallowed a sigh.

It *was* right; he'd been right about that. She loved him with a ferocity she never would have imagined, and it wasn't because of how he made her feel, but that he'd made her feel at all.

Dragging his lean body over hers, sliding between her legs and lifting up and over her, Hunter bent his head to kiss her again. His mouth was hot and sweet, and she closed her eyes and gave herself to the sweep of raw emotion that coursed through her. His arms were braced on the bed, his erection hot and soft and hard all at the same time, brushing between her thighs. He paused at her entrance, the sweet heat of him nudging the folds of her body in a teasing caress. Susan arched unthinkingly.

Hunter moved with a low, masculine growl of satisfaction when she opened for him, her arms curling around his neck to draw him closer as he mounted her. He penetrated with a swift, hard thrust of his body, throwing his head back as she arched to meet him.

"Ah . . . God—Susan, sweetheart," he muttered in a thick groan as her body convulsed around him. She felt his heat inside her, the strength of him driving into her; he thrust in and out in shattering moves that made her ache all over again, ache and yearn and reach for that elusive goal.

Pinning her to the mattress with slow, deliberate thrusts of his body, Hunter watched her face, caught her eyes and would not release them. Susan saw the measure of her response reflected in his green eyes, saw her gasping, arching pleasure mirrored on his face. The soft light made his golden hair gleam dully; he looked to her like a great, tawny lion, all smooth, graceful muscle and muted gold.

And the sensual glitter in his eyes beckoned her, coaxed her to follow where he led, to yield all to him. Susan felt the surge of desire pound through her, vibrating and so intense she shuddered with it.

It was a heady madness, a soaring promise that lingered just beyond reach. Hunter's hands curved over her shoulders in an iron grip; he drew back and rammed into her again and again, filling the throbbing core of her with deep thrusts and making her cry out. He moved ruthlessly against her, until she was sobbing and whimpering and pulling at him for more.

"Hunter, Hunter, please."

Beads of sweat glistened on his face and shoulders as he looked down at her, a strangely taut expression hardening his face.

"Please what, love?"

She gasped as he stroked slowly, using his body to tease her, to bring her to the brink of satisfaction but not give it to her.

"Please what?" he asked again, softly, shoving into her with his weight behind it, making her reach for him, her hands fluttering helplessly around his shoulders, his back, his waist. "What do you want, sweetheart?"

"Oh, God . . ." She shuddered, and he bent his head and took her nipple in his mouth, sucking gently at first, then more strongly. Her fingers slid down his back, grazing the slick, bare skin with her nails, and she felt him flinch and then drive into her again. "Hunter, oh, Hunter," she moaned as he swept her up into the hard, driving rhythm of his lean body. It was exquisite torment, pain and pleasure at the same time.

And when he growled roughly and spread his hands under her hips to lift her, slamming his body into her in a compelling force that took her with him, she heard herself cry out her love for him. Then his mouth covered hers, and he inhaled her love and gave it back to her with his body.

Susan sobbed her love for him into his naked shoulder, over and over again, whispering fiercely, "I love you, I love you."

And then the release took her, shatteringly, coming in great huge waves and rolling over her until she shuddered with the force of it. She heard, dimly, Hunter echo her words in a harsh grate of breath, then thought she must be mistaken when it rolled into a groan of release. The sound filled the shadows of his bedroom in a ragged wave of pleasure as he stiffened and exploded in a pulsing surge of life. Or death, the little death that comes with love.

Chapter 15

"YOU'RE NOT GOING anywhere." Hunter's arm tightened around her waist when Susan tried to get up. His long body coiled around her, surrounding her with strength, with warm sensations that made her uneasy. The arm he'd thrown over her so casually held her in a hard embrace. She felt him all down the length of her, his muscled frame nudging against her back and thighs, an erotic scrape of heat and skin. Susan flung him an exasperated glare.

"Don't you think this has gone far enough?" she snapped at his closed face. His eyes were shut, his mouth curved in a blind smile.

"Not far enough, I'd say."

"Oh, really?"

One eye opened, and he peered at her through the thick curtain of his lashes. "You mad again?"

It was said wearily, as if he was put upon enough by her moods.

"No, *still* mad."

A deep chuckle rumbled in his chest, and his arm flexed enough to mold her into him, pressing her into the hard angle of his chest and thigh.

"I like the way you get mad, sweetheart," he said, both eyes opening to stare at her with amusement. When she stared back at him, he glanced at the long furrows she'd raked into his skin with her nails. Susan flushed.

Squirming back a little, she felt the heavy heat of his body against her thigh, felt him stir at the memory. Her flush deepened painfully, and she swallowed.

"Hunter, you know this can't go on. I have to go back. I have to find Pete. He'll be wondering where I am, and if I'm all right. He'll be worried."

"Barton will likely tell him. Or anybody else who saw us. Which means half the town. The other half knows by now, I'm certain."

Susan stared at him. He looked totally unconcerned. A slow, hot light burned in his eyes, and she saw a faint smile press the corners of his mouth. Her voice shook slightly.

"Do you care so little for my feelings that you'd make me a whore in front of the entire town?"

His mouth tightened. "No one would dare call you that."

"Not to your face maybe, or even mine, but they would behind my back." She dropped her lashes and couldn't stop the flow of words from her mouth. "Hunter, I can't marry you, I just can't. I'd like to in a way, but it would never work and you know it. Not now. Not after everything that's happened. You'd never know why I married you, and I would never believe that you wanted only me." She paused and gasped when his hands tightened painfully on her upper arms and added quickly, "You know it's true! You know it!"

"Dammit, Susan, that's *not* true." His eyes were bleak and cold, and she saw his rage replace the lights of desire. "If you would just stop and think for a minute instead of being so damned worried about what everyone's going to say, you'd see that I've wanted you since the first day we met. If I just wanted to buy or lease your damned land, would I have gone to all this trouble? Do you think I'd have done this if Mrs. Johnson or Mrs. Purdy owned it? Can you see me out courting either of them under the full moon?"

He gave her a rough shake when she giggled. "Oh, Hunter, I didn't think of that!"

"You didn't think, period." He released her with a slight shove and lay back on the pillows again. Curving one arm behind his head, he frowned at her with irritation.

Susan sat up. She looked at him for a long moment. "I should go back anyway," she said. "Pete *will* be worried about me. Especially if someone tells him that you literally dragged me down the middle of the street to your lair."

"Lair? You make me sound like a wolf."

"Lion," she said, remembering her earlier impression of him. "A golden, fierce lion."

A slow smile slanted his mouth. "Isn't there some sort of nursery rhyme about that? About what big teeth you have, or something like that?"

"That's Little Red Riding-Hood and the big bad wolf. You don't qualify, I'm afraid." Susan's head tilted to one side, and she raked his long, golden body with an assessing gaze. "In fact, I'm not certain which fable you would qualify for. I don't see you as the lion with a thorn in his paw, or the fox—wait. Yes. That's you. The fox who fools the gingerbread man into climbing on his back on the pretext of taking him across the stream, then gobbling him up."

His hand flashed out to curl around her wrist and drag her toward him. "Do you think so?" he murmured against her mouth when she lay across his chest, her breasts rubbing against him.

Her heart leapt. "Yes," she managed to say around the sudden lump in her throat, "I do. Foxes are full of guile and trickery."

"So are black-eyed Susans. . . ."

"Hunter—oh, God, Hunter," she gasped when his head bent, and he flicked his tongue across the erect peak of a nipple grazing his chest. She arched backward. "I really . . . should be . . . going. . . ."

"Later." His mouth moved to her other breast, leaving a trail of hot, moist kisses in its wake. She shuddered, and he put a hand on her shoulder and pushed her slowly back to the mattress.

"But Pctc will be wondering where I am," she protested again, weaker this time, her voice fading slightly on the last word.

"He knows where to find you." Hunter drew in a sharp breath that created a cool wind on her wet breast and made her arch sinuously beneath him. "He can come here."

"Oh, my God!" Susan pushed hard at him, using the heels of her hands. He was immovable and just lifted his head to look at her through narrowed eyes.

"What?"

"If Pete comes here—well, he just can't. I would die. It would be mortifying. And he might . . . might draw on you." She looked up, her eyes huge, dark, and shining. "Would you kill him like—would you?"

Hunter's mouth twisted. "Like I did who? Franks? Not unless he left me no choice. I don't think Sheridan's that stupid."

Half sobbing, she tried to wrench away. "Oh, God, what have I done? I should never have fallen in love with you, never have let this go so far. . . ."

His hands tightened on her, and his voice was hard. "I intend to marry you, Susan. We wouldn't be the first two people to rush the wedding day a little bit."

"I told you—"

"No. Don't say it. I don't care what you think now,

you know you want to marry me. It's just all that stupid land rights stuff that has you in a heat about it. It'll blow over."

"And if it doesn't?"

"It will." He slid an arm under her hips to pull her up into him when she tried to twist away. "I told you—you're staying with me."

Her voice came out all wrong, quivery and faint instead of forceful. "I can't . . . Pete . . . there will be trouble."

Hunter rolled onto his back with a groan and bent an arm over his eyes. His mouth tightened with frustration. "I wish a damn blizzard would hit," he snarled, "then I would not have to listen to you whining about being found in bed with me. You're the damnedest female I ever met—you'll do it, but won't admit it, and won't marry to make it right."

That stung, and Susan rose to her knees to snarl back at him, "And you expect me just to fall into bed with you whenever you drop your pants?"

His arm lowered. He glared at her. "It'd be nice."

Spluttering furiously, she opened her mouth to tell him what she thought of that, when a strange noise pattered on the roof. Instead of saying what she'd intended, she said, "What was that?"

Hunter had already swung his legs over the side of the bed and was striding toward the window with his gun in his hand. He stepped to one side, gave the shade a tug and a snap, and it rolled up with a flapping noise. Gray light flooded the room, putting his muscled body in sharp relief. Susan was so busy staring at him that it took a moment for her to drag her attention to what was outside the window. It was Hunter's soft laugh that gained her attention.

Her eyes widened when she swung her gaze around.

"Snow! In July? Is it snowing?"

"No. It's hail. But the biggest hailstones I've ever seen." He turned and slid her an amused glance. "Not quite a blizzard, but the next best thing, I think."

Susan opened her mouth to argue but could find nothing to say. Closing it, she smiled instead.

Hunter pulled the shade back down and crossed the room to her, tossing his gun back on the bedside table to scoop her up into his arms. "Does that satisfy your worries for a few minutes?" he muttered in her ear, and she nodded against the angle of his neck and shoulder.

"Yes. You must have a guardian angel that was listening to you. I've never seen a wish granted so quickly."

"Take it as a sign, Susan," he breathed against her ear in a warm, husky gust of air that made her shiver. She still knelt on the mattress, and he had one knee on the bed and the other foot on the floor. His body rubbed against hers, and he knew she could feel his growing arousal. It nudged against her bare belly, hard and insistent.

Twisting, he took her with him as he lay back on the mattress, holding her upright. He looked up at her face, at the glowing dark eyes and wild tumble of sable curls that rioted over her shoulders and down her back. God, she was so beautiful. And sweet. And maddening. Half the time he didn't know if he wanted to kiss her or smack her. Kissing always won out.

"Make love to me, sweetheart," he urged, sliding his hands down her arms to her wrists and bringing her hands to his lips. He kissed the palms, then each finger, his tongue wetting the skin and tasting her. He saw the brief flash of confusion on her face and smiled against a hand.

"Like this," he said and dragged her hands down over

his chest, sucking in his breath sharply at her touch on him, groaning aloud when she took the initiative and curled a hand around him. His body leapt beneath her untutored caress, and he shoved upward. "Yeah," he said in a panting moan, "like that."

Stroking her hand up and down his rigid body, Susan gave him a shy smile when he stared up at her hazily. He knew she had to see the pleasure in his eyes. It had to be obvious. Curling his fingers into the bedsheets, he fought for control as she held him and caressed him, and when she bent her head to kiss him, touching him lightly with the tip of her tongue, he clenched his teeth to keep from groaning aloud.

Exquisite arrows of pleasure shot through him, from his head to his toes and all that was between throbbing with hot need. He couldn't help the small thrusts of his hips up at her, the rhythmic strokes of his body that mimicked the sex act; his hands slid up her arms again, and he cupped her breasts in his palms, feeling the weight of them, teasing the taut nipples until he heard her gasp.

Shifting, he reached for her to push her back into the mattress and mount her, but she avoided him. Shaking her head, she put a hand on the flat ridge of muscles banding his belly and held him there while she straddled him. Hunter sucked in a deep breath. Positioning a knee on each side of his thighs, she lifted her body over him and slowly sank down.

He did groan aloud at that, a long, husky sound of pure pleasure that vibrated like the throaty purr of a lion. His lashes half lowered over his eyes as he looked up at her, watching her face, the intense concentration that knit her brow and made her bite her lower lip between small white teeth. That fascinated him; the press of her teeth into the smooth, satiny surface of her lip, the slight quiver as she gasped and closed her eyes.

When he moved to grasp her around the waist and bring her down hard, Susan grabbed his wrists in her hands and held them out to the sides, smiling at him. He allowed her to hold him, a faint, lazy smile curling his mouth. Still holding him, she began to lift up and down, her breasts swaying over his chest, occasionally grazing the skin with her tight nipples. Hunter held his breath, swallowed a loud groan, and glanced down to see himself disappearing inside her. It jolted him, made him throb with an urgent need to dominate her, to pull her up and down on him in a rhythm of his own choosing, and he had to hold back.

Sweat glazed his skin as he restrained the desire to set the pace, and outside the hail beat down on the roof in a driving noise that drowned out everything but the fierce surge of blood through his veins. Hunter dug his heels into the bed and surged upward when she was coming down, ramming his hard body into her, grunting with the effort to hold back. He was almost crazy from it; the need to pound into her was setting him aflame, and he ground his teeth.

"Susan . . . God—you've got to let me . . ."

She looked up at him. "Let you what?" She lifted her hips and drove down again, impaling herself in a silky, hot slide. "Don't you like this?" Her breasts raked over his chest again, and he coiled forward, grasping a nipple with his lips and tugging until she moaned aloud. He kept at it, watching her face; her eyes drifted closed, and her mouth opened and her head tilted back.

Hunter brought his arms up and put his hands at her waist at the same time as he rose up into her, slamming her down onto him in a move that was pleasure or agony, he wasn't certain which. It tore a groan from him, made his back arch up toward her again. Sliding his hands from her waist to her buttocks, he drove up again and again, his breath coming hard and fast, rattling harshly in his lungs.

Susan cried out, arching her back, moving atop him in a wild, thundering ride as he held her. Her thighs spread to take in more of him, and he felt the rushing heat of his release sweep up; he held it. Clenching his teeth, he held her as she rocked back and forth, her breath coming in short, fast pants for air. He waited, waited until he felt the hot, silken convulsions of her inner body tighten around him; when she cried out again and went still with a strangled gasp, he dug his hands into her soft skin and heaved upward again, letting his body explode inside her.

It was pain, pleasure, sweet release. It was love, and he knew it. He held her in his arms while his breathing gradually slowed, while she sagged over him with her face pressed against his neck and shoulder. A fierce surge of protectiveness enveloped him, and he knew he'd never let her go. Never. She was his.

He held her until she finally stirred, lifting her head to gaze down at him with lazy, dark eyes.

"Has anyone ever died from that?" Susan asked in a thick drowsy voice, and Hunter laughed softly against her cheek.

"Not in my arms, I'm afraid."

"Oh. Then I'm the first."

"Are you dead?"

"I think so." She was silent for a moment, then said, "I hope not. I want to do it again sometime."

Stroking back the damp tendrils of hair from her temple and forehead, Hunter tightened his arm around her. "I think we can arrange that."

She lowered her head again. "Good."

Curling her feet under her, Tabitha looked down at the huge hailstones littering Los Alamos. "Did you see all those people run for cover? Looked like fleas on a burning dog, didn't they?"

Horatio stifled a sigh. "What a quaint comparison— yes, I did see them, Tabitha. Do you think you've succeeded?"

"Lord love a duck, I hope so!" She shook her head. "I have rarely seen two such reluctant, star-crossed lovers!" She paused. "Well, unless they were in one of Shakespeare's plays. Have you noticed how much more popular he is dead than alive, by the way?"

Ignoring her question, Horatio asked, "How do you propose to solve the rest of her problems?"

Tabitha stood up and shook dirt from her skirts. "I don't. Leave that up to the cowboy. He's capable enough. Besides, he owes me. If I hadn't sent that blizzard he asked for, he'd be sitting there counting his toes while Susan trotted off up the street."

"So you've solved everything?"

Heaving a sigh, Tabitha said tartly, "Since you keep bringing it up, I suppose I haven't. What's wrong now?"

"Just bringing them together like that doesn't solve the problem of the brooch and Evan Elliott. Has that occurred to you?"

"Obviously not." Tabitha shrugged with annoyance. "Can you point out the error of my reasoning?"

"Reasoning, no. Ways, yes." He ignored her irritated mutter of "How kind!" and pressed his fingers together at the tips to form a steeple. "Perhaps you should direct your energies toward erasing the danger to Miss Whitten instead of assuring her marital bliss. Though I agree that Mr. Carson seems quite capable of taking care of her in many ways, he is not omnipotent."

Tabitha snorted. "Omnipotent! You would use a two-pence word like that! I thought I was limited in what I could do and how I could arrange matters. Now I'm supposed to sweep down there and carry Elliott or Thorne off in a blazing chariot or some such thing? Poppycock!"

"You're to do no such thing." Horatio looked insulted. "I merely pointed out the flaw in your plan. It is up to you to devise a method of rescuing your descendant without upending the affairs of man."

"Affairs of man. Affairs of man." She rolled her eyes. "Whatever happened to the art of communication? Why must I *arrange* rescue?"

Horatio gave her a long-suffering glance. "Your last effort at communication did not exactly convey the correct message. Miss Whitten thought you meant she was not to trust the very man she was supposed to trust."

"She's an idiot. I can't help that. I should have been given—wait. That's not fair. She's not an idiot. She's just confused." Tabitha sighed. "Very well. Let me think."

She stared glumly down at the town, propping her chin in her palm and resting her elbow on her knee. The hail had stopped, and people were coming out of stores and houses, looking up at the sky, exclaiming excitedly and picking up the frozen precipitation from the street. Some of the horses had been caught out in it and bolted, and now their owners trekked off to find them. Pete Sheridan came out of the general store and looked up and down the street, found the wagon and team hitched up under an awning at the loading dock of the granary, and set off.

Tapping her toe into the dust, Tabitha blinked at the fine grains boiling into the air, drifting on the wind. She looked up with a smile. Horatio watched her warily.

"I've got it," she said. "The perfect solution."

Evan gazed at the plump, garrulous woman sitting across from him with a pained expression. Then he slid an incredulous glance at the bartender behind the long, curved bar.

"How long did you say you'd been working here, ma'am?" he asked politely, looking back at her with a sigh.

Smiling, the woman chirruped, "Only a few days, but I have big plans. Yes, big plans. I want to stay here. This is a town on the rise, I can see that, yessirree, a town on the rise. Why, I'll bet—"

"A few days, huh?" Evan interrupted with a shake of his red head. "I haven't seen you." He managed a polite smile. "It was nice meeting you, though, and I'm sure I'll see you again." He put his hands on the table palms down and started to rise, and the woman stopped him. There was something compelling in her gaze, in the shrewd blue eyes that caught and held his.

"You don't want to leave yet. I have something to tell you." She moved in a rustle of red satin, and the feather in the wide hat she wore bobbed over her eyes.

He stared at her uncertainly. "You do?"

"Yes. About Susan."

Evan sat back down, looking at her suspiciously. "Why do you think I'd want to know anything about Susan?"

"Odd," the woman mocked, "you don't *look* stupid."

Flushing to the roots of his sandy red hair, Evan's mouth tightened. "All right. Tell me."

"There's been a lot going on out at the Lazy W.

Someone has been stealing Susan's cattle."

Evan blanched. "What's that got to do with me? I don't know anything about it."

"No one said you did. Or maybe, someone just suggested you might know." Silence followed that statement, then she added, "Susan always protects her friends anyway."

Evan nodded slowly. "Does she know who stole them?" he asked after a moment and narrowed his eyes at her when she shook her head.

"No, but the sheriff said he thought he did. And I think Hunter Carson intends to try and catch them."

His lips curled in a sneer. "Carson? That ought to be funny. I bet he couldn't find his ass in a snowstorm."

The woman blinked at that, then shrugged. "Well, I do think people are watching out now. It's said that she has a man guarding her all the time."

"Susan?" He seemed startled. "Does she need a guard? I don't know anyone who'd hurt her—except Carson, and she's too starry-eyed to listen about him. Or was. He won't give her the time of day now, and she's still cold as—aw hell, it don't matter." The last was said in a bitter voice.

"That's the way it is with young girls." She waved a blithe hand. "Some handsome fellow comes along and turns their heads, and they fall in love. Won't listen to friends who've listened to them for years." Her eyes grew misty with memory, and she stared past Evan at a distant spot on the saloon wall. "Then jealousy sets in, and before you know it, poof! Someone gets pushed down a flight of stairs and ends up with a broken neck. All over a stupid brooch—"

Jerking to a halt, she blinked and looked at Evan. "Sorry. I believe I got distracted by another story."

He was looking at her closely, his face white and set in grave lines. "Did you?" He leaned nearer. "You have an odd accent, ma'am. Mind telling me where you're from? I just happen to know somebody who talks sorta like you. You might know him."

Flustered, she said quickly, "Oh, I'm sure I don't. I don't know hardly anyone around here. Just Susan. I was acquainted with her mother a long time ago. I think I've wasted enough of your time. Hope you'll help her if you can. She's a nice girl."

"Wait—"

"Later. We'll talk later. Must go now."

Evan sat back in his chair and stared after the woman as she got up and scurried across the floor. She stepped behind the curtain that separated the private rooms from the rest of the saloon. No one remarked on her absence, and even though he waited, she didn't come out again. Finally he got up and crossed to the bar.

"Riley, where's that older woman who works here? You know," he added impatiently when the bartender stared at him, "the one with the frizzy hair?"

"Naomi? She's right there."

"No," Evan said with an impatient shake of his head. "Not her. Don't you think I know her by now? This one said she's only been here a few days. She's new, kinda plump, real thin eyebrows—"

"I don't know who you're talking about, Evan." Riley shook his head. "We ain't hired anybody new in months. Still got the same whores we've always had."

Leaning against the bar, Evan got an uneasy feeling in his gut. He didn't like it. And he didn't like hearing that Susan had been losing cattle. He had this inescapable feeling that he knew who was behind it, and he didn't like that, either. Dammit, he almost had things worked out. He sure didn't need another complication. There had been too many spooky things happening lately. Made him wonder if he shouldn't just give up. But he couldn't. He was in too deep now.

He pushed away from the bar and crossed the saloon. The double doors swung wildly when he went through them, and his spurs rattled as he strode down the wooden sidewalk. He found Peter Thorne reading a newspaper in the hotel lobby.

Looking up as Evan entered, Thorne smiled. "Hullo! I didn't expect to see you this early. Quite an unusual bit of weather we're having, what?"

"You been rustlin' cattle, Thorne?" Evan demanded in a low voice, his eyes fixed on the Englishman.

"Whatever are you talking about, old boy?"

Evan plucked the newspaper from Thorne's hands. "Susan. Cattle. Lazy W." He tossed the crumpled paper aside. "Put it together for me, will you?"

A slightly hard expression tightened Thorne's smile and made him look suddenly dangerous. "Really, old boy," he said silkily, "if I was, this would hardly be the place to discuss it, now would it?"

Evan sat down in a threadbare velvet chair and looked at Thorne. "It's true, then. Why?" His voice was strained and obviously distressed.

"Don't carry on. In the first place, I never said I was responsible for any missing cows. In the second place, if someone has taken it upon themselves to filch a few of her bloody cows, that can only help you."

"How do you figure that?"

He waved an airy hand. "Simple. She needs cattle to make money. Less cattle, less money. Less money, the better the chance she will part with the brooch." His gaze grew hard and cold. "Have you even asked her about it?

Do you know where she keeps it?"

Evan looked away. "I haven't asked her about it, but I know where she keeps it." His spurs jingled when he shifted his feet. "I think it's best if I don't ask her. Then she won't be suspicious of me when it comes up missing."

"I suppose you know," Thorne said after a moment, "that there are rumors Miss Whitten intends to allow the railroad access to part of her land."

Evan's mouth tightened. "Yeah. I heard that. If she does, she won't need money, that's for certain."

"I also heard," he went on as if Evan hadn't spoken, "that Hunter Carson has been given the boot. That allows you in, old boy. If you play your cards right, as you Texans say."

Evan looked thunderstruck. "He has? I knew that Susan hasn't seen him in three weeks . . . from what I've seen, he's been mean as a snake lately. How'd you find out she's not going to marry him?"

"One should always keep a finger on what is going on with underlings. Cowboys talk, I've discovered, and rumor in this case seems to be true." He smiled at the look on Evan's face. "I see the knowledge pleases you."

"Yeah. It pleases me a lot. I thought about drawing on Carson, but . . ." A bitter smile curled his mouth. "Charley Franks made the mistake of bracing him a few days ago. I saw it. Charley never cleared leather before Carson shot him." He rubbed his jaw. "I always thought Charley was pretty fast. Now I know how Carson got that gunslick reputation. He's fast. Damned fast. And cold as ice in January. He didn't flick an eyelash. Just shoved in new bullets and walked off like nothing had happened."

"Do I detect fear?" Peter Thorne mocked, and Evan shook his head.

"No. Respect, maybe, same as I'd respect a rattler."

"I see. It's fortunate that Miss Whitten no longer has him hanging around her, then."

Evan looked up with a speculative gleam in his eyes. "Yeah. I'd call that fortunate for somebody."

Sitting forward, Peter Thorne said softly, "I think we have wasted enough time. I think it's time for us to collect what is due us."

Evan shrugged. "I just hope we get what we're hopin' for, not necessarily what's due."

"How fatalistic." Thorne's eyes narrowed. "Are you beginning to feel faint about this?"

"I don't like the idea of stealing from Susan, no. But I think I'll be doing her a favor in the end." He met the Englishman's cold gray eyes. A frown knit his brow. "Do you know a woman who talks like you here in Los Alamos?"

Thorne sat back. "I beg your pardon?"

"A woman, plump, talks a lot. Has an accent like yours. Do you know her?"

Looking faintly startled, Thorne shook his head. "No, I have no idea whom you may mean. Why?"

"Oh. No reason. She's just—odd. Says funny things." He raked a hand through his sandy-red hair, then tugged his hat back on his head. "All right. Tomorrow. I'll get it from her then. Are you going to leave town with it?"

"My dear chap, as soon as you put it in my hand!" A faint grimace crossed his aristocratic face. "I detest all this blowing sand and dust and heat. Even the brief relief today made it worse. Now it's muggy."

"Guess you have to be used to it." Evan stood up. "I'll get back in touch with you as we'd planned."

"Good idea." He paused, smiled. "Until then, why don't you think about how grateful Miss Whitten will be that you still want to marry her?"

"Grateful?"

"I can't imagine that dallying with Hunter Carson has enhanced her reputation any—have I erred, Mr. Elliott?"

Evan had taken a menacing step forward, his hands knotted into fists. He sucked in a deep breath. "Yeah. Don't mention her name again. All right? I'll get you the damned brooch, you give me the money, and we're quits. Got it?"

"Got it."

Peter Thorne stared after Evan until he'd disappeared from sight. Then he rose from the settee and went down the street to send a telegram. There would be a lot of wheels set in motion once he had the brooch in his hands.

Chapter 16

PETE SHERIDAN LOOKED from Hunter to Susan and back. His eyes were hooded, his muscles tense. "Reckon we need to talk, Carson."

"Pete—" Susan began quickly, but Hunter's hand on her arm tightened.

"No. He's right. We need to talk. And we don't need you in here," he added when she moved toward a chair. He tucked a finger under her chin and kissed her quickly, smiling a little at her blush. "Don't worry, sweetheart. It's not a killing matter." His cool gaze over her head dared Sheridan to disagree, and he didn't.

But when Susan had disappeared from the neat, sparsely furnished study, Pete turned to Hunter and asked abruptly, "What are your intentions, Carson? Straight out."

"Straight out?" Hunter's smile was faintly ironic. "I'd marry her now, if she'd do it. I'd have married her three weeks ago if she hadn't gotten some damned notion in her head that I was out to cheat her." His gaze was direct. "Is that what you wanted to know?"

"Among other things." Pete raked a hand across his jaw. "I already told you how it stands for me. I've got an obligation to her, sorta. I want to know what you plan for her future."

"Whatever she wants. Within reason." He pushed away from the desk. "I don't need to tell you that Susan is a strong-willed female. You know that already.

I've got a few businesses to run, and sometimes I have to travel. She can go with me, or she can stay here. The Lazy W is hers, plain and simple, out and out. I can help her, or I can stay out of it. It doesn't make much difference to me. It's her decision."

"And the railroad?"

"Ah. The railroad." Hunter shrugged. "That's a bit of a problem. I'm just an investor, see, and I've got partners. I may not care whose land those tracks cut through, but you can bet there are those who do." He frowned. "I thought of offering a deal to Elliott, but I don't think he'd take it. Not now. And besides that, it's eight miles out of the way to use his land."

"Have you talked to Susan about this?"

"Partly. Not in detail."

Pete looked down at his feet. "You might want to do that. She's got ideas of her own, you know."

"Yeah, I know."

Silence stretched for a moment, then Pete looked up at Hunter. "I know your reputation as a gunslick, Carson. And I don't care. You hurt one hair on that girl's head, I'll come after you. I mean it."

"I know you do. And if I ever hurt her, I'll deserve killing."

Pete grunted. "Huh. She's liable to tie you up in a bunch of knots so fast you won't know what hit you. I might be warnin' the wrong person."

Grinning, Hunter said, "I'll take my chances."

Susan gave Blaze her head. She felt lighthearted, almost carefree in spite of everything. Maybe she wasn't as sure of Hunter as she'd like to be, but she was sure that he loved her. Even Pete had said—in his offhanded oblique way—that he knew Hunter would take care of her.

The first embarrassment about Pete guessing the extent of her involvement with Hunter had faded at his matter-of-fact acceptance of it. She should have known. Pete Sheridan was a man who took the world the way he found it and expected it to do the same for him.

And she had told Hunter she'd marry him, said it against his chest, the words muffled by his cotton shirt and the flex of his muscles. He'd lifted her face and kissed her and infuriated her by saying he hadn't doubted it for a moment. Before she could say the angry words on the tip of her tongue, he'd kissed her again and then delivered her to Pete with a smile and a reassuring squeeze.

"Take care of my woman for the next few days, Sheridan," he'd said casually. "Then I'll come after her."

He was coming after her, and she'd be his wife. . . .

Susan leaned over her mare's neck, nudging her with the heels of her short boots, letting the horse run with her neck stretched out and the wind whipping across them. In a few days she'd be married to Hunter. She'd be his wife, and then . . . and then they'd face whatever the future held as man and wife.

It filled her with anticipation at the same time as it did a spurt of fear. The world was so uncertain at times, so precarious a place to be. Could she risk loving so much? Everything she'd deeply loved had been taken from her. No, she realized a moment later, it hadn't. There was Doris. And Pete. And even that silly pig she loved. She still had them.

Reining her mount to a slower pace, Susan sat up and pushed her hat back so that it dangled against her back.

A cloud passed in front of the sun and shadowed the land for a moment, and she half turned in her saddle to look back at the slower wagon. Pete had yelled at her when she'd first taken off, but she'd ignored him. Now they were just distant specks against the burning land around them, the scrub and mesquite and flat-topped ridges on the horizon. She'd ridden farther than she'd intended and knew Pete would be furious with her when she rode back to the wagon.

Sighing, Susan wheeled Blaze around and nudged her into a gentle lope down the brush-studded slope. Dust rose in a hazy cloud, and she pulled her neckerchief up over her nose and mouth to keep from choking on it.

A pair of roadrunners skimmed across the land in front of her, startling Blaze into snorting and half rearing, and Susan concentrated on keeping the horse from bolting. Silly mare, she thought irritably, as if she hadn't seen hundreds of the small brown birds in their rides! But now the horse chose to rear and snort and plunge, dancing sideways in a series of hops that carried her over a clump of cactus.

Cactus grew thickly in places and lay scattered over the slopes in a random pattern, cropping up unexpectedly. Prickly pear and beaver tail cactus sprouted haphazardly, catching unwary horses and horsemen.

Blaze screamed as the sharp, spiny needles scraped the tender flesh of her fetlocks, and Susan fought to control the panicked mare. When the horse reared up again, Susan wheeled her around with a mighty effort, and the horse came down on her forelegs in a hop that jarred Susan's teeth. The chin strap of the bridle got caught up under the mare's lower lip, and taking the bit in her teeth, Blaze struck out in a maddened run across the prairie. Susan swore under her breath, using one of Pete's favorite phrases. She was in for a time of it if she didn't get the mare slowed.

Grimly hanging on, Susan was vaguely aware that Pete was pounding after her, spurring his quarter horse gelding into a dead run. She caught the glimpse of movement, could barely hear his shout over the pounding hooves and rasping breath of her mount, and thought that she was doing good just to hang on. She tried to bring Blaze's head around to the side, to turn her in a run, wide at first, then tighter until she finally slowed, but her efforts were having no effect. A loud crack in the air startled her, sounding like a shot. She felt her horse falter, slow, stumble.

Dammit, Susan just had time to think before there was a hard jolt, and she knew that Blaze must have fallen. Then there was no more time to think, no time to do anything but try to stop her own headlong flight through the air. There was the empty sensation of weightlessness, a searing fall, then a jarring crash, and everything went black.

Coming slowly out of the painful black shrouds that clung to her, Susan opened her eyes. It was dark. She hurt. She couldn't see anything, and she blinked, wondering for one terrified instant if she was blind.

But then she knew it was only night, for she saw the faint shadowed movements around her grow clearer. A groan slipped from her, and her head throbbed mercilessly.

"Awake, huh?" an unfamiliar voice said from somewhere just above her, and she shut her eyes again.

It hurt to think, and somehow, she knew that voice was not friendly. There was a hint of malice in it, of enjoyment in her discomfort. When Susan tried to move her hands and found that they were tied together at the wrists, she realized the danger. She opened her eyes again.

"Where am I?" she asked in a voice that didn't sound at all like hers. "Who are you? Why am I tied up?"

"Curious little bitch, ain't ya?" the man muttered. "I ain't telling ya nothin'. And don't go yammerin' at me. It won't do ya no good, and I'll gag ya if ya do."

Susan believed him. There was grim satisfaction in his tone. Her head ached, her body throbbed in several places, and her muscles screamed protest every time she tried to shift to a more comfortable position. Blinking against the pain that scored her every movement, she tried to see if she recognized anything.

Shadows filled the room. A low fire burned in a small stove, and she could smell coffee. That started her stomach to rumbling, and she closed her eyes again. It looked like one of the line shacks built at intervals for cowhands to use as refuge when out with the cattle. But she had no idea who it belonged to. It could even be one of her own, for all she knew.

She was lying on a rough cot; a blanket had been tossed carelessly across her lower body. Ropes bound her wrists, harsh against her tender skin, chafing her. Her neckerchief was still around her neck, and she thought suddenly of her mare. Blaze. Had they shot her?

"Who shot my horse?" she asked, and the man turned toward her again, a darker shape against the light of the fire, his face shadowed by night and the brim of his pulled-down hat.

"What's it matter?"

"Damn you, that was a good horse!"

Derision fringed his words when he said, "Still is. I'm a good enough shot to keep from killin' if I don't wanna."

Before Susan could feel any relief over the fact that her mare had not been killed, the man added, " 'Sides, I took a likin' to that mare. She's fast, if a little spooky at times. I kin git that outa her."

"She's my horse, not yours," Susan said, more to keep him talking than anything else. He might accidentally drop a hint as to where she was or why she was there if she could keep him talking to her. "You won't be able to keep my horse. She's too much for most people to handle."

Snarling a curse, the man spat on the floor. "Don't be tryin' to git my back up, lady. You ain't gonna have a damn thing to say about who gits that mare. You ain't gonna have a damn thing to say about anything."

"Don't be too sure of that. When my foreman comes after you, you'll wish you'd left me alone." Pain throbbed in hot waves, blurring her world with a red haze as Susan tried to focus on her captor. He was laughing at her.

"Shit, lady—*Miz Whitten*—Pete Sheridan don't have a clue where you are. You kin rot here, and he'll never know it."

She heard the creak of leather as he rose to his feet, caught a quick glimpse of double holsters hanging on him, had an impression of medium height. There was something vaguely familiar about the man, but she couldn't think, couldn't recall what it was. Closing her eyes again, Susan gave in to a wave of pain before she forced herself alert again.

"Maybe you're not aware of this," she began much more coolly than she felt, "but Hunter Carson is a friend of mine. He won't be too happy when he finds out you've taken me like this."

The man gave a grunt that Susan took to mean he hadn't known that. She wiggled around on the cot to stare at him in the shadows. "He'll come after you," she added softly and was startled by the short bark of laughter.

"That's th' general idea, Miz Whitten. That's th' general idea." Laughing, he shook his head and struck a match along the floor. He held it up to a cigarette jutting from his mouth, and the spurt of flame illuminated his face as he lit his smoke.

Susan's heart dropped. Duncan. Greet Duncan, the man she had fired months before. Revenge, then? But how? Why? And why would he care about Hunter? She hadn't even known Hunter existed then, hadn't fallen in love with him.

She stared at him in the dark and wondered if her fear showed on her face. Greet Duncan was the kind of man who'd do sneaky, evil things if he thought he could get away with it, the kind of man who'd hurt helpless animals. He wasn't the kind of man to plan and carry out a scheme of revenge. Or at least, she'd never thought so before now.

Taking a stab in the dark, she asked, "Who's your boss in this?"

The match flame extinguished in a blur as he shook it, and the tip of his cigarette glowed orange-red in the dark. "Don't make no difference. Don't git any big ideas. You're here and you're gonna stay here until I say different."

That answered her question. He was working for someone else. Someone who could plot and execute a daring kidnapping right under the nose of her foreman and three of her men. The pain at her temples radiated outward, making her eyes burn and mist.

Susan lay quietly, listening as Duncan rose to his feet and stoked the fire, keeping it burning low, heating the tin coffeepot over the glowing coals. He poured himself a cup of coffee; the liquid sound goaded her thirst.

"May I have some water?" she asked, and he swore softly.

"Yeah, in a minute. Don't git in a hurry, 'cause I sure ain't."

Susan bit her lip. She should have known better than to ask. He'd enjoy making her wait. Clamping her lips together in a thin line, she decided not to ask for anything else. It would only give him satisfaction.

By the time Duncan brought her a dipper of warm, musty water, Susan was too thirsty to even consider refusing it. He allowed her only a swallow or two before he took it back and said that was enough. She didn't argue, but her eyes burned into him.

Rocking back on his heels, Duncan met her gaze and a dark scowl knotted his brow. Susan felt it more than saw it, even as her eyes had adjusted to the shadowy light. He'd deliberately kept it dark in order to keep her from knowing him, to keep his identity a secret. He thought she didn't know, that she was stupid as well as fumbling in the dark. A faint, bitter laugh welled in the back of her still-dry throat, and Susan looked away.

"Hoity-toity bitch," she heard him mutter under his breath, curling to his feet. He crossed the room and dropped the dipper back into a bucket. She heard the splash and tried not to think about water.

She tried not to think about how tightly her wrists were tied, too, and how her head ached and how frightened she was. It had been midafternoon when they'd finally left Los Alamos, hours ago. Judging from the depth of the shadows in the one-room shack, it had been dark for some time. So, if Pete was looking for her— and she was sure he was—why hadn't he found her?

Closing her eyes, Susan tried to imagine the scene, tried to think how it had been so easy for someone to take her like that, right from under Pete's nose. And she wondered if Hunter had been told, and if he even knew what had happened.

Hunter, Hunter, where are you? she couldn't help but plead silently.

Almost dancing in her anger, Tabitha paced the hill with short, jerky steps. "Kidnapped! Abducted! Snatched away like a prize bauble! O, how faithless are those souls that plot and burn!"

"Tabitha, you sound like very bad prose from Master Shakespeare." Horatio met her irate gaze calmly. "Are you going to hop about all night like a frenzied toad, or do you intend to lend assistance in some small way?"

"And you say *I* have a way with words," she muttered. "Frenzied toad, indeed! Aye, Horatio, I do intend to lend assistance. I intend to go after that dangerous cowboy and set him on the trail."

"I assume you mean Hunter Carson?"

"Who else?" Tabitha ground a fist into the palm of her other hand, groaning. "That dreadful man has her prisoner, and he looks a scurvy sort of villain to me."

"I daresay he is." Silence greeted that observation, then Horatio suggested, "Perhaps you should go at once. I do not like the looks of the situation."

"Aye," she said darkly, "it looks dire."

She still stood there, and Horatio lifted a brow. "My dear Mrs. Tidwell—or should I say Saint Tabitha?—may

I inquire as to why you are so reluctant to go?"

Sighing, she said, "He makes me nervous."

"Nervous? Hunter Carson?"

She glared at him. "Yes, *nervous*, Hunter Carson! It's his eyes. I don't see how the girl stands up to him at times. He's positively frightening."

"What can he possibly do to you, even if he thinks you are batty?"

"Oh, nothing, and I know that. But still, there's something about a man with eyes like that—well, you'd have to be a woman, Horatio, and you're not."

"Quite observant of you. But I think you need to make haste. If I am not mistaken, our abductor's cohorts are even now approaching. . . ."

Tabitha muttered something Horatio didn't quite hear, then closed her eyes and concentrated. When she opened them again, she was standing on Hunter Carson's front porch. She sucked in a deep breath and gave a sharp rap on the door.

Heavy footsteps echoed inside, and Hunter swung open the door and looked down at the plump woman. "Yes?"

"May I speak to you about an urgent matter, Mr. Carson? It's quite important, I assure you," she added when he gave her a narrow stare.

"If it's about a bill for your feed—"

"No, no, no, nothing like that." A placating smile curved her lips. "It's about Susan."

That got his attention, but his mouth flattened and his eyes narrowed. "What about her?" he demanded in a hostile tone that made her take two steps back. "If this is about gossip, by God, I think you'd best—"

"Lord, no!" came out in a gasp. "Truly, this is life and death!"

Hunter swung the door wider. "It had better be." He didn't see the shudder that rippled over her as she stepped inside. "Who are you?" he asked bluntly, and she gave him a weak smile.

"Tidwell. Tabitha Tidwell. Married name. Once a Lynnf—no matter. Look, Susan is in danger."

"Danger?" The single word cracked out like a pistol shot, and Tabitha leapt again.

"Pray, don't be so violent! Yes, danger, and she needs you. Her horse ran away—oh, I don't know what I can say and what I cannot—and she was taken. Her foreman has not been able to find her, and . . . where are you going?"

He'd turned away from her and was striding into the room just off the entrance hall. Lamplight flickered over him as he snatched up his gunbelts and hat.

"You'd better not be playing a prank of some kind, Mrs. Tidwell, or I won't be too happy." The warning came as he buckled on his gunbelts, and Tabitha nodded weakly.

"No prank. Danger, like I said."

"Who sent you?" He tugged his hat on and was striding swiftly toward the door, putting an arm beneath her elbow and turning her with him as he yanked open the door again.

"Let's just say I took it upon myself to come." She gave a shrug when he looked at her closely, and she sucked in a deep breath. "Ask Doris about me sometime."

Satisfied with that answer, Hunter nodded. He escorted her down the short walk where he'd pulled Susan earlier, then left her at the gate of the neat fence. "Can you find your way back home from here?" he asked impatiently before he left her, and she nodded.

"Oh, yes. I found my way here, didn't I? Just *hurry!*"

Hunter didn't need to be told again. He half ran to the stable for his horse, saddled him, and was gone in a blur of dust down the street. Light from a nearly full moon glittered on his fair hair and silvered his silhouette as he rode east toward the Lazy W.

"Well," Tabitha said, pleased with herself. "That was neatly done." Then she stifled a small scream when she felt someone behind her. "Horatio!" She glared in the shadowed light. "Why did you sneak up on me?"

"I didn't sneak." He leaned against the white fence. "I see that you were able to get your point across this time."

"Yes, I did well. And I don't think I said too much." She frowned. "Of course, I do believe you keep changing the rules on me. No matter. Do you think he'll get there in time to keep her from harm? Oh, of course he will. His kind always does."

"Do they?"

Startled, Tabitha looked at him. "Well, nearly always. Oh, dear, you do say the most terrible things!"

Chapter 17

HUNTER FOUND THE Lazy W in chaos. Doris, usually so calm and practical, was almost frantic with worry, and Pete Sheridan lay groaning on a pallet in the house. He refused to be taken to a bed upstairs, and Doris refused to let him go to the bunkhouse. It had been a stalemate of sorts, from what Hunter gathered, with Pete ending up in the parlor.

Kneeling beside Pete, he lifted a brow. "So, how'd you get yourself into this kind of fix, Sheridan?"

Pete ignored Doris's indignant gasp and grinned weakly. "Lettin' Miss Susan have her own way, of course." He gave a short cough, and Doris leaned over him anxiously with a wet cloth and spoonful of medicine. He flashed her a quick stare that plainly said "leave me alone" and looked back up at Hunter. "That damn crazy mare of hers. Took off, got the bit in her teeth, then spooked. There was a shot. Threw her down a hill. . . ."

When he broke off to cough again and Doris pressed forward with determination and medicine, Hunter lifted his icy gaze to one of the other hands. "So where is she now?"

Murdock shifted uneasily. "There was some shootin'. Two of our men got hit, it took us by surprise so quick. They got Pete first, because he'd almost caught up to her." Shaking his head, he muttered, "Then bullets came from everywhere, and there we were in the open. We couldn't lift our heads without riskin' hot lead cleanin' out our ears. By the time we managed to get to where she was, she was gone. They hit her mare, I think. Blood everywhere." He gave an eloquent shrug. "Hell, we never even saw 'em, only the empty shells and the cut-up ground after."

"You don't know how many?"

Pete answered. "No. Maybe ten, maybe less. It was the surprise of it that caught us off-guard." He had a disgusted look on his face. "This is the first bullet I've caught in over fifteen years. And I've fought the Comanche and Apache more times than I can count. I guess I was just so mad at Miss Susan for racin' off like that . . ."

He let his voice trail into silence, and Hunter nodded grimly. By God, when he caught up to her—well, no sense in thinking like that now. He'd know what to do once she was safe again.

Rising in a smooth curl of long-muscled legs, Hunter looked down at Pete. "You better worry about what she's going to say when she gets back. You know she's liable to put the blame on you for not chasing her down earlier."

Laughing softly, Pete nodded. "Yeah, I reckon she might at that. Knowing Miss Susan."

Beckoning to Murdock, Hunter drew him aside and told him what he'd need for the morning. "How many guns we got?" he asked when Murdock nodded, and the man reeled off the names of seven men. Hunter grunted. "That'll have to do. I want them all saddled and ready to ride at first light."

Murdock flicked a glance toward Pete, and Hunter's lips flattened into a cold smile. "You can check it out with him if you want, but I'm riding early. It's up to you who goes with me."

A faint flush reddened Murdock's face. "You gotta understand, Carson, he's the man who pays us."

"I understand. But like I said, I'm riding out at first light, and if you want to go, be ready."

Murdock shoved his hat back, tugged it forward again, sighed. "Yeah. Well, I reckon you'll have us behind you. I heard of you, Carson, and . . . uh, well, we'll be with you."

Hunter's stiff stance slowly eased. "Good."

When he went out to stand on the front porch, Doris came to join him. Her soft brown hair was in wild disarray, and she had never looked quite so worried.

"You've got to find her, Mr. Carson." Her throat worked for a moment. "I can't stand to lose two of the people I love . . . most." Her voice cracked on the final words, and he moved awkwardly to put an arm around her shoulders. This didn't come naturally to him, but he felt the same as she did. He liked Pete Sheridan, respected him, but God, if he lost Susan . . . it didn't bear thinking about.

"I'll find her. I'll find her."

It was all he could say. All he could think. But he knew there had to be some reason, someone who wanted her so badly they'd risk anything to take her. And he still could not see what good it would do. Hell, the Lazy W was in as bad a financial situation as most of the other ranches in Callahan County.

Shoving his fist against the wooden porch post, Hunter felt something brush past his boots and leapt back. An odd snuffling sound relaxed him. "Stupid pig." When Doris looked at him, he pointed down. "Arthur."

She smiled slightly. "I guess I should feed him. It's past his suppertime, but I was so crazy when they brought Pete in and then told me about Susan—" She put a hand on his arm. "Do you think it was Evan?"

"Evan?" His brows snapped down. He didn't want to tell her that's exactly who he'd thought it was at first. Not until he was sure. He knew that Doris had the same kind of indulgent affection for Evan Elliott as she did Arthur. "I don't know," he compromised, and she looked at him sideways with a slight curl of her lips.

"You think it, too. Lord help me, I don't know why, but I have this feeling that he's involved somehow. And when he was here today, I tried not to be hateful or say anything about the last time he and Susan had that—"

"He was here today?" Hunter interrupted. "When?"

She sighed. "At about three or three-thirty. Somewhere about the same time as Susan was . . . was abducted."

"Neat alibi," Hunter muttered. "How convenient for him."

Leaning back against the post, Hunter cursed the dark and cursed the delays. He was helpless until sunrise. And he felt it all through his body, that curling tension that made him want to do like the Comanche and get on a horse and just ride, going nowhere, just riding for the sheer hell of it.

He dug into his vest pocket and drew out the small tobacco pouch he carried. He didn't smoke often, but he sure felt the need for it now.

"I'm going back to see what I can do for Pete," Doris said after a moment, and he noticed that she wasn't calling him Mr. Sheridan anymore. He smiled into the dark.

"All right. He looks like he's going to be okay. Hit him high on his shoulder. Unless he gets the fever . . ."

"I know. I've cleaned it, and it looks pretty good. All pink, with no bones hit." She paused. "Mr. Carson, I just want to say . . . well, I think you really care about Susan. I can see it in your face. If anyone can bring her safely home to us, it's you."

He stuck the rolled cigarette in his mouth and stared into the distance. "I'll do my best."

"I know you will."

He heard the door open and close behind her and bit down on the cigarette and lit it. Smoke curled into the air in a thin stream, flattening against the brim of his hat. It stung his eyes, and he narrowed them against it.

Jackknifing his long legs, Hunter sat down on the steps of the porch and smoked his cigarette. He considered the possibilities and came to the inescapable conclusion that Evan Elliott was somehow tied up in it. He had to be. No one else would take Susan. There just wouldn't be anything to gain from it. He flipped the cigarette butt into the air and watched it make a reddish arc before it hit the ground. Then he got up and went inside.

"Miss Wheeler," he began, and Doris looked up at him with frightened eyes. "No, it's okay. Nothing's happened. I just want to ask you something—" He took her arm and moved her away from where Pete lay drowsing. "What did Elliott do when he was here today?"

"Do?" She looked confused. "I don't understand. . . ."

"When he came today and Susan wasn't here. Did he stay? Did he wait for her or go out to the stables or anything like that?"

"No, no—oh, he did go into Mr. Jake's study to get a book he left here. But that was all."

"A book. Did you see him leave with it?"

Doris shook her head. "No, he stuck his head in the kitchen door before he left and said he couldn't find it. I didn't see it in his hands, so I guess he didn't."

"Does Susan keep anything important in that study— like the brooch Elliott wanted her to sell?"

"Well—" Doris pinkened. "Yes, she does," she finally said in a rush, and Hunter realized that she was reluctant to talk about it. His mouth hardened.

"I think you can trust me enough to—"

"Oh, it's not that! It's just that I'm not really supposed to know about the safe, you see, and yet I do. I can't help but know about it. I clean the house, and it's so easy to find—I'm sure you know what I mean."

Amused, Hunter nodded. "Can you show it to me?"

Hunter wasn't at all surprised to find the safe open, the clasp on the metal box snapped, and the wooden box with the brooch missing.

"You're sure it was in here?" he asked, and Doris nodded grimly.

"I'm quite sure. I saw her put it back in the box. We talked about it. She was laughing about a curse and told me about a Lady Tabitha Tidwell who was supposed to have been murdered for it . . . oh, God, the curse!" Doris paled, and Hunter smothered an impatient oath.

"If there's a curse on that brooch, it's probably one of rank stupidity," he said sharply, and Doris flashed him an indignant glare. He relented slightly. "Or maybe greed. I don't think it's anything worse than that."

Raking a hand through his tawny hair, Hunter slid the metal box back into the safe and covered it with the stone. A faint frown creased his brow. "What'd you say the name of the murdered woman was?"

"Lady Tabitha Tidwell. Or maybe Lynnfield. I can't quite recall. She was a Mrs. something and a Lady something and I can't keep it straight."

"Sounds familiar. Maybe I read about it."

"I don't think so. It happened in England several hundred years ago. Susan told me."

"Oh. Well." Hunter turned his mind to the present. He hated the delay, hated the inactivity. He wanted to be doing something to find her, and it galled him that he had to wait. Pacing impatiently, he didn't even notice when Doris left the study and closed the door behind her.

As the night dragged on, Hunter knew he'd have to get some rest. He stretched out on the rug where he'd made love to Susan and closed his eyes, thinking he'd never be able to sleep.

When he woke, it was almost dawn and the pig was curled up next to him. Hunter slanted the animal a wry glance. It snuffled blearily, opening one eye to gaze at him as if asking why he was being disturbed.

"Damn pig," Hunter muttered but slid a hand down over the soft skin in a brisk rub. Arthur groaned and stretched his legs out, rolling a little to one side to allow Hunter free access to his pudgy belly. His hooves scrabbled wildly in empty air when Hunter found an itchy spot, just like a dog would do, and Hunter grinned. "Damn pig," he said again, and Arthur seemed to regard it as highest praise. He stuck his snout up under Hunter's hand when he stopped rubbing him and sat up. He rubbed him idly for a moment.

Curling to his feet, Hunter raked a hand across his beard-stubbled jaw, then headed for the kitchen. He could smell coffee and knew Doris must already be awake.

By the time the eastern sky had a faint brushing of pearly pink to outline the hills, Hunter was saddled and ready. Eight men rode with him; seven guns plus Murdock. He nodded once and touched his spurs to the chestnut he rode. It sprang forward, fresh and eager, and clods of dirt flew up from beneath its hooves. The yard of the Lazy W was cut up by the thunder of hooves as the men rode out, and Doris stood on the front porch and watched anxiously.

"Dear Lord," she said aloud, pressing her hands to her mouth, "bring her home safe to us. . . ."

Susan was still awake. She'd slept fitfully, off and on all night, tossing and turning on the hard cot and keeping a watchful eye on her abductors. Sometime during the night more men had ridden in, and she felt definitely uneasy. It was obvious that something was going on, and she didn't know what.

Her hands were numb. Someone—not Duncan—had given her some more water, a full dipper this time. That had brought on the uncomfortable necessity of using a convenience, of which there was none. She held it as long as she could, and when sunrise began to show in the eastern sky and she knew that it would be even more embarrassing in full daylight, she finally conveyed her desire to one of the men.

Grumbling, he had a brief conference with Duncan, and to her horror, it was he who escorted her out to the nearest clump of bushes. She was dragged to her feet and shoved roughly to the door of the shack. Sagging from the painful surge of blood into her cramped muscles, Susan felt him yank her back up.

He laughed harshly. "Don't look so high and mighty now, do ya? Hell, ya don't look that fine at all to me. Bet you lay there all night thinkin' about how scared ya are, and ya should be."

Susan drew herself up, fighting the wave of dizziness that washed over her. "No," she managed to say calmly, "I lay awake thinking how dead you're going to be."

That seemed to jolt him, and Duncan drew back a hand to slap her. Someone else spoke up quickly, "Better wait on that. Mark her up and there's liable to be trouble."

"Like there ain't already?" Duncan snarled, but he didn't hit her. His hands tightened viciously around her arms, and when he shoved Susan into a clump of bushes, he refused to turn around. "Naw, and give you a chance to git away? Go ahead and do what ya gotta do. I seen it all anyway."

She stood her ground. "Not mine, you haven't!"

"Yeah, well keep arguin' about it, and that kin change, too. . . ." She capitulated at that, and he grinned, watching her step into the scrubby bushes.

Gritting her teeth, Susan managed as well as she could with her hands tied in front of her and Greet Duncan's eyes never leaving her. Thankfully, the bushes hid the most private functions, but his smirk still made her face flame.

She took as long as she could, surreptitiously scouting the countryside for familiar landmarks. East she could pick out quickly because of the faint glow on the horizon; dark shapes scoured the rolling hills, some of them flat on top, like the ridges beyond the Lazy W. She frowned. The single flat-ridged peak sliding gradually down to flatter land looked familiar. Brushy Creek slid past several hundred yards ahead; she recognized it from the stands of mesquite that stood in clumps along the banks.

Quickly bending her head, she fumbled with the buttons on the front of her skirt and stood up again. It took her several minutes to manage it with her hands tied, but she finally succeeded. Duncan was still watching her, a sneer curling his mouth. Susan met his gaze coolly. He spat deliberately at her feet.

"Reckon you know well enough now who I am, don't ya?"

"Polecats, Mr. Duncan, have a smell all their own. I knew you at once, I'm afraid."

Jerking her roughly along with him, Duncan wore an ugly look on his face as he half dragged, half shoved her into the shack. One of the men looked up from the card game being played on the crude table.

"She got yer back up again?" he asked in amusement, and the others laughed as Duncan's face suffused with color.

He gave Susan a jarring push toward the cot, laughing when she stumbled and half fell on it. She managed to roll to one side, flinging him a nervous glance.

Light pushed through the cracks in the windows, and she saw now that they'd been covered. Then she recalled that she hadn't seen any horses outside the shack, no evidence that anyone was there. An air of waiting hung over the men, showing in the occasional glances they shot at the door or windows, the air of expectation in the way they straddled the chairs around the table.

Susan couldn't help but wonder who else was involved in her abduction, even while she racked her brain to think of a reason for it. There just couldn't be a good reason; this entire situation defied logic.

With the sunrise, it began to grow hot and stuffy in the shack; she sat motionless, working her hands under the bite of the ropes, keeping them covered by the blanket. With the heat, tempers rose between the five men. Cards were dealt and shuffled, money tossed down. Susan slid an apprehensive glance at the table when one of the men snarled an accusation at another.

As the quarrel erupted, one of the man leapt back, his hand on the butt of his gun, voice raised in anger.

Susan flinched back as guns were drawn and oaths hurled in the tense air. Men grabbed at them as the chairs were overturned, and in the close quarters the report of a pistol sounded as loud as a cannon. Susan couldn't help a small scream, and she turned her face to the wall. Drawing her knees up, she tensed in preparation for flight should the opportunity arise.

A new, harsh voice cut across the scuffle, and the sharp crack of a whip sliced the air. Susan pressed back against the wall over her cot and tried to see who had come in to break up the quarrel. She was terrified; if she didn't die from a stray bullet, she was liable to be killed for some other reason. Neither prospect left her feeling as if she had a chance at all.

But then she saw the man who had come in with the whip, and her heart leapt. Evan. He had come to rescue her.

It took a moment for the realization to sink in that these men knew Evan, and that they followed his orders. And that led to the final conclusion that he was responsible for her being there.

Anger sparked in Susan, slow and hot and filling her with a rage she hadn't known she could feel toward her childhood friend. By the time he'd settled the quarrel and told the man that the shot had probably alerted half the county, she was quivering with fury. He turned toward her, and a frown flickered on his face as he dropped the whip.

"Duncan!" Evan crossed the room, throwing the man a furious look. "She doesn't look as if she's been treated as I left instructions for her to be."

"What do you expect? Hell, she'd try to run if we didn't tie her, and besides, she's got a tongue like a razor." Duncan's smile was nasty. "She's lucky I didn't gag her to boot."

"No," Evan said tautly, kneeling beside the cot and reaching for Susan's hands, "*you're* lucky you didn't gag her."

Susan snatched her hands away from him, fighting the angry tears that stung her eyes. "Don't you touch me!"

He looked startled, then annoyed. "SuSu, listen to me a minute—"

"No. I think I've listened to you too long, Evan." Her words came out in a hoarse whisper. "You're weak. You're just what you said you hated, and I didn't want to believe it. Oh, Evan, how could you do this to me?"

"To you?" His mouth tightened. "I did it *for* you. Don't you see that?"

"Obviously not." Her chin lifted, and she pulled as far away from him as she could get. Nausea welled in her, and she fought against it. He had a stricken look on his face, but she couldn't find it in her to feel sorry for him. No, not anymore. This was too much to stomach.

"Look, SuSu," he was saying impatiently, "you don't understand. This will be the end of our problems. I'm going to be rich, don't you see that? You won't have to do or sell anything you don't want to. You can marry me. I'll take care of you, like I always wanted to do."

"With blood money? With stolen money?" She laughed and felt the edge of hysteria rise. "I guess you think

I've got some hidden away to ransom myself with, but—"

He grabbed her shoulders and shook her. "Don't be stupid. No, I'm not—that's not why I did this. It's not your money. It's . . . not."

She flung her head up to glare at him. "I suppose you made a bargain, like Hunter told me. You've tried to get me to sell the brooch I inherited, and now you're going to make me pay it to go free. Well, I won't! You'll just have to kill me, Evan."

Staring at her, his blue eyes were pale flames in his face. "Does the damn thing mean that much to you? You never acted like it did. You laughed and said it was worthless to you because it wouldn't save your ranch."

"I know, but that didn't mean I would part with it. It is my legacy, Evan, just like the Lazy W. If I could have used it to help the ranch, I would have, but I couldn't. I would never sell it."

Releasing her shoulders with a shove that sent her back against the wall, Evan stood up. He looked down at her, his face tight with frustration. "Dammit, you should have said so!"

"I never thought my friend would steal from me!" she shouted back at him, ignoring the wary looks on the faces of the other men. "I never thought you would be so cruel as to kidnap me, have me terrorized all night, then waltz in here and expect me to be happy about it." She choked on a sob. "Evan, how could you?"

That last wail made him swear softly, and he turned to look at the men listening. "Wait outside," he said tersely, and they exchanged doubtful glances with one another.

One of them finally spoke up. "We ain't here by your orders, Elliott. We take our pay from—"

"I don't give a damn!" Evan snarled, taking a step toward the man. "If it wasn't for me, none of you would be here. Now wait outside!"

After a long moment's hesitation, the men began to file outside. Susan noticed they left the door open, and that long shadows fell across the light streaming in. It was obvious that they had no intentions of surrendering easily.

"Evan—" she began, but he cut her off.

"No. Don't say anything else, Susan. I don't think I can stand it if you do."

She looked at him miserably. His face was pale, and his eyes were dull and glazed with fatigue. He leaned against the table and stared down at the playing cards scattered over the floor. Finally he lifted his head again and turned to look at her.

"I guess I'll take you back. But tell me—are you in love with Hunter Carson?" His expression was stiff, waiting for her answer, and she looked away.

"Yes."

She heard his sigh, long and drawn-out. Then he said, "I thought you'd called off the marriage. At least, that's what I was told."

Sliding across the cot, she stood up and went to him. "I did, or at least, for a while I was too upset to think about it. We . . . got things straightened out between us." She held up her hands, showing him her wrists. "Would you untie me now, please, Evan?"

A crooked smile curled his mouth, and he began to tug at the rough ropes binding her wrists. The knots were tight, and he reached for the knife he had in his boot top to slice them. When he straightened, he looked over Susan's shoulder and gave a start of surprise.

"What are you doing here? I thought you were going to wait fo—"

"What, pray tell, are you doing, Mr. Elliott?" came the smooth, cultured voice, filling the room with menace. "Do you intend to set her free?"

Evan stiffened. "Yes." His glance was defiant, and he slid the knife up under the ropes around Susan's wrists.

She looked at Peter Thorne and saw the faintly amused press of a smile at the corners of his thin lips. He was wearing a suit, looking incongruous in the heat and dust and desolate location. Then her glance drifted downward, and she saw the small, two-barreled pistol he held in his palm.

Gasping, she said, "Evan!" just as Thorne pulled the trigger.

Evan staggered a step, then the pistol cracked again, and he slid sideways, the knife dropping from his hands before the ropes around Susan's wrists had been severed. There was a funny, shocked expression on his face, and two holes had been punched in his chest. Blood seeped slowly down his shirt.

Susan screamed, then screamed again and again, until Peter Thorne stepped forward and brought the palm of his hand across her face once, twice. Her head snapped back, and she stumbled to the cot again.

"Do gain control, my dear. I believe enough noise has been made up here to alert the militia."

Susan stared up at him in disbelief. Tears raked her cheeks, and the skin smarted and burned. She looked down at Evan lying on the floor half under the table, surrounded by playing cards and quite still. His eyes were closed, and he was lying on his side. She didn't see his chest moving at all. A pang of grief hit her, grief for what he'd meant to her at one time.

"You killed him," she whispered, and Thorne shrugged.

"I would have had to sooner or later. It might as well be sooner, since he'd obviously had second thoughts about the role you are to play in this little scheme."

She stared at him dazedly. "Role?"

Thorne smiled. "Quite. Who do you think engineered this complicated play, my dear Miss Whitten? The dull-witted Mr. Elliott? No, no, no. I assure you, he only went along with what I wanted him to do. I told him as little as possible."

Susan watched as Thorne flicked a speck of dust from his immaculate gray sleeve. His starched white collar and vest and gold fobs seemed fantastically out of place in the shabby line shack. So did Evan, sprawled at her feet. A sob caught in the back of her throat again, but when Thorne gave her a narrowed look, she quickly swallowed it.

He smiled. "Very good, m'dear." Bending, he flipped open Evan's vest and took something from the pocket. With a strangely satisfied smile on his face, he picked up one of the overturned chairs and steadied it, then sat down. His gaze riveted on the object he held, and Susan's eyes slowly shifted to focus on it.

She gave a start, and he laughed. "So, you recognize this, do you, Miss Whitten?"

"My brooch."

"Aye, your brooch. Now *my* brooch." He flicked open the lid of the wood and velvet box, and gave a soft sigh of pleasure. "I've waited some time for this to be returned to my family, you know."

She stared at him numbly. "I don't know what you're talking about."

"Don't you?" He smiled and lifted the brooch from its bed of velvet. "That's the trouble with Americans. None of you ever bother with your history. It's valuable to know about such things. Gives one a sense of continuity, of belonging to the past and present and future. Ah, but what would you know of that? You're brash, arrogant, thinking only of what's now." He snorted derisively. "This, m'dear, is what means something. This brooch has a most fascinating history—would you care to hear it?"

"I already have," Susan began stiffly, fighting the tremors that racked her body. Thorne seemed so comfortably chatty, completely ignoring Evan's body at his feet. After the first pistol shot, one of his men had appeared in the doorway, grinned, and disappeared. Now it seemed that her fate rested in the Englishman's hands.

Thorne waved an impatient hand. "I daresay you have not heard it correctly." He leaned forward, his pale eyes glittering. "I know the history, for my family helped forge it!"

She stared at him coldly. "I'm certain your family was responsible for the murder that brought on the curse then, if I must judge them by you, Mr. Thorne."

Laughing, he appeared to enjoy her chilly reply. "That is probably so. You see, this diamond was originally part of the treasure stolen from an Indian rajah back during the Crusades. The original stone was one hundred and seventy-two carats. Pity, but a clumsy cutter reduced its size to a mere one hundred six carats. At any rate, after King Richard gave it to your illustrious ancestor Lady Catherine of Lynnfield, it began to acquire an even greater attraction." Thorne frowned slightly. "You see, 'twas my ancestor who'd discovered it, but it was taken from him to help enrich royal coffers. After

Richard's release from Austria, my ancestor, Baron de Warenne, petitioned for its return. Obviously, it was not returned to him. Some furor about de Warenne's plotting to keep Richard in Austria or something. At any rate, it was never the countess's diamond to begin with. We have tried to recover our property for hundreds of years, without success."

"I find this story too fantastic to believe," Susan said stiffly. "You came all the way over here to steal back a brooch that you claim belonged to someone almost seven hundred years ago? I think not."

"Ah, you doubt me. I'm devastated." Thorne's smile did not reach his eyes. "No matter. Even if I had not listened to this legend of wrongdoing from my cradle, I would still want the brooch. It is *worth* a king's ransom, my child, and I have it now."

"And so you kill to take it, kill to keep it." She met his arrested gaze with a scornful stare. "I am well aware that you cannot let me live now."

"Well, well. You are more clever than I had thought. I agree. You are the last of your line, the last Lynnfield. I cannot allow you to live. I intend to get rid of those gentlemen outside before I arrange a fatal lover's quarrel. It will be perfect. With the advent of Mr. Carson, the motive as well as the means is at hand. Poor, impetuous Evan. He truly loved you, I think."

Susan's throat tightened. She tried not to look at Evan as he lay on the floor. She focused on survival; if she let herself think of Evan, of Thorne and his twisted plots, she would succumb to hysteria.

"And now that Evan forced you into jumping the gun, so to speak," she said calmly, "how do you plan on dealing with 'those gentlemen outside'? Wholesale slaughter?"

"What a vivid imagination you have. No, nothing of the sort. My plan remains intact; I just need to enforce its effectiveness with a little judicious flight. And of course I will need to remove you and your dead lover at once. This is not the most remote place to be conducting such affairs. But so much for that." Standing, he pocketed the brooch in its wooden box.

Susan looked up at him and thought that she had never seen such complete evil in a human being before. It was a terrifying sight, to glimpse such ugliness behind a serene, smiling countenance.

"Sir Reginald Thorne!" Tabitha smacked a curled hand into her open palm. "Of course! Rogue, scoundrel, lecher, and murderer! How could I have not made the connection?" She looked at Horatio's impassive face. "Sometimes I don't really listen to people as I should, I'm afraid. I get an idea in my head, and that's all I think about." She groaned loudly. "By the holy rood, I cannot believe I have been so single-mindedly obtuse. . . ."

"Enough, Tabitha." Horatio's voice flowed over her like warm silk. He sounded more kind than he'd sounded since she had embarked upon her one-woman crusade. "You'll help her. Just think."

"Think. Yes, yes, of course that's what I must do." A frown curled her brows into a knot. "Sir Reginald did murder for the brooch—was it he who pushed me, by the way? I seem to recall seeing him on the stairs, along with Lady Emily—no matter. His descendant will surely not hesitate at murdering poor Susan. Ah, and her cowboy is on the way to save her, but will he be in time? Will he be able to stop that wretched Thorne? Thorn in my side, is what he is, by the rood, a bloody thorn in my side!"

Horatio coughed, and she paused in her diatribe to look at him.

"A clear trail, Horatio. He must have a clear trail. I know I'm carrying on, but it helps me think sometimes. Is it allowed that I leave some sort of sign for him to follow her?"

When Horatio didn't reply, Tabitha gave an impatient shake of her head. "Never mind. I think Carson can follow the tracks they left behind. I'd best turn my attention to seeing that Thorne does not harm her until he reaches them."

Chapter 18

HUNTER FOLLOWED THE tracks, the faint smears of dried blood from Susan's horse, a drop here and there on a rock or a blade of dry grass. Disturbed rocks, topside bleached by the sun and now lying on darker sides, gave him a guide. Crushed blades of grass, the deep-cut half-moons where horse hooves cut into the softer ground in places, all led to a remote line shack on the farthest perimeter of the Lazy W.

Mouth tightening, Hunter called in the men with him, and they advanced on the rough wooden shack. They didn't ride in shooting and yelling, though it might have worked if not for the fact that Susan was probably in the shack. They could have poured enough hot lead into the ramshackle hut to kill anyone in there.

From the outside it looked empty and deserted. But Hunter knew that they were in there. He'd seen a flicker of movement at one of the black-covered windows. And behind the shack, in a natural corral of high red rocks, he heard a faint whicker from horses. Yeah, they were in there.

Every instinct sharpened, and Hunter motioned quietly for his men to dismount a half mile from the shack. They approached on foot, stealthily moving from cover of rock to rock, clumps of sage and cactus disguising their approach. It was hot. The sun was rising overhead in a scorching ball of fire that wet their shirts with sweat and made palms too slick to hold their guns without gloves on.

On his belly on a flat outcropping of rock that jutted out like a shelf, Hunter squinted against the press of searing sunlight. Rocks dug into his chest and stomach, and the stock of his rifle was hot to the touch. He'd filled one hand with his Colt.

Drawing up his Winchester with one hand, Hunter settled it against the rock and waited, sighting down the barrel. He waited, while the sun beat down and no wind blew, and an occasional insect crawled over the sweat rolling down his body. A fierce exultation filled him; he was going to kill Evan Elliott. He wouldn't risk this again. And he'd enjoy doing it. If Susan had so much as a scratch on her, he was going to take his time killing him. . . .

"Carson."

The whisper came from his left, and he turned slightly. "Yeah?"

"Dust to the north. Riders, I think."

"Coming here?"

"No."

Hunter shifted his attention to the dust cloud Malone was talking about. It hung in a faint haze in the distance, and when he saw four horses, he swore softly.

"Think they're going for help?" Malone asked in the same soft whisper, and Hunter shrugged.

"Won't matter. By the time they get back, it'll be too late."

A sudden wind sprang up, blowing dust devils through the air in a whirr of grit, and the men all drew their neckerchiefs up over mouths and noses. It seemed as good a time as any to draw fire from the men in the shack, and Hunter rose to a crouch.

When they were only a few yards from the shack, a shot rang out, zipping past Hunter so close he could feel the heat of it. He smiled, paused, whipped up his rifle, and put a bullet through one of the windows. There was the sound of breaking glass and a hoarse cry, and that broke the oddly quiet tension.

Bullets began popping, and the men with Hunter fired, ran to cover, fired again, peppering the windows with controlled shots. Hunter got as close as he could to the shack, diving behind some water barrels.

"Send out the woman!" he shouted in a lull in the shooting. "Send her out unharmed, and we'll back off!"

There was silence from inside, then someone shouted back, "No! We'll kill her if you don't ride out. . . ."

Hunter's reply was a carefully squeezed shot, and he swore softly under his breath. Sweat trickled down the side of his face, wetting his hair and shirt and chest.

He had to get Susan out of there. He couldn't risk her being shot, but he didn't trust them not to use her as a shield. Damn Evan for a coward, hiding behind a woman's skirts.

"Elliott!" he shouted again. "Don't risk her. Send her out and we'll talk."

After a long moment crawled past, the voice came again. "Elliott's dead. We've got the woman, Carson. You'd better back off if you want to keep her healthy."

Hunter felt a spurt of fear for Susan. If Elliott was dead, she didn't have anyone to protect her. Men who would throw in with Elliott to take a woman sure wouldn't care about keeping her alive.

His head lifted, and he squinted into the distance again, thinking. Then his cold green gaze shifted back to the shack. He turned with his back to the barrels and saw two of the Lazy W men looking at him from behind a rock.

"Murdock, Malone—keep me covered."

"Hell, Carson, you ain't thinkin' about—"

"Do it."

While the men kept up a steady stream of gunfire, Hunter ran crouched over to the back of the shack. It was a solid wall, with small chinks where the boards didn't quite meet. No windows, no door. Pressing against it, his rifle in one hand, his pistol in the other, he sucked in a few deep breaths. Then he dug at the dried mud filling one of the cracks between boards, and peered inside.

She wasn't there. Susan wasn't in there. That was the reason for the dust cloud then. The men were keeping them occupied while Elliott took Susan and ran. And he had wasted time trying to smoke them out. Rage seared him, hotter than the sun overhead, and Hunter took out his pouch of tobacco and matches.

When he'd stacked dry grass and sticks along the back wall of the shack, he struck a match and lit the tinder. It caught immediately, blazing up in a scorching flame that quickly, greedily, ate through the wood wall. Then he moved around front and waited.

Choking on dust, her hands still tied in front of her, Susan fought back her despair. Greet Duncan and Peter Thorne pulled her horse with them in a brisk trot, apparently set on reaching their destination in a hurry. It was all she could do to hold on, with her hands tied.

She tried not to look at the other horse, at the body slung facedown over the saddle, jouncing with every jolt of the horse. Evan. Poor Evan. God, she wished it hadn't ended like this. He'd been at fault, yes, but she found she could not hate him for it. And now he was dead.

Hot tears streaked her cheeks, making mud out of the dirt on her face. But when Thorne slanted a glance back at her, her eyes blazed with hatred at him, not tears. He only laughed.

"Such a fiery little termagant. I almost regret the necessity of killing you, Miss Whitten."

"I doubt that."

Greet Duncan sliced Thorne a grin. "I'll take care of it for ya, boss. Ain't no love lost between me and her."

"I know that." Thorne's tone was cold, and he dug his heels into the sides of his mount and sent it up the next incline before he added, "But I have no intention of letting this look like anything but a tragic ending to an ill-fated *ménage à trois*."

"A what?" Duncan stared at him blankly, and Thorne gave an ugly laugh.

"Never mind, Duncan. Just follow orders."

By the time they reached the small shack on Elliott's land, Susan was nearly falling from her horse with heat and thirst. Only grim determination kept her from allowing the welcoming shadows that hung at the edges of her conscious mind to claim her.

She was vaguely aware of Thorne pulling her from her horse, of Duncan slinging Evan's body carelessly to the ground with a thud, of being half dragged into the shack. Lack of food had made her weak and dizzy, and she clung to the edge of the cot where she was pushed without really seeing anything.

It was cooler in the shack, and the windows weren't covered but left open for cooling breezes to filter in. She stared dully around her, not really seeing the table and chairs, the potbellied stove. Thorne was busily arranging items in the room, making it look comfortable. She stared at him without comprehending, and he caught her look and smiled.

"See, we must make this look like a lover's nest. That is so the sheriff will think you and Evan were most . . . uh—close—before you fell into a quarrel and shot each other."

"Are you waiting for my approval?" Susan asked in a sharp tone when he paused and looked at her expectantly. "I asssure you, I never approve of insanity!"

Drawing himself up, Thorne glared at her. "I was not asking for approval, m'dear. I don't need it. I have all I need already."

"Do you?" Her smile was nasty, and she gathered her courage and defiance into a hard, glowing knot inside her. If she was going to die, then she would give Peter Thorne something to think about, to worry about. "I'd suggest that you enjoy yourself while you can, Thorne, because when Hunter Carson finds you, you won't live long enough to be so pleased with yourself."

"Carson?" Thorne laughed shortly. "I daresay he's dead by now, too. If those men I left behind have done what I told them to do, he looks like a sieve now."

Susan felt a sick lurch of her stomach but kept her chin lifted and her eyes cold. "I don't think he's that easy to kill."

Snorting, Thorne leaned back against the table and let his pale eyes drift over her. "Not unless he lets himself be, which is what I counted on. The noble Mr. Carson would not let anyone harm you and would trade himself for you."

When Susan stiffened, he laughed. "Ah, you see it now, don't you? Of course you do. And of course, if he doesn't, he will merely remove all my witnesses for me anyway. Then it is simply a matter of him being hanged for murdering you and your lover in a fit of jealous rage."

"Why do you think anyone would believe this?" Susan tried desperately. "It's too farfetched to work!"

"Because I have very carefully laid the groundwork for this in Los Alamos, m'dear. A few words here and there in the right ears . . . oh, yes, people will believe it readily. In case you haven't noticed, people are always ready to believe the worst. Gossip does fuel a few fires."

Remembering the rumors that had spread through the town and Hunter's dragging her down the main street in full view of everyone, Susan closed her eyes and shuddered. It would be believed. How horrible. Hunter had shot a man in the middle of the street only a short time before, and he had a reputation as a fast gun. Yes, people would be only too ready to believe that he was responsible for their deaths.

"You're mad!" she whispered, opening her eyes to look at him, and he laughed again.

"Yes. Probably. But it's the mad ones who always win out, m'dear."

Susan stared at him, and when Greet Duncan came into the shack, she hardly noticed. Her former cowhand dumped Evan onto the floor. His body sagged with a heavy thud, and she looked away. The blood had dried on his shirt. Except for a small, thin trickle that oozed from a blackened hole in the material. Susan frowned.

Then she glanced up quickly at Duncan when he came to stand in front of her, his legs braced and his thumbs tucked into his gunbelt. He was grinning, and when he saw her narrowed glance, he laughed softly.

"Boss," he said over his shoulder, "don't you think she should look more like she's been rollin' around with her boyfriend? 'Less she looks a little more . . . used . . . people might not think they were—"

"I get your drift, Duncan." Thorne's face held a hint of distaste, but his pale eyes looked thoughtful. "Perhaps we should make it a bit more—intimate."

As Duncan glanced at Thorne, then back at Susan, she realized what they meant and reacted. One booted foot came up in a swift reflex, catching Duncan square in his crotch. He doubled over, cursing and retching, cupping himself with both hands as he sank to his knees on the floor. Through the haze of rage and fear that gripped her, Susan heard Sir Peter Thorne's choked laughter.

"By God, Miss Whitten! What a rare jewel you are! I do think you are truly a descendant of those damn Lynnfield bitches after all. . . ."

Tucking her feet up under her in a tense crouch, Susan stared back at him, not moving, keeping a wary eye on the man on the floor. He sprawled close to Evan's body, still gasping with pain and fury, his eyes narrowed and promising when he looked up at her. She shuddered again.

Crouching above the shack on a rocky ledge, Hunter tried not to think about the raw, oozing wound on his arm and seared across his temple. They burned but didn't hamper him. A grim smile curled his mouth. He was still able to fight, and if Thorne had counted on his death, he'd been sadly mistaken.

It hadn't taken him long to track them; they'd made no effort to cover their trail. Guess they'd counted on the others delaying them long enough to get away, counted on his thinking Susan was still there. Hunter's eyes were cold and deadly as he shoved more bullets into his Colt Peacemaker and snapped it closed with a whirring click.

Only Murdock had come with him. The rest of the men were wounded too badly to fight; one had been left behind to take care of the bodies and ride for the sheriff. He figured that he and Murdock could handle Thorne and Duncan.

A curl of smoke drifted from the black pipe jutting out of the shack's roof. They were in there all right, and he glanced at Murdock.

"Ready?"

Wetting his lips with the tip of his tongue, Murdock nodded. "Yeah. You think Duncan will come out and fight? I've got a score to settle with him. . . ."

"I doubt it." Hunter glanced at the shack again. "No wild shooting. I don't want to risk Susan." He squinted at Murdock. "You all right?"

"Yeah. It's just a burn." He indicated the shallow red streak across one shoulder that was seared away by a bullet and grinned. "I've had worse."

"There might be three of them, if that bastard was lying and Elliott's still alive," Hunter said with a grunt. "If he is, leave him for me."

Murdock snapped his revolver shut and whirled the chamber with his thumb, then picked up his rifle. "He's all yours. Let me have Duncan. He's the bastard that stole my roll one payday."

"I'll try to draw their fire," Hunter said, "and you pick off anyone who comes out that door. Make every shot count."

But doing it was not as easy as saying it, and Hunter crouched behind a jumble of rocks stacked higher than his head and swore softly. They weren't taking the bait. Thorne had called out the door saying he had Susan and wouldn't hesitate to kill her; Hunter knew it was true.

Gritting his teeth with frustration, Hunter tried to decide whether to risk her now or wait until he could get a clear shot. Either way was dangerous. Thorne meant it. He would kill her if Hunter didn't back off, throw down his gun, and come in with his hands up.

"All right, Thorne!" Hunter yelled down after a minute, motioning for Murdock to stay hidden. "I'm coming down."

"Bring in your men with you!" came the reply. "Or she's dead. I swear it, Carson!"

"It's just me, Thorne. I came alone."

"I don't believe you," came the amused response. The words echoed off the rocks, and Hunter considered for a long moment.

"How do I know she's not already dead?" he yelled back, motioning for Murdock to circle around behind the shack. "I haven't seen her. I may be wasting my time for nothing!"

"Stop stalling, Carson." Thorne's voice held an edge of anger in it. "Stand up and show yourself, and I'll let you see her."

Hunter waited a moment. His belly curled. He knew if he stood up, he risked getting a bullet in his chest. But the man sounded edgy, and he was risking Susan with every moment that ticked past.

"All right!" he yelled back when Thorne demanded he show himself again. He glanced in the direction Murdock had gone and slowly eased himself out from behind the rock. He made an excellent target, standing silhouetted against the hot burning sky behind him, in his tan denims, white shirt, and black vest, and he knew it. It was an agony to move into the open, to hold his arms out at his sides to let Thorne see that he wasn't holding a gun. It took every ounce of his self-control to stand there while Thorne took his time getting to the door.

Susan appeared in the opening, her face pale, her eyes huge and dark in her face. He felt his gut tighten for her and tried to make his voice calm and reassuring.

"You all right, honey?"

Her voice was a choked sob. "Hunter, please run! He's going to—"

She was yanked back inside, and Duncan filled her space, his hand filled with a gun, a smirk on his face.

"Move up a bit, Carson. You don't look so damned mean now, when you ain't got a gun in your hand."

Staring at him coolly, Hunter felt the hard ridge of his Colt at his back where it was tucked into his belt. He itched to go for it but waited. He didn't say anything, just looked at Greet Duncan.

Duncan shifted uneasily. He had the advantage, but the bastard wasn't squirming. He just looked at him with those cold eyes, eyes that he'd never seen before on a man, eyes that made him look away. Death lurked in those cold, clear, emotionless eyes, and Duncan felt another spurt of fear. Damn him. Damn Hunter Carson, who could make him shudder even when he stood in the open without a gun in his hand.

Waggling his gun, Duncan snapped, "Over there! Out in the open more, where I can see you good."

"Afraid?" Hunter mocked, taking two steps sideways, his eyes never leaving the man in the doorway. "Send Susan out. Let her go and it'll be just you and me. I'll give you first shot, Duncan."

Where was Thorne? Why hadn't he shown himself? And what was he doing with Susan? And Elliott?

Susan screamed suddenly, a soft sound that was quickly choked off, and Hunter tensed. Rage flared hotly in his eyes, and he swore loudly.

"Damn you, Thorne, if you've hurt her—!"

"Stay put!" Duncan snapped, shifting position in the open door and glancing over his shoulder, then back.

His finger tightened imperceptibly on the trigger, and he said in a soft mutter, "I don't trust him—give me a minute."

Tension curled tightly in his belly, and when Hunter took another step, he sensed rather than saw Duncan thumb back the hammer on his pistol. Throwing himself to one side in a reflex action, he knew that he didn't have enough time to draw. He'd been thinking about Susan instead of Duncan, and it had cost him.

But a bullet from up and to one side plowed into the air in a screaming whistle, hitting Duncan in the middle of his chest and sending him backward in a stagger. *Murdock,* Hunter had time to think before he hit the ground in a roll and filled his hand with his Colt. Duncan's pistol had fired a recoil, and he heard Murdock give a shout of pain.

Then Hunter was up and running, leaping over Duncan and kicking his pistol from his hand as he crashed into the shack. He stopped short just inside the door. Evan Elliott lay in a boneless sprawl on the floor and looked quite dead. His gaze flicked to Thorne and Susan.

The Englishman was holding her in front of him, and he had a gun pressed against her temple. He smiled at Hunter.

"Hullo! Looks like a checkmate, my friend."

"I'm not your friend, and you'd better let her go," Hunter snarled. "You're a dead man, Thorne."

"Ah, but not as dead as young Elliott. Not yet. And I do not intend to be." Bringing the arm he held up under her breasts tighter around Susan, Thorne moved a step to the side. "If you value her life, you will put away your weapon at once. I will not hesitate to shoot."

"No, Hunter," Susan said in a half sob, "he'll kill me no matter what! Don't do it!"

"Ah," Thorne said quickly, "you may listen to her last words, if you like, but I assure you that I will not die by myself. And she will be just as dead, whether you kill me or not. Suit yourself, but remember—I must have a live hostage in order to bargain."

It was a good point. Hunter stared at him coldly and saw the nervous flicker of Thorne's lashes over his pale eyes. Thorne was afraid of him, and a frightened man was as unpredictable as they came.

Slowly he lowered the barrel of his pistol. Susan sobbed. A tight smile curled his lips.

"Looks like you win this round, Thorne."

"I never doubted it," came the cool reply. Thorne gave Susan a rough push forward, his arm still tight around her. "Throw your gun down, Carson. By the barrel, slowly. That's right. Now back up against the wall."

Hunter slowly let his gun fall to the floor, then shoved it away with his foot as Thorne instructed. Then he backed up against the far wall, keeping his cold eyes trained on Thorne and Susan. Susan sobbed softly, tears running down her cheeks.

"Very good, Carson," Thorne said and smiled. "Now, if you will be so good as to put your hands in the air and clasp them over your head, please. Ah. That's right. Like that."

"Let her go, Thorne," Hunter said stiffly. "Let her go, and this can stop here. Keep the damned brooch, or whatever you came after."

"But why should I?" Thorne asked mildly. "I have it all now. I have you where I want you, and I have the brooch. And I also have my safety guaranteed by Miss Whitten's presence." His finger tightened almost imperceptibly on the trigger of his gun. "I don't need you anymore, that's for certain."

Susan struggled, and Thorne tightened his arm around her until she gasped for air. "In fact, Carson, you're a bloody nuisance." The gun leveled even with Hunter's chest, and Thorne smiled evilly.

Tabitha shrieked with impotent fury. "Do you see that? Do you see it? And here I am, not doing a blessed thing! Is that fair? Is that what you wanted of me, Horatio?"

Shaking his head, Horatio said imperturbably, "No, not at all, Tabitha."

"Then what am I to do? Stand here and watch while he slaughters him? Oh, how can I stand it?"

"Tabitha," Horatio said mildly, "I never suggested that you could not offer assistance. I only said that you could not arrange emotions to your own desires."

She stared at him. "You didn't?"

"No," he said, "I didn't."

"Oh. Well, then, I think I'll go down and see what I can do." She paused. "Er, Horatio—I can't really be killed again, can I?"

"No, of course not."

"Not shot, or stabbed, or anything violently painful like that?"

"No, Tabitha, not even where you can feel it."

She smiled. "Very good. I'll be back."

Standing with his back to the wall, Hunter looked at Thorne, then Susan, and tried to think how big a chance it would be to jump him. He'd only get one shot off, and then it would be over with. But if Hunter didn't manage to kill him, Thorne would have Susan at his mercy.

In the split second it took for him to think that, he heard a clink of metal and saw from one corner of his eye the astonishing sight of a woman garbed in green hose and some sort of leather gown, brandishing a sword over her head and smiling gleefully. He stared, not knowing what to do or say and saw Thorne half turn at the same time.

It was the woman who had come to his house to tell him about the ambush, and Hunter looked at her bewilderedly at the same time as Thorne gave a startled cry and stepped back. Leaping forward with a glad cry, Tabitha Tidwell, Lady Lynnfield, or Lynnfeather, as she was known in the present company, shouted, "En garde!" at the amazed Thorne. Light from the window and door made runnels of silver along the length of the blade, sparkling in brittle splinters.

In his shock Thorne loosened his grip on Susan. She gave his arm a push and flung herself at Hunter, who closed his arms around her. Thorne's attention swung immediately from Tabitha and her wildly swinging sword, back to Hunter.

A smile curved his mouth, and he deftly sidestepped the awkward lunge from the sword at the same time as he put his thumb on the hammer of the pistol and drew it back. Hunter shoved Susan to one side and down, then turned in the same movement to fling himself backward out of the path of the bullet. Firing first at Tabitha, Thorne then swung toward Hunter, thumbing back the hammer again for his second shot.

But Tabitha paid no attention to the bullet that plowed through her green leather jerkin. She bellowed, "Swine! Coxcomb! Blackguard! Vile villain!" The sword tip flashed again, backing Sir Peter away from her. He looked stunned. Another pass with the sword sliced through Thorne's coat, nicking his upper arm and slashing through the gold fob he had swagged over his chest. He let out a squeal of rage and pain and thumbed back the hammer again. The bullet passed harmlessly through Tabitha's jerkin again, and Sir Peter stared wildly. It should have hit her. He was only a few feet away.

"Who are you?" he screamed, backing away, his terrified gaze swinging from the green-clad female swordsman to Hunter and back. He looked faintly disbelieving and pulled the trigger of his pistol again. Another loud shot rang out in the small room, and the smell of gunpowder was sharp and acrid.

By this time Hunter had managed to edge toward his pistol still lying on the floor not far from Evan Elliott's body. But Sir Peter saw him from the corner of his eye, and the gun barrel waggled toward him again. He looked dazed, slightly bewildered, and pale.

"Move," Sir Peter snarled, "and I'll put every bullet in this gun into you. Who is this woman?"

Half on his side, Hunter looked up at him, gauging his chances. "I have no idea. Isn't she a friend of yours?" he asked, tense with the effort not to move. His pistol lay just out of reach, tantalizingly close. The handle of the Colt lay almost under Evan's stiff, cold fingers, and he swore softly. Good thing he was dead.

The sword flashed again, gaining Thorne's attention, and when he glanced back toward the woman, Hunter stretched for his pistol. To his surprise, Evan's hand curled around the handle and gave it a shove toward him, sliding it across the wooden floor.

Not hesitating, Hunter grabbed his gun. He brought it up in a smooth motion, using the edge of his other hand to slam down on the hammer and fire it.

The loud report shattered in the room, and Thorne gave a grunt. The pistol in his hand wavered, then slid from his fingers to the floor. He sank to his knees, then fell.

Hunter rose in a swift, lethal move, grabbing Thorne in a fierce grip and wrestling him to the floor. When Thorne struggled, fumbling at a knife in his boot, Hunter brought his boot down hard on the Englishman's wrist. Bones cracked loudly, and Thorne screamed.

Susan looked away, shuddering. She crawled across the floor to Evan, and lifted his head to her lap. He blinked a few times, managed a smile, tucked his fingers into her hand.

"I waited, SuSu," he whispered hoarsely. "Couldn't let you be . . . alone . . . until I knew Carson was here. . . ." His eyes closed briefly, and he struggled for breath with painful gasps while Susan stroked back his damp hair and fought her sobs. When Evan opened his eyes again, he murmured, "Dyin' ain't so bad. Kinda peaceful. Lots of bright light . . . sorry to leave you, but know Carson will take care . . . of . . ."

His head sagged to the side, and Susan held it for a long time. Sobs racked her, and her tears wet Evan's shirt.

"He's better off now, dear," came a soft voice, and she looked up through blurred eyes to see the lady she knew as Mrs. Lynnfeather. A faint smile touched her lips. "I know he is, child. He would have been miserable watching your happiness. Hell is often of our own making, you know."

Susan felt Hunter come up behind her, felt his strong, warm hand rest gently on her shoulder; she thought of having to watch him love another woman, and understood. She nodded.

"Yes, I understand," she whispered.

"I knew you would. And he's paid his dues with the greatest penance a man can give, I think—selfless love.

At the end he became what he wanted to be all along. Some people never reach that goal."

Susan gently laid Evan's head on the floor and stroked his eyes closed. After a moment she looked up at Tabitha with a confused expression, and said, "Mrs. Lynnfeather—what are you doing here?"

"Doing, my dear? Why, I came to help you." A big smile curved her mouth, and she looked quite pleased with herself. "Didn't you need my help?"

"Yes," Susan said. "Of course we did, but—"

"Then that's why I'm here. I came to help. And it looks as if your cowboy has managed to take care of the rest of things by himself. All I did was provide a little diversion for him. Didn't I do well?"

Moving to stand over Sir Peter, Hunter looked up at Tabitha as an amused expression warmed his jade eyes. "I'd say you did damn good, lady."

"Why, thank you." Tabitha preened. She slid the sword into the sheath at her side, managed to get the tip of it stuck between the slats of a chair back, and pulled it free before she added, "You didn't do so badly yourself."

Hunter shrugged. He looked at Sir Peter kneeling on the floor, blood flowing from a wound in his arm. Blood already covered his sleeve from the sword cut, and he still looked dazed and confused, holding his broken wrist.

"Who *are* you?" Thorne asked in a hoarse whisper, his eyes fixed on Tabitha. "Who?"

Tabitha glared at him. "I believe I knew a kinsman of yours once, Sir Peter. He was just as dislikable a fellow as you. And about as honest. All you Thornes seem to end up as gallows bait, and I daresay that you will make a particularly ugly corpse."

Sir Peter blinked. "I don't know you," he said.

"No. You don't. But I knew Sir Reginald. A vile, blackhearted wretch if ever I've met one. Ended his days on the block."

"On the block?" Sir Peter muttered. *"On the block?"* He seemed to absorb this information, then shook his head in a helpless denial. "But the last Sir Reginald was executed by Queen Elizabeth over three hundred years ago. . . ."

"Enough chitchat, Thorne," Hunter said brutally, not even bothering to listen to the dazed man. "The sheriff will be here soon. You can chat with him." He looked up when another man appeared in the doorway, and Susan saw Murdock nod at them.

"Howdy, Miss Susan. Looks like there's been some kinda trouble today, don't it?"

Susan dragged a blanket over Evan and stood up, meeting Murdock's grave stare. "Yes, there certainly has."

Murdock looked at Hunter. "Riders comin'. Looks like Barton, all right. A few of our men are with him."

"How's your arm?"

Shrugging, Murdock winced at the pain that brought and said, "Fine. It'll heal."

Leaning down, Hunter grabbed Thorne by one arm and jerked him to his feet, ignoring his cry of pain. "Come on. You can figure this out later. You'll have a lot of time where you're going."

"Oh," Tabitha said in a plaintive tone, "does that mean he won't be executed?"

Hunter looked slightly taken aback, and Murdock stared at her dumbly, his amazement plain. Susan put a quick hand over her mouth. The expression on Tabitha's face was so disappointed that it was ludicrous.

"No," Hunter said slowly, "it means he'll get a fair trial."

"And then they'll hang him?"

A faint grin pressed at the corners of his mouth, and Hunter shrugged. "There's a very good possibility of that."

Tabitha smiled. "Good. One must pay for his crimes, you know. It's expected. And necessary. If he doesn't pay in this life, he'll certainly pay in the next."

Susan sank down on the floor, her back sliding against the wall as Hunter dragged Sir Peter outside. Murdock went with him, backing out, his gaze riveted on the strange lady in green leather. Susan looked at Tabitha curiously.

"Mrs. Tabitha Lynnfeather—is that your name?"

"One of them, I suppose." Tabitha's face grew pink. "I'm afraid I haven't been completely truthful with you, dear."

"Oh." Susan blinked wearily; shock and fatigue were beginning to show on her face, and she looked sadly at Evan's body. "Things have gone so badly. So terribly wrong. I don't know how they could have been worse."

Tabitha tilted her head to one side. "Don't you, dear? Are you sure?"

Startled, Susan looked back up at her. "Well," she said slowly, "I guess they could have. I mean, I could have lost Hunter, too."

"And your own life. Don't forget that."

Susan stared at the floor. "Without Hunter, I have no life."

An odd smile creased Tabitha's face. "Yes. I do think you have discovered something worth having, Susan. He's a man who won't be dissuaded by circumstances. He's strong. He will be there for you in good times and bad." She paused before adding softly, "And his love is strong enough to live for all time, I think."

Catching her breath, Susan pushed her hair out of her eyes and met the blue gaze regarding her with such kind affection. "Do you think so, Mrs. Lynnfeather?"

"I know so, my dear." The sword caught on a table leg as she turned abruptly, muttered "God's teeth!" then gave it a jerk. The table slewed sideways with a grating of wood on wood, and Tabitha sighed. "Well, I've had my fun. Do you think you can take care of your cowboy now?"

Crossing her arms over her knees, Susan nodded. "I am quite certain I can take care of him. If he'll still have me."

"The key to a successful relationship is communication, you know." Tabitha nodded wisely. "Listening is equally as important as what is said. If you have your heart and mind open, you will hear so much more than when you only try to convey your own thoughts. In fact, I've only recently discovered that truly listening to others is absolutely *vital*." She seemed struck by that revelation and gave a short nod. "Yes, vital. Well, Susan, I must go now. I hope to see you again."

"But . . . but how did you get here?" Susan frowned. "And how did you know where we were?"

"Oh, I just followed everyone else. Easy enough to do." A bright smile flashed, and Tabitha walked to the door with a clank of her sword, her leather gown swishing loudly around her legs. The green hose ended in short leather boots like none Susan had ever seen. She followed her to the door.

"Mrs. Lynnfeather," she said, "I know this is odd, but I feel like I've known you all my life. You really are a nice person, and I'm glad you came to visit me."

Coloring, Tabitha gave Susan a quick hug. "You've no idea what your words mean to me, m'dear. And I shall never forget you. Not for all eternity."

They smiled at each other, and when Hunter appeared in the doorway, Susan was saying, "Stay with us a while."

"Oh, no," Tabitha said quickly, correctly reading the expression on Hunter's face. "I don't think that would do."

"Will you come to our wedding?" she persisted.

"Perhaps. I'll get in touch with you. I don't know where I will be—if I cannot come, I will be certain to send you something."

"I'd rather have you there."

Tabitha pressed her hand. "I know. I truly do. But I have to go now. . . . Why, what is that you have, Mr. Carson?"

He held up a small wood and velvet box. "This is Susan's heirloom. I don't think Thorne will need it."

A strange expression crossed Tabitha's face. "May I— do you mind very much if I see it?"

When Susan nodded, Hunter held out the box and Tabitha took it in her hand. With trembling fingers, she lifted the lid and took out the brooch. Sunlight slicing through the open door glinted off the exquisitely wrought gold filigree and made the diamond sparkle so brightly the entire room took on a faint glow. Tears sparked Tabitha's eyes, and she cradled the brooch in her palm reverently.

"It's always been the most beautiful piece . . . take good care of it, Susan. Now that earthly justice has been done, I do not think that bad fortune will follow those who own it."

She placed it tenderly back in the box, closed the lid, and handed it to Susan. Laying a cool hand on Susan's warm cheek, she said so softly only Susan could hear,

"Lady Catherine would have been very proud of you, I think."

Susan stared up at her, feeling an odd, tingling glow. Mrs. Lynnfeather's face seemed to take on a glow of its own as she stared at her, and when she had gone and Hunter came to stand beside her, Susan rested her head on his shoulder.

"Nutty old woman," he muttered, and she shook her head.

"No, I don't think so. I did at first. Now I think she is probably a lot wiser than I dreamed."

Hunter shrugged. "Sheriff Barton is riding over the hill about a mile away. He ought to be here shortly. He can take your Mrs. Lynnfeather or whatever her name is back to town."

Turning in his loose embrace, Susan traced a finger over the old scar at the corner of his eyebrow, then the new red streak on his temple.

"All right."

He looked at her. His eyes were narrowed, his mouth flattened. "All right? No argument?" When she shook her head, he grunted, "That's unusual."

"Get used to it."

A faintly amused gleam lit his eyes. "I know you make that promise in the heat of the moment, but I hold no hope that you will ever be a meek, quiet wife, Susan Whitten."

"Just so I'm *your* wife, does it matter if I'm quiet?" She brushed her fingers over his fine, sensual mouth in a light flutter that made his eyes flare with hot lights. His arm tightened around her.

"No. It doesn't matter. Not to me. Just so you're mine, sweetheart."

"Now, that, Hunter Carson, is a promise I intend to hold you to," she said against his lips.

Chapter 19

THEY SAT ON a high ridge overlooking a grassy valley. A grove of oak trees shaded the crest, and along the north slope blackberry bushes grew thickly, heavy with fruit. A ripe promise lingered in the air, and the wind blew softly around them as their horses grazed contentedly nearby.

A blanket lay in lumps on the grass, remnants of a picnic still littering the quilted squares. Hunter knelt with one knee on the ground, chewing on a sprig of grass, watching Susan stare into the distance.

"What about the railroad, Hunter?" Susan turned to look at him with large, bruised eyes. Doubts shadowed her face for a moment. "I mean, I would still lease you the rights, if that's all you—"

"Don't say it." His eyes were narrowed and hard. "Just don't say it. I told you before, and I'll tell you this last time, then I don't ever want to hear anything about it again, dammit." His hands moved to grip her upper arms, and he stood up, bringing her up off the ground in a smooth flex of his muscles. She caught a brief glimpse of blue sky and white clouds before his face blocked it out. "I don't give a damn about land rights, or credit extensions, or gaudy pieces of jewelry, or any of that other stuff you seem to think I'm so hot after."

His mouth was only inches from hers. She stared into the hot lights flaring in his eyes and nodded. "All right," she managed to whisper. "All right."

"No, don't say all right like that if you don't mean it when you say it."

"I mean it. I swear I do." Susan put a hand on his chest. "It's just that—"

"God, I knew you wouldn't let it rest."

Her chin lifted slightly, and she saw the angry lights fade in his eyes as he looked at her with a faint softening of his mouth. She felt her heart lurch. "It's just that I want to be sure. I don't want anything between us."

"Nothing between us?"

"No, nothing."

Susan blinked when he grinned, and then she saw his eyes rake down her body in a positive leer. She flushed, but it wasn't with distress. This flush started deep in the pit of her stomach and radiated outward.

"Agreed, sweetheart. I don't want anything between us, either. Especially annoying things like too many clothes."

"Hunter—" She took a step backward, pulling free of him. "It's broad daylight, and we're—"

"And we're out here in the middle of nowhere, with only a few hawks to watch." He advanced a step, smiling slowly at the quick leap in her eyes. "Why do you think I brought you out here?"

"You said to look at a spot to build our new house." A faint accusation tinged her voice, but there was that slow fire in her eyes that beckoned him forward. He took another few steps, and her nerve fled at the look in his eyes. Heat simmered with raw sensuality in his gaze, and his voice was deep, husky, vibrating with masculine hunger.

"We looked at it."

"Is that why you came out here that day—to look for a place to build?" she asked, putting her hands behind her. A tree halted her retreat, the bark rough beneath her palms.

He stopped and looked at her as if sensing her sudden reluctance. "No. You know why I came out this way. I was trying to find a new route to cut that railroad spur."

She looked away from him, inexplicably nervous. There was so much to think about, so much to come between them if she let it. Did all women have doubts about the men they'd decided to marry? she wondered. Not that she did, really; not about Hunter himself. It was those other things . . . her brow furrowed. What was it that Mrs. Lynnfeather had said? Oh, yes, *communication.* Leaving her heart and mind open, and really hearing what was said.

Looking back at him, Susan saw the wary look back in his green eyes and suddenly knew that she couldn't allow that to happen.

She ran a finger down his chest, smiling when he sucked in a sharp breath. "And did you find one?" she murmured. "Or do you intend to allow me to lease my land for the spur?"

The wariness was still in his eyes, but he only said, "I think something can be arranged."

"Umm." She flicked open one of his shirt buttons with a finger. "And this land you've bought for a new house—what do you intend to do with it?"

"Raise cattle and children."

He was breathing heavier now, his features blurring with desire as she flicked open two more buttons and slid her hand inside his shirt. Her fingers caressed the smooth flex of muscle, then slipped down to release the last two buttons. His shirt gapped open. Brown skin showed beneath.

"Where do you plan on getting those?" she asked when he didn't elaborate.

"The cattle or the children?"

"Both."

"I know a lady who owns six thousand head of prime cattle." His muscles contracted as she tugged his shirt free of his pants and slipped her hands around his waist to his back. "*God . . .*"

"And the children?" she murmured, lifting on her toes to press her mouth against the smooth tanned skin of his throat. She could feel his heart pounding in his chest, and a strong pulse beat beneath her lips.

"The same lady . . . Susan, if you keep that up, I'm going to push you back on that blanket and make love to you right here."

"Ah, promises, promises," she said into the angle of his neck and shoulder. There was a split second before he reacted, then she felt the coil of his muscles an instant before he lifted her into his arms with a low growl.

"You asked for it," he muttered into the hair at her temple, and she laughed.

"So I did."

His movement had brought her breasts up against his bare chest, and she shuddered at the light, rasping scrape that made the peaks tauten. Her blouse was a thin cotton, short-sleeved in the heat, her riding skirt just as light.

Hunter pressed his mouth against her temple as he lay her back on the blanket and bent over her, his eyes going a deep, hot green beneath the thick brush of his lashes. Her hands curved over his shoulders, and she could feel the powerful flex of his muscles beneath her fingers. When his mouth covered her nipple, wetting the thin cotton blouse and making her gasp, her nails dug into him in a reflexive clench. She arched into him and groaned.

Lifting his body, Hunter unbuckled his gunbelt and lay it aside, keeping it within easy reach. Susan watched, her body feeling achy and heavy as she waited. He reached for her again, tangling his hands in her dark hair, curling his fingers into it to drag her face up to his and kiss her. He filled her entire being with him, with the feel and taste and smell of him.

Matching the fervent strokes of his tongue in her mouth with her own, Susan felt him shift to unbutton her blouse, still kissing her. The warm wash of air over her bared breasts made her shiver, and he lowered his head to take an aching peak into his mouth, curling his tongue around it in a tantalizing motion. Hunter groaned, and she felt his arms tighten around her.

Susan lifted her hips, unable to stop that primitive reaction to what he was doing, gasping when he moved to the other breast, then trailed hot, searing kisses down her ribs and back up.

"Hunter . . ."

He lifted his head, and his eyes were glazed with passion. His hand drifted downward, sliding between her legs to caress her through her skirts, then shifting to the buttons at the waist. When he had them undone, she lifted her hips and he peeled away her skirt, stockings, and boots.

It seemed so right, somehow, to be lying beneath the sky and clouds and making love. She watched through hazy eyes as he sat up and shrugged out of his shirt, working deftly at the buttons of his pants to free himself, then coming back to her. He moved between her legs, pushing them apart with his body, lying across her in a hot meeting of bare flesh. His belly rubbed against hers in a hard ridge of muscle, and she felt his arousal.

Susan's nerves were stretched so tautly that she almost cried out when he didn't take her at once; she shoved her hips up at him.

"Slow down, sweetheart," he murmured, lavishing kisses along the line of her throat, his teeth nipping at the soft skin. One hand moved down to guide his body into position, but he didn't enter. Sliding arousingly against her, he let her writhe and twist beneath him, encouraging her to a higher pitch with his hands and mouth, until she dug her nails into his back and almost screamed with need.

"Hunter, oh, God . . . please . . ."

Answering her plea, he penetrated slowly, his thrust deep and sure, making her gasp and clutch at him as she arched to meet him. Her eyes flew open and she looked up into his deep green gaze with smoky need in her eyes.

"Is that what you wanted?" he muttered thickly and did not wait for her reply before he began moving in stronger, harder motions. "Sweet Susan, black-eyed Susan, love . . . God, I need you."

His face was close, his words and breath feathering over her cheek, stirring the dark tendrils of hair over her ear. He pushed into her until he could go no further, using his body to give her all the pleasure he knew how to give. Sweat beaded on his face; warm air coasted over his body as he watched her face, watched her bite her lips and close her eyes and give herself into his strokes.

A shudder racked him when her thighs clenched around his hips in a convulsive movement, and he clenched his teeth against it and buried his face in the sweet curve of her neck and shoulder. Susan felt his shudder, felt his effort to hold back, and could not keep her body still.

When she pushed up into him hungrily, seeking to take him inside her in a driving need to have all of him, heart and soul and body, as deeply as she could get, Hunter dug his hands into the quilt beneath them and braced himself. His thrusts grew harder and deeper, and he groaned as he took her mouth again, plunging his tongue inside and matching the movements of his body. Susan's hands moved to his hips to hold him, to pull him into her.

Panting, slamming into her eager body, Hunter drank in her cries of pleasure with his mouth. When Susan shuddered and jerked upward, her heels pressing into the quilt and ground as she strained toward him, toward that elusive peak that seemed just out of reach, he met her. This time her cry rose above them, up into the trees and sky, mingling with the soft keening of the hot prairie winds as she found what she sought.

Before her shattering convulsions had trembled into memories, Hunter found his own sweet pleasure, arching back with his neck corded as he exploded into waves of release. When he rested his weight on his elbows and knees, she felt a sweeping rush of love so deep and intense tears came to her eyes.

He lifted his head after a moment, blond hair dark with sweat, his eyes soft and hazy. Rubbing a thumb across her wet cheek, he murmured, "Tears, sweetheart?"

She nodded. "Yes. For you, for me, for us. Happy tears, I think."

He smiled. Then he kissed her again, at first sweetly, but the kisses subtly altered, and she felt him grow strong in her again, lifting her, taking her with him in spite of the fact that she was still limp and shaking with reaction.

And now, and now, when he rocked against her, taking and giving and making her alive and vital, she heard him say in a voice husky with need and longing and relief, "I love you, sweet Susan. God, I love you."

She was drowning, drowning in sensation and the wild, heady pleasure of hearing him say he loved her, and Susan gave him back the words with her entire heart and soul.

"I love you, Hunter. . . ."

The Departure

TABITHA SIGHED HEAVILY. "The wedding was lovely, don't you think?"

"As weddings go, it was most—unusual."

Tabitha eyed him. "Unusual? Oh. You mean the pig. That was not planned, I don't think. It was the cakes that drew him." She frowned. "Ate some of the best ones."

"Are you satisfied, now that you've attended their wedding?"

"Perhaps I should be asking you the same thing." She smiled at his quizzical glance. "After all, I was asked to help, and I've done so. Are you satisfied?"

Horatio rocked back on his heels. He looked from Tabitha down at the ranch, saw Hunter and Susan climb into a buggy and leave in a blur of dust and laughter. Then he saw Pete Sheridan come up behind Doris and put an arm around her waist, his good arm. Bandages still draped his other one, but he was up and around.

"I take it there is to be another wedding?" he murmured, and Tabitha nodded.

"Yes. Pete and Doris plan on running the Lazy W while Hunter drags Susan over the countryside with him. When they come back, their house will be built." Sliding a foot over the ground and stirring up faint clouds of dust, she said in a sly tone, "The brooch is going back to England, you know."

"Was that your suggestion?"

"Heavens, no!" Tabitha shot him a startled look. "I only said that Queen Victoria recently added the Kohinoor diamond to the collection of British Crown jewels, but that it would pale in comparison to the brooch. Susan decided to loan it to them, with the stipulation that should a Lynnfield heiress ever desire its return, it would be done. I thought it quite fitting."

"And safer."

Tabitha nodded. "Much safer. Not only for the brooch, but for Susan. Who knows if there's another greedy lunatic like Sir Peter in the Thorne family? Having known Sir Reginald, I would not doubt it at all."

"But Sir Peter has gotten his just deserts, I would say."

"Oh, yes. Deportation to England, a trial for murder—I am sorry that poor old Graves was killed for what he knew about the brooch and Susan. Wondered how Thorne knew about her."

"Well, Tabitha, I must say that you have done quite well." Horatio smiled at her pleased expression. "Even with the rather theatrical swordplay you indulged in, matters turned out satisfactory."

"Yes, they did, didn't they? And I thought I was a fair hand with a sword. Watched a few duels in my time and can still recall that handsome devil Raleigh dashing about with his sword." She sighed. "Men were men in those days, I tell you. Of course, Hunter Carson is quite a man, too, I must admit. Strong, forceful, but capable of being gentle. Not bad for an American."

"So, you don't think Americans are too bad now, do you? I'm glad."

She stared at him suspiciously. "Why?"

Horatio began walking, and up ahead of him a dark cloud appeared on the horizon, whirling down and stirring up choking clouds of dust. He walked toward it.

His voice floated back to her, and she trotted after him to hear.

"You see, you've done so well, Tabitha, that I think you can be trusted to help another. . . ."

"What?" It was a shriek, and Tabitha's legs pumped furiously as she tried to catch up. "What do you mean? I've missed God only knows how many concerts, and I've missed my soft cushions . . . Horatio! Come back here! Whatever are you talking about?"

Pausing, he turned back to her with a conciliatory smile that did nothing to lessen her irritation. "It's Ian. He's only been with us for a short time, and I fear that he needs someone to show him how to manage things. See, he had a problem on earth before, and it was never resolved. Well, you have learned, Tabitha, that all unresolved problems must eventually be—"

The cloud descended in a loud roar that drowned out what he was saying, and she stared in exasperation.

"Of all the nerve! Well, if he thinks that I'm going to spend my time tutoring some wretched—wait! What problems are unresolved?" She stepped into the cloud. "Not that I'm going to help, mind you. I'm just curious. I've earned a rest. You said so yourself. Didn't you? Horatio . . ."

411